# Woman at War

# Woman at War

*DACIA MARAINI*

TRANSLATED
FROM THE ITALIAN
BY
MARA BENETTI
&
ELSPETH SPOTTISWOOD

ITALICA PRESS
NEW YORK
1988

This translation first published by Lighthouse Books,
55 Mint Rd., Liss, Hants, UK.



ITALICA PRESS, INC.
625 Main Street
New York, New York 10044



**Library of Congress Cataloging-in-Publication Data**

Maraini, Dacia.
Woman at War.

Translation of: Donna in guerra.
I. Title.
PQ4873.A69D5813 1988 853'.914 88-81204
ISBN 0-934977-12-7 (pbk.)

Printed in the United States of America
5 4 3 2 1

Cover Art: Alexandra Eldridge

*I watch a woman dare*
*I dare to watch a woman*
*Watch me learn to dare*
*My arms and legs feel awkward*

*Jean Tepperman*

*ADDIS*

# *Addis*

*1st August*

Giacinto has gone fishing. He got up at seven. Even before washing his face he lined up his fishing tackle on the floor and cleaned it item by item with a rag dipped in paraffin.

Then we had coffee in the yard, in the shade of the banana trees. It's Sunday and the neighbours were still asleep. Giacinto slipped on his black swimming trunks, swallowed the last morsel of bread dipped in milk and made for the small door that gives on to the road. I watched him walk: his powdery skin, his long legs covered with blond curly hair, his stringy neck, his thin shoulders. He looked like a lonesome, uncertain boy.

"What do you want for lunch?"

He didn't answer. He went off dangling his yellow canvas bag against his skin.

I got dressed. I cleaned up the house and tidied the trunk, taking out all the fishing tackle, rubber suits, guns, harpoons, knives, masks, snorkels, flippers, and a grid to fry the fish on. By the time I'd finished it was midday. I hadn't stuffed the peppers yet and I still had to wash the salad. My legs ached and I had shooting pains in my back. I settled myself into a deck-chair in the courtyard, with my head in the shade and my legs in the sunshine.

I fell asleep and dreamed a mole was digging a tunnel through my stomach. I woke with a sudden stab of pain. A dull intense ache was welling up from deep down inside me and something warm was wetting my thighs. I took a deep breath to overcome the tension in my belly. I didn't feel like moving, I just let the blood trickle down my thigh, sweet and lukewarm.

Later I shall have to wash the canvas of the chair, I told myself, I shall have to scrub it with soap, I shall have to leave it out to dry. Later. Just now I don't want to stand on my feet.

I close my eyes and the sun shines scorching and vicious on my naked legs.

So starts my holiday. A reassuring trickle of blood, the joy of being in the open, the pungent smell of basil. School is a long way away. Giacinto will come back later with the fish. I've tidied the house. This evening I'll iron his shirts, prepare the sauce, do the washing up.

Just now I don't want to think of anything. I am content. I am happy.

*Midnight*

For dinner we ate Giacinto's first catch — an ugly-looking scorpion fish with brown, mottled scales. Then we lay back in the deck-chairs in the yard and stared up at the sky, dense with stars, and listened to the blaring of our neighbour's television.

These neighbours of ours are from Naples and they spend their time squabbling. I don't know how many of them there are; the children's screams are interrupted from time to time by the husky voice of a woman. When they aren't quarrelling, they play football. Their ball fell into our yard several times today. On the first occasion I took some time returning it and five of them arrived on my doorstep: they turned the yard upside down, trampling on the young basil plants with their clogs, and breaking off the stems of the tomatoes. Now, as soon as I see the ball fall on our side I drop whatever I'm doing and run to fetch it, and throw it back to them straight away.

At ten I started clearing the table. I washed the dishes, scoured the saucepans, rinsed the glasses. I haven't yet got used to the long narrow kitchen with its floor paved with broken tiles. The house we've rented resembles a tadpole, all head and no body: a bedroom with two windows, a dark kitchen, no bathroom. The toilet is a filthy hole: to wash yourself you have to use the kitchen sink or the garden hose.

To make up for it we have a beautiful courtyard, enclosed by a ten foot wall, as secret as an Arab garden. In it grow basil, alfalfa, mint and tomato plants. There are also some white and violet geraniums, zinnias and windflowers. On one side there are two tall orange trees with grey trunks and intensely green leaves, which produce small, hard, bitter oranges. Against the street wall there is a tall, thick fig tree, whose twisted branches have managed to grow several feet above the brick inside wall. In the centre, like a green, glistening heart, grows a cluster of banana trees; lustrous and pale, the leaves rustle with a noise like brushed rubber.

*2nd August*

Today Giacinto went out at six. I cleaned the smelly toilet and mended the black curtain that separates the kitchen from the bedroom. Two wasps buzzed insistently over the sugar bowl.

At eleven I went shopping. The market is nearby, along the road that leads down to the harbour. I stopped to look at a narrow shop window crammed with bread, small white pizzas and maize-flour biscuits. A hand tapped me on the shoulder.

"Bread? You shouldn't buy your bread here."

"Why not?".

"This Mimi, he killed his wife with a fork and spent eleven years in jail. Then, out of spite he married a whore with a stack of money as soon as he was free."

"But I must buy bread somewhere."

"If bread has been touched by poisoned hands it becomes poisoned too. Mimi got married for fear of his foster-brother who put a spell on him from beyond the grave. Then with the money he bought himself this shop. Now do you see?"

She was a fat, stumpy woman with a dishevelled face and amused, insolent eyes. She grabbed me by one arm and dragged me off to another shop. She walked at my side, aloof and dignified.

"Are you from the village?"

"Born and bred here, me. My name's Tota and I work as a part-time cleaner. And you? Are you a cleaner too? Part-time or full-time?"

She insisted on treating me to a large pistachio ice-cream, after which she walked home with me.

"If this is where you're staying you must be on a pauper's holiday. This is Pisshead's house, we call him that because he's always pissing himself with fright and it completely fucks him up. It's not very comfortable, though, this place, the only nice thing about it is the yard."

"The landlord's called Di Bartolomeo."

"How much is he charging you?"

"35,000 liras."

"That's a hell of a lot. He's eating you alive, the scoundrel."

She stalked off down the road with a quick, rigid walk. I took out the heavy iron key and unlocked the garden door, just about doubled up so as not to drop my parcels. I pushed the door open with my foot. Among the tomato plants I caught sight of a yellow plastic bag. I put the shopping down and went to pick it up. It stank. It bulged with fish intestines, egg shells, fruit peel and torn-up paper. It couldn't have come from anywhere but next door — it was right under their wall. I picked up the bag and went to knock on their door. An elderly woman, wrapped in a torn, greasy smock opened the door and looked at me anxiously.

"Is this your rubbish?"

She muttered a few words. Then she went back into the house and returned a moment later with a younger woman who gave me a cold smile. She invited me in, but I refused. I was feeling annoyed and I asked her whether the rubbish was theirs.

"It certainly isn't ours. Let me see."

She took the bag in her hands. She turned it over and over in her fingers. She sniffed it. Then she returned it to me and repeated:

"It isn't ours, for certain."

"But it could only have come from your yard, it fell right where the ball always falls."

"I'm telling you it isn't ours. Don't you believe me?"

She gave me an arrogant, brazen look. I couldn't think of an answer. After all, she could be right. The old woman drew near to us, whimpering, and the woman sent her away with a brusque gesture. Then, without saying goodbye, she slammed the door in my face.

*4.00 p.m.*

Giacinto's asleep. He's curled up naked on the bed, hiding his genitals between his thighs. His hunched back, his head deeply set between his shoulders, his bent legs, all express a tenacious self-defence. Against what, I wonder?

His freckled back is covered with a transparent down that disappears at his buttocks. There his skin looks more naked. The freckles thicken up on the two rosy crescents like a small child's face: two smiling, innocent cheeks, and hidden away between the creases a red capricious little mouth.

I bend down to kiss him and he wakes with a start. He looks at me fearfully as if I have come to steal something from him. His dark eyes stare at me half-blind with sleep. He opens his mouth to speak but changes his mind and doesn't say anything. I have the feeling that at that moment he hates me.

But a cup of coffee is enough to make him recover and become his usual amiable pensive self.

*10.00 p.m.*

At seven we went down to the piazza to have an ice-cream. Our neighbour's entire family was there: grandfather, grandmother, four children, two of them with their spouses, and nine grandchildren. Bending over herself the grandmother was sucking an ice-cream. When she saw me coming she stopped sucking and followed me with suspicious, malevolent eyes. The mother smiled with forced cordiality.

We sat in a corner, in the shadow of a mulberry tree that grows right against the fountain, and ordered two ice-creams.

"I've discovered a grouper fish and a murena, where they live, I mean. Tomorrow I'll start stalking them, but I'll have to be patient: the sea-bed's clear and the rocks go down a sheer hundred feet, but they're cautious, the bastards, they're afraid."

I couldn't follow his underwater saga, I was too distracted by the continuous coming and going of people in the square. At the tables sit large families of holiday-makers who resemble our neighbours down to the minutest detail: fat women chatting idly in low voices; flabby, pot-bellied men, their shirts opened up on their hairy chests. With indolent intentness they follow all the girls who pass by and comment on them in loud voices. The sons are mostly lean, restless, sun-tanned, encased in extra tight-fitting trousers, their buttocks conspicuously in evidence. They wear dark glasses and brightly-coloured T-shirts. The daughters are plumper and more wary. They move about in groups, unsociable, ill at ease, talking amongst themselves in low voices. They wear their hair shoulder-length, no make-up, thigh-length skirts and sandals with very high heels.

The parents sit around chatting as they gulp down huge quantities of ice-cream, beer and aperitifs. The boys are restless as grasshoppers as they dart and scurry about us. They swarm out of the square and then return in twos and threes, sit down to have a drink and a moment later they're off again in groups of five or ten. They grab their mopeds and beep their way through the crowd, then they reappear together with other boys on bikes. They prop their mopeds up against the trees, join the the girls, devour soft ice-cream, then once again they're on their feet ready to run off somewhere.

The foreigners can be spotted a mile off. They look lost but happy. They come to the café straight from the beach without getting changed, a little triangle of white paper stuck on their noses, plastic flipflops on their feet, their arms and legs red from the sun. The rich stay closeted in their villas along the coast and the village sees little of them. They send their servants to do the shopping, and when they want to go out for a drink they go to Casamatta or Porto Cane where the yachts are moored.

At half-past seven a quaint, somehow unfashionable trio arrives: a very beautiful disabled girl, a bony boy in a white tennis suit, and a woman in her forties with burning eyes and a grey plait that dangles on her chest. The girl plods forwards on her crutches, sweeping her soft, provocative eyes over the scene. She is dressed in red and wears jasmine in her hair.

Everyone's gaze is now fixed on the strange trio with a mixture of compassion and curiosity. One or two children burst into laughter but the three do not seem to take offence. The girl threads her way through the tables, stumping her crutches on the asphalt with her muscular shoulders, holding her head up, her hair as soft and fresh as a waterfall. They sit down and order lemon water-ices and biscuits. They don't talk much, though now and again they exchange a few words in an incomprehensible, guttural language.

The noises of the mopeds had become deafening. I suggested to Giacinto that it would be better to go back home, but he wanted to stay.

"I don't notice the noise, so it doesn't bother me how much there is."

"It gives me indigestion."

"It's probably because I'm used to noise: at the garage it's much worse than this." He spoke slowly. He thrust the ice-cream spoon into his glass, methodically separating the strawberry from the pistachio.

Suddenly I heard squeals of suprise. A Neapolitan family stood up gesticulating. I looked up to see a white-haired man with a monkey on his shoulder arrive and sit at one of the tables. All the boys in the square crowded together round the old man. They struggled to touch the monkey on its belly, its legs, its sexual organs, and to pull its tail and whiskers. The monkey squeaked with fear, hopping from one of her master's shoulders to the other as a little boy tried to force an ice-cream down her throat. The man smiled awkwardly, ill at ease, trying gently to keep the crowd away. Holding his pet tight against his chest he spoke to her softly, in English.

Ten minutes later the monkey had been forgotten. The boys went back to their mopeds, and the grown-ups returned to their idle or irritable chattering.

There was something sensuous and sickly in the stifling atmosphere of the square. Mulberries fell suddenly without a sound, to be crushed under people's feet, leaving a violet stain on the ground. In the distance could be heard the noise of the waves as they toppled heavily against the rocks.

*3rd August*

This morning the ball fell into our yard a dozen times. Every time I rushed to where it had fallen and returned it immediately. On my way back from the shops I found the usual bag of rubbish and flung it into the dustbin.

In the market I met Tota. She ran up to me and it was obvious that she'd been waiting for me. She started talking straight away in a carefree, natural way as if we were two old friends. She came with me to buy salad, bread and detergent. Then she dragged me to see a friend of hers, someone called Giottina who works in the launderette by the harbour. Giottina looks just like Tota! Her body is a bundle, she has short, strong, sun-tanned arms, an ageless face and large, listless eyes.

The launderette is a long, dark room, carved out of rock and containing two enormous washing-machines. Against the wall there are two shelves covered with piles of dirty washing, and two chairs with broken backs. The clean laundry hangs from the ceiling, drying on nylon lines.

As I entered I was assailed by a violent stench of ammonia that took my breath away. Giottina stands behind a long table that cuts the room in two. She irons dresses and shirts, digging her arms into the mountains of dirty clothes to clear a space, and as she irons she talks. She has a hoarse, thick voice and from time to time she bursts into shrill, rasping laughter.

"The richer they are, the more their flesh sizzles. Their flesh fries, you know, and they shit figs. Haven't you seen them yet, the people from the Villa Trionfo, haven't you seen how they walk when they come down to do their shopping? The mistress walks in front with banknotes stuck to her fingers, each finger a thousand-lira note like Pompei's Madonna on her Feast Day. Behind walks the maid with two silk shopping bags in her hands. I'm surprised you haven't noticed them, everyone watches them, the mistress is a beauty and the maid has the sort of eyes that make your guts churn to look at her. They come down and buy a whole lot of stuff, all aphrosiacs."

"Aphrodisiacs, Giottina, the right word is aphrodisiacs. Giovanna here, she knows, she's not stupid."

"I know, I know she's not. Why, she's a school teacher."

"They buy eggs, lots and lots of eggs, they buy red peppers, butter, anisette liqueur, capers, lobsters, you know what that means, don't you?"

"The next morning their sheets are soiled with men's filth, that's what Rosalie, the girl who goes over to do the cleaning, told me."

"And then they sleep all day and in the evening they shut themselves in and lock all the windows so that no one can see them."

"One night the gardener saw them strutting round the house all naked and they screwed each other like animals, up their arses, everything, men with men, women with women, you know?"

I listened to them without saying a word. I could see them getting more and more carried away, swallowing their saliva with excitement, their bright eyes shining as if they were chopping onions. They took turns telling their stories without ever overlapping.

I was suffocating. The ammonia burned my nose and I was enveloped in a nauseating fog of steam. I stood up and said I must go. Tota held me back by one arm as I picked up my bag full of vegetables. Then she followed me all the way home.

*10.00 p.m.*

Giacinto came back at three o'clock with a grey mullet dangling from his waist, strung to a metal line through its gills. The fish's blood dripped on his leg. He told me in an excited voice how he had stalked the beast and followed it for hours through the rocks and sea-weed. He had waited for it, tricked it with false movements and finally routed it out, cornered it and then killed it with a harpoon shot through its back. When he talks about fishing he becomes handsome, his eyes, normally dull, become brighter, his lips gain colour and his pale cheeks become flushed.

We ate the fish and afterwards we made love. Quickly, as usual, without giving me time to come properly. I tell him to wait for me, but he says that if he doesn't hurry he loses momentum and then he can't make it. He's in a rush to grow big, to become red-hot, flesh against flesh, to be swallowed up. He's in a hurry to explode as if he'd lose something if he hesitated. He says if he pauses a moment he'll turn soft and slack, he'll fall asleep. So he rushes on, pursued by the fear of God knows what, he clings to me in a frenzy, bites, jerks, screams. I can't stop him or restrain him, and when I grab him he's already come. The hot liquid trickles down on to the sheet. I come half-way, panting and frustrated. He falls asleep in his usual contracted position, his legs and arms bent under his chin. I'm overwhelmed by a sense of futility.

I got up and went into the kitchen. I cleared the camp-bed we use as a sideboard, moved plates, cutlery, pans and jars of pickle down on to the floor and stretched out on the rough canvas. The smell of onion and anchovies gave me a sense of excitement and I started playing with my pubic hair with closed eyes and a pulsing throat. A sweet feeling of warmth spread slowly from my belly to my breasts. The orgasm came from far, far away, like a painful thrust deep within me. I became drowsy, unconcerned by the mosquitoes that flew heavily around me with a threatening hiss. I fell into a dark, sweaty sleep.

*4th August*

When I think of going back to teaching this winter I start feeling sick. Back to that terrible school in Zagarolo. The bus to the station. Then the train. Then another bus. To find myself eventually in front of the headmaster's stupid face, his voice distorted by anger, his eyes stained yellow, his mouth dirty with coffee.

"Signora Magro, you are three minutes late."

As they wait for me the boys are telling one another dirty jokes. Their desks are full of pornographic comics. I'm not a good teacher, I know. Instead of fighting against ignorance and boorishness I adopt a lethargic apathy. I avoid my colleagues, talk to no one. I keep right away from the headmaster.

I let the children do what they please. I teach what I'm supposed to teach mechanically, with no enthusiasm, no sympathy. My only consolation is Fidelio. To get to school he has to walk five miles every morning. He is dark, surly, serious, silent. He isn't a good pupil, he isn't quick, he's always the last one to understand. He can hardly speak proper Italian. His black eyes conceal a confused intelligence, something hard and disquieting which distinguishes him from the others. I go to school only because of him. I enjoy waiting for him to arrive after all the others are already at their desks. I start calling the roll. I hear the door screech. Light, troubled steps. I know it's him. I don't turn. I wait until he's taken his place. I lift my head. He's there, rigid, humble, introverted, sullen, tired from the walk. He spends the afternoons working in the fields with his father. He's never talked to me about it, but I can tell from his hands, which are large, strong and hardened by callouses like the hands of an adult.

On the last day of term I called him to my desk. It was just after the one thirty bell and all the others had gone. I gave him a big book of short stories by Conrad. He didn't say a word. He clutched the book and hid it inside his shirt. He stood there awkwardly, embarrassed, not knowing where to look. I asked him whether he would read it. He raised his dark questioning eyes and gave me a sad, uncertain smile that amazed me. I saw him to the door. I grasped his head in my hands and kissed him on the mouth. His lips were narrow, cold, his tongue shy and very delicate. It was a kiss of love. We left each other without a word.

*3.00 p.m.*

In the market I met Tota and she dragged me to the launderette. I went in holding my breath. Giottina was ironing and the air was heavy with the smell of detergents. The humid heat glued my shirt to my breasts. I took a stool and sat by the open door.

"At the Villa Trionfo love-making has turned into whoring."

"Whoring has turned into sperm."

"Sperm turns into poison."

"The maid becomes the mistress."

"She carries golden coins sewn into her dress."

"And walks like the devil, on tiptoe."

"Did you see them when they came down for a stroll?"

"The mistress in front, like a queen, her husband three steps behind, and the maid last with her tinkling bangles."

The voices alternate with each other, swift, darting, without ever overlapping, a joyful, undulating rhythm. I listen to them, forgetting the heat.

"She wore bangles round her ankles like a Muslim slave."

"A slave who eats up her masters."

"She bewitches them."

"In the morning they go out boating, the three of them, and they row and row."

"As soon as they're well out to sea they undress and embrace each other."

"The two women, that is, the maid and the mistress, he stays at the oars and sweats, all dressed in black, shirt, tie, waistcoat, shoes, socks, everything."

"And the two women, stark naked, kiss, hug and caress each other madly as if they were spell-bound by the full moon."

"They are far out to sea, but there's always someone watching them through binoculars, they are the lenses of conscience, and rumour flies all around Addis."

"The man doesn't do anything, poor sod, just stays still, all dressed up like that, and the two serpents kiss each other, pet, rub against each other, and he rows on, the prick, his shirt soaking with sweat, his tie dangling down, he doesn't say a word, the idiot, he just rows and rows."

"He stares at them, though, and when his mouth becomes as hot as a furnace he dips his hand into the sea and splashes his face a little."

"Then the two women take out a dinner fit for a king: fried chicken, roast rabbit, smoked ham, shell fish, ice cream, melon, and they start eating."

"Now and then they take pity on him and hand him a tiny morsel of fried chicken."

"Or a dab of ice cream, and he thanks them with a nod like this, and the two snakes laugh at him because he's really so funny and stupid and can't eat without dribbling down his chin."

"And then after that they fall asleep with their arms round each other in the bottom of the boat, the mistress and the maid, and he carries on rowing in desperation."

Giottina was gazing at me with her eyes full of sensuality and malice. Her fat arms moved back and forth in a cloud of whiteish steam.

I was swallowing down the hot, pungent air. I sat listening to their words, interrupted by the regular thumping of the iron. Underneath my bottom my skirt had stuck to the bench. I stood up and went outside. I sucked in the cool sea breeze, I drank large gulps of it avidly. I looked back into the shop. Behind the steamed-up shop window I saw the clumsy bodies of the two friends moving about, heavy and white.

I won't go back there again, I told myself. But I knew I would. It's like a dark theatre where they improvise disturbing fantasies, reckless games full of bitter sensuality that fascinate me in spite of the nausea.

*10.00 p.m.*

Giacinto came back at three o'clock with a tall blond lad. He kicked open the garden door, calling "Is it ready, Vanna?"

He had some fish strung together on a metal ring, but instead of lifting up the fish he lifted up the arm of the young lad in the swimming costume.

"This is Santino. Lay another place for him."

I watched him as he came forward, his fair wet hair dripping on his dry neck. He was tall, taller than Giacinto, with the beauty of a spoilt child. I laid another place on the table and cut the largest bit of meat in half. Meanwhile I was observing the boy: fair, almost white-haired; blue eyes, a bashful smile. He must be German, I thought, though his name is from around here. We sat down and ate hard-boiled eggs and a tomato salad seasoned with oregano. The boy didn't speak: he ate smiling to himself and keeping his legs crossed under the table. Giacinto talked about his job with cheerful enthusiasm and Santino listened to him, serious, attentive, his eyes wide open. Meanwhile I was running from the kitchen to the table and back.

"Is your garage large?" I heard him ask with the slurred drawl of the Neapolitan.

"I don't really know whether it's large or small, it's my home, I've been there since I was sixteen. There are twenty of us mechanics, and then there's him, Vargas, the boss. It's like a family, or so he says. He's not too bad as bosses go. He's been a worker too, he's put his whole life into it, always on the work floor, but then when the moment comes he's as hard as nails, and what annoys him more than anything is the Union. He doesn't want to know about rights and duties; if you ask him for something like you ask your father then maybe you'll get it, he's willing to do you a favour, he cares about being good-hearted, but if you talk to him about Unions, strikes, laws, he gets angry and that's it, finished, good bye to it all."

Santino eats greedily, with delicate movements, lost in thought. I put some soft golden apricots as big as eggs on his plate, and watch him split them open, hardly moving his long, delicate fingers. He swallows them after melting them in his mouth. Afterwards he and Giacinto stretched out on the deck-chairs in the shade of the banana trees. I cleared the table, did the dishes, and made the coffee. When I went out again, Giacinto was asleep. I put his cup on the ground. Santino picked it up, bent over his friend, and woke him up by a gentle touch of his finger on his eyelids. Giacinto drank down the piping hot liquid in two gulps and then went back to sleep. I was left alone with the boy. I did not know what to say.

"Are you from the island?"

"Yes."

"From Addis?"

"Yes."

As a matter of fact he did have the narrow, quick way of speaking of the islanders.

"What do you do?"

"I'm a waiter, though at the moment I'm out of work."

"Your father, what does he do?"

"He's a fisherman."

"How old are you?"

"Twenty."

"Giacinto's asleep. I feel sleepy too. What do you want to do? Stay or go? You can have a nap as well if you like."

"Can I stay? It's nice here, I like it. May I?"

I stood up and went to lie down on the camp bed in the kitchen. But I couldn't sleep. Behind the curtain I could hear Giacinto's heavy irregular breathing and the rustling of the banana leaves, but I could not hear Santino. His silence unnerved me.

At seven we went down to the square. Santino wouldn't come. As usual the boys were there at the café, darting back and forth, furiously revving their bikes. At half past seven on the dot the quaintly dressed trio arrived: the paralysed girl in a lemon yellow dress trimmed with red lace, a bunch of wild roses in her hair; the furious-eyed little boy in his white tennis suit; and the woman with grey plaits dressed in a lilac-flowered jacket with starched collar and white piqué cuffs.

People stared at them with curiosity. They followed them with unsympathetic looks as they made their way through the tables. They nudged each other and one person pointed at them sniggering. But there were plenty of other distractions and the three were soon forgotten. The babble of voices broke off, halted and rekindled at every new arrival.

Giacinto went on reading his newspaper without lifting his eyes to look at the strange apparition. When he'd finished reading the last page he asked if I wanted to go home. He was hungry. I begged him to stay a little longer. I had heard from Tota that the 'beauties' would arrive round about eight and I wanted to see them. And in fact just after eight, there they were. They arrived in twos, strolling along idly. They are young men in their twenties, affected and sophisticated. They wear tight-fitting trousers, shirts open to their tanned chests, wedge-heeled clogs, silver chains at their wrists, gold trinkets at their necks. They look around without seeing, with dreamy languid eyes. Their hair is lightened with camomile rinse and they wear it down to their necks or in shiny curls falling indolently over their eyes.

They make their way through the tables, feigning indifference. But their roving eyes track down what they're after in a flash — some smartly-dressed middle-aged women who are sitting alone in a dark corner. No greetings, no visible sign, but suddenly one of the women gets up, pays the bill, and walks towards a car parked round the corner. The chosen youth follows her, gets into the car. They drive off silently without even exchanging a look.

They are the wives of businessmen from Munich, Hamburg, and Berlin, who come to the island to rest and make love. Their husbands join them from time to time, arriving on a Saturday only to fly back the following Monday. They own the most sumptuous villas on the coast, but unlike the well-to-do Italians they lead a solitary life, and so they don't think it beneath them to come down to the village. The young men are the sons of local peasants and fishermen. During the winter they sign on as mechanics or as cabin boys on ferries and trawlers, and during the summer they sell their bodies to the foreign tourists.

I know how much they charge too. The newsagent told me yesterday morning as I waited for him to untie the roll of newspapers. He saw me watching one of the 'beauties' and he put on a smiling conspiratorial look.

"Do you know how much that beautiful fruit costs?"

"That young lad?"

"The round figure of ten thousand liras. But if it's only a quickie, during the day, you might get him for as little as five."

He stamped his two huge swollen feet in their check woollen slippers on the floor, and burst into laughter. Nervously he struggled to unravel the knot with his red chapped hands.

"He's handsome, that boy, don't you think?"

The lad was coming towards us. He walked with a vacant air, eyes lost in a vacuum, body softened by sleep, a bouncing yellow quiff on his radiant forehead. He entered the shop, picked up a sports magazine, rolled it up and slipped it under his arm. Then he struggled to take money from a pocket glued to his thigh. He couldn't. He said: "I'll pay tomorrow" in a soft, musical voice and left with a cheerful tick-tack of his clogs.

"Do you want to meet him?"

At last the knot came loose. He handed me my paper and leered at me. I didn't answer but he insisted, moistening his lips:

"You should see him naked, he's a real beauty. Don't you really want to meet him?"

I paid, but as I was about to leave he continued:

"Sometimes he does it free."

As I walked out of the door he continued to snigger with a sly, lascivious look.

*5th August*

The heat is sweltering. I woke up at six, my body sweating, my face swollen, a bitter taste in my mouth. I got up and opened the window that looks on to the yard. Outside the air is as warm and motionless as stagnant water. Mosquitoes skim indefatigably, searching for their prey. The pungent smell of basil drifts in with the mosquitoes. I walked back to bed. Giacinto was sleeping, curled up naked. He slept fitfully, the rhythm of his breathing irregular: sudden rushes followed by pauses like death-rattles.

At eight he went out. I was still half asleep, my head aching. I got up and had a cup of piping hot coffee and some bread and butter. My back felt sore and I did the washing reluctantly. I read a few pages from a book on Byzantium. Then I went shopping. In the market I met Tota. She was waiting for me and I walked with her down to Giottina's. The asphalt was softened by the sun, and the heels of my shoes sank into it. Tota fanned herself with a folded newspaper. The launderette window dripped with condensation. Giottina was ironing with vigorous movements, her fat body floating in the acrid vapours. I refused to go in, but Tota took offence.

"It's cool inside."

"It's sweltering."

"If you don't come in you'll hurt Giottina's feelings. She's waiting for you."

"It's too hot, honestly."

She looked at me with a sudden hard and unfriendly expression. She turned her back and disappeared into the launderette. I went back to the market. I had to finish my shopping. The vegetables were wrinkled with the heat: the lettuce leaves yellow and limp, the tomatoes too red and soft; they split open at a mere touch and sent a spurt of warm yellow liquid dripping between one's fingers.

At three Giacinto came back with Santino. We had their fishing booty for lunch: two one-pound octopuses, and a little mullet the size of your hand.

Giacinto treats Santino like a child. He teaches him how to use the gun, the mask, the flippers; he peels his tomatoes for him and fillets his fish. Santino doesn't take offence, not even when Giacinto tells him how stupid he is. Instead, he smiles and sinks his head down between his shoulders with an air of contrition. He drinks his wine in small sips and when he swallows a slightly larger sip he lifts his hand to his throat and blinks his eyes. He hardly ever speaks. He eats slowly, bringing the food to his mouth with calm, delicate gestures.

"Why is it that we never see you in the square in the evening, Santino?"

"That's when I look for work."

"In the evening?"

"I go to the restaurants to see if they can give me a job, sometimes a waiter or a kitchen assistant doesn't turn up so I stay."

"Where do you go to find work?"

"To Lago Morto, Casamatta, Porto Cane, all over the place."

"How do you get there, do you walk?"

"I can always find a friend with a scooter."

"But where do you live?"

"In Via San Perfido."

"Just near the market?"

"Yes, right there."

I thought I had seen him around the market stalls. It might not have been him, though, but someone who looks very much like him: the same light blue eyes, the same long legs with knobbly knees, but shorter, walking with long relaxed strides, wearing a ragged T-shirt and a pair of shorts too large for him.

"Do you have a younger brother?"

"Yes, Orio."

"That must be him I see all the time in the market, he looks very much like you."

"He does the shopping for my mother."

"How old is he?"

"Fourteen."

I didn't know what to ask him next. If you don't ask him questions he doesn't talk. He sits there silent, with a vacant smile on his half-parted lips. Fortunately Giacinto takes him along wherever he goes. They sit together and Giacinto hands him the fishing tackle and gets him to clean the salt-stained metal, always talking to him in an affectionate way.

At seven the boy left and we went down to the square. There was the usual crowd of indolent Neapolitan families chattering away, and the boys and girls with their scooters. The disabled girl and her companions were there too, as well as the German women waiting for their 'beauties'. There were also two new arrivals, a German family and a French family. They are on a cheap holiday and are staying in bed and breakfasts for 3,000 liras a day like the Neapolitans.

At eight thirty the 'beauties' arrive. They've spent the day sleeping at home, crowded together with their sisters, cousins, brothers, aunties, grannies. Then at sunset when the air is cooler they emerge slowly out of their shells like snails, placid and sensual, leaving a trail of cheap scent behind them. The fair, severe-looking German women wait for them, pretending to read. As soon as they spot one they fancy they slip their books into their handbags and walk nonchalantly towards their white Mercedes or flame-coloured Jaguars parked along the Via Bianca di Savoia.

Meanwhile the mopeds come and go remorselessly. Everyone minds their own business, or so it seems. But that's just a pretence — in fact everything gets round in a flash. The café waiter told me about the two new arrivals:

"They are insignificant people, just ordinary workers in their own countries." As he spoke he smiled at me superciliously as if to imply that we were insignificant too and that it was especially magnanimous of him to treat us so kindly. He isn't unfriendly because he likes chatting and joking about the bills which he calls "just a little dear." But when he deals with the people from the villas his face changes: it opens up into an ecstatic grin. His body which is normally hunched and clumsy stretches out and becomes lithe and elegant; his voice, usually graceless and spiteful, becomes soft and genteel and utters expressions you'd never expect to hear from him: "S'il vous plait," "por favor," "as your lordship wishes."

Giacinto was restless. He kept mechanically stirring his ice cream in the glass, his eyes fixed on his shiny dessert spoon. He asked me about the book on Byzantium.

"That Justinian was a real son of a bitch wasn't he? What did he do next?"

I told him about the chapter I'd just been reading — about Belisario and Totila and their battles with the Romans.

"What about Theodora?"

"She was the daughter of a bear-tamer called Acacio."

"That must have been a shit of a job."

"There were lots of bear-tamers, so many that to hold down his job Acacio had to keep inventing new gimmicks all the time."

"Weren't the bears enough?"

"One day he laid his daughter naked on the ground in the centre of the arena, covered her all over with grains of wheat and then sent in a swarm of hungry ducks."

"What about the people?"

"Oh, they loved it."

"How old was the girl?"

"Five or six, I'm not sure."

"I wish I'd lived in those days."

"And worked as a bear-keeper?"

"No, just as a nobody, a craftsman maybe, just do my job and then stand in the doorway and look at people and eat . . . by the way, what did they eat?"

"The poor ate maize fritters, chicory, rats, salted cod; the rich, chickens, pheasants, sturgeon, pork, beef."

"I'd like to live in a different place from here, a different time. I'm fed up with being myself, here, today. I don't mind working, I don't want to live like a king, but just to have a bit of change. Tell me some more."

I told him what I had just read, about the merchants, the priests, the warriors, the prisons, the hard labour. He listened to me quiet and engrossed as if all the people in the café had disappeared.

"Do you remember the history lessons?" He gave a soft raucous laugh. I remembered all right. It was during the first period of our marriage. He was fed up because I knew more than him. He hated my books, he wanted to chuck them out of the window. Then he decided that he would start reading too: history, geography, philosophy. He read at night, in the loo sitting on the pan. He even bought himself one of those third-rate encyclopedias on the never never and started reading it straight through, from the letter A. He was straining his eyes over it. On Sundays, instead of going out for a stroll he'd lie on the bed with one of these huge volumes and read for hours on end. But when he got to the letter C he became fed up. For three days the volume stayed on the floor open at an early post-war picture of Como. Later he lined up the volume with the others on the shelf in the living room, and never opened it again.

At a quarter to nine we stood up and slowly started off home. As we went up the High Street we stopped in front of the shopwindow of Pussy Pussy Bang Bang, a boutique which displays all the latest swimming costumes. Every night there's a new display: costumes hanging from coral branches, or placed carefully on a white sea-bed, or floating on a stormy sea. The shop is small and expensive, and therefore not much patronised, even though everyone stops in front of its shiny window. The owners stand upright in the doorway watching the people pass. They are a married couple in their thirties. She's Venetian, he's Neapolitan. They are both handsome, sun-tanned and dressed in a well-to-do, sophisticated way. They greet the

German wives, the holiday-makers from the villas along the coast and the village notables with large smiles. But for the rest, those who dress poorly or look down-trodden, they don't even give them a disparaging glance, they just look straight through them as if they were made of glass.

Giacinto is fascinated by these vividly coloured sea-beds. They are an iridiscent mirage in the middle of which dangle tiny inviting garments and mysterious bits of fabrics. I tug at his arm, feeling the disapproval of the two stuck-up owners. We drag ourselves away from the shopwindow, only to stop again a little further on in front of another shop. This time it's a showcase full of fishing gear: black and yellow masks, light blue flippers, red and green diving-suits, plastic knives that will float. It's always the same stuff, but Giacinto never tires of looking at it piled up in a chaotic heap. His eyes are transfixed by the jewel of the display — a chromium-plated respirator with silver cylinders fitted into canvas sacks, a big mask with an accordion-shaped contraption of pipes, laces, levers, hooks, buckles, everything varnished in brilliant colours.

"One day I'll buy it, fuck me if I don't."

"What's it for?"

"With that you can walk on the sea-bed as easily as down the High Street, you can breathe calmly, chase fishes as easily as chasing a chicken, wait, hide, turn round, then *zap*! you strike and you've caught it."

"It's much too expensive, though."

"I know it is, shit, but next year I'll get it, I only need to put by a few thousand liras a month."

"We're always in debt."

"It's all my bloody mother's fault, otherwise I'd do it."

"You could give her a bit less."

"Shit, she's my mother after all, I can't throw her out into the street, can I?"

"Why don't you pass her on to your brothers for a bit?"

"Franco and Rito live in Germany, they never even dream of sending her a lira. Peppina and Gianni both have hordes of children, they can't cope as it is. Besides they say that Mother is more attached to me than to any of them. Okay, it's just an excuse, but the net result is it's always me that ends up having to look after her."

Every evening he says the same thing. He makes complicated

calculations tracing the figures on the glass with his finger. He gets angry, groans and starts again. But standing in his way there's always his mother whom he pretends he can barely tolerate although in fact he's very attached to her. He's at the mercy of her every whim: she's only got to make the most hare-brained and unreasonable demands and he turns all weak and submissive and gives in. Last Christmas she asked him for a gold table-lighter shaped like a cannon that cost 25,000 liras and off he goes and buys it for her.

*6th August*

This morning Giacinto woke up feeling randy and decided to make love. He pulled me violently against him while I was still asleep. Naked and sweaty we embraced under the sheets that smelt of bleach. When I was nearly ready to come, he came first. He bit me on the neck, screamed and then fell asleep with his mouth on my shoulder. A quarter of an hour later he got up, singing happily. He shaved and went out almost immediately without even having a cup of coffee. I lay there on the jumbled bed, alone. The sun shone on my naked legs, the aroma of mint wafted in through the open window. I shut my eyes and against the dark background of my eyelids the nervous, soft, fair body of a young boy materialised. I screwed up my eyes even more. I stretched my hand to my belly. I clutched a curl of hair with my fingers. Now the boy's soft skin is touching mine. A painful heat invades my throat. My cheeks burn. My heart pounds. I breathe with difficulty. His light lips brush my skin, caressing it with fragile tenderness. I had a small, sharp orgasm.

At eleven I went down to the market and met Tota who had obviously been waiting for me. I couldn't refuse the invitation to follow her. She came with me to buy potatoes, bread, lettuce. Then we went down to the harbour.

"While you sleep, people are rushing about, the boats return to harbour, the hotels put out their mattresses to air, I iron . . . and you snore." Giottina looked at me as cold as ice. She was ironing slowly, her fat arms shining with sweat. I sat on the usual bench.

"I'm on holiday."

"So what? Do you want a coffee?"

"Do you know what *she* does?"

"Who's *she*?"

"That American miser who lives all alone on top of the mountain, without any conveniences, anything, inside a stone house that's falling apart."

"She sleeps on a straw bed, never washes or cooks. She eats nothing but figs and onions."

"As for dressing, all she wears is a cloth wrapped round her waist. She's just eccentric, she's a looney."

"She's probably made a vow of poverty." Tota laughs. She has two gold teeth and when she laughs they glint cheerfully.

"What vow of poverty? She's got the money, she just doesn't like spending it."

"Those who've got plenty don't have to like it. Those who've got next to nothing, they like it all right."

"She's just a bit weird."

"And a bit stupid."

"When the moon comes out, she crawls out of her house on all fours like a wolf and rolls on the ground and rips out roots with her teeth."

"Have you seen her?"

"No, I haven't, God forbid, but two holy eyes have."

"A servant of God, I mean a priest who's ill and bedridden. He's got nothing to do all day so he spies on people from his window with a pair of binoculars. He saw her."

"Did he see her at night then? Can he see in the dark?"

I contradicted her just for the sake of it. I know that the more I contradict her the more excited the two of them become with their crazy obscenities.

"Don Antonio has owl's eyes, at night he can see where no one else can."

"He's seen yellow devils roaming the mountains stark naked."

"Don Antonio is a saint. He's got perfumed honey instead of blood."

"Do you know what he saw one night under a full moon?"

"Two foreigners, a man and a woman, eating each other's privates."

"What . . . what do you mean?"

"The man was lying naked with his head on her cunt and the woman was lying with her head on his prick and they were eating each other and afterwards she didn't have a cunt any longer and he didn't have a prick, they'd swallowed them up."

"Then the devil arrived and carried them away dancing."

"That man, the priest, is a bit psychic — he can see into things like a prophet, without using his eyes or his brains, just straight through with his holy spirit."

The sickly-sweet smell of burnt cloth broke the spell and Tota gave a scream. Giottina had burned a pair of trousers listening to her. Giottina rushed to fetch some water and threw it on the burn-mark.

"It's all your fault, you lousy cow, because you can't control your tongue. So now the Saint's punishing us."

"It's your fault, you bitch. Who started the story about Father Antonio?"

"You bastard!"

"You fucker!"

"Whore!"

"You're the whore, we all know that, you're messing about with that van-driver, a married man with four kids."

"Go and fuck the van-driver!"

"It's true!"

"What about you, then, you touch up your own nephew who can't even get a hard on yet, so what are you then?"

That started them tearing each other's hair. I tried to separate them and got a scratch on my forehead for my pains. It was only thanks to the greengrocer next door who came running in, closely followed by her husband, that we managed to separate them. It took the full strength of the three of us to pull them apart.

*10.00 p.m.*

Giacinto arrived home with an enormous shiny brown skate; Santino was carrying a netful of black sea urchins which glistened with green and violet reflections. Slowly they waved their spines in search of something to grip on. Santino picked one up and placed it in his curved palm. With his other hand he thrust a knife with a precise clean blow between the quills, causing them to shoot everywhere. The sea-urchin split open squirting a clear watery liquid on his hand. Santino put the knife down and with a thin horny finger scooped out the dark brownish pouches that fill the shell and threw them away.

"Those are the intestines," he explained in a slow voice. He rinsed the half valve with the eggs attached to it and put it into my hand. The filaments formed the shape of a star against the smooth grey enamel of the shell.

"Go on, suck them up."

I tried, after some hesitation and embarrassment. It was the first time I had tasted them. They had a strong pungent taste, initially as disgusting as the taste of a sweaty armpit. Then, once melted in my mouth, it became pleasant, sweet and sour like wild grass. Santino was watching me with his gentle blue eyes, and laughed at my grimaces. He was exultant, happy. He cooked the skate on a charcoal fire. As soon as its glistening skin began to curl up and crack Giacinto said it was ready. We ate it with lemon juice and olive oil. Its flesh is fatty and slightly bitter. After dinner Giacinto went for a nap. A little later I followed him. Santino stayed staring at the wall in front of him. He has the ability to stay in the same position absolutely still, like a cat. I know he isn't asleep. If I go out and come back I always find him with his eyes open, his legs and arms like stone, his chest so steady and quiet it looks as if he isn't breathing at all.

*7th August*

Tota came up to me looking like a prize fighter with a scar on her lip and a large blue bruise under her left eye.

"She tried to kill me, the bitch. I did worse to her, though, I ripped a piece of flesh this big from her neck."

"So your friendship is over, is it?"

She gave a sudden sour burst of laughter, her two gold teeth sparkling between her bloodless lips like two stars.

"Guess what we'll do now."

She dragged me by an arm, with an air of complicity.

"Come on, we'll buy some cakes and eat them in the shop."

So that's what we did.

*4.00 p.m.*

Giacinto is asleep. Santino is resting, lying on a deck-chair in the yard. I'm not sleepy. The thought of the school at Zagarolo comes into my mind and I wonder whether I should ask to be transferred. I hate that school, above all I hate its headmaster, his horsey face, his bulging eyes swollen up with stupidity.

If it wasn't for Fidelio I'd have left already. But I can't bring myself to leave him. His dark suspicious eyes, his bashful laughter, his horny hands, his droopy ears, his thick, straight, pitch-black hair. He's the only person who can compensate me for another year of boredom and hard labour.

Teaching like this is meaningless. I feel contaminated by my hatred of the school — a hatred that everyone feels, from the pupils to the teachers, from the caretaker to the headmaster, a dull dense hatred, utterly destructive because it isn't matched by the will to change things. The headmaster talks of "social duty", but doesn't believe in it. The only duty he fulfils with any enthusiasm is that of the cop: to control the timetable, to control discipline and to control our political beliefs. Last year he called me into his office to tell me off for bringing a "bolshevik newspaper" into the classroom. I don't know who could have spied on me.

"We are non-political here," he shouted, lifting up his arm in a gesture of despair. Then in a more subdued tone he spoke of "moral responsibility" towards the pupils, of a "balanced education", of "judicious caution" and other similar idiocies.

I'm running down a railway track of inertia like a train, and I can't see whether I'm surrounded by fields or lawns or houses or ruins. I'm deafened by this thundering, compulsive rush towards a destination I don't know. I follow the syllabus like everyone else, automatically, without thought . . .

Giacinto woke up. He came close to me. He kissed me on the nape of my neck and called me his "baby".

"Tonight we'll go to Santino's for dinner."

"Santino's? To his home?"

"We've been invited. His mother has invited us. Okay, just you and me? Don't you want to come?"

I said I thought it strange of her to invite us without knowing us. He shrugged his shoulders. He was cheerful and satisfied after a good morning's fishing. Santino had coffee with us, then he apologised with a gentle smile and went home.

"He's going to cook for us," Giacinto said, looking at him with pride.

"We should take something, some wine, don't you think?"

"No, no, I don't think so, they'd be offended. They are simple village folk."

## ADDIS

*Midnight*

At half past eight we are standing in front of Santino's house. Giacinto looks up at the steep staircase that leads to the first floor. The house is over a century old, of white stone, with small windows, thick walls and damp patches staining it all along its length. The doors are red and full of woodworm. We ring the bell. The boy I'm always seeing at the market comes to the door.

"My brother's sleeping. I'll go and wake him." He smiles amiably. His voice is as opaque and soft as Santino's.

"Sleeping? He said to come at eight o'clock." Giacinto speaks in a hard, annoyed tone of voice. I pinch his arm to stop him taking it out on the boy.

"You're Orio, aren't you?"

"Yes."

"Well, go and tell Santino we're here."

But Orio doesn't seem to have any intention of obeying him. He ushers us into a rectangular room with organdie curtains at the windows. He gestures us towards a sofa lined with imitation leopard skin. Next to it there's a red plastic armchair on which sits a big blond doll with its legs wide apart.

Orio closes the door behind him, leaving us there on our own. The house is quiet, there's not a sound to be heard. I stare at the sideboard in front of us. Inside its frosted glass I can indistinctly see plates, glasses, enamelled bottles, all neatly arrayed. The top is highly polished and on it is an array of garish objects: a madonna inside a gigantic shell, a ceramic boot filled with artificial flowers, a bottle of perfume shaped like an apple, an ashtray like an Egyptian boat, a cigarette lighter in the form of a small brass cannon. On the walls hang small paintings representing seventeenth century damsels strolling round the gardens of the royal park of Naples. Giacinto is nervous and looks repeatedly at his watch. He smokes a cigarette, then stubs it out on the boat-shaped ashtray which immediately capsizes. I pick up the cigarette ends and bend down to blow away the ash. At that moment the door opens and Orio comes in bearing a tray of glasses.

"Did you wake your brother?"

"No, I didn't."

"Why not?"

"Because when he's asleep, he doesn't like being disturbed. He'd probably give me a thump round the earhole."

"But where's your mother?"

"In the kitchen."

"Is there anyone else at home?"

"My father and my brothers."

"What are they doing?"

"I don't know."

"Then I'll go and wake up Santino."

Orio puts the tray down quickly and goes and stands in front of the door as if to bar the way. Giacinto gives up the idea. Orio goes out and locks the door behind him. I stand up, pick up the apple and sniff it. It exhales a sickly sweet perfume of tuber rose. I go back to the sofa and bend down to pick up my glass. I lift it to my lips and a yellow, sticky liquid burns my tongue. I drink two sips of it, staring through the window at a triangle of white sky.

"Aren't you drinking?"

"No, I'm not."

His eyes are sullen and menacing. He faces the door, motionless and rigid.

"Why get angry? They'll be here soon."

"Guests should be greeted. They should be made welcome, not left alone as if they were in a dentist's waiting-room." I laugh and gulp down another sip of the sweet orange-flavoured liqueur. A minute later Orio enters and beckons us to come. We follow him down a long, dark, cramped corridor and emerge into a large roomy kitchen with tall, narrow windows. The furniture is modern, made of wood and formica. The floor is paved with flowery, majolica tiles. A large mahogany fridge with a madonna on top of it towers against the back wall. Opposite it, the cooker stinks of frying fat. A short, chubby woman comes towards us with a friendly smile. She has a very beautiful, serene, clear face, with two bands of grey hair framing her full cheeks. In her hands she holds a plate of fried fish. She invites us to sit down.

"My son has told me a lot about you. Do take a seat."

"But where is he?"

"He's coming."

Meanwhile her husband has entered: a tall, lean, white-haired man with turquoise blue eyes. He shakes our hands energetically without a smile. Then he sits down at the head of the table, grabs a bottle of wine, fills up his glass, and at once puts the bottle beneath his chair. Santino's brothers follow him in and sit down: tall, thin, dark, they look cocksure and confident. They have listless faces, strong features and swimmer's shoulders, but none of them is as good-looking as Santino or Orio: there is a hint of brutality tainting their youthful faces. With them comes their sister: a plumpish girl with smooth, delicate features. I wonder to myself where these lads were while we were waiting in the lounge. We heard not a sound, not a voice, not a footstep. They all greet us, but without any feeling of friendliness. At once they begin to eat everything their mother brings to the table, silently and voraciously.

"Where's Santino?" asks the father, raising his head from his plate. He has sparkling, white, wolf-like teeth.

"He's coming," replies the mother, hardly turning. She concentrates on frying the fish in a large black frying-pan.

"If he doesn't turn up within two minutes, I'll throw him out."

The mother stirs the pan on the stove, without saying a word. The man looks at her with annoyance. He swallows his wine in a few gulps, pours himself out some more, and immediately returns the bottle to its hiding-place beneath his chair. No one takes any notice of us, except the mother who fills our plates every time they are empty.

Giacinto eats staring at his knife and fork, frowning to himself. I get the feeling that maybe it's one of us who should start the conversation, so I turn to the father and ask:

"What's the fishing like around here these days?" It's a bit of a silly thing to say, but I can't think what else to talk about. Giacinto looks daggers at me. The man turns to me slowly, and then answers in a dry tone of voice:

"I haven't been fishing for twenty years."

"But Santino told me . . . "

"Santino is a liar. Don't believe a word that bastard says."

"Do your sons go fishing?"

"My sons go fishing? No way. Gigi is a mechanic, Toto is a wholesale dealer, Armando is studying to be a land surveyor, Laura goes to a girls' boarding school run by nuns. They are all home on holiday just at present."

"What about Orio?"

"Orio goes to school, but he's a lay-about. He's just like his mother, he's a good-for-nothing."

"What about Santino?" Giacinto suddenly asks, looking at the man defiantly.

"Santino does nothing. He's a loafer, he's got no backbone."

"But he works, doesn't he? He works as a waiter."

"Oh yes, he does, he does. Once every six months, for a couple of weeks."

"Could I have a little wine, please?" Giacinto holds out his glass. The father looks at him with astonishment: apart from him no one in the house drinks, not even the mother. He reaches for the bottle under his chair and fills Giacinto's glass with ill-concealed rudeness. He doesn't offer me any. Immediately he conceals the bottle once again under his chair.

"Switch on the radio, Laura!"

A shrill voice is advertising detergents. The mother brings over a dish brimming with sweet and sour aubergines. At that moment Santino comes in. Without saying a word, the father picks up a knife and throws it at him. Santino dodges it and the knife sticks into the door-jamb. Santino extracts it, wipes it clean on his trousers and takes a seat between his sister and Orio. He looks round, his pale blue eyes smiling. There is a red blotchy mark on his cheek from where he was lying on the pillow.

"There he is, the lout, that's him," says the father, his mouth full, pointing at Santino cheerfully with a fork. Santino rests his hand open on his plate and stretches his mouth into a huge yawn. I can't avoid looking at his teeth which are clean, small, and very white. The mother brings her son a bowl of pasta. Self-absorbed and gloomy, the brothers carry on calmly eating. Giacinto is upset, I can see from his eyes which are cloudy and resentful. He finishes his wine, but doesn't dare to ask for more. He looks round at the other glasses, all filled with water, and resigns himself to drinking water as well. I turn to the girl who is the only one to show any interest in us and who looks at us from time to time shyly and enquiringly. A little curl the colour of ripe corn coils over her plump, white forehead.

"So you go to a convent boarding school?"

"That's right."

"What grade are you taking?"

"The sixth form."

"Oh, you're a good student then?"

"She's the best student in her class," the father intervenes proudly.

"Will you go to university?"

"God forbid!" Again, it's the father who answers while he pours out more wine for himself. "University? What university? She's already engaged, you know."

"Oh. Does her fiancé come from Addis?"

"He's the son of a friend of mine. Well, he's my partner, we share a small vineyard together. The boy's a good lad, really."

Laura opens her mouth to say something, but then changes her mind and carries on eating, her fork clutched between her pale fat fingers.

"Are any of your sons engaged too?"

"Engaged, huh! Their interests are quite otherwise. Eh, Toto?"

Toto winks at his father and the man sniggers. Laura titters. The mother serves another steaming dish.

"This island is nothing but a brothel, that's why I don't let Laura stay in the village. It's a whorehouse, all these German women who descend on us to go man-hunting. Switch off the radio, Lauretta!"

The speaker's voice is snapped off in the middle of pronouncing the words: ". . . the Greek Colonels". The father turns to the eldest son with a cheerful, inviting tone of voice:

"You tell them, Gigi, what you did to that eighteen-year-old English girl."

Gigi lifts his head, swallows the mouthful he's chewing and clears his throat. He prepares himself like an actor about to recite his lines, and his voice emerges harmonious and alluring.

"I bump into this bird as she's swimming alone a hundred yards from the shore. She's got no top on, only her pants, the whore. I say 'coming up?' — I was in the boat with Orio, see? It was stifling hot, it was one of those really scorching days. She says 'no thanks', the bitch, and swims off. I make a sign to Orio and we get closer again. She sails along like a fish and we follow behind. We were gradually edging her off shore. She swims and swims and tosses about, then when she's really tired we hoist her bodily into the boat. She was a sort of livid blue colour and her teeth were chattering, so I say: 'Do you see now that it's no use running away from a handsome lad like me?' First I dry her well, then I grab her by the neck with one hand and pull her knickers off with the other."

Giacinto stops eating and looks at the young man with a scowl of surprise on his face. Laura laughs softly, a napkin pressed against her mouth. The others go on chewing, their sleepy eyes expressing approval. Only Santino looks uneasy.

"She started wriggling like an eel, biting and scratching. I say: 'Okay then, if that's how you want it. You know what I'm going to do? Throw you back into the water. Why, first you go swimming around half-naked all alone, then you close your legs. You're just a prick-teaser, that's what you are.' I grabbed her and slung her back into the water and I said 'Well, cheerio, we're leaving you here.' Meanwhile we'd gone a really long way out and the sea was getting rougher. I say: 'Bye bye, and watch out for the sharks, the sea's full of them round here.' She got really scared, she was struggling and panting, taking in mouthfuls of sea-water, crying and swallowing her own tears. Orio says: 'If we're not careful that one really is going to croak.' I say: 'Wait just a little longer, till the peach is fully ripe, then we'll pull it on board and I'll eat it up.' When I see that she really can't cope any longer, I heave her up into the boat, dry her and screw her right there in the bottom of the boat. Well, it was all the same as screwing a dead fish."

The father extracts a fish bone from his mouth and smiles with delight. The mother brings on another casserole of chicken stew and peppers. But she still doesn't sit down. Her plate of pasta is there on the table, getting cold, untouched. She goes to the fridge, takes out a bottle of water and brings it to the table.

"Fine exploits indeed!" she burst out.

They all look at her. But she's once more at the stove, turning her back on us. The smoke rising from the frying pan wraps her head in a cloud. But the attention lasts for a moment only. The father is talking and everyone's eyes return to him.

"One lesson isn't good enough for those whores. There's no stopping them. Every year that goes by they become more and more revved up and shameless. They descend on us like vampires to suck our poor islanders' blood."

"They take 20,000 a night, though, those poor islanders" says Giacinto tartly.

"Yes, so they do. Bloody hell, if there wasn't a demand there wouldn't be the trade, would there? Go on, Toto, tell us what you did to the German woman who wanted to buy you."

Toto pretends to look shame-faced. He waves his hands in front of his face, nibbling his food rapidly, and casts cunning glances all round out of the corners of his eyes.

"Come on now, I'm your father. If I tell you to do something, you've got permission and you do it."

Toto gulps down a sip of water and wipes his mouth with a napkin. He starts telling his story in a warm, husky voice.

"Just like now, I was on holiday at home: eating, sleeping, swimming. One evening at the Del Mondo café this German piece comes up to my table and starts flirting with me. To cut it short, she says: 'I want to have it off with you' I say 'How much?' She says: '5,000 liras.' I say: 'Thanks very much. What do you think I am? An Irish wolfhound?' She says: 'I'll make it ten'. He interrupts the story to toss a breadcrumb into his mouth. His olive complexion has brightened, his cheeks are flushed. The father watches him indulgently. His brothers carry on eating indifferently, but their silence is like that of an attentive audience doting on their favourite actor in the darkness of a theatre.

"Anyway, after a bit of bargaining we fix it for 20,000. So I say: 'Let's go.' She pays off the waiter, takes me to the car and off we go. We arrive at her place up near San Andrea — all arches, flowers, flights of steps — the real thing! Meanwhile, before leaving the café I'd beckoned my brothers to follow us, in fact as I went into the house I saw our blue Fiat already parked alongside the garden wall."

"Do you really think this is interesting our guests, Toto? They certainly won't want to know how it continues. I've heard it a thousand times and it's disgusting."

Infuriated, the sons turn to their mother. She has broken the spell and now she stands by the stove, nervous and frightened. Her husband hurls a napkin at her.

"Why do you always have to poke your nose into other people's business?"

The woman looks at Santino seeking his support, but her son is looking vacant as if he were still asleep. He eats slowly, bent over his plate, moving the food to his mouth with obsessional delicacy. Of the others only Orio looks a little ill at ease. But he tries to cover up his embarrassment, of which he clearly feels a bit ashamed. He shovels enormous pieces of chicken into his mouth with nervous gestures. The sauce trickles down on to his quivering chin. Toto looks round to make sure he can count on his brothers' support, his father's complicity and his mother's silence. Then he continues with his story. He takes no notice of us, they've mistaken our dismay for admiration and our embarrassed silence for approval.

"Anyway the German woman ushers me in and offers me a vodka. 'Nice,' I say, 'thanks, so kind of you.' It was ice cold and she asks me if I want a slice of lemon in it. Okay, why not? I was getting closer and I start kissing her on the neck. She was all perfumed like a vase of flowers. I say: 'You smell okay.' She says 'Well, I've just had a foam bath.' I say: 'That's it, you smell of foam.' She laughs and I throw her on to the floor. She says, 'No, wait, let's go on the bed' I say: 'To do what, on the bed?' She laughs again, and meanwhile I've pulled out one of her tits, it wasn't bad either for a fifty-year-old. I say: 'Pretty good tits you've got.' She slides her fingers down to the buttons of my flies, so I say: 'Just a minute, baby, I must have a slash first'. But instead I go to the window and beckon my brothers in. Then I go back to her, tear off her clothes and get on top of her. As soon as she sees my brothers coming in she gets scared and tries to stand up. But I keep her down even though she wriggles and screams — she was as strong as a bull, the bloody whore. I say, 'Come on Gigi and Armando, you keep her down while I screw her!' Then Gigi and I kept her down while Armando screwed her, anyway in the end all three of us screw her, actually four of us because Orio was there, but he was too scared, poor fish, he couldn't get it in, so we helped push it in for him."

Orio lowers his head. His forehead is blushing, his lips pale, and the morsel of chicken stuck between his teeth doesn't seem willing to go up or down.

"She screamed as if she was being slaughtered, and I say: 'What are you shouting about, you silly cow? You've had four of the best pricks in the whole island, what more do you want?' 'I'll report you, I'll denounce you to the police,' she shouts, 'murderers, murderers.' I say: 'You thought you could buy me, Toto Pizzocane, for 20,000 miserable liras? You ugly German slut, you revolting bitch!' I spat on her and we walked out."

"She denounced you though, she wasn't kidding." The mother is holding a piece of bread dipped in oil. She has found renewed courage and speaks in a hard, accusing voice.

"So what? Father soon put things right, seeing the police sergeant is a friend of his."

"Oh sure, but he had to pay up all the same. The sergeant doesn't keep his mouth shut for nothing, you know."

"It was well spent money, all for the best. A lesson like that should be administered at Government expense."

"After all, we didn't hurt her, Mother!"

"She had four men for the cost of just one aperitif, all young and in their prime."

The brothers are now laughing with their mouths full. Only Santino refuses to participate in the performance, but in a passive, detached way. Laura shows her approval by laughing a bit uncertainly. The father looks at them with his eyes sparkling as if to say: "now you can see what my sons are capable of."

The only one who shows open dissent is the mother, but it's obvious that her opinion counts for nothing — all she's good for is to clear away the table. Giacinto and I sit there as stiff as ramrods, undecided whether to go or stay. In the end, I don't know whether out of curiosity or cowardice, we decide to stay. We make the decision without speaking, a rapid exchange of looks is enough. The mother carries the dirty plates to the sink and returns with some clean bowls. None of her sons helps her apart from Orio who now and then takes away a plate, clacking on the floor with his clogs. Every so often Laura stretches out her plump fingers and picks up a large piece of ricotta stuffed with candied fruit and thrusts it greedily into her mouth. Toto and Armando squabble over a piece of cake. The father makes a sign and Orio gets up and switches on the radio again. A husky, sensual voice accompanied by violins and electric guitar gushes out an inane song.

"Is that Purea Willey?"

"Sure it is."

"What a cunt!"

"She's singing in the village tomorrow."

"We're not blind, you dope, we can read the posters too."

"I think she's really beautiful."

"She sucks up men like eggs."

"She wouldn't suck me up, I can tell you."

"She would just eat you up in one single mouthful, you turd."

"I'd give her a kick in the mouth if she tried."

"Can we all go and see her tomorrow at the Ciao Ciao, Father?"

"No, we cannot."

"Why not, Father?"

"Because I say so."

"I know why. Because of the owner. Father wanted to buy the land next door off him and he refused. Didn't he, Father?"

"'I'll sell it to you, Peppino Pizzocane, for 3,000 per square metre', he says, the scoundrel. I say: 'Go and fuck yourself, you mingy bugger'." He makes a gesture with his hand. The sons laugh. This time the mother laughs too. Santino goes on eating, absorbed, his eyes white, motionless, mottled like milk.

"I reported him, though, to the harbour office for unlawful occupation of public land and he got a handsome fine, the bastard." Orio has fallen asleep, his head leaning on his folded arm. Laura removes the plate from under his cheek. The father stretches, stands up and yawns noisily.

"And now everyone to bed. Good night. By the way, what do you do for a living, young man?"

"I'm a mechanic."

"Ah. And what did your father do?"

"He was a farmer."

"You haven't gone a long way in your family, have you?"

Giacinto is about to open his mouth, but the man doesn't give him a chance to speak. He gives him a slap on the back, shouts "Good luck, mate!" and makes his exit followed by his sons. In the kitchen there remains Santino, the mother and Orio, who is still sleeping. Santino finishes his piece of cake and smiles absentmindedly. His mother goes up to him and pours him some wine from the bottle which the father kept hidden. She pours some out for Giacinto as well but he doesn't drink it. Santino raises his head and asks:

"Are you going to Punta Zafferana tomorrow?"

"Yes."

"Okay, cheers."

The woman sees us to the door and shakes hands with us solicitously: "You must excuse my husband and my sons, they're a bit heavy-handed, but underneath they're good-hearted, they don't mean any harm."

We take our leave. Outside the air is tepid. It smells of the sea. Giacinto bursts into nervous laughter, takes my hand and we run home.

*8th August*

At six thirty I was woken by a loudhailer announcing Purea Willey's arrival on the island. She's singing tonight and tomorrow night at the Ciao Ciao night-club, accompanied by 'The Frantic Babies'. At the market people are talking of nothing else. I met Tota in the doorway of the newsagents, cheerful and excited, with hair newly permed.

"Are you coming to the Ciao Ciao tonight?"

"What for?"

"To hear Purea Willey, of course, the Jaguar of Busto Arsizio."

"No, I don't think I'll go."

"They're giving me a reduction because sometimes I go and do the cleaning there! I know the manager. Do you know Signora Virginia?"

"No."

"That woman from Friuli who doesn't wear knickers. Well, everyone knows that. Sometimes they pay me to go there and clap to order, but this time there's no need for that. They're giving me a ticket for the first row, only 10,000 liras."

"10,000 liras, that's a lot."

"That's what you think. Do you know what an ordinary first row ticket costs? 30,000, and on the black market 50,000."

"Is Giottina going with you?"

"No, she prefers opera."

"So do I."

She looked at me, surprised. She shook her head with a gesture of commiseration. Then she went off to doll herself up.

*10 p.m.*

There was a lot of bustle and activity in the square. The mopeds were going back and forth making even more noise than usual. The Neapolitan families were raving about the singer, whose picture was on the front page of the Naples daily paper.

"That Purea makes me cry."

"Did you see her in 'Don't Ever Leave Me'?"

"I saw her in 'Disappointments in the Night'. But you know, she's certainly no beauty, she looks like a gorilla."

"It's her voice that stuns you."

"Yes, with a microphone to help it along. But have you noticed how she holds it? She puts it in her mouth, in between her teeth, on her tongue. Even a whisper sounds like thunder that way. It's just a put-up job."

"What about her legs though?"

"What about that flabby stomach then?"

"Well, after eight abortions what do you expect?"

"Who says eight abortions? Are you crazy?"

"I read it in headlines that big."

Giacinto was not interested in all this gossip about the singer. He separated the pistachio from the strawberry meticulously, his eyebrows knitted, his eyes far-away.

"What are you thinking?"

He lifted up his pale face, puckered by a sad smile. He didn't answer. He went on digging into the ice cream with his dessertspoon, engrossed in something distant and painful. When he's like this, it's better not to insist. I gazed down the dark alley from which the 'beauties' emerge. I like following their movements — so predictable and yet so full of surprises.

*9th August*

I was coming out of the bakery and bumped into Tota. She was carrying some bags bulging with dirty linen. I took one off her and walked with her to Giottina's. On the way I asked her about Santino's family.

"Who, Peppino Pizzocane? As cunning as a fox. Do you know him then? He's out to grab and cheat as much as he can, and he always gets away with it."

"What do you mean?"

"For instance he used to catch fish with depth charges. You know, bombs as small as your little finger which you throw into the water and then you catch a hundred, two hundred kilos of fish."

"That's forbidden, isn't it?"

"Of course it is, but he doesn't give a damn! With the sort of contacts he's got, he's okay, even when he gets reported he gets off scot free."

"And what does he do now?"

"He's bought a piece of beach and rents it to some boorish people from up North, but mainly he works as a sort of dealer, a front-man. He works hand-in-hand with this Di Gennaro character who's bought up all the plots of land at the foot of the mountain. Now he's done a deal with the Mayor and they're going to build him a council road and in exchange he's giving them a percentage on the sales. The result is the plots have shot up to 5,000 a square metre already. He's no fool, is he?"

"But what does 'front-man' mean, what does he do?"

"It means he's a sort of dogsbody, he goes ahead and sniffs out what's in the air, keeps the labourers quiet, looks after public relations, works with the authorities when the boss doesn't want to expose himself. If there's any little job that needs doing, like a fire, or cutting a few animals' throats as a warning, it's him who does it. In exchange he receives protection and also of course a rake-off — he isn't stupid!"

"What about his children?"

"The children have got him in the palm of their hands. He's pure gold. When they were little they lived on dry crusts, now they stuff their faces and dress up to the nines. He's sent his daughter to boarding-school, she's a beauty, as plump as a chicken. The sons too are well-built, strapping fellows. All except one, Santino, he's turned out bad, he doesn't like work, he doesn't like anything, he's good for nothing! He keeps running away from home, he doesn't care for anyone, his father sent him to work as a waiter, but he's no good, he'll end up in jail with an iron ball round his ankle, poor little sod."

"What about the mother?"

"She struck lucky. She ought to light a candle to St Francis."

"What do you mean?"

"If he hadn't married her, she'd still be eating off the pavement."

"Why?"

"He got her out of a brothel, didn't he? Because of a vow he'd made that if his sick mother recovered he'd marry a prostitute; his mother got better in spite of having cancer, and he kept his vow. There's no doubt he's a man of honour, that's for sure."

"Do the children know?"

"Do they know? Of course they do! When he's angry, he throws it all back in her face, he shouts so loud you can hear him from the harbour. 'I picked you out of a brothel, you whore!' Sometimes he punches her with his fists — he's a violent man. He isn't bad, though, he's a decent man, rich, pious, good-natured. You should see them when they go to Mass on Sunday, the whole family together, they're the best people in town, good-looking, devout, hard workers, oh yes, they're a very respected family."

"I'll just hand this stuff into the launderette now. I must go, I've so much to do at home."

"Wait, I must tell you about last night, about Purea. One of her shoulder-straps broke off in the middle of a song and . . . "

"No, I can't stay, it's late, I'll see you again."

She said goodbye, but she was disgruntled and her lips curled in a way that made her look like a fish.

*Midnight*

Santino hasn't come today. Giacinto is in a bad mood. He went out at ninc and came back empty-handed.

"Didn't you catch anything?"

"The water was too muddy. I got close to two marble-fish but then I lost track of them, and I almost got bitten by a murena that sprang out from behind a rock like a dart."

At five he went for a nap and didn't wake up till eight. I thought it was too late to go down to the piazza for ices, but he insisted, and when we arrived it was already half-past-eight. We sat at a table at the end of the square almost next to the public lavatory and ordered two melon-flavoured ices. Some of the tables were empty as most people had gone home to dinner. The Englishman with the monkey sipped a gin, sitting by himself with a book. From time to time he took a peanut from his pocket and handed it to the monkey. The animal squatted on his shoulder and diligently shelled the nut looking round with furtive, suspicious eyes.

As soon as we sat down, one of the 'beauties' arrived on his own. He was wearing a pair of egg-yolk yellow trousers, a mauve T-shirt tight at the waist, and a belt five inches thick with a golden lion's head as a buckle. He walked nonchalantly, letting his peroxide-blond quiff dangle on his forehead. He knew that all eyes were following him and he preened himself: he held his neck upright, thrust his chest forward and gently swayed his hips, rippling his stiff muscles beneath his tight trousers. His face is anything but beautiful, it reminds you of a pekingese: small, worried eyes hidden by thick eyebrows, snub nose and a large, lipless mouth. His body though is splendid. It makes you want to touch it, to dig your teeth into it.

"What happened to Theodora then?" asked Giacinto.

"What happened was that Acacio had to invent some really resounding spectacle, so he made his daughter copulate with a bear."

"In the circus?"

"Oh yes, it was the most eagerly awaited event of the season. The bears no longer drew the crowds, you see. You know what it's like — standing up on their hind legs, dancing with tambourines, a saucer in their mouths, or devouring live rabbits two at a time, it was all stale stuff. They wanted something new. Acacio was on the point of being sacked, especially now that everyone was talking about this extraordinary Libyan lion-tamer who had taught his beasts to eat up Christians in stages, first tearing off their genitals, then one buttock, then the other, then their head, and so on. So he thinks up this never-before-dreamed-of-stunt: his eight-year-old daughter having intercourse with a bear."

"How the hell does a bear manage to copulate with a little girl, I'd like to know?"

"The book doesn't say."

"They must have used a bench, or a couple of mattresses, or something."

"I don't know."

"A stool perhaps."

"Maybe."

"These fucking historians go on about wars and kings and popes, but never ever about young girls being forced to copulate with bears. I wish I could have lived then, so that I'd know better about that sort of thing."

"So that you'd have had to work like a mule?"

"Yes, up to my ears in debt, hanging about in doorways, whiling away whole afternoons watching the camels carrying slabs of salt from the desert, the women going to the well."

"How would you have paid off your debts then?"

"I wouldn't."

"If you didn't pay, they'd confiscate all your belongings."

"And if I didn't have anything to confiscate?"

"They'd sell your children."

"And if I didn't have any children?"

"You'd be made to work for nothing, you'd become a slave."

"And if I couldn't work?"

"They'd throw you down the bottom of a well."

"And if I spat on the State laws?"

"They'd lash you to the stake."

"And if I defended myself?"

"They'd crucify you."

"And if I minded my own business?"

"Somehow they'd catch up on you and make you pay, because you're poor and ignorant."

He started laughing. Then all of a sudden large drops of rain began to fall on the tables, creating havoc all around. The sky had become dark, there was a great clatter of shifting chairs, overturned tables, and laughter and squealing. The boys on the mopeds flew away like a swarm of birds, leaving a trail of purple smoke behind them. The German women stood up and without hurrying took shelter inside the café. The Englishman with his monkey walked off all hunched up along the Via Casamatta. He staggered and laughed to himself at the acrobatics of his little pet which had slipped inside one of his sleeves for fear of getting wet, and was squeaking petulantly. Only the disabled girl stayed where she was, looking round her with a haughty air. Her companion with the grey plait covered her head with a newspaper. The white-clad young boy laughed out loud at the people fleeing in panic. The Neapolitan families ran off, forgetting their bags on the tables, losing their clogs, and squealing as if they'd been caught in an earthquake. Giacinto didn't notice the rain until a drop landed in his cup of half melted ice cream.

"It's raining, Giannina."

"So I see."

"Let's go home, shall we?"

"Yes, let's go."

"What's for dinner tonight?"

"There's braised aubergines with bread-crumbs and tomatoes."

"Why don't we have a few of those almond biscuits those two women with glasses sell?"

We ran all the way up Via San Antonio at great speed, sheltering under the balconies, and keeping close to the walls. Giacinto stopped for a minute in front of the Pussy Pussy Bang Bang shop. Some pink floral slips fluttered from the mast of a cardboard ship, like a sail. The two owners stood behind the shopwindow, tastefully dressed, perfectly suntanned, well combed, gazing with melancholy down the empty street. Via Maramaldo, Piazza Trimuggia, Via Garibaldi, we ran all the way because by now it was raining cats and dogs, until there we were in front of the cake shop. Mother and daughter stood behind the glass door. Inside there's always a nice smell of cloves and caramel. On the counter are rows of trays loaded with cakes and pastries. Against the wall, on shelves of light-coloured wood, is a row of glass jars filled with sweets — silver, pink, light blue and red. The mother and daughter look so much alike you'd think they were sisters. They both have shapeless bodies, with breasts and bellies that merge into one single large protuberance. Each head is a ball of tight curls wedged between broad, bulky shoulders; their skin is pale and smooth, their teeth white and clean, their lips narrow and childlike, and their hazel eyes short-sighted and magnified by their glasses. They differ only in the colour of their hair, the mother's grey, the daughter's brown. They dress alike, in black. They wear the same tortoise-shell glasses. They laugh alike, tilting their heads timidly towards one shoulder.

Giacinto examined the trays closely one by one, enquiring about each different cake, what it contained, how it was made, what it tasted like and how much it cost. The two women answered in unison, smiling contentedly, not at all put out by this cross-examination.

"And what are those?"

"Ladies' fingers."

"May I taste one?"

The two women bent down simultaneously and bumped their heads together. But instead of being put out they burst into cheerful laughter. Automatically they both took off their glasses, cleaned the lenses on the hems of their dresses and put them back on their noses with the same placid gestures. The daughter passed the tongs over to her mother who bent down to pick up the cake. With trembling hands, as if she was about to catch a butterfly, she delicately closed the two silver tongs around the cake and offered it to Giacinto. At that moment the door opened with a jingle and the Englishman came in with his monkey. The two women gave a start of fear. The Englishman reassured them with a smile, and held his pet tight in his arms, as if to say that he would not let it damage their beautiful glass jars. The monkey looked at the cakes with shining eyes and emitted little shrill squeaks of anticipation. Then it stretched out a minute wrinkled black hand towards the counter, not insolently but with a look of humble supplication. Its master gave it a little rap on its arm. With a gesture of sympathy the two women simultaneously picked up a biscuit each and held it out to the monkey. For a moment the monkey gazed at the two biscuits, confused, not knowing which one to take. It turned to look up at its master's face for guidance, then it stretched out both its arms, grabbed both biscuits and thrust them into its mouth. The two women laughed with their mouths wide open, clapping their hands. The Englishman had to struggle to keep his balance on his large, wet feet. His small, bloodshot eyes were half-hidden beneath his heavy eyelids.

We went out with our box of cakes. It was still raining, though not so heavily. We arrived home, bathed in sweat, with wet hair and muddy shoes. From the yard rose a refreshing smell of damp soil and ripe tomatoes. I watched Giacinto's back as he arranged the cakes on a plate. I began to feel randy and wanted to make love. I told Giacinto and he replied "Let's have dinner first." We had baked potatoes with butter, salt and pepper. We stuffed ourselves with cakes. I was in a cheerful mood, I don't know why. Maybe because of this rain which had cleansed the air after a day of sultry heat. I helped him undress, taking off his trousers, his wet socks, his sopping wet shirt. I stroked his chest. I kissed his nipples that are so delicate and sensitive. Until a few years ago he was ashamed of letting me kiss them. He believed that only women's nipples should be kissed. He seemed to think it was very shameful to have sensitive nipples. Now when I take them between my lips he closes his eyes, arches his back and smiles happily. I warmed up his cold feet by rubbing them with my hands.

"Stroke my back, Vannina, will you?"

He lay down on his stomach. I sat on top of him, astride, and massaged his neck and shoulders, and then down his back, tracing his spine along the vertebrae with my fingers, loosening up his stiff muscles. I could feel him relax, abandoning himself to it with his eyes closed, motionless, satisfied. Little by little his arms grew heavier, his breathing too. When I bent over to kiss him on his ear, I saw he had fallen asleep. I lay down next to him and took his wrinkled penis in my hand. I watched him sleep. He had curled his lips into a childlike pout and some drops of saliva trickled out of the corner of his mouth. He seemed distant and elusive, yet so close and yielding. I felt I had never loved him so much.

*10th August*

Giacinto went out at nine. At ten I went shopping. I looked for Tota and found her chatting with the fishmonger. I stood waiting for her at the counter which was covered with seaweed and fish. The fishmonger, who wore a blue singlet and shorts, was cutting the head off a shark. Tota was talking to him about some common relative of theirs, and at the same time staring spellbound at the knife as it cut into the white flesh of the fish. Also on the counter, turned over flat on its back, there was another shark with its mouth half open, shaped like a crescent moon. A tiny red stain the size of a coin stood out in the centre of its broad, snow-white breast.

As soon as Tota had finished we went round to Giottina's. By now I don't take much persuading. Indeed, it's me who makes the first move to go to the launderette. The two women's extravagant tales relieve me of the boredom of my solitary mornings.

"I'll tell you something, last night Purea Willey went to Villa Trionfo and I got my brother to go after her."

"Your brother Pietro?" asks Tota eagerly.

"No, the little one, Pasquale. Maybe I did wrong, though, because he saw things there he shouldn't have seen."

"How old is he?"

"Eleven in November."

"Go on then, what did he see?"

This time Tota knew as little as I did. Giottina gave some heavy thumps with her iron on a pair of lilac briefs, her fat arms quivering with each thump. On her sweaty chest glittered a thick gold necklace with the head of the Madonna in light-blue enamel.

"That man, poor little fellow, they've bewitched him. He's got no freedom any more, he's bound to them hand and foot."

"He's bewitched, bewitched, I told you so, didn't I?"

"Just listen. Purea goes in and the first thing she does is to take off her wig!"

"Are you joking? That amazing hair of hers, its not real, it's a wig?"

"Too true. Underneath that glorious mop her skull's as smooth and white as an egg."

"Shaven?"

"Shaven. She hasn't a single hair anywhere on her body, the shameless creature, it's as if she's made of marble, all clean and white and powdered."

"For all the world like a holy nun."

"She wasn't always like that, you know. She was born as hairy as a baboon. She had so much hair on her chest that she sweated like a tropical jungle and mushrooms used to grow out of it."

Tota took out a paper bag full of sweet green olives and poured a dozen into the palm of my hand.

"That's why her voice is so deep and stormy, because it comes from that jungle like the sound of a boa-constrictor."

"And your brother, what did he see next?" asks Tota, leaning forward.

"I can't tell you, it's too disgusting, it makes me feel sick."

"Go on Giottina, tell us."

"It gives me the creeps."

"We are all friends here."

"There's something weird about that woman's body, she isn't normal. In short, she's . . . the fact is she isn't a woman."

"There! I've always thought she wasn't a real woman, you can tell from her voice, there's something diabolical, unreal about it," said Tota chewing another olive, and speaking very slowly as if preparing herself for some mysterious ceremony.

"For dinner they gave her a huge dish of sole as big as a tray — swordfish, lobsters, oysters, the lot. They went on shoving it back for two hours till everyone was worn out and bloated with food. Then Purea went into the beautiful pink bedroom and the maid followed to help her undress. She stood there as stiff as a ramrod, and the maid took off the shimmering red lamé dress she had on when she sang at the Ciao Ciao, then she took off her wig and then her bra — it seems she's got very large handsome white breasts with coal-black nipples." Giottina stopped, seized by a sudden dizzy spell. She put down the heavy steaming iron and bent double with a groan.

"What's up? Are you feeling sick?"

"I suddenly came over all faint."

"Can I get you a glass of water?"

"Just let me rest a little. I'll be better in a tick. There now, my heart's pounding, feel!" She grabbed Tota's hand and thrust it inside her dress on to her sweaty breast. Tota kept it there motionless, biting her lips with an air of perplexity. Then she resumed eating her olives, spitting out the stones on to a small square of newspaper. I dashed to open the door that gives on to the road, which is the only ventilation there is, and I was met by a gust of hot, fresh air. The sea breeze swept into the room, dispersing its poisonous fumes and making the clean dresses which hang from the ceiling dance and twirl about. Tota rushed to the door and closed it again.

"Leave it open, one can't breath in here!"

"No, Vanna, no. Fresh air is okay, but it's no use at all. It's not the air, it's just exhaustion. Do you know how long Giottina works in a day? Twelve hours, twelve terrible hours, sometimes even fourteen, and do you know how much she earns? 50,000 liras a month. Do you see now, if she didn't cheat her customers a bit and fiddle the bills here and there she'd starve to death. Do you understand now?"

She drew close to her friend and thrust an olive into her mouth. Giottina recovered her equilibrium. She spat the olive stone to the ground, clutched the iron and resumed ironing energetically, looking at us with her two dark lustrous eyes.

"Then the maid took off her panties, and out came everything: a beautifully white swollen opening, just like a woman, but from it poked another thing that was really out of place."

"What was it, Giottina, darling?" Tota stretched forward with wide-open eyes and her hands clasped in between her thighs. "Tell us, dear friend."

"A long white worm."

"Oh, Mother of Mercy! How terrible, how ugly!"

"Purea is made like that, half man, half woman."

"And the maid, what did she do when she saw that?"

"When she saw she had that limp worm dangling between her legs, she bent down and kissed her reverently, as you'd kiss the holy wafer."

"But why?"

"I don't know that."

"And Purea?"

"Purea was a bit bashful, but she didn't say anything."

"Then?"

"The maid helped her lie down on the bed, then she went and called her mistress."

"Go on."

"The two came back together and there was Purea fast asleep, stark naked, beautifully white, hairless, perfumed, all powdered on her privates which looked like a little mountain of white sugar." The story was interrupted by the arrival of a customer. The two women looked at her with hatred. Giottina grabbed the bundle of dirty linen off her and pushed her out.

"Isn't that the chambermaid at the Pensione Stella? Iolanda from Pozzuoli?"

"Yes, that's her, the shameless cow, she has it off with Ciccio Canna, who owns the chip-shop on the sea-front."

"Ciccio Canna is a decent guy. They all say he killed his wife with rat poison, but who knows — you can't be sure, it's just village gossip."

"You must be careful, Vannina, this village is so riddled with gossip and scandal, whatever you do is everyone's business."

"All villages are the same."

"No, here it's worse because we're an island, we're on our own, even when the place is chock-full of tourists we're alone. We know each other too well, we're all related, we're one flesh."

"And Purea Willey, Giottina, what about her? What did the mistress do when she saw her like that, naked?"

Tota was anxious to hurry back into those sleazy waters we'd been immersed in before the interruption.

"The mistress and the maid stood there together looking down on her as she slept. Then the mistress turned to leave, but the maid transfixed her with blazing eyes, so she began to undress rather hesitantly."

"And the husband?"

"The husband stood on the balcony, watching through the window. He was crying."

"But how could Pasquale see all this from the garden, in the dark?" I asked.

"There was a full moon, that's how."

"Then?"

"The maid, fully dressed, pushed the two naked women against each other, belly to belly. Then she got hold of Purea's worm and thrust it with her fingers into her mistress, who was trembling all over as if she was half dead."

"She's crazy, she's crazy, it's a bad omen, even worse than St Eustachio's black garlic."

"The husband watched and cried, poor thing, his tears formed a little lake on the floor but he didn't even notice. He stood there with his feet all soaking and peered at the three women with vacant eyes: the snow-white one all powdered and floury, like a sole, the dark one with her dyed hair, rolling about together like two poisonous snakes, and the third one, like an evil dwarf, fully dressed and made up, directing the whole operation."

"And Purea Willey, the saintly creature, did she wake up?"

"One of them was kissing her on the mouth, the other was holding her worm between her fingers, but she never stirred: until the maid gave out a perfidious scream when she found that beneath that worm there was nothing. Then she woke up."

"Nothing, what do you mean nothing? Nothing what?"

"Nothing at all. No balls, no sperm, nothing, so the worm would just stay being a worm and would never change into a butterfly."

"Poor Purea, poor thing. What did that crazy maid do then?"

"She started kicking her up the arse."

"And Purea, poor child, what did she do?"

"She fell into a deeper and deeper sleep, she tossed and turned, she stuck out her beautiful white bottom which shone like a lantern."

"What a sight, what a sight!"

"It shone so bright that my little brother got dazzled staring at it."

"And then?"

"Then, I don't know, because Pasquale got scared and came back home."

Tota sighed. Giottina closed her eyes, once again seized by a dizzy spell. I stood up, mopping the sweat off my neck. I was in desperate need of a breath of fresh air. I opened the door and went out. The light outside made my eyes smart. The sea air was very cool and caught the back of my throat painfully.

*Midnight*

Giacinto came back at three, with two live octopuses hanging from his belt and dripping black ink. He dropped them in the kitchen and went to lie down on the bed. He seemed to be in a foul mood.

"Have you seen Santino?"

"No, I haven't."

"I wonder where the hell he's hiding."

"Perhaps he's found a job."

"Have you got any of those cakes we bought yesterday?"

I fetched the few that were still left. He thrust them greedily into his mouth, two at a time. I picked up the octopuses. They were still moving and the smaller one stretched out its soft sticky tentacles and clung to my arm. Its pads sucked at my skin. I hit it against the floor, but I couldn't kill it.

"Bite its head."

Giacinto was watching me from the bed, chewing cakes. He was enjoying himself. He wanted to see how I would cope with the situation. I brought my mouth near to the shiny frozen head of the octopus. I met two tiny livid wet eyes, savage with fear. I didn't have the courage to bite it. I took hold of a knife and gave it a mighty blow on its head, and cut it in two. But it still kept on moving, and with its head all smashed lying on its side, the tentacles groped their way towards the edge of the table, clinging to the plate and grasping my fingers. I grabbed the two pieces and threw them into the boiling water, and turned away to concentrate on chopping up the parsley. From the frothy water I thought there rose a wheezing gasp like a death-rattle.

I put the lid on the pan. Giacinto fell asleep and all was silent. The only sounds I could hear were the crickets and the distant murmur of the market. Then the silence was suddenly broken by a strange hissing. I looked out into the yard and saw that a bundle of rubbish had fallen just under the wall that separates us from the neighbours. This time I had seen it, they couldn't deny it had come from their side. I picked it up and went to take it back to them. I rang the bell. The old woman came to open the door. She sniggered. A moment later the young woman arrived and I told her I had seen the bundle fly over the wall. She looked at me in dismay as if she didn't understand. Then she grabbed me by the arm, dragged me into their kitchen and made me sit down on a chair. She took out a whitish liqueur, some ricotta cheese heaped up on a saucer with a floral design, a glass and a teaspoon. She looked at me with such thoughtful tenderness that I didn't know what to say. I tried to swallow a piece of ricotta, but didn't like it. I plucked up courage and confronted her.

"Excuse me, why on earth don't you throw your rubbish into the dustbin?"

"We don't have a bin, my dear."

"Well, buy one then."

"How can we? You can see for yourself, there are ten of us, we've hardly enough money to buy food let alone dustbins."

"A dustbin isn't expensive."

"Who's going to give us the money, my dear, if you knew how hard it is for us!"

I was about to say that they have the money to stuff their faces with ice creams every evening, but I couldn't say a word. The woman picked up the teaspoon, filled it up with ricotta and thrust it into my mouth as if I were a child.

"Isn't it good? It comes from the mountains. Come on, my dear, eat it, eat it up."

And what about the motorboat they squabble about from morning till night, and all those fishes whose heads I catch glimpses of inside the rubbish bundles? Can it be true they haven't got enough money to buy a dustbin? The woman didn't let me talk. As soon I finished one mouthful she scooped up another spoonful and pressed it against my lips. To stop her I had to get up and rush away leaving the bundle behind on the table. But she caught up with me in the doorway. She clutched my shoulder with an iron hand, her eyes stared straight into mine with a look of ferocious determination and she put the bundle into my arms.

*11th August*

Santino is back. He came back at three, all dressed in black, smiling serenely, his golden tuft hanging over his clear eyes.

"What's happened?"

"Why?"

"You're dressed in black."

"Oh! My father died."

"Oh dear, I'm very sorry."

"He was a good father."

"I had the impression you hated him."

"I didn't kowtow to him, but I didn't hate him. Now there's going to be a big row."

"Why?"

"He didn't leave a will. Gigi has produced a piece of paper that says he left everything to him as the eldest son. Toto says he's hand in hand with the notary, who is his godfather, and wrote it himself. Armando took a pot shot at him with dad's pistol, but missed. Now they've dragged in the lawyers and everyone's at daggers drawn."

"And your mother?"

"In Gigi's will she isn't even mentioned. Toto says that's proof it's a fake because Gigi hates my mother, whereas father loved her."

"What's going to happen then?"

"We've got to wait, haven't we, while the Judge decides whether the will's a fake or not. If it is Gigi will be sent to jail, and if not Toto will."

Giacinto arrived. When he saw Santino his expression changed. He burst into laughter, hugged him and asked why he hadn't shown up. Santino told him about his father and the family bust-up. Giacinto listened to him as he cut open the fish's belly. He ripped out its entrails with impetuous, good-humoured gestures.

"Your brothers seemed to be all good friends."

"Before father died, yes, they were. Now, they're not."

"Has he left a lot of property?"

"I don't know. I think yes, he's left quite a bit. He never told us what he owned, there's the stretch of beach, the house, some money in the bank but I don't know how much."

"They'll end up agreeing amongst themselves and you won't get a halfpenny."

"But I've got my mother. While father was dying she carried off a box full of silver and gold things he kept hidden under one of the floorboards."

"Don't your brothers know about it?"

"Maybe they do, but now it's buried in a vineyard up in the mountains and no one knows where it is, only mother and I."

"And the house?"

"Laura says the house is hers, my brothers have promised it to her. It isn't worth much anyway, it's old and falling to pieces, but anyway they say she can't have it because she's under age."

Giacinto watched him with a look of surprise, as if he was discovering a new Santino, quite different from the one he knew. We had roast grouper and tomato salad with oregano and basil. Giacinto and Santino between them knocked back the bottle of red wine which he hadn't touched for the past three days. Santino talked more about the will. He was excited, he took off his dark jacket because he was so hot. A thick black band was stitched to his white shirt at the level of his heart. He rolled up his sleeves and ate greedily everything I put on his plate. Before he went he invited us to go to his father's funeral which takes place tomorrow morning at ten. I said I wouldn't go, but Giacinto said yes, he would.

*12th August*

Half the village turned out for Peppino Pizzocane's funeral: relatives, friends, the parish priest, the police sergeant, the choir of the Daughters of Mary, the butcher, the grocer, the barber, and many others.

The widow, calm and beautiful, with a round violet hat on her head, followed the coffin leaning on her two eldest sons, Laura sobbed on Santino's shoulder, Orio was pale and grave and there were traces of dried tears on his cheeks. Armando carried the inlaid mahogany coffin along with three other sturdy youths whose faces were blistered by the sun. We passed in front of Giottina's launderette. I looked inside but I couldn't see a thing. The windows were steamed up. We moved up Via Garibaldi, the midday sun shining straight down on us. The graveyard is wedged between two small, rocky hills. Its gates were wide open. We slowly made our way between the tombs of bluish-grey stone which comes from the quarry at the foot of the mountain. Tota says they sell it as holy stone because once upon a time the whole mountain was thought to be holy and people used to climb the steepest rocks to beg God for grace. We stopped at a corner right next to the boundary wall. There were no cypresses in that corner of the graveyard, only some stunted lemon trees with dark leaves that gave off a pleasantly astringent scent. The coffin was lowered into the grave. The widow stared transfixed at the hands of the labourers who were controlling the rope, she didn't take her eyes off them for a moment. In her tired swollen eyes there was a hint of joyful relief. I looked down to the sea at the bottom of the valley. I could see the village, grey and compact in the centre, white and spread-out towards the outskirts. A silvery thread crossed right along its length, disappearing out of sight towards Punta Zafferana. In the background was the sea, thick and muddy. It becomes lighter towards the horizon, so light that it merges into the pale blue sky.

They started shovelling earth into the grave. Two women began to cry loudly. Another woman gave a deep, sinister scream like a hungry wolf and this was repeated by several other old women. Then there was a bustle of dark bodies, some kneeling on the ground, others starting to tear their clothes. The funeral was on the point of turning into an archaic primitive ritual. The priest came forward, patient but determined; he restrained the women and suppressed their screaming; he whispered some prayers, holding the prayer book tight between his fingers like a flag. The women drew back. The solid citizens crossed themselves. The ceremony was over.

We traced our steps back to the village. In Via San Perfido they insisted on dragging us all into their house, where there was a reception with refreshments. I would have preferred to go home, but Giacinto wanted to stay. Laura, once again her smiling self, was passing round a tray loaded with cream cakes. Orio followed her with a trayful of glasses. The people huddled into small groups in the corners of the room, talking softly and mournfully. The widow had taken her place in a velvet armchair with patched arm-rests from which she accepted the condolences of relatives and friends who paraded in front of her and kissed her hand. Her mouth was twisted with grief, but her eyes were mocking and contemptuous as she stared up at the false faces of her guests. Gigi, Armando and Toto stood next to her, dressed all in black, like three large, gentle but threatening angels. Santino ate one cake after another, sitting comfortably on his father's bed. With one foot he trampled on the white mosquito-net that had protected the corpse from flies. From time to time he raised his gentle, pale blue eyes and nodded a greeting to someone, as he kept on chewing.

*Midnight*

Giacinto is in bed with a temperature. He says he's got a sore throat and he can't breathe. He sent me to the square to buy him an ice cream. I told him that ice cream is bad for him, but he made such a fuss that I slipped on my shoes and went down to the Café del Mondo. I picked my way between the crowded tables and went in. I ordered a pistachio and strawberry ice. As I was paying for it, I heard excited voices. In the doorway I found myself face to face with Purea Willey. I stood there gaping at her, unintentionally blocking her way in. Her head was wrapped in a scarf of red silk. Beneath her marble-white forehead her pale face was pierced by two dark, determined, hard eyes. She's much taller than me and her slim, supple body gives off a strange scent of oriental spices. I looked carefully to see whether she really was bald, but she didn't appear to be. Her face is smooth, compact, without a trace of powder. Meanwhile, the crowd thronged behind her, pushing and cheering. Three powerful-looking young men spread their arms and enclosed her in a protective circle. But Purea sent them away fearlessly and entered the café alone, spreading confusion among the waiters. Her admirers followed, pushing and trampling each other and shouting.

"Purea!"

"Purea, sign this photograph."

"Purea, please give me a kiss!"

"Purea, go on, sing something for us."

"Look, Pinuccia, look love, that's Purea, the television star, look at her!"

"Yes, it's her, it's Purea. Wow! Look at her eyes."

"Purea, you're so beautiful. Give me your hand, darling, I've dreamt of holding your hand for years."

"I've got your picture here, please sign it."

The crowd swelled. The bodyguard couldn't keep back the people who stampeded forward to touch her, kiss her, talk to her. Someone tore a piece of her dress. Immediately someone else snatched her red scarf leaving her bare-headed, her platinum blonde hair stuck to her skull. Someone's hands clutched her organdie blouse. They ripped it in two leaving her bare-chested. Purea got scared and started screaming. Other feverish hands were tearing at her black cotton skirt. As she screamed her bodyguard started punching and kicking so violently that in no time they'd managed to hack their way through the crowd. They grabbed the singer and carried her away bodily, lifting her over the counter and through the back entrance. The crowd was now yelling furiously. The waiters were trying to clear off the children who had climbed on to the counter. I had received two elbow-blows in my stomach and a punch on my shoulder. Heaven knows what had happened to Giacinto's ice cream. Amidst the confusion glasses and bottles had crashed to the floor, strewing it with broken glass. When the hall finally cleared, I saw a large bundle dumped against the wall. I looked closer: it was our neighbour's old lady. She stood there hunched up and trembling. She had two chocolate ice creams squashed on her chest, a few bits of glass in her lap and a smear of blood on her cheek. Her white hair was loose and tangled and one shoe was missing. She was holding one of her arms and moaning. I went to try and help her. She bit my hand.

*13th August*

Giacinto still has a slight temperature. All the same he insisted on getting up and going down to the square for an ice cream. We sat in a sheltered corner, next to the fountain. We gave our usual order, a pistachio and strawberry ice for him and an iced lemon drink for me. At eight o'clock the trio arrived and went to sit by the fountain. The disabled girl was dressed in white and wore some red geraniums in her hair. She ordered a lemonade. As she sipped it I noticed she was looking at me. She stared at me with smiling eyes. But my thoughts were far away, I was scanning the scene for the arrival of the 'beauties'. Shortly afterwards they emerged from the alley, one at a time. First came the blond with the gold cross, then the very slim one with a face like an ape, locks down to his shoulders and a silver bracelet on his wrist. Behind him was another one called 'The Star', with black eyes, raven hair and a dark, thick-set body. There were two solitary German women sitting aloof, magazines open on the table, aperitifs in their hands. Of the two, one was quite old, her hair very obviously dyed, her fat thighs encased in tight-fitting fondant pink trousers. Her face had a look of desperate, hard sensuality. The other one looked younger, she must have been around fifty. By the style of her clothes, the cheerful smile on her face and the way she wore her hair combed back on her neck there was something simple and genuine about her.

Giacinto played with the teaspoon inside his metal cup. He didn't look around, he seemed absorbed in some jealously-guarded secret.

I kept feeling the eyes of the disabled girl fixed on me. Suddenly I saw her stand up and come limping towards our table. Giacinto noticed her only when she started speaking. He dropped his spoon on the ground in surprise. He stood up and offered his seat to her, but she didn't want to sit down.

"I would like to talk to you for a moment, may I?"

I said yes, of course she could. I went with her to the end of the square, walking slowly to adjust my pace to the rhythm of her crutches.

"I've been looking at you for days. Haven't you noticed?"

"No, I haven't. I did today, for the first time."

"You have a very sweet face. You're shy, aren't you?"

"Well . . . .Yes, a little, I suppose."

"Do you know Santino Pizzocane?"

"Yes I do."

"Has he ever told you about me?"

"No, he hasn't mentioned you."

"I know he goes to your house every day. He's fascinated by the man who lives with you. Your husband, is he?"

"Yes, Giacinto."

"He's always talking about him."

"I didn't know you knew each other. He's never said anything to me."

"We sleep together. I'm in love with him, but he doesn't love me. Not much anyway. Where are you from?"

"We live in Rome, but I'm Sicilian by birth. And you?"

"I live in Naples. My mother's English, my father Turkish."

"Are you here on holiday?"

"Do you know that Santino worked as a waiter at my place, did he tell you?"

"No he didn't."

"I've had infantile paralysis and I can't walk without crutches, my legs are paralysed from the knees down. Sometimes I have to wear splints, but I hate them, I'd rather use crutches. One leg is much better than the other, the right one, but altogether I'm quite a wreck. All the same I have a beautiful body. Do you think so?"

I nodded assent. I looked at her delicate sun-tanned hands gripping the tubular iron handles. As she talked she threw her head backwards, shaking her long chestnut hair. Her face is very beautiful, unsymmetrical and feline: her forehead wide, her grey eyes long and narrow, her nose small and straight, her lips fine and her chin rounded with a little dimple in the centre. She speaks with the high-pitched voice of a little girl.

"Santino is good-looking, isn't he?"

"Yes, very good-looking."

"Do you think he's in love with me?"

"I'm sorry, I really don't know."

"Will you do me a favour if I ask you?"

"What sort of favour?"

"Talk to him about me, try to find out whether he loves me."

"I'll try to, if you like."

"I'm not jealous of you, it's your husband I'm jealous of. I think Santino has fallen for him in a big way." Her smoky-grey eyes rested for a moment on my face, anxious and questioning. She was studying closely the effect her words were having. I thought she must be a bit neurotic and had invented the whole story to attract attention. She's the sort of person who must be the centre of attention, I thought to myself: those garish clothes, flowers in her hair, her quick, impulsive way of talking. All of a sudden I found her disagreeable and ridiculous. She was watching me, and she seemed to read my thoughts. In fact she said immediately in a sad tone of voice: "You're thinking I'm a crazy exhibitionist and you don't like me."

"Well, it's true, I was thinking just that."

"Can I ask you another favour?"

"That is?"

"Don't tell your husband what I've just said to you?"

"What am I to tell him instead?"

"Tell him I'm in love with you and I've asked you for a date."

"Why should I invent such a complicated lie?"

"He'll believe you straight away. He's the type that believes anything. He's not interested in anything except himself. I don't think he loves you much, you know, he couldn't care less. I'm sorry you're so unfortunate as to have a husband who's that uncaring, you might just as well not have one at all."

"You're wrong, Giacinto loves me a lot, and we're very happy together."

"Well, let's go back now. Don't forget your promise, and tomorrow I'll come and see you."

I invented a different story to tell Giacinto. But he wasn't at all curious about my encounter with the disabled girl. He continued to occupy himself with his own secret thoughts.

I now realise that I forgot to ask the girl her name.

*14th August*

I was woken up by the thud of the neighbour's rubbish bag. Today, though, there was a bottle inside the bundle which broke as it fell, shooting slivers of glass everywhere.

I got up. I picked up the bits of glass, wrapped them in a piece of newspaper and threw them back over the wall.

At midday, when I got back from shopping, I found the yard a complete mess. While I had been out, the neighbours had had a field day, throwing dozens of bottles everywhere. One of them had shattered against the window, breaking it. Another had sliced a large, beautiful banana leaf clean off. Splinters of glass were everywhere, even inside the kitchen.

"It's better just to ignore those people; if you react it just makes things worse." So said Giacinto, and I had to admit he was right. Today he's in a good mood: he came back from the sea with his belt loaded with fish. Santino was with him, wearing electric yellow trunks and a blue and white striped T-shirt.

We had lunch out in the yard, in the shade of the banana trees. Later, Giacinto went for a nap. I cleared the table, did the dishes, washed the pans, wiped the cutlery, polished the kitchen-sink: then instead of lying down on the camp-bed in the kitchen, I sat in a deck-chair beside Santino.

"Listen, what's the name of that disabled girl I keep seeing at the Bar Mondo?" I asked him.

"Suna."

"What sort of name is that?"

"It's Turkish."

"Do you know her well?"

"So so."

"Why haven't you ever told us about her?"

"I've never had occasion to."

"But she is a friend of yours, isn't she?"

"Yes and no."

"Do you like her?"

"Yes, I do."

"Do you make love to her?"

"Sometimes."

"Are you in love with her?"

"I don't know."

"You mean to say you don't know whether you are in love with someone or not?"

"I don't know."

"Does she love you?"

"Who knows?"

"But you see each other often?"

"Every day."

"So when you leave here you go to see her?"

"Sometimes yes, sometimes no."

"But why haven't you ever told us about her?"

"You've never asked me."

"And the two of you talk about us?"

"Yes, when she wants to."

"She's very attractive and she moves beautifully in spite of her crutches. Do you mind her having to use crutches?"

"No, that doesn't worry me."

I was asking stupid questions, I was aware of it. I was going round and round in circles. I felt I was being boorish and interfering. As I was trying to think of something to change the subject, I heard Giacinto's voice calling. I went into the bedroom. He was curled up naked and looked at me frowning.

"What have you and Santino got to talk about?"

"Does it worry you?"

"I can't get to sleep. Stay here with me." He seized one of my hands and drew it close to his mouth. He kissed my wrist, bathing it with saliva. He fell asleep like that, my hand between his, a frown on his forehead, his lips tightly clenched.

*Midnight*

At seven thirty we went down to the square. Immediately I spotted the entire family of our neighbours. They took up two tables and a dozen chairs. I was about to go up to them and complain about the bottles, but they pre-empted me by greeting me with great cordiality. They smiled warmly as if I were one of their closest friends, and I lacked the courage to go and confront them. The old woman had one of her arms in plaster. She glared at me with malevolent eyes.

Suna wasn't there. We had an ice cream and talked about Theodora and the Byzantines.

Giacinto doesn't like reading, but he loves me to tell him what I'm reading. At times he gets quite obsessed about a story and he forces me to tell it all chapter by chapter, and then he asks questions and makes comments.

"Pope Virgilio went all the way from Rome to Byzantium? Good God, that's a long way, isn't it? Wasn't it dangerous?"

"They were the bosses after all, Italy was packed with Byzantine soldiers."

"They could have butchered him like a pig!"

"They'd made him Pope because he was obedient and did what he was told."

"Then why did they want him in Constantinople?"

"Because he had disowned the Monophysites protected by Theodora, and they wanted him to change his mind."

"And what about Totila, that son of a bitch?"

"As soon as the Pope left Rome, he invaded it, but Belisario went after him and kicked him out."

"But how did a mechanic like me, a working-class yob, manage to survive? I bet your book doesn't tell you that."

"You're right, it doesn't."

I saw Tota on the other side of the road. She was waving her hands and beckoning me. I went over to say hello.

"You don't show up any more, why's that?"

"I couldn't, I've been busy."

"Giottina told me to give you a message: Watch out for the evil wings of the one who can't fly."

She threw these sibylline words in my face and then walked off, an enigmatic smile on her fleshy lips.

*15th August*

Giacinto went out at eight. At nine I heard a knock on the door and went to open it. It was Suna, together with the young boy dressed in white.

"This is Oliver, my brother."

She was wearing a light blue skirt and had no flowers in her hair. She looked even more beautiful and glowing than when I see her in the evening at the café. From close to, her narrow lips look like a scar on her bronzed skin. There is something painfully sad in the expression of her mouth, but when she smiles she becomes sweet and childlike. Her teeth are very white and even.

"Did you talk to Santino?"

"Yes I did."

"Do you mind if I make myself a cup of coffee? Oliver, go and buy me some lump sugar."

"I have sugar, as much as you want."

"I prefer lump sugar." She handed a 1,000-lira note to her brother, and he ran off hopping on his light blue tennis shoes. Suna went into the yard to look around. She went up to the banana trees, bent to pick a basil leaf, and broke off a caper from the bush that clung close to the bottom of the wall.

"Then what did he say?"

"He said he doesn't know whether he loves you or not."

"Do you think he's sincere?"

"I don't know. To tell the truth I don't like this role you've forced on me."

"I've given him lots and lots of money, I don't know how much, it could be half a million liras."

"What on earth for?"

"Just because . . . well, once he wanted a moped so I bought him one, but then he lent it to a friend who smashed it up against a tree. Another time I gave him some money to buy his mother a ring."

"A ring, but why?"

"He wanted to give her an aquamarine. Mind you, he didn't ask me for the money, he isn't grasping at all. When he's got money he just throws it away. I know his father has made a fortune on the black market with all his swindles, but he doesn't give him a penny, he sends him off to work as a waiter."

"His father died a few days ago."

"Did he? That's strange, Santino hasn't said anything to me. He's so good-natured and affectionate, I suppose I've lost my head over him. But he's so good-looking — have you ever seen him naked?"

"No, I haven't."

"He's so fair, so smooth and tall, he has such slim hips, a bottom that sticks out so sweetly, and a wonderful golden prick. Do you think I'm going to lose him?"

"I don't know."

"I like everything about him, I can't get angry with him. Do you think that spying on people is a sign of great love?"

"Probably not."

"Thank goodness. All the same, to ask you to find out if he loves me is bad, don't you think it's bad? Do you think a proud person would act like that?"

"No, I don't."

"That's it, you see. Have you ever made love with another woman?"

"No, I haven't."

"I have, it's nice, what I like about Santino is that he's like me, a bit man and a bit woman."

"Are you sure he likes men?"

"He likes women, but yes, he likes men too. Perhaps women more than men, who knows? When I first met him he was making love to a waitress from the Pensione Vista-Mare, some girl called Stella, then I found out that at the same time he was having it off with an Austrian tourist, a boy with a pock-marked face from Salzburg. Then the boy left, Stella got married, and he came to my house to work as a waiter."

"Did he stay long with you?"

"Almost three months."

"Why did he leave?"

"He didn't leave, Marta threw him out because he never lifted a finger, he spent all his time with me and didn't do a thing in the house. Do you think you could make love to me?"

"I don't know, I've never thought about it."

"I don't think I could, you're not my type. Have you seen that plump English girl with puffy eyes and almost white hair who comes to the Bar with her parents? Well, she's my type, I like her, but she's too young, she's only about thirteen. I'd like to seduce her actually, but I think you're nice even if you do look a bit dead. There's not much life in you, you're like a burnt-out candle, why are you always so fagged out?"

"I don't know, it's how I am, I suppose."

"I bet you don't get on with Giacinto at all."

"You're wrong, I do."

"Because you do what he tells you, that's not getting on with someone, it's passivity. I'm sure Giacinto doesn't satisfy you sexually."

"How can you say that?"

"I can see from the way he holds your arm when you come to the Bar, I can see it from the way he talks to you, the way he looks at you. I'm sorry to tell you this, but your husband is not in love with you in the least. He's fond of you, maybe, but his mind's elsewhere."

"Look, didn't you come here to talk about Santino?"

"We must become friends, mustn't we? And to become friends we must get to know each other."

"You haven't asked me a thing, you've just made a lot of wild guesses."

Our conversation was interrupted by Tota. She said I must come at once, she had something urgent to tell me. I couldn't say no. I said goodbye to Suna and went down to Giottina's with Tota.

But she didn't have anything to tell me at all. It was the usual stuff about the orgies inside the luxury villas. I asked Giottina what she meant yesterday by her mysterious warning, but she wouldn't tell me anything more about it, just that I would understand in time.

*16th August*

Giacinto went out at eight with the bag full of fishing gear and I got up too. I didn't feel like sleeping any longer so I started washing his shirts. I was still holding the bar of soap in my hands when I heard a thud. I went out. I thought it was the usual bundle of rubbish. Instead, it was a half-dead cat. I picked her up in my arms. She trembled and her nose was bleeding. I cleaned the blood off her with a little water and poured out some milk in a saucer. When I put her down on the ground she fell helplessly on her side and continued to bleed from her nose and mouth. She kept one of her paws bent up in pain. I dabbed her nose with hydrogen peroxide. She let me do this, gazing up at me with two dull, lifeless eyes. Her upper lip was split in the middle and revealed sharp, yellow teeth. I offered her some more milk but she refused it. I moved her into the shade. The flies sucked the blood on her nose and I shooed them away. I tried to lift up her head. She was wheezing like a death-rattle. Then she stiffened and fell backwards. I got up, mad with rage and ran round to the neighbours. The same old woman came to open the door. The plaster on her arm was covered with coloured graffiti, her face looked sick and her apron was greasy and dirty. However, this time she didn't run away, she came up to me hesitantly, grasped one of my hands, and kissed it ingratiatingly. As soon as she heard her daughter's steps she screwed up her face in terror and scuttled into the kitchen.

"You threw a cat into my yard. Now it's dead. You'd better come and bury it."

"What cat, my dear? We don't have any cats here."

"It was flung over the wall into my garden in exactly the same spot as your rubbish always falls."

"It must have been the kids from the street, they're capable of anything. Do you think we'd hurt a poor cat? They're God's creatures, like the rest of us. Would you like a cup of coffee, I'll go and make one immediately."

She was about to rush into the kitchen, but I stopped her and said that I didn't want any coffee. I was about to slam the door and go when I heard the old woman muttering in the other room.

"If she died she asked for it, because she's a crooked cat. First she steals, then she miaows, the thief."

"You see, even your mother says it was you."

"Don't listen to that crazy old woman, she doesn't think straight, she's sick. She's sick, I tell you, do you want to see her file when she was in the loony bin? Wait, I'll go and get it. She's had ten electric shocks, she's crazy, she's a burden to us, a misfortune. How can I make you believe me, a real calamity, she even eats the children's biscuits and their powdered milk. She's worse than a mouse, she empties the fridge completely, she gobbles down the crusts of parmesan cheese, and all the jam, a jar every three days, she's worse than a leech. Shall I show you the certificate?"

"No, thank you. I'm going back home now."

She didn't take much persuading. Gently she shut the door behind me. I stood there bewildered, staring at the doorplate on which the name Ciancimiglio was written in gold letters. I was about to leave when I heard a turmoil behind the door. The woman was slapping her mother, who whimpered softly, moaning like a little child.

I gave a mighty kick on the door and shouted: "Pigs! Swine!" I really hurt my toe. The noise of the slaps stopped abruptly.

At home I found the cat on its feet licking the saucer clean. The blood was still pouring out of its nose, dyeing the milk pink.

*Midnight*

Today Santino didn't come to lunch. He came about four o'clock with a friend of his: a very dark young man with a big head, black curly hair and a discoloured beard that hid his mouth and cheeks. Giacinto immediately became moody. He exchanged a few words with the guest and went to sleep. Santino was hungry and asked for something to eat. I gave him some bread, and some figs left over from yesterday. He picked up a fig, cut into its skin with the nail of his index finger and peeled it as you'd peel a banana, without soiling his fingers. His friend asked for a coffee so I made him one. He was looking at me stealthily. I asked him his name.

"Vittorio".

"Where are you from?"

"Naples."

"Are you here on holiday?"

"I don't like too many questions."

I was struck dumb by his confident, metallic voice. Perhaps I've offended him, I thought stupidly. I kept silent and watched him. He took a packet of cigarettes from his pocket, drew one out and offered it to Santino. With slow, meticulous movements he struck a match. He blew the cigarette smoke through his nostrils with a pensive air, wrapped in thought. Now and then he scrutinised me with two piercing eyes.

"Your husband is a mechanic, isn't he?"

"Yes, he is."

"And you are a teacher?"

"Yes."

"How did this mixture of classes come about?"

"What classes?"

"A proletarian and a petit bourgeois."

"Well, we met six years ago and . . . "

"I don't want to know your personal affairs. Are you a socialist?"

"I'm a communist."

"What a joke."

"Do you want some figs?"

"No thank you, they're bad for my teeth."

His teeth are in fact all decayed and stained with nicotine. That's why whenever he smiles he twists his mouth and stretches his lips to one side. Santino looked at me with a gentle smile, while his beautiful supple hands fingered the violet figs. He had already eaten half a dozen.

"Are you an activist?"

"No, I'm not."

"A-political, uncommitted, couldn't care less, only worried about earning your bread and butter. I know the type. They let themselves be outwitted by the proletariat every time — look at Santino."

"Santino isn't interested in politics."

"How do you know?"

"Are you interested in politics, Santino?"

Santino stopped eating. He wiped his mouth with the back of his hand. He stretched his large pale blue eyes wide open and smiled blankly. He didn't answer.

"Santino is exploited and he knows instinctively who his enemies are," said Vittorio sternly.

"And you, what are you?"

"My father is a criminal lawyer, born and bred in the slums of Naples, my mother is a shopkeeper from Palmanova, near Venice. It's up to you to decide what I am."

"Are you a student?"

"I study and I work."

"What sort of work?"

He crushed his cigarette underfoot and took out another one, holding it delicately between his hairy fingers. He lit it and started smoking. Santino had resumed eating the figs, splitting them open with slow, pensive gestures.

"Why don't you go and see what your friend is doing?" Vittorio asked him all of a sudden, taking a peeled fruit out of his hands.

Docile and obedient, Santino stood up, licked the sugar off his fingers and went into the bedroom. Vittorio followed him thoughtfully with his eyes. Then he put his cigarette down on a brick, leaned towards me and said in a low compelling voice:

"You're a friend of the disabled girl, aren't you?"

"Her name is Suna."

"I want you to introduce me to her."

"Why?"

"Don't keep asking why, it's insufferable."

"Santino knows her too."

"I want you to introduce me."

"But why?"

"That's none of your business."

"What a bully you are!"

"You're right, I am a bit provocative. Take it as a residue of my petit bourgeois background."

His deep-set eyes widened and his sallow face turned sad. Nervously he drew a few puffs from his cigarette. Then he relaxed his lips into an amiable smile.

"How much do you get a month?"

"120"

"You're almost a proletarian too. What differentiates you is your education, a bigoted, antiquated, chauvinistic education."

"Why do you think I'm bigoted and chauvinistic?"

"You aren't, it's the education of your class that is bigoted and chauvinistic."

"What do you mean?"

"I mean the culture that gave birth to the ideals of the Risorgimento a hundred years ago and to the fascist aberrations of thirty years ago."

He was dazzlingly self-confident. It doesn't take more than a few words to make me unsure of myself and all of a sudden I felt excluded from his world of intelligent and courageous people, condemned to the mediocrity of a class which, due to my inertia and stupidity, I would never be able to break away from. I had accepted him as my judge, the arbiter of my life. I had put him on a pedestal, heroic, daring, his wings unfurled in reckless flight.

"It's possible to free yourself from this culture if you really want to, of course you can. I'm certainly no determinist, you can break free from it, but only through political struggle. Passivity makes you an accomplice, it fucks you up without you knowing it, because you're not only an accomplice you are also a victim, you're a flea that can't live without the blood of the rich. Besides, you're a woman and women are even more inclined to be passive and masochistic, they are even more messed up. You need to make a qualitative leap, but it's not easy, you could end up with both your legs broken." His commanding voice and stern, staring eyes had something fiery and infectious about them. "Well, then, are you going to introduce me to her, or not?"

Giacinto and Santino came out of the kitchen and stood chatting together.

"Why don't you introduce yourself to her?"

"I've done that already, but she doesn't want to know: she's suspicious, like everyone who's well loaded, she's scared someone might take her money away from her."

"But what do you want from her?"

"Between your class and that of your husband there's a very small distance, a mere inch, but it's that little inch that fucks you up."

Santino came up to us and said he had to go home. Vittorio stood up. Before leaving he bent forward and whispered in my ear: "Well then, I'll come back tomorrow at eleven o'clock. I want you to have the disabled girl waiting for me here." He gave me a look of complicity and a warm restless handshake. It was difficult to stand out against the excitement of his persuasive brutality.

*17th August*

I cleaned the kitchen and made the bed. I was about to go and do the shopping when there was a knock on the door. It was Suna. Alone, without her brother. Her face was pink and flushed. I offered her a chair but she shook her head. She didn't want to admit she was tired. She stood there leaning on her crutches, a warm smile on her thin lips.

"Yesterday a man came here who wants to get to know you at all costs."

"His name's Vittorio, isn't it? I know him and I don't like him."

"Why?"

"Because he's a big-head."

"He has a seductive voice."

"I didn't notice."

"His eyes are attractive too."

"In other words he's made a conquest of you."

"I like the way he talks."

"It's all gloss, can't you see the way he treats women as if they were so many vegetables?"

"I don't know how he and Santino can be friends, they are so different."

"Is he a friend of Santino's?"

"Santino brought him here."

"Are you sure?"

"Of course I am."

"Where is this Vittorio now, then?"

"He said he's coming back at eleven o'clock this morning."

"Well, I'll stay then. I want to see him."

I persuaded her to sit in a deck-chair, in the shade of the banana trees. She threw her withered legs to one side of the chair. When she noticed I was looking at them she covered them up with a swift movement of her hand. She was wearing an old-fashioned pale lilac skirt with lace frills.

"Is it true you are very rich?"

Her red patent leather shoes gleamed from under her skirt. They were fastened on one side with a button and they reminded me of the shoes of a doll I had been given when I was a child in Palermo.

"My father has made lots of money on the black market. He's handsome, very charming, as soon as you see him you'll fall in love with him, but he's frivolous and irresponsible, he only cares about dressing smartly, eating well, parading around and being admired by women."

"What about your mother?"

"My mother ran off with a bathing-attendant a few years ago, now she lives in Sorrento, has four children and starves."

At eleven on the dot Vittorio arrived. From a distance he looks foreign: leaden, opaque skin; pitch-black hair; an aquiline nose; dark burning eyes, and swollen purple lips. He advanced swinging his skinny legs, shook hands with Suna with studied indifference, and sat down next to her on a small black stone.

"I'm pleased to see you. You're very beautiful."

He really looked pleased. He gave her a cheerful, slightly embarrassed smile, revealing a row of broken yellow teeth. Suna didn't respond to his inviting smile. She sat rigid, staring haughtily into his face.

"Do you know what Büchner says in his 'Danton'?" Vittorio attacked her resolutely. Suna lowered her eyelids slightly and wrinkled her nose. Vittorio lost some of his confidence but nonetheless he carried on.

"Danton believed that it was a bourgeois revolution, Saint-Just conceived of it as a proletarian democracy, and was wrong, Robespierre was killed by his extremism. 'The people don't want blood, Robespierre, they want bread,' says Danton, and the play finished up with the question: to what extent is it permissible to use violence in order to enforce civil virtues? What do you say?"

"I say you are an exhibitionist."

"Didn't they teach you to hold back your stools as a child?"

"So what?"

"Isn't that a form of violence too? Isn't it a way of repressing the child's spontaneity? Of nature? There are some forms of violence which have become so common that nobody recognises them any more. Education is a form of violence. Did you ever go to boarding school?"

"Yes, I went to a convent."

"Didn't they teach you that you must repress and sacrifice yourself?"

"So what?"

"Isn't that violence?"

"What is it you're trying to prove?"

"Have you ever been in jail?"

"No, I haven't."

"Have you ever worked as a building labourer on top of a nine-storeyed house without any protection, and walked up and down rotten joists with your arms loaded with bricks?"

"No, I haven't."

"Have you ever been on the point of bleeding to death after being turned away by all the hospitals because you can't afford a private bed?"

"No I haven't."

"All that is a form of shitty social violence. Don't you understand, it's a display, a shop window full of acts of brutality; just as the butcher lays out the sirloin, the fillet steak, the liver, the brains, so every morning society displays all in good order the state assassinations, fraud, robbery, theft, all committed by the state, fully sealed and officially countersigned."

"Yours is violence too. You're attacking me with such a chauvinistic tone of voice it makes me want to vomit."

"There's a legitimate type of violence, on the side of change, and an unjust type on the side of the status quo."

Suna didn't reply. She looked at him thoughtfully, irritated, but perhaps also intrigued. Vittorio's face burns with a fire that holds you spellbound. His voice glissades into your ears in mellow, compulsive waves.

"Get me a glass of water, Vannina."

He turned towards me with a tender smile as if he were proposing to me. I jumped to my feet and dashed into the kitchen. But I heard Suna telling him off.

"What the fuck do you think you're doing? You're even giving orders now. Go and get the water yourself."

When I went back outside I found them silent. Vittorio was frowning. He drank the water in large noisy gulps. Suna carefully observed him as if she was trying to discover the mechanism of his attraction. Then she confronted him in a firm, measured tone.

"What does your mother do?"

"Nothing, she stays at home."

"Do you have a maid?"

"No, we haven't."

"So how can you say your mother doesn't do anything?"

"Well, she stays at home, she does the housework."

"You mean, she makes your dinner, she makes your bed, she washes your dirty underwear, she irons your shirts, she does your shopping, she cooks for you, she washes your dishes. Doesn't she? Isn't this what you mean?"

"My mother is a country woman, a peasant. At one time she went hungry, now she has a little money, not much, just enough to eat and afford a house with central heating and a movie on Sunday afternoon."

"Do you have any brothers?"

"Yes, two of them are still quite young."

"Who looks after them?"

"My mother."

"Has your mother ever had a lover?"

"What are you jabbering about? If you saw her you'd understand that's a bourgeois question, this mother of mine is an old hag, she isn't a woman."

"That's it, you've said it. An old hag, without sex and without brains, an old hag that wipes all your bums clean."

"Typical female logic. You have the stubborn arrogance of the rich, you're like a princess, it's impossible to talk rationally with you."

"Okay, I'm rich. But just listen how rich I am. It's my father who has all the money and he keeps it tightly tied to his balls. He gives me so much a month like a kept woman. That's how it is, I earn and own nothing, and it's not me who decides how and when to spend that money, I have no power whatsoever. The Turk holds everything tight in his hand, and do you know what he wants? He wants me to get myself a husband as soon as possible so that I'll be off his hands and out of the way. But unfortunately with these legs of mine it's not going to be so easy. So if I want to buy myself a dress, a pair of shoes, a book, I must ask him. And if I want ten liras, and I mean ten to spend as I want, without giving him an account of it, I have to tell him a pack of lies, I have to cajole him, win him over, and then feel guilty because of it. He is my fucking father and I am his beloved daughter, his pet, but if I ran off with a bathing attendant like my mother he'd pull the gold tooth out of my mouth that I had put in thanks to him last year. He'd take away the stockings and panties I'm wearing for the injury I'd caused to his bourgeois prick. Handicapped, that's fine, it doesn't matter, he even feels sorry for me, but what he's looking for is some dolt of a husband to foist me on to, never mind if he's boorish and ugly so long as he's well loaded and is willing to take me without making too much fuss, and that's it, finished, finito."

"What a tirade. I know all this and frankly it bores me to tears. These nonsensical excuses, they are just bourgeois, provocative, unreal."

We were interrupted by Giacinto who arrived back scowling, with no fish and a long wound on his thigh.

"What's happned?"

"The sea was rough today, I got bashed against a rock and almost split my head open."

I rushed into the house to get some iodine. When I came back Suna and Vittorio had left.

*18th August*

Today I haven't seen either Vittorio or Suna. While Giacinto was away fishing, Tota and Giottina came to visit me. They were excited and had a mysterious air. I was puzzled to see the two of them there, all dressed in black, with boots on. They invited me to go with them.

"Where are you going?"

"Put on your walking shoes."

"But why?"

"Never mind why, let's go."

I slipped on a pair of rubber-soled shoes, locked the door behind me and followed them. Along Via San Antonio and Via Maramaldo, across Piazza Trimuggia, through the Papparlardo Quarter, we eventually emerged on to the stone-flagged road that leads to Maiola. It was hot and we were tormented by flies. We passed the graveyard, and the road narrowed until it became just a rough path of yellow earth. Our footsteps raised a cloud of fine, light-coloured dust that settled on our sweaty bodies and stuck to our skin. There was a chalky smell of dry mud burning in the sun, mingled with the scent of mint. We kept on climbing, leaving the village behind us and making our way through vineyards with still-unripe grapes and orchards enclosed by walls of grey rock.

I would have liked to stop and have a rest, but they held me by my arms, one on one side and one on the other. I had no option, I was forced to keep up with their rapid steps.

Eventually we had to stop in front of a dog stretched out right across the path. Giottina gave it a kick. The animal raised its head with a start. Tota lifted up her foot to kick it too. The dog dragged itself to its feet with its tail between its legs, and went off to curl up under the bamboo wind-break, by a small public fountain.

"Can I have a drink of water?"

"This fountain hasn't given any water for fifteen years, love."

Above the dried-up fountain there was a minute niche made of bricks. Inside was a small statue of the madonna with such a riddled face that it looked as if she was suffering from small-pox.

"Let's sit down for a while, I'm all sweaty."

They looked at me as if I were a spoilt child. Giottina took out a wrinkled handkerchief and passed it over my neck with abrupt maternal gestures. Then we carried on our climb, pounding on the dust-laden earth. We were walking in the direction of the mountains and eventually the vineyards, the orchards and the peasants' houses came to an end. Instead there were only bare naked rocks. The parched earth was broken here and there with patches of prickly grass.

The path became narrower and we had to walk in single file, Giottina in front, myself in the middle and Tota behind. There were no trees, no shrubs, no shade, only brambles which scratched our legs, and suffocating sunshine.

"But where are you taking me? I'm worn out."

Instead of an answer Giottina kissed my hand. In that kiss there was such fervour, such humility, such affection that I didn't have the courage to insist. I carried on walking quickly. After more than an hour of non-stop climbing we arrived at the edge of a short dense scrub of acacias, junipers, scrub pines and wild fennel bushes. I immediately threw myself down on the ground. Tota burst into laughter, but after a moment she came and sat down too. Giottina stood there on her feet fanning herself with a fig leaf she had broken off along the path.

"But where are we going?"

They looked enigmatically at each other, as if they had some secret from which for the time being I was excluded. They stood there still and silent, without deigning to answer me.

In the distance the valley opened out as it sloped down towards the sea: the houses, the streets, the vines lined up in orderly rows, the tomato fields, the almonds, the lemon trees, and along the coast, the brash white luxury villas rising sheer above the sea.

The harbour gleamed like a square of green glass encircled by silvery rocks. Further on the sea became light and clear, embellished with white feathers.

All that air, the wind, the wide open horizon, made my head spin. Accustomed as I was to being shut in between the walls of my courtyard, I was overcome by the sense of space. I had a pain in my chest and the fierce light assaulted my eyes. I closed them and immediately felt the grip of two friendly hands. Giottina and Tota pulled me to my feet and we started uphill once again. Now the greenery was becoming gradually more dense, one had to bend double to force one's way between the tangle of branches. We climbed over fragments of rock, slipping on the moss, thrusting our way through the leaves.

Now that they'd slowed down, Tota and Giottina had acquired something stately, almost sacred in the way they advanced, as if we were about to reach the end of a holy pilgrimage.

With our arms and legs pricked by thorns, we eventually emerged into a small clearing covered with wild ferns. There in front of us, as if it had materialised out of thin air, was a stone hut with a straw roof. It had only one window, which was covered with a piece of yellow plastic. The door opened into a dark interior where thousands of flies seethed and buzzed.

Giottina and Tota stiffened, holding their breath with an air of reverence and fear. Then Giottina crossed herself and Tota spat cautiously on the ground three times. We went in. The house smelt of putrid watermelons and dried fish. I couldn't make out a thing, all I was aware of was the flies crazily hissing around me. After a while my eyes got accustomed to the darkness and I saw Giottina and Tota go towards the corner under the window. I followed them slowly for fear of tripping over some object lying on the floor.

"Poor innocent soul, afflicted heart, may your death be peaceful."

"Holy Mary, help her to free herself from her body."
"The blood is heavy, the soul is weeping."
"Jesus, seize her hand."
"Heart bleeding."
"Hands nailed."
"Feet crucified."
"Temples tormented."
"Chest poisoned by gall."
"Mouth burned by vinegar."
"Take her, Lord, my Prince."
"Take her away with You."

When eventually my eyes had become accustomed to the darkness I was able to make out the thing lying in front of the two kneeling friends: the broad-shouldered, bulky body of a woman, her two long legs clad in a pair of orange trousers. Her long grey hair lay on the rush matting, her mouth was gaping, her eyes were wide open, shiny and green. The horror made my legs go weak at the joints. I fell on my knees beside the two women who were absorbed in reciting aloud a long lament in monotonous, relentless voices. When they had finished they crossed themselves; then Giottina closed the woman's mouth and Tota lowered her eyelids. But her eyes slowly opened up again and seemed to stare straight at me. I recoiled.

Giottina motioned me to keep quiet. She stretched out her hands to the dead woman's shoes and untied the long white laces with hasty, delicate movements. The white tennis shoes came off, one after another, exuding a faint smell of damp rubber. Meanwhile Tota was unbuttoning the blue and white check shirt. She took the woman's two swollen white breasts in her hands as if she were weighing them. Then she began to search for something: her wrinkled fingers slid along a thin string that the dead woman wore round her neck and descended to the left of her breasts into her trousers. Tota tried to take off her shirt, lifting the woman up by her shoulders. The grey head with its wide open eyes slipped onto Tota's lap spilling a trickle of saliva, but she remained unperturbed. She carried on working with light delicate hands until she had succeeded in undressing her. Then she remained still, with the dead woman's head on her lap, her arm wet with saliva, staring at her with quiet curiosity. Giottina was dealing with the trousers. Her plump, horny hands moved with great dexterity, without embarrassment, neither too fast nor too slow. She unzipped the trousers in one go and then grabbed them by their hem and pulled them off, hardly shifting the dead woman at all. The woman wasn't wearing panties. Her genitals, naked and brown, appeared suddenly in the middle of a tanned, skinny, wrinkled belly. Giottina folded the trousers automatically, as she would do in the launderette. Then she bent forward to seize the string that had ended up twisted around behind the dead woman's back.

She beckoned me to give her a hand, but I pretended not to understand. I didn't feel in the least inclined to touch that lifeless body. Quickly Tota took my place, and together they turned over the corpse with one single skillful movement. A shiny curved object lay under her, crushed against the dark flesh. In a flash, Giottina laid one of her hands on the jewel. She gave it a sharp wrench and broke off the string. She drew it close to her eyes and stared at it for a long time with fascination. Then, with an abrupt gesture of collusion, she thrust it into my hands. It was a large gold phallus from which a small silver net dangled. Inside the mesh I caught a glimpse of something red. I pressed the two ends of the clasp and there in the palm of my hands were two coral eggs the size of beans. Tota and Giottina stared at the extraordinary object as if spellbound. Then all of a sudden Giottina snatched it off me and slipped it into her bosom beneath her sweaty bra.

They stood up and began to rummage amongst the woman's luggage: a wicker trunk, a wooden box, some plastic bags. They pulled out creased dresses, woollen socks, dirty towels, and other unrecognisable rags and tatters, as well as books and letters and sheets of paper covered with writing.

I stayed beside the corpse. I couldn't take my eyes off that large, bony, luminous body. I wondered how long she could have been dead. Not long. The smell given off by her flesh wasn't bad, indeed it was pleasant, like wild herbs and ploughed earth.

From behind, with her suntanned skin, one arm bent around her head, her legs stretched out, she looked as if she was asleep. Her head was covered with filmy hair, her cheek pressed against the matting. From beneath her hair stared out one large still green eye that gazed sardonically at me.

Tota came up to me and put the woman's passport into my hands. I opened it. Her name was Georgia Ringrose and she came from Nevada. She was fifty six.

The photograph was dusty and I cleaned it with one finger. Against a dazzling white background stood out a long melancholy face with something deranged about its clear eyes.

Tota gave me a gentle kick on my back. It was time to go. I stood up and followed them out of the hut, their arms loaded with booty.

"You'll be found out in no time."

"Shut up, Giovanna, mind your own business."

"I don't understand why you've dragged me up here, just to help undress a corpse."

"Can you read English?

"A little."

"Read these then."

Tota thrust some letters and receipts into my hands. I started reading them. While I was skimming though the papers they dug a hole with a short garden spade.

"Is there any money, a cheque, something?"

"No, there's no money, only letters and a few receipts for parcels."

"Read the letters."

"Why?"

"Go on, Vannina, read."

I took out a sheet of flimsy paper covered with large rounded handwriting. I read it aloud, translating as I read:

> Dear Mother
>
> Stella and I are setting off for Los Angeles. We are taking the dog with us: Stella's due in a few weeks and wants to go back to her place for it. We are so happy we can't stop drinking, I wonder if all this beer might be bad for the baby, but Stella doesn't think so.
>
> Lots of kisses,
> Yours,
> Michael"

"Carry on, Vannina."

> Dear Mother
>
> Today George was born, we called him that because of you. I know that you don't care but it's a way of feeling close to you. Stella is fine but the dog got run over by a car on the same day as George was born, so I'm happy and sad at the same time.

You know that Puffy has been with me for the last seven years and we loved each other dearly.

My work progresses all right. My paintings are getting larger and larger, and more and more full of anguish, but no one wants to know. Sometimes I wonder whether I went wrong from the very beginning.

Lots of kisses,
From your son,
Michael

"See if there's a picture of this Michael."

I rummaged through the letters but I couldn't find any picture.

"The earth is bloody hard here." Giottina rubbed her aching back. "Read on, Vannina."

I took out another sheet of the flimsy light blue paper, scribbled over with green ink.

Dear Mother

Little George died, no one knows why, five days after he was born. It happened suddenly, without a moan or a whimper. He was so plump and well. Stella doesn't want an autopsy. I do, because I want to know why he died. Stella says she doesn't care, that the baby's body mustn't be touched.

She's started drinking again, she insults me all the time, as if it was my fault. Tomorrow we'll go back to New York.

Lots of kisses,
Yours,
Michael

I heard a sob, and lifted my eyes. Giottina was crying. Tota was sniffing too and her eyes were shining.

"Read on, Vannina."

Dear Mother

New York is no better than Los Angeles. Stella has turned really nasty, she drinks from morning till night, doesn't want to make love any more, she calls me a failure, says that she only married me because of my money. I try to convince myself that she's beside herself because of George's death, that I should not give in to her provocation, but then I always swallow the bait and we end up vomiting the most disgusting things at each other. The other day I grabbed her by the neck, I didn't hurt her, but now she treats me as if I were a murderer. I begin to feel disgusted by her filthy body, swollen up with beer, I feel like jumping out of the window.

I'm sorry to take it all out on you, Mother, but you're the only person I can talk to.

Goodbye,
Yours,
Michael

"What a cesspit."
"Yes, read on, Vannina, read on."

Dear Mother

At last I'm going to have an exhibition. The manager of the art gallery is enthusiastic about my gigantic 'States of Mind'. We'll have to mount them inside the gallery, because the frames won't go past the doors. I'm getting the invitations printed, my period of crisis is over, it seems. I've met a wonderful girl called Marion, she's a philosophy student. I've regained the five kilos I lost in these last horrible months.

To be absolutely truthful, the exhibition at the Bauer Gallery is being paid for by me, but one must start from somewhere. I'm sure I'll sell all the 'States of Mind' and with that money I'll make up the expenses.

Stella torments me because she doesn't want a divorce, she spends her days shut in at home drinking, and when she sees me she clings to my neck and cries. At twenty five she looks like some old idiot woman. I promised her some money, but she doesn't want any, she says I've destroyed her, that I've dragged her away from the South and made her live in this horrible foggy city, that I married her just to have someone to cook for me while I'm painting (but I've always helped her, Mother, you know that) and that I've destroyed her self-confidence, that she's given me everything, and now without me she feels abandoned.

I just don't know what to do about her. I'll put the whole matter into the solicitor's hands, I want to get rid of her as soon as I can, she ruins my peace of mind, and destroys my concentration.

Goodbye, my dearest,
Yours,
Michael

"These people must be stinking rich."
"There's no money here, though."
"Only a lousy twenty dollars."
"What a bloody swindle."
"But why are you burying all that stuff?"
"We certainly can't take it down in broad daylight, can we? We'll come and get it another time, once the body has been taken away."
"Who's going to take her away?"
"Within an hour the whole village will know."
"Who's going to tell them?"
"We will."
"Yes, so you get caught straight away."
"We're not going to tell people to their faces, we'll spread it around as if we'd heard it from someone and they've heard it from somebody else, so that the rumour spreads and soon the police get to know and organise an expedition to the mountains, with hand-cuffs, guns, machine-guns, stretchers, the lot."
"Won't they realise she's been undressed by someone?"
"Everyone knows she never wore clothes, even the priest has seen her naked through his binoculars."
"They'll notice that the money and the pendant have gone."
"What pendant? No one knows about it."
I helped them tidy up everything inside the hut. I followed them down the mountains, walking rapidly in silence.

*19th August*

Giacinto came back at eleven beside himself, covered with blood, holding his ears with his hands.
"Have your hurt yourself?"
He lay down on the ground swearing. His nose was bleeding, he had bruises on his body.
"What's happened to you?"
"A depth charge, I almost got killed, the bastards!"

"But where?"

"At Punta Zafferana. They were on a boat, I was under water, I didn't know a thing. Suddenly I heard a roar and then I felt a terrible pain in my ears as if they were being pierced with nails, I saw the fish shoot out of their lairs dead, and I felt punches all over my body. If I'd been closer I'd have been smashed to pieces, the bastards!"

"Did you see them, who were they?"

"There were five of them. They apologised of course, and then shot off to drop their charges a bit further away. By the time they'd finished you couldn't find a fish alive even if you'd paid its weight in gold."

"Wasn't Santino with you?"

"He was sunbathing on the rocks, he says he didn't hear anything, and that he doesn't know any of them, but then I saw him wave surreptitiously to one of them, a fellow with only one hand."

"I'll take you to the First Aid Centre."

He refused to let me. He stretched out on the bed and fell into a heavy sleep straight away. I took a sponge and some lukewarm water. I wiped the blood off him and gently massaged his aching limbs with some oil. He carried on sleeping — or maybe he pretended to, I'm not sure. His prick swelled up and I held it between my oily fingers. I only had to caress it a few seconds for it to explode into a sudden quick orgasm. The sticky white liquid spurted on to my bare arms.

Santino arrived at one o'clock. He wore his usual black salt-stained shorts and a light-blue T-shirt that matched the blue of his eyes. He gave off a nice scent of rose water. He sat down at the table and ate two large pieces of sword-fish in silence; then he stretched out on a deck-chair in the shade of the banana trees. I cleared the table, did the dishes, cleaned the kitchen sink, swept the floor. By the end I had a sore back, so I lay down on the camp-bed in the kitchen.

I couldn't sleep though, it was too hot.

I got up and went barefoot over to Santino. I saw he was sleeping quietly, with his mouth half open and his hands resting on his thighs. I went and sat in front of him.

The sunshine danced on his face, filtering through the fringed leaves of the banana trees. Stretched out and relaxed as he was, his beauty was soft and delicate. The only thing missing was the opalescent blue of his eyes and the white gleam in his pupils that gives his face its look of disquieting beauty.

I like watching people asleep. It gives me a sense of excitement, of liberation. I fixed my eyes on his large sturdy feet. They are feet that are not used to wearing shoes, they are more often bare, their soles hardened and their toes suntanned, soft and slightly swollen with small dark creases on their joints.

From there my glance explored upward, travelling as light and anxious as an ant along his slender fragile ankles. A tiny light-blue vein encircles his ankle like a sleepy little snake. Further up his skin becomes amber-coloured, tight-stretched.

His relaxed muscles showed through the lean flesh like slackened ropes. Further up his sturdy round thighs are slightly spread apart and rest on the striped canvas of the deck-chair. Some small blond curls gleam on his sun-burnt skin.

As my eyes ascend further they are arrested by his black woollen trunks, stretched over his body. I tried to identify the shape of his genitals. His penis is not very prominent, on the contrary there's something tender and delicate about it that makes it look like a swallow nesting between his thighs.

My body was gradually catching fire, my eyes went up to his pouting mouth, his receptive arms, his vulnerable neck. I felt a strong desire to embrace him.

I dropped my bathrobe to my bare knees. I put my hand on my hot belly. A sharp scorching taste filled my throat. I kept staring at that sleeping, vulnerable body. I had a slow, quivering orgasm.

Relaxed and calm Santino carried on sleeping, with his mouth wide open, gently snoring.

I began to laugh softly at my own daring. I'd never have dreamt I could act so shamelessly with such a danger of being seen. Besides I don't have the least intention of making love to Santino.

*Midnight*

I slept till seven. Giacinto went down to the village for a walk. I stayed in to make supper. Santino was still in the yard, and I asked him if Vittorio was a close friend of his.

"So so."

"How long have you known him?"

"A few months, I used to work with him."

"Where?"

"In Naples when I went around on my moped to deliver leaflets."

"What leaflets?"

"Stuff for the Movement."

"What Movement?"

"Proletarian Victory, it's called. Ever heard of it?"

"Does it have a lot of members? Is it large?"

"I don't know. Vittorio says there are members all over Italy, thousands of them."

"Where do they get their money from?"

"I don't know. Vittorio is a good chap, though, last year here in Addis he screwed a couple of German tourists, they gave him 200,000 liras each, and with the money he bought a second-hand duplicator."

I was about to ask him a few more questions, when he suddenly got up and left. I put the saucepan to simmer and switched on the iron as I had to iron one of Giacinto's shirts.

While I was ironing my thoughts drifted to the school at Zagarolo. Once again I saw the headmaster's worried, sickly face, I heard his harsh voice right in my ears. He spoke of salaries, timetables, marks. Instinctively I stepped aside as I always do when I'm next to him. His mouth smells of rotten fish, and he seems to enjoy blowing his rank breath right into my face. His smooth well-manicured hands move slowly over the class register in search of mistakes. His fussiness is obsessive. According to him, a teacher is good when he keeps the register in good order. If he discovers a smudge or an erasure he's capable of making a violent scene, only to apologise later in a not very convincing manner.

Behind his greasy body I saw my colleagues' laughing, vulgar heads sticking out. I heard the warm voice of Tania, the most conscientious of the lot, the only one who is not given to gossip and who is keen on her job. She's short and ugly and her chin is always red. Our colleagues call her "Little Red-beard". They maintain that her chin is red because she shaves every morning. Once again I heard her clear gentle voice, immediately crushed by the shrill, uncouth voices of the others. In the corridor everyone is complaining about the caretaker who turns the school into a street market, selling doughnuts, chocolates, pizzas and nougat; about the pupils who bring pornographic comics into the classroom, destroy the desks with their pen-knives, and soil the walls with graffiti; about the parents who don't give a damn, about the State that is always late paying our wages, about the Provincial Education Office, and most of all about the headmaster who torments everyone with his obsession about tidiness, and is incapable of achieving it anywhere apart from the class registers.

The voices become strident and aggressive and they whirr in my head like a swarm of locusts. By the time I'd finished ironing I was stupefied and exhausted. Amidst all the confusion I tried to visualise Fidelio's sad, pouting face. For an instant I caught a glimpse of his youthful, untamed eyes and that made me feel better.

*20th August*

At seven o'clock I was woken by a heavy knocking on the yard door. I got up and went out. As I passed through the yard I was struck by the neighbours' bundle. It hit me on my back and then fell on to a young basil plant, crushing it.

I felt a surge of anger that left me breathless. I picked up the bundle intending to throw it back but then I restrained myself.

Tota was at the door, with a beaming smile on her pale lips. Her two gold teeth sparkled.

"Why so early, Tota?"

"Come with me, Giottina wants you."

"I'll come a bit later."

"No, come now, later the shop will be full of people and we won't be able to talk in peace."

"Just a minute, then, I'll get ready."

I left Giacinto there sleeping. I didn't even have a coffee and I couldn't stop myself from yawning.

The launderette was cool and humid, the smell of detergent hadn't spread through the room yet. Giottina was ironing away wearing a dress with a gigantic floral pattern which made her look fatter and more imposing than usual. As soon as she saw me she put the steaming hot iron down and came to give me a hug. Her cheeks were cold, her mouth was hot.

"Do you have something to tell me?"

"Have you thought about what I said the other day?"

"What was that?"

"The message I sent you through Tota."

"Oh yes, beware of the evil wings, but what does it mean?"

"Beware the evil wings of those who can't fly."

"What does it mean, though?"

"You don't know what friendship is. We are your friends. Those vile people you go around with are not."

Tota sat frowning and nodded at her friend's reproaches.

I looked at them with gratitude. Their savage, possessive friendship gives me a sense of elation. They wanted to tell me that they were jealous, that they needed me.

I spurred them on to talk about my new friends: meanly, because I knew that they would slander them brutally.

"That friend of yours from Naples, what's his name?"

"Vittorio."

"That ugly little fright goes around the island banging his drums like a tinker."

"What drums?"

"He drags along a trail of freemasons, people with no religion, no morals, who want to chuck out the Virgin Mary and put Satan in her place."

"Do you want some of these pizzas?"

Tota took some steaming hot small pizzas out of a bag of greaseproof paper. She put two into my hand. They were soft and tasty and had a strong flavour of oregano and anchovies.

"They're nice, aren't they?"

I nodded. Tota thrust one into Giottina's mouth. She ate it without interrupting her ironing.

"His hand is like a snake, he rummages and rummages, he's so slippery."

"What do you mean? Where does he rummage?"

"Under women's skirts, that's where. He slips his hand in, he's shifty, last year he used to get up to his dirty tricks with this German girl in the street in front of everyone."

"In the street, yes, I saw him too."

"He got her to take her panties off in the café without anyone seeing so that afterwards he could boast of having raped her."

"But there's always someone who sees these things and then the ugly devil pokes his hand around and searches — oh, he's a dirty snake."

"And then?"

"He touches and rubs and strokes and then he sniffs his hand like a dog."

I laughed. Tota got angry. She said I had no respect. In the excitement an anchovy slipped out of her mouth and fell on her sweaty chest. She picked it up and put it back angrily into her mouth.

"And then he goes out preaching to the peasants, he says they've got to get together, burn the landowners' vineyards, kill their animals, throw the rich out of the villages, take their women, their goats, sheep, everything, and then drink themselves to death."

"That crippled girl is of bad stock too."

In Giottina's voice there was a veiled, nervous hatred. Tota scowled. They were watching me to see how I would react.

"She's a very nice girl."

"If you only knew what that whore gets up to."

"Her name is Suna."

"She lies on her terrace in the sun as naked as a worm."

"What's wrong with that?"

"And as the sun gradually cooks her all over she drinks wine and eats almond biscuits."

"So what?"

"Then she calls the waiter of the month — because you see in that house there's a different waiter every month. She calls him, she makes him kneel in front of her like a pilgrim and kiss her down below, then she pours wine on his head so that he drinks wine and eats her flesh like a priest at the altar."

"I know where Suna lives and there's no terrace."

"There is one, there is, I tell you, she just keeps it hidden."

"How can one hide a terrace?"

"You're a goose, you don't understand anything about anything, you don't know that the only people who can give you real friendship are the two of us because we really care about you, the others are just trying to con you, they aren't genuine, they're creeps, they're swindlers."

"Beware the evil wings of the one who can't fly," repeated Giottina with a sphinx-like expression on her face.

"What does it mean?"

"Keep away from the bird with tattered wings, that Turkish girl you take into your house, betraying our trust."

"I've got to go now, Giacinto is sick and he needs me."

Reluctantly they let me go, but first I had to promise I'd come back tomorrow. Outside there was a great hubbub, cars driving along head to tail leaving no space for those who wanted to cross the road, horse-drawn carriages loaded with tourists making their way through the throng, cracking their whips. My heels sank into the asphalt.

To avoid the confusion I took the long way home, passing by the harbour. The fishing boats had been dragged ashore for quite some time. The villa dwellers' rubber dinghies and sailing boats swung sluggishly to and fro on the filthy, greasy water.

*11.00 p.m.*

In the late afternoon we went down to the square. The air was sticky and heavy. Crowded round the tables whole families of holidaymakers chatted indolently as they ate their ices. The mopeds roared about as always, but with less insistence than usual. Everything repeated itself mechanically and predictably as if it were a film I'd seen through before.

At eight o'clock the 'beauties' arrived. No one deemed them worthy of a glance except for two German women who sat by the boxwood fence affectedly sipping red liqueurs.

Giacinto stirred the ice cream in his glass more vacantly and absentmindedly than usual. His body is still sore and his ears partially deaf from the underwater explosion. I asked him if he'd like to know something about the last chapters of the book on Byzantium, but he didn't respond. I asked him if he had seen Santino in the morning. He said he had. Then he resumed beating the ice cream in his glass till he had reduced it to a mush the colour of mud.

At half past eight Suna, Oliver and their companion with the grey plait arrived. They walked towards a table by the fountain, far away from ours. But then they changed their minds and came to sit with us. Suna leaned her crutches against the hedge and sank into the chair, covering her legs with her skirt.

"This is Marta, our housekeeper, our companion in boredom. You've already met Oliver." We greeted each other listlessly. Giacinto lifted up his face, twisted with annoyance. He was not too pleased at being disturbed in his meditations. Suna made fun of him, laughing cheerfully, but he continued to busy himself with the glass of ice cream.

"Don't you ever go for a swim, you're as white as a nun!"

Delicately Suna took my hand in hers.

"I don't like the sea. I don't like salt water and if I stay in it for longer than ten minutes I get covered in red splotches, my eyes puff up and I feel sick."

"If I had your legs, I'd be rushing into the sea instead of sunbathing on the terrace all by myself like a twit."

"Is there a terrace in your house?"

"It's an extension of the roof that I've transformed into a terrace. I put up matting all over so that no one can see me and I sunbathe there in the nude. If you want there's room for you too."

"I don't like the sun, it gives me a headache."

"Your wife is a bit of a wet blanket." Suna turned to Giacinto with a shrill laugh. Giacinto smiled at her foolishly, without putting his spoon down. He looked stubborn and longfaced. Then all of a sudden he stood up. He said he was going to see some fishing tackle at the corner shop and disappeared. Marta and Oliver went off to buy a pair of sandals, so Suna and I were left together on our own.

"Giacinto isn't happy, he looks like someone who's just about to drown."

"He's like that."

"How long have you been married?"

"Six years."

"Do you have any children?"

"We've decided against having any."

"Why's that, because of money?"

"Not only that, it's also because Giacinto doesn't care for children, and I don't much either. As soon as we got married I became pregnant. I took great care during my pregnancy, I was happy about it. Then the baby died as soon as he was born and after that I decided not to try again."

"Has Giacinto always been so sad?"

"He's cheerful at times."

"He's got something stirring inside him that's swallowing him up."

"He's been like that ever since I first met him: he doesn't talk much, he broods over things, he's longfaced — then he has bursts of happiness and gaiety, with Mario for example: sometimes they stay up all night laughing."

"Mario?"

"A friend of his who used to work at the Atac as a driver, but then he gave it up. He's very fond of mountains, his father was a member of the Alpine troops, he came from Udine. The two of them spend their time talking about women."

"Male solidarity."

"When I arrive they stop talking and become serious and boring, then as soon as I go to bed I hear them laughing, they chat and drink, they go on till two or three in the morning. With him Giacinto is a different person, he acts like a school-boy, cracks jokes, makes up all sorts of stories."

"He's very distant."

"That's the sort of person he is."

"Do you think he loves you?"

"I don't know."

"Would you be upset if he didn't give a damn about you?"

"Yes."

"Do you love him?"

"Yes, I do."

"You think you love him, because you submit to him. You look after him, you take care of him, you put up with him, but that isn't love."

"What is it then?"

"It's duty, you're in love with your sense of duty."

"I couldn't live without him."

"But you don't get on sexually, do you?"

"Not really."

"Can't you see?"

"Giacinto says that sex doesn't matter much when you love someone."

"He says that because it suits him."

"He means it."

"And you, what do you think?"

Nothing. I thought nothing. I didn't know what to say. I take what Giacinto says and make it my own. I never even think of contradicting him. I think he is better than me, that he's right, that what he says is good enough for both of us.

*21st August*

I was still in bed, but I wasn't sleeping. I heard the noise of the crutches on the bricks, and a hand drew the shutters apart from the outside. I opened my eyes. At the window appeared the smiling face of Suna, breathless after the climb, her hair glued to her forehead, her neck perspiring.

"Hullo."

"Hullo."

"Did you see what those swine have thrown into your yard?"

"What is it?"

"Take a look."

She bent down. With two fingers she picked up a transparent rubber pouch half-filled with a whitish liquid.

"I don't know what to do, if I go and complain they fill my yard with empty bottles and rotten fish."

"You're too soft-hearted, even when you're angry you don't scare anyone. You're too timid, you always feel unsure of your opinions, even when they're obviously right."

"That's true."

"All this dumping their rubbish on you is just a way of telling you that they're not afraid of you, that they are superior and that they don't like you because you haven't been friendly towards them."

"How do you mean not friendly? They've always chucked their stuff over from the very first. Besides, they haven't got any friends, they always keep themselves to themselves, within their own family."

"They still expect you to make friends with them, nonetheless."

"Well, there's a nicer way of telling me that than chucking their rubbish over the fence." Suna went into the kitchen and washed her hands in the kitchen sink. She poured some cold coffee left over from yesterday into a small pan. I wanted to help her, but there was no way of persuading her to accept any help. She turned on the gas, took a small cup down from the shelf and opened the bag of sugar.

"Have you heard that Santino has gone to Naples with Vittorio?" she asked casually.

"What for?"

"I don't know. Santino is the Movement's big conquest — a real live proletarian, semi-literate too, that really makes an impression."

"When are they coming back?"

"Who knows? Do you think I ought to give him money?"

"Who?"

"Vittorio, for the Movement."

"I haven't quite understood what it's all about."

"If I could give Marta the sack I could give him the money from her wages. I do everything myself anyway, I don't need her."

"Would you do that, get rid of her?"

"I've told you, I can't decide anything. Anyway, it's my father who pays, so it's him who calls the tune."

"Don't you have any money of your own?"

"I spent all I had buying Santino the moped and the ring for his mother. My father gives me anything I want, but it's him who has to buy it and pay for it, he says that Marta is there to help me, but actually he put her there so that she can spy on me, every week she has to send him a letter reporting what I've done and what I haven't done, she's just a fucking spy."

"What about your brother?"

"Oliver has strong legs but he's neurotic. He gets into terrible rages that leave him breathless."

"How old is he?"

"Thirteen. He's too thin, you can count his ribs, he has a beautiful prick though, once I even held it in my hands to see how large it was. I said to him: 'Do you know, you've got a nice body, Oliver,' but he ran off frightened and now he's shy with me."

"What do you mean, he gets into terrible rages?"

"For example, I mean he gets up one morning and discovers that his trousers haven't been ironed and he starts screaming, and if by any chance Marta isn't around and I give him tit for tat, he gets vicious, grabs anything in sight and flings it against the wall. Marta is very patient with him."

"So she's useful to him, anyway."

"My father employed her for me, but since Oliver's been having these fits she looks after him more than me, luckily. But the Turk doesn't know anything about it, Marta hasn't told him, I haven't either, so he thinks everything is okay and that suits me because it means I have more freedom."

"Don't you live with your father in Naples?"

"No, he lives with his other wife and his other children, Gabriele and Lina. We live in a small flat in a nearby road and every Sunday we go to their place for dinner, lace everywhere, home-made cakes — well, to put it in a nutshell it's an incredible drag."

"Does your father love you?"

"Yes, he does love me as a piece of his property, he dearly loves anything that belongs to him, as soon as he doesn't own it any longer he forgets all about it."

"And you?"

"I loved him so much, more than I'll ever love anyone else, I think, he was my first real love, now I hate him. But let's stop talking about him, it upsets me. I could sell my watch, couldn't I?"

"Do you want to stay for lunch? I'll grill some fish if you like."

"I don't feel like facing Giacinto's antipathy."

"I'm sure once he gets to know you better he'll change his mind."

"He'll never change his mind, because I'm a crow and he's a mole; we'll never get on."

"You aren't like a crow at all."

"I'm impertinent, pigheaded, impatient and vain, you couldn't be more crow-like than that."

She burst into laughter. Her fresh, joyous laughter was infectious and I started laughing too.

"Do you want to come shopping with me?"

"No I can't, I must get home to help Marta."

"Didn't you get another waiter to take Santino's place?"

"Yes, Stefanino did for a while, but he was always in front of the mirror sleeking his hair, he wore my mascara, my eau-de-Cologne, and as soon as we went out he'd let in this lover of his called Gold Tooth. In a nutshell he didn't do a thing and Marta got rid of him, now she does everything herself, I help her a little but not much because I hate housework. But since she's started cleaning and cooking Marta has become insufferable."

"She looks so sweet and gentle."

"She's sweet and she's shy, especially with strangers, but at home she becomes hard and wicked, I don't know, maybe she's jealous of Oliver, with him she's kind-hearted and tender, with me she's impatient and bad-tempered."

We said goodbye to each other in the doorway. I watched her walk quickly towards the sea, beating her crutches on the stone slabs. She stopped for a moment by the stall selling melons to buy a slice of red water melon. Just before going round the corner she turned and gave me a joyful glance of complicity as if we shared a secret.

*Midnight*

Today's been an uneventful day. Santino's absence is oppressive. Giacinto is gloomy, his ears always on the alert, waiting to hear the noise of Santino's steps on the road.

We went down to the square early at six. The Bar Mondo was half empty. It was still too hot. Stupefied and intoxicated, flies landed on our hands and necks. The square was invaded by children playing tag and making a hell of a noise. A few of them were playing in the shallow fountain and splashing each other with water.

At seven Giacinto was already fed up. He raised his eyes at the arrival of the Englishman with his monkey who came down slowly with a silly smile on his face. His pet clung to his head like a hat, its light blue tail dangling down his back. Giacinto burst into silent, long-drawn-out laughter. When he calmed down, he had tears in his eyes and he was coughing. He asked if we could go home.

We stopped in front of the shop that sells underwater gear. He came out with the usual complaints about his mother, he says he hates her but in reality he doesn't, he can't do without her. I told him off for being too soft towards her, then he got upset and accused me of being jealous.

Meanwhile we had arrived at Via Maramaldo. The cake shop stood with its doors open, empty and cool, and we went in to buy some cakes. Giacinto asked for some soft chocolate-covered brioches sprinkled with minute silvery balls. Santino likes them very much. He can eat a dozen all by himself, one after another.

But Santino didn't come tonight either and we had dinner by ourselves, in silence, the neighbour's television blaring in our ears. Then, while I was clearing up I heard a thud. I walked a few steps towards the neighbour's wall, stumbled over a huge rotten watermelon and fell flat on my face, my hands soaked in the gummy liquid reeking of acid. As I fell I hit my knee on a block of stone and the pain took my breath away. I lay there like a drunkard, face downward in the stinking liquid, hungry flies whirring all around me, waiting for the pain to pass off. Giacinto helped me to get up.

I was crying with anger. Giacinto said not to make an issue of it. But I didn't listen to him. I went inside, limping, blood trailing down my leg, and grabbed two, three, four empty bottles and hurled them over the wall. At each crash I felt such a sense of relief that I went back inside to get another four and threw them over too.

From the adjacent yard there was not a voice, not a sound. They were all inside watching television. Giacinto says that by tomorrow our garden will have been destroyed, our house set on fire and we'll all have been stabbed to death.

I washed my face and my mud-splashed legs at the tap in the yard. My shirt was filthy with that stinking liquid and I put it to soak. I disinfected and bandaged my knee.

We were already in bed when there was an insistent knocking at the door. I asked Giacinto to go and see what it was. He replied with a grunt and turned over. I put on my dressing-gown and went to the door. I was sure it was our neighbours, and prepared myself for their outburst of anger. Instead I found myself confronted by a policeman in uniform with a sheet of paper in his hands. He lifted up his sleepy face and showed me the piece of paper.

"Are you Signora Magro Giovanna?"

"Yes, that's me."

"This is a charge of nocturnal disturbance, aggression, grievous bodily harm, deliberate damage, injury, housebreaking, acts of violence and theft."

"Violence? Theft, did you say? Who on earth can have accused me of that?"

At my question he smiled shiftily. He scratched his head. He couldn't have been older than eighteen.

"You must appear in front of the police sergeant tomorrow at seven o'clock. I'm not allowed to tell you anything else."

"Was it Ciancimiglio who made the accusation?"

He raised his mild eyes and looked at me doubtfully. Then he nodded assent. He handed me the sheet and asked me to sign it. Then he went off swinging along on his short legs.

I expected Giacinto to be angry with me. This time, for once, I was wrong. He railed at our neighbours calling them delinquents, hooligans and murderers.

He hugged me affectionately. We ended up making love — but in a rush, our eyes shut, as usual. Half way through he left me, and came alone, with a small stifled cry, stubborn and solitary. He turned over, kissed me delicately on the corner of my mouth and went back to sleep.

*22nd August*

I went to the police station. They were all very kind. They said: sit down, please, take a seat, wait a minute, would you like a cup of coffee? I felt relieved. Thank goodness, I thought, the whole business will come to nothing. But later the trouble started. The ten minutes waiting turned out to be fifty and their politeness faded away as soon as they started questioning me. The policeman asked me questions and I answered them. The pig-eyed man, with his legs stretched out underneath the table, typed out my answers with two fingers.

"Now I'll read it to you, then you'll sign it and everything will be over. Well then: 'I hurled bottles numbering seven on the forecourt of the adjacent house with the intention of gravely injuring the occupants of the aforementioned house, whom I dislike because of disagreements that have previously occurred between us.' "

"But, excuse me, I didn't say that, I didn't throw the bottles with the intention of injuring anyone."

"If you throw a bottle without first looking to see who is standing in the place where you are throwing it, obviously you aim at injuring and perhaps even killing someone."

"But the yard was empty, there was nobody there, they were all in front of the television set. There was no noise, nothing, if those people are anywhere you know they're there all right from the noise they make. I can tell when they're out in the yard and when they're not, there's no danger of making a mistake. I only wanted to make up for all that rubbish they had chucked at me."

"But undoubtedly, my dear lady, you couldn't have the mathematical certainty of it, could you? So obviously you are in the wrong and there is a crime."

"What about them, then? What certainty did they have all those times they hurled bottles, tins, melons, and muck of all kinds, even used condoms, at me?"

"A condom, my dear lady, can't injure you. A condom may offend your morals, even you could say your sense of decency, but it does not cause an injury, therefore it is a different matter."

"They hurled lots of bottles, even when I was out in the yard in broad daylight."

"Did the bottles they hurled injure you?"

"No they didn't."

"You see? Obviously they made sure that you weren't within reach of their missiles, so that they wouldn't hurt anybody, ergo logicus est."

"But I didn't hurt anyone either, or else I would have heard screams or something."

"And there you're wrong, my dear lady, you did injure someone, ergo et simpliciter. Signora Stella di Pepe, an elderly lady and the aforementioned Ciancimiglio Giuseppe's mother-in-law, who as a consequence of said injury, indeed of the said fracture, had to have her arm put in plaster."

"But she's had her arm in plaster for several days, she broke it one day at the bar when she got trampled on by the crowd pushing to see Purea Willey. I remember that occasion very well, everyone in the village knows that!"

"My dear lady, it seems to me that you're trying to pull the wool over my eyes."

"Everyone saw her, why don't you ask around, she already had her arm in plaster the day I went to complain about the cat. You see they'd thrown a cat over to my side and they almost killed it. Later they threw a rotten melon which I stumbled over, injuring my knee."

"Did you likewise report the incident to our office?"

"No, I didn't."

"You see, it's plain and simple, here in front of us we have Signor Ciancimiglio's report and we must deal with it. So did you or did you not hurl bottles into your neighbours' courtyard?"

"But I tell you there was no one there, the yard was dark and silent."

"Did you or did you not throw them?"

"Yes, I did."

"Therefore, Galvano, write the following: 'I likewise hurled bottles numbering seven, empty of any liquid' — were they empty or full, my dear Signora Magro?"

"Empty."

"'Empty of any liquid into the adjacent courtyard, precisely in order to hit Signora Stella di Pepe, the aforementioned Ciancimiglio Giuseppe's mother-in-law, whom I dislike due to previous occurrences of disagreement'."

"No, excuse me, I didn't say that."

"This is what appears to have happened, what must be written down. I write down the facts, my dear Signora Magro, you want to change the facts. If Signora Di Pepe was injured it means that the bottle hit her, if the bottle hit her it means that you likewise aimed at the old lady, whether you intended to or not is a difficult matter which the judge will have to ascertain."

I came out at midday with a bitter taste in my mouth. I had a headache and I needed to pee. The sergeant said I'll have to appear in front of the Magistrate's Court in Naples when they summon me.

*Midnight*

On my way home I stopped at the market to buy potatoes and salad. My shirt was glued to my back, my eyes were smarting, I was in a daze. I stared at the chicory and couldn't for the life of me recognise what those long white shapes with their green tops were, even though I was quite familiar with them.

I felt a touch on my arm and jumped. It was Orio, Santino's brother.

"Hullo."

"Hullo!"

"What's wrong with you? Aren't you feeling well?"

"I'm okay. I was miles away, that's all."

"Give me your basket and I'll carry it for you."

"Oh, don't bother."

He gave me a shy, beaming smile, grabbed the two raffia handles with a confident air and started walking in front of me with quick agile steps.

I followed him without taking my eyes off his boyish body, so delicate and robust. His dirty tattered trousers were held up by a plastic belt with gold studs. His white shirt had a hole in the back. On his head he wore a blue fisherman's cap of thick coarse wool. He walked with one arm rigid from carrying the basket, the other swinging to and fro, his head pushed forward. His short blond hair shone from under his beret. The back of his neck, suntanned and salt-stained, expressed both obstinacy and shyness. He reminded me of Fidelio and suddenly a sharp wave of excitement constricted my chest.

I had to stop to catch my breath. He turned, smiling gently, his pale blue eyes lightened by the sun, and I beckoned him to wait for me. When I reached him I put my hand on his arm. His skin was dry and soft.

"Have you heard from Santino?"

"He's in Naples. He's coming back tomorrow."

"And your brothers, what are they doing?"

"The case comes up in October. Meanwhile Gigi's staying with Uncle Giusseppe, Armando's gone to stay with friends in Positano, Toto's gone off on holiday with a Swiss girl, and Laura's gone back to her boarding school."

"What about you?"

"I'm at home with my mother."

We had arrived home. I wanted to take my shopping bag off him, but he insisted on carrying it all the way into the house.

"It's no trouble at all, I've got nothing better to do."

He came in, looking at everything with curiosity. He sat on the edge of a chair, took out a huge green crumpled hankie and wiped the sweat off his neck and forehead. He didn't have the nerve to ask me for a drink.

"Would you like a coffee?"

He nodded. I poured the coffee into the percolator, turned on the gas, filled the pan with water and put it on the ring. I got out two cups, teaspoons and sugar.

"Do you go to school?"

"I'm behind. I'm only in the third form."

"Don't you like it?"

"It's a drag."

"But you still go all the same?"

"I go when I feel like it. The headmaster's a friend of my father's so he'll pass me anyway."

"But now that your father's dead what are you going to do?"

"That guy is still your friend even when you're dead."

"So what do you do instead of studying?"

"I read."

"What do you read?"

"Comics. 'Messalina', 'Diabolic', 'Sexflash' ".

"Don't you do any work at all?"

"I do when I feel like it, but to tell the truth I never feel like it."

"What do you like doing then?"

"Nothing."

"There must be something, surely? You like comics, for instance. What else?"

"I don't like comics either, you know. I only read them because I find them in my hands."

"You find them in your hands? How's that?"

"Because I trade in them."

"You mean you buy and sell them?"

"Yes, that's it."

"And, besides this, what else do you do? Do you have any friends, do you go around anywhere, do you play games?"

I sounded false. I knew I was being very much the teacher, nagging and pedantic. I felt like laughing, but I didn't know what else to say — it was just a way of making conversation. He was shy and so was I. I would have liked to lick his light blue eyes.

"No, I haven't got any friends. I had one, but he was drowned."

"Only one?"

"Sure, only one."

"Haven't you got even a single friend now?"

"No, I haven't."

"What do you do by yourself?"

"Nothing."

"Do you like being with your mother?"

"Yes, a little."

"Are you upset about your father's death?"

"A little."

"Did you love him?"

"Not a lot."

"Why not?"

"I don't know."

"Do you get on with your brothers?"

"No, I don't."

"Why not?"

"Because they're arseholes."

"Santino too?"

"Yes, Santino too."

"What do you think? Did your father really leave all that money to Gigi?"

"No, he didn't leave anything to anyone. He thought he'd live for ever."

"So you have no friends, nobody. Don't you get bored always being on your own?"

"No, I don't."

"Do you ever go swimming?"

"No, I don't."

"Why not?"

"Because the water makes my skin shiver. I always have a pain in my guts, too."

"What sort of pain?"

"A pain."

"Have you seen a doctor?"

"One doctor says I've got an ulcer, another says it's kidneys, and a third says it's just growing pains."

"How long have you had these pains?"

"More than a year. Sometimes I faint too."

"Have you had any treatment?"

"I've swallowed more pills than the worst hospital case."

"Did they take any X-rays?"

"Twice. They say maybe it's cancer and there's nothing they can do about it."

"What do you think?"

"I think all the doctors are a load of arseholes and all they're after is your money."

"Do you say that or is just what your father said?"

"He used to say it and now I say it too."

I put the cup of coffee in his hands. He lifted his pale gentle eyes. He didn't look sad, though, only thoughtful, with an intent quiet seriousness.

"I hope this coffee doesn't disagree with you."

"I drink more coffee than a Turk."

"That's probably what gives you pains in your stomach."

"Coffee is only bad for me after a meal, or at night when it unsettles my stomach and stops me getting to sleep."

"Do you want more sugar?"

"Yes please."

I put two extra teaspoons into his cup. I sat down and sipped my unsweetened coffee. I was staring at his pale face with its miniature features, long eyelashes, and deep eyesockets like those of an adult.

"Do you believe that when you die everything is finished?" he asked suddenly, turning his head over his shoulders.

"I don't know."

"Once a German man told me that after one dies one comes back to life as a different person or maybe as an animal."

"That's called metempsychosis."

I always behave just like a teacher. I could hear my voice coming out of me, stupid and boring. I would have liked to stay here and look at him in silence, but I was afraid he would leave.

"This German told me that if I was good I could be reborn as an elephant."

"Would you like that?"

"Hans says that when you've been good you're reborn rich and handsome, when you've behaved like a shit you're reborn poor and ugly."

"So what if you are born poor but handsome?"

"Hans says that a poor person must have done something really bad in his previous life."

"Who is Hans?"

"A German guy who used to come and pick me up from school."

"Was he a schoolboy?"

"A schoolboy — he's got white hair! He used to give me money in exchange for letting him feel my cock."

"How often did you do that?"

"Whenever he came to the school. He didn't come every day because he was scared of my brothers in case they saw him and beat him up. But they'd done the same with him though."

"The same what?"

"Let him feel their cocks for money. Gigi even gave it him from behind. But Hans only likes little boys, once they grow up he doesn't even deign to look at them; they call him an ugly pouffe and throw stones at him, but the moment they need money they go with him."

"You don't need money, do you?"

"My father was as tight as they come with money. My mother never had a penny. Luckily though I make money by trading."

"How much did this German give you?"

"Once we split his head open so badly he was in hospital for five days. He kept shouting 'Stop it, that's enough, boys, have mercy.' He jumped up and down on his short hairy legs and held his broken head in his hands, bleeding all over the place, but before we agreed to stop he had to fork out all the money he had on him, 1000 marks."

"Where is Hans now?"

"He only comes here in the spring, around April; then in July he leaves again. Last time he gave me 1000 marks, do you want to see them?"

He drew a crumpled blue note out of his pocket and showed it to me with pride. The palm of his hand was soiled with earth.

"Did Santino go with Hans too?"

"Yes, he went with him even more often than me, he got a lot of money out of him. My school-mates did too, almost everyone did. For letting him have a feel he gave you 5 marks, and 20 if you let him give it you from behind. He pays well, he's a decent man all right."

"But doesn't the fact that you make love to a queer make you a queer too?"

"No it doesn't. To be a queer you have to enjoy it."

"How do you know who enjoys it and who doesn't?"

"It's simple. If you're a real man you don't enjoy it."

"What about you, are you a real man?"

"Sure I am."

"But you got your 20 marks, didn't you?"

"Only once. He hurt me, the bastard, so after that I said to him 'feeling only, nothing more.' His prick weighs a ton."

"Have you ever made love to a woman?"

"Well, yes, to that German woman my brothers picked up. But I couldn't get it up and they were laughing at me. They pushed it in for me so that doesn't really count."

"Would you like to try?"

"You bet."

"Would you like to do it with me?"

"What if you don't want to?"

"I'm suggesting it to you."

He lowered his head, embarrassed. He blushed and bit his lip. I went up to him. I took his head between my hands. I kissed him on the mouth.

I felt his full salty lips tremble. His tongue, as rough as that of a cat, tasted of coffee. His breath was bitter and acid.

As soon as my tongue touched his, he trembled. He opened his arms and drew me up against him impetuously. Through our clothes I could feel the shape of his firm, slender body.

I took his hand and led him behind the curtain to the bed. I knew Giacinto might come back at any minute but I didn't care. As a matter of fact I hoped he would so that he could catch me with Orio.

I undressed him. With a flick I knocked off his blue woollen beret. I unbuckled his belt with its gold studs. His baggy trousers collapsed onto his shoes. He wore a pair of red nylon pants. I lowered them too. His hips were narrow and bony, his genitals were like a man's. We lay down on the bed. He looked at me carefully. He was waiting for me to tell him what to do. He let me kiss his chest and neck with his eyes shut, a smile on his lips. I took hold of his sweet swollen prick and guided it inside me. He moved slowly, adapting himself to my rhythm. I was doing the same.

I clasped him tight in my arms in a violent torment of love. I had a total and uplifting orgasm. Orio came a few seconds after me. He gave out such a scream that I was scared. He rolled his eyes, clenching his teeth as if he'd had a sudden attack of fever. Then he sank into my arms like a corpse.

"Are you all right?"

He didn't answer. Then he jumped out of bed, got dressed quickly without looking at me and disappeared.

Giacinto came back a few minutes after Orio had left. He had caught a large brown octopus so he was in a good mood. He flung it on the kitchen table and went off to have a shower in the yard, using the garden hose.

I stretched my hand out to the octopus. It was still alive. A row of wet suckers clung spasmodically to my bare arm and I winced with disgust. Giacinto saw me from outside and burst out laughing. He came in dripping wet, grabbed the octopus with both hands and bashed it several times against the floor until it stopped wriggling.

"If you put it to soak in salt we can eat it tomorrow." I was about to tell him that Santino is coming back tomorrow but he went back into the yard and started splashing water over himself again. We had lunch just after half past two. We had boiled potatoes with salt and butter, tomatoes and mozarella cheese with a dressing of oil, oregano and basil fresh from the garden.

"Santino's coming back tomorrow."

"Who told you?"

"Orio."

"Who's Orio?"

"He's Santino's younger brother. Don't you remember him?"

"No, I don't."

"He looks like Santino. He's a handsome boy but he's ill. He says that the case over the inheritance is going to be in October. We had coffee together, chatted a bit and then made love."

Giacinto lifted his head. He didn't look upset, only surprised.

"You made love with a child?"

"He's fourteen. Don't worry. I didn't corrupt him, he knows all there is to know about sex, his brothers forced him to rape a German woman. Besides he often lets an old guy masturbate him for money."

"Why do you tell me?"

"Because it's true."

"Stuff that up your arse. Don't drag me into this affair of yours. I don't understand it and don't want to understand it. Haven't you even a little bit of shame?"

"Does it upset you that I made love to him?"

"I'm shitting myself with jealousy!"

"You don't give a damn, do you?"

"Jealousy is a lot of crap. You are my wife, there's nothing to argue about, it's just plain and simple. I don't intend to act the jealous husband, you're free, just don't bother me with your fucking truths, that's all."

"What about sex? You and me make love so badly together."

"Sex is always a bit of a mess. It comes out all right only once in a while, by chance, and one doesn't know why. In any case it's got very little to do with marriage."

"When you make love you only think of yourself, you don't give a damn about me. In spite of being only a boy Orio showed me more consideration than you ever do."

"Oh fuck off, you stupid cow. I don't want to know a thing about what you do with that kid. I just don't want to know, all right?"

I would have liked to carry on, but looking at his face it was clear that he wasn't prepared to talk about it any longer. I started washing the dishes. He went into the bedroom. I heard him bustling about with his spear gun. Then all of a sudden, as I was wiping down the kitchen sink, I felt a punch in my back. I didn't have time to turn round before he came at me like a savage dog. I lost my balance and fell over, breaking two plates. He covered me with punches, kicks and bites. Then suddenly he put his arms round me and hugged me.

*23rd August*

Vittorio is back. Without Santino though. He came with a sad-looking friend of his called Faele. He is a young man with a long body and very short legs. When he's sitting down he looks like a normal sized man, but when he's on his feet he looks like a dwarf. He has large black eyes, a protruberant nose, thick fleshy lips and a mouth crammed with small very irregular teeth. Giacinto was glad to see Vittorio again, even though he says he doesn't think much of him. He invited him to lunch, together with his friend.

They arrived at two o'clock carrying a bundle of papers and pamphlets which they put down on a chair in the kitchen.

"This is for you, Giacinto."

"I don't read much, it gives me a headache."

"Why are you so disinterested in us people who work for you lot?"

"You lot who?"

"You workers."

"I am myself and that's all."

"The trouble with you is that you think of yourself as a loner, instead of which you are just one amongst millions of other exploited workers."

"Even if that were true, it wouldn't make any difference."

"How much do you get a month?" asked Faele aggressively.

"180."

"And how much does your boss, the owner of the garage, get?"

"Listen, don't bother me with this shit. I know I'm exploited, all right. You don't need to tell me that."

"Giacinto is right, Faele. It's no use acting like a fucking hero. After all, you don't risk your job, do you?"

"For Chris' sake, if people aren't prepared to take risks, we'll end up with a fascist state, believe you me."

I had to go into the kitchen to fry the squid. I left the door open, but I could only hear fragments of their conversation. They were talking about the Communist Party.

". . . . it's taking in water everywhere, the fucking thing . . . instead of changing the world all they try to do is patch it up, a bit here, a bit there . . . fucking reforms, sure, but also private property . . . collective management of course, but also centralised administration . . . come to terms with the Catholics in order to set up a shitty bourgeois republic that panders to the rich as much as to the poor, the exploiters and the exploited . . . Giovanna, bring us some wine! . . . they've sold themselves, they don't give a shit . . . about the people, I mean, about the masses . . . Are you bringing us the wine or not?"

I took out the wine and the glasses. Stretched out on the ground, Faele was talking with his eyes shut, his face turned towards the sun. Lying in a deck-chair, Vittorio skimmed through the papers. Giacinto looked at them, frowning.

"You should pull yourself out of this trap."

"Trap? What trap?"

"This social democratic bullshit."

"Don't pester me with your fanaticism. I'm in the Communist Party and I'm satisfied. I've never even thought of leaving it."

"That's like saying — I've only got one mother, my mother is mine and I like her as she is."

"If you don't stop getting at me I'm going to chuck out the lot of you."

Faele and Vittorio sighed and looked at each other disconsolately. I had to run back into the kitchen to prevent the squid from burning. I turned off the gas and emptied the slices of octopus, dripping with oil, into a dish and served them.

They ate them avidly, together with large slices of coarse bread. From time to time they glanced at Giacinto with disapproval, then they resumed their greedy chewing. I kept running in and out of the kitchen carrying clean plates, pouring the wine, making the coffee, and catching bits and pieces of their discussion.

"Right, you interiorize the norm and then, even if you're on the left, deviant behaviour like — well, theft for example — is perceived as an abstraction."

"Hell . . . deviant behaviour, what's that for fuck's sake?"

"Anything that infringes the authority of the state, in other words anything that the state regards as everlastingly valid, as if somehow history had created it for all time rather than history being created by it . . ."

Giacinto was watching them with an expression of annoyance. Sleep was pressing down on his eyelids and he twisted his mouth to prevent himself yawning. He would have liked to send them away and go to bed, but he didn't dare. For their part the two were completely oblivious of his impatience. I started cleaning the table. The two friends sipped their coffee. They were talking to each other in irritable, careless voices. Giacinto asked me to make him another cup of coffee. Vittorio made a gesture to indicate that he wanted one too.

I went back into the kitchen and rinsed out the cups. I put some coffee into the percolator, turned on the gas, filled up the sugar bowl and dusted the tray. I did everything in a rush, overcome with a feverish nervousness. I was sleepy too, and irritated by Giacinto's restlessness.

I went back with the piping hot coffee. Vittorio was still stretched out in the deck chair. He was smoking a cigar that gave off a sweet smell of dried figs. Faele was standing by the banana trees. Giacinto gulped down his coffee.

"Well then, I'm going off for a sleep," he said finally, in a temper. He got up and went towards the house.

"Giacinto, listen a minute . . ."

Faele swallowed a sip of boiling hot coffee and pointed one of his fat fingers at him. But Giacinto had already disappeared through the door.

The two stayed there sipping their coffee in silence, while I cleared the table. Then, just as I was about to go for a nap, Vittorio stopped me with a peremptory question: "Have you seen Suna?"

"Yes, I saw her yesterday."

"Did she say anything about money?"

"She says she'll have to sell something because her father won't give her any."

"Of course he won't! She's as tightfisted as all the rich, but we'll squeeze something out of her. How much do you think she'll be able to scrape together?"

"I've no idea."

"That father of hers must be very fond of her underneath it all. Why don't you tell her to enforce her rights as a disabled person?"

"Her father has another family."

"She should turn to her mother then."

"Her mother hasn't got a penny, she lives in Salerno with this man who works as a bathing attendant during the summer and collects mussels during the winter."

"Another crazy, ragged English woman. I've met so many of them, after a few months they get fed up and go back home to get their neuroses ironed out."

"They've been living together for twelve years and they've got four children."

"One hair of a man's prick is stronger than a hundred oxen, did you know that?"

They burst out laughing. Faele broke a piece of shiny banana leaf and crumbled it nervously in his fingers. Vittorio put out his half-smoked cigar against a stone and slipped it into his pocket.

"I've fallen in love with your beautiful Suna, did you know?" he said, looking at me challengingly.

"Weren't you after her money?"

"From what you know of her, do you think she's an easy lay?"

"I don't know what you mean!" I answered plucking up all the courage I was capable of. I wanted my voice to come out indignant and angry; instead, it sounded feeble and embarrassed.

"Listen now, there's a little job that needs doing, Giovanna. Come here." Vittorio put some sheets of paper into my hands and carried on in his over-seductive, patronising voice: "You're an intelligent girl, you'll find it easy, you only have to separate the sheets of the pamphlets. You put those with 'the revolt of the unemployed' written on them on top, and those with the 'people are on our side' underneath. Is that clear?"

I wanted to say no. But I let myself be carried away by the pleasure of saying yes, of being ingratiating, carrying out a task without question, so that I could then be rewarded with the approval of those who were cleverer and more confident than myself. It was just what they expected from me, naturally, it was my role as a woman. Meekly I set about doing what Vittorio had demanded of me.

At that moment I heard the yard door open, and I turned round. It was Suna. She stood at the far end of the garden, dressed all in white, with a posy of yellow daisies pinned in her hair. She looked round cheerfully, as if to say: "Here I am, it's me, beautiful, disabled, proud — but one insolent word from anyone and I'll thrash the lot of you."

She came down the courtyard hopping lightly on her crutches. Her brusque movements clashed with her old-fashioned and slightly affected outfit. She went and sat down on the deck chair with a delicate movement that emphasised the suppleness of her body.

Vittorio dashed out to help her, but she shooed him away with a look of irritation. She wanted me to give her a kiss. She greeted Faele with an unfriendly smile while with one hand she delicately covered up her withered legs.

"Are you a member of the Movement? What do you do?" she asked him.

"I'm a student, I live off my parents if that's what you mean. My father's a surveyor but at sixty the poor devil's never been able to set up his own business. He's a failure who can't even scrape together enough money for the daily shopping. In other words he's a bit of a prick, especially considering there are nine of us — just think, nine products of his conjugal bed."

"He found the money to pay for you to study, though."

"By skimping and scraping on everything, eating dry bread and boiled potatoes like beggars."

"What about your brothers, don't they study?"

"I've only got sisters. Three are married, one works, another one helps my mother around the house, the youngest is five."

"So the entire family sacrificed itself to send the only son to college. I guess your sisters must be really happy about this sacrifice."

"They adore me."

"What does your father think of your political ideas?"

"Between him and me there's no communication — no relationship at all. I study because it's my privilege and I'm not giving it up. But at home we never speak to each other, he's a monarchist, but really he's just a cretin, there's no hope for him."

"You must have got all your intelligence from your mother then."

"My mother's even more of a cretin, they're a perfect couple. The greatest event in their life was a trip to Portugal to see the King, together with three hundred other monarchists from all over Italy."

Suna stopped questioning him. She turned her head imperiously towards Vittorio and confronted him in a calm tone of voice.

"Do you want me to join the Movement or is it enough if I give you the money and that's that?"

"Give us the money, and after that . . . then we'll see . . . " Faele was interrupted by a furious look from Vittorio. Suna burst out laughing.

"Faele is absolutely wrong. It's just not true that we only care about money. First of all it's people, then it's money."

Vittorio spoke with his warm, persuasive voice, his eyes fixed dreamily on Suna's tense face.

"You must agree that a bourgeois like her, quite apart from the fact that she's handicapped, isn't going to be very much use to the Movement."

"Shut up, Faele, why do you always manage to say the wrong thing at the wrong time? You're a clumsy clot, you never get it right, do you? Besides being middle class, Suna is first of all an innocent young girl who needs to understand herself."

"Leave all these fucking distinctions to the intellectuals."

"What do you think you are, you fool?"

"I am an activist in the service of the people."

"The hero has spoken."

"Okay, take the piss out of me, but what's that got to do with it?"

"It has everything to do with it because you are bourgeois too, and so am I, and so is Giacinto, and so is everyone else, it isn't so easy not to be bourgeois in a stinking shitty bourgeois world like ours."

"Are you toying with nihilism now?"

"I'm a pragmatist, that's what. You fly up in the air and I keep my feet on the ground, you half-wit."

They started quarrelling and shouting at each other, just as if Suna and I weren't there. At one point Vittorio ordered a cup of coffee by snapping his fingers at his empty cup. Suna listened to them, thoughtful and serious, sitting straight upright, her legs thrown to one side. The tips of her flame-red patent leather shoes peeped out from underneath her large white skirt. They were discussing the pros and cons of letting her join the movement. By now they were insulting each other openly, calling each other 'bourgeois', 'reactionary', 'bastard', with harsh choked voices. At one point Suna got up and leaning heavily on her crutches walked out into the street. She crossed the yard without either of them noticing her.

*Midnight*

Vittorio and Faele stayed there arguing the whole afternoon, sitting outside in the garden. They swore at each other, then they made it up. Eventually they began to plan something in low voices, tracing some drawings on the back of a poster.

At six Giacinto and I went down to the square. We ordered two pistachio and strawberry ices. Suna didn't come. The 'beauties' weren't there either. Giacinto was nervous and insisted on going back home before eight o'clock. The two friends were still there writing out God knows what document. I rushed into the kitchen to see whether there was enough to eat for all of us. I was short of bread, and Giacinto said he'd go down and buy some. I set the table and put on some water to boil for the pasta. I prepared a sauce, chopped the tomatoes, washed the lettuce, grated the parmesan cheese. Just as we sat down Santino arrived, all dressed in dark blue, with a white shirt and a red tie. I hardly recognised him. He had lost that air of a village boy, he looked almost adult. He hugged everyone, then he sat next to Giacinto and began to eat the pasta and sauce avidly.

Giacinto was happy. His eyes sparkled, his brow was smooth. Even the two bitter wrinkles at each side of his mouth had vanished.

I was happy too because when Santino is here everything becomes easier and lighter. We dined cheerfully, drinking and laughing, then we all went to bed.

*24th August*

I got up at eight o'clock and found the yard strewn with rubbish. There were fish heads scattered everywhere, even among the leaves of the banana trees. Two wet nylon stockings dangled from the branches of the fig tree. Some tar-soiled cotton rags lay among the pots of basil. Two bottles had shattered against the wall shooting splinters of glass over the geraniums and the deck chairs. There were watermelon rinds, tins with their lids off, mouldy bits of bread, egg shells, empty milk cartons. As I put on my rubber gloves and started picking up all the filth, there were tears of anger in my eyes. I thought of going to the police station and reporting them, but just the idea of having to speak to that fox-faced sergeant made me change my mind.

Underneath the marble-topped table which we use to clean the fish on I saw something greyish. Gingerly I stretched out my hand. It was a dead mouse, with clotted blood on its black snout.

I heard the yard door open. I turned, still holding up the mouse by its tail. It was Suna, followed by Oliver.

"What the hell are you doing?"

"If I hadn't thrown those bottles the night of the watermelons this wouldn't have happened, and I wouldn't have been reported either."

"They'd do it anyway."

"Not like this, they'd throw the usual bundle which I've just about got used to putting in the bin anyway."

She wasn't convinced. She settled into a deck chair and looked at me with a teasing smile.

"Whatever you do, you never succeed in scaring anyone, you're too meek."

"So what?"

"So nothing. You'll just have to resign yourself to putting up with the rubbish, that's all."

She had stretched out her snow-white legs in the sun. My eyes shrank for a moment, repelled by the sight of that repulsive shrivelled flesh. She noticed my look, but didn't do anything to cover her legs. She stayed there motionless, smiling. Meanwhile Oliver had gone into the kitchen to help himself to some fruit.

"Don't look at my legs like that."

"I'm sorry."

"I'm worried, Santino is avoiding me."

"Why?"

"Maybe he's bored with me, maybe not. Something's worrying him, though. According to him, it's just politics."

"Don't you believe him?"

"Yes, I believe him, but I think he's deceiving himself. Maybe it is politics, but it's also something else and I don't know what."

"He's probably enjoying the company of the other lads in the Movement. He was always by himself before."

"Maybe."

"He came to dinner here last night."

"I know. I go past his house a hundred times, trudging on my stupid crutches, and I saw him arrive. Do you think he doesn't want me any longer?"

"You are so beautiful, Suna."

"Yes, up here as far down as here, like a fucking mermaid. Sometimes when we are naked in bed I see him look at me: my beautiful breasts, I know all about that, my beautiful belly, yes, my beautiful hips, hmmmm hmmm, then all of a sudden his pupils go ghghghgh and shrink in disgust, instead of legs I have a stiff leathery cold tail. What can you do with a mermaid in bed — you tell me?"

"A mermaid is sexless."

"I have a splendid cunt, did you know that?"

Her way of talking about her own body disconcerted me. I smiled stupidly without knowing what to say.

"Would you like to come to Naples with me?"

"What for?"

"Santino is going back there in two days time."

"By myself, without Giacinto?"

"By yourself, of course, what are you afraid of? I'm sure he wouldn't give a damn, besides you don't need his permission, do you? You tell him you're going and you go."

"If he doesn't want me to, I can't, I would feel too bad about it."

"You aren't his property."

"Besides, we have to go back home in a few days."

"Even better, you stop over in Naples with me, he goes back to Rome and you join him later."

"I'll have to discuss it with him."

"You're scared, you're just fucking scared."

"Where would I sleep in Naples?"

"In my house. Do you know Naples?"

"Very little, I've passed through it a few times, I don't know it really."

"I'll take you around. It'll be very hot, but who cares. I'll tell my father that I need to go and see my doctor, that I'm not well, that's the only valid excuse for me to move an inch: my health. Well then, are you coming?"

All of a sudden, to go and be Suna's guest in Naples seemed to me a fantastic and exciting thing to do.

"I'll talk to Giacinto about it."

She kissed me on the forehead, and left with her brother who was nibbling away at another peach. Giacinto came back at two with four small scorpion fish hanging from his belt. Santino was still with him and they were both in a good mood. They insisted on cleaning the fish themselves, and also on setting the table. They tossed the plates, glasses and cutlery at each other with cheerful laughter.

At three Vittorio and Faele arrived. They picked at our left-overs. Those two are always hungry: Vittorio says he has no time to think of food, Faele starts off by saying no thanks and then he eats up everything in sight. We opened a can of butter beans and one of tuna fish. They finished up the bread which was meant to last until tomorrow and cleaned out the bowl of squid left over from yesterday.

"Why don't you come to Naples, Giacinto? We have a big project there in mind."

"I've got to get back to work."

"Well, before going back, stop over with us for a few days."

"That's all very well, but what do I tell Vargas?"

"Tell him you're ill."

"Who's going to believe that? At the end of August, the second the holidays are over, one is taken ill. We aren't still at school, you know!"

"Santino's coming too."

"I know."

"Recently we've increased our membership," said Faele, sucking the tentacles of a squid dripping with sauce. "Two students from Pozzuoli, an unemployed guy from Naples, and an Alpha worker. If you came we'd introduce them to you, so that you can get a better idea of what's going on with your own eyes."

"I can't. Besides, I really can't see why I should join your fucking movement when I'm already in the CP. I believe in big-scale, well-established things."

"These massive solid movements end up never moving at all, that's the trouble: they sink from their excessive bulk, like the Palace of Justice in Rome."

"The Palace of Justice is sinking because it's badly built: what meaningless nonsense, what has this stupid analogy got to do with the CP?"

"Who told you that the CP is not just meaningless nonsense the same as the Palace of Justice, and that it's not sinking and collapsing headlong into the shit?"

"Listen, I don't like discussing politics with you lot, okay? The CP is my party, and I don't want to hear you slinging shit at it, is that clear? And if you don't jack it in, I'll throw you all out of the house, you fucking pain-in-the-arses."

"How touchy you are, Giacinto."

"You eat my food, then you spit into my plate, so now you can go and fuck yourselves."

"So you throw that in our teeth, the few measley bits of fish we've got from your table, just like any bourgeois turd worried to death about his property."

"I have no property, only a spear gun and a pair of flippers. Who pays for all this food you eat? I do, don't I, and I pay through the nose as a matter of fact."

"Do you know what your trouble is, Giacinto?" Faele jumped at him, his face twisted up in anger, his mouth full of beans. "It's that you're as corrupt as a rotten pumpkin."

"It's you who's corrupt, not me, you lump of shit."

"Faele, cool it, give him a break." Vittorio put on a serious face. He crushed his cigar beneath his clogs and turned round with a conciliatory air.

"If Faele is so hard on you it's only because he wants to shake you up, Giacinto. You are one of us. Indeed you are one of those we are fighting for, the archetypal proletarian who must demonstrate a sense of solidarity towards other proletarians or he'll end up playing right into the hands of the bosses."

"No one is against you, Giacinto. On the contrary, it's because you are a worker, because you're exploited and you know what the class struggle is that we want you to join us."

"Well, you've chosen the wrong method. I believe only in what I see, I don't give a damn about castles in the air, and now I'm saying goodbye because I must go and have a nap. I'm sleepy."

He stood up and went. Vittorio and Faele stretched their hands towards the last few apricots and gobbled them up. Santino had fallen asleep in a deck chair with his shirt open on his tender delicate neck. Vittorio asked me to make him a coffee.

*11 o'clock*

At seven we all went down to the square for an ice. Suna greeted me from a distance. She didn't join us. Santino had left at five o'clock without saying goodbye and we hadn't seen him since. The square was crowded. I caught a glimpse of our neighbours' family busy stuffing their faces with huge ice creams swimming in fresh cream. Wearing a pair of shorts and a blue T-shirt Ciancimiglio sat sprawled under the mulberry tree laughing and slapping his hands on his thighs. On his hairy chest glistened a gold cross studded with precious stones. As I looked at his hands with their sturdy fingers covered with black hair, I wondered what his job might be. Vittorio guessed what I was thinking and in a low confident voice answered my question.

"That man made a fortune manufacturing liqueurs at home: he

used to collect empty whisky and vodka bottles and fill them up with some poisonous rubbish which he'd sell at street corners without a licence. It was mainly orange-flavoured methylated spirit, real graveyard stuff. When they came looking for him to take him to court, he'd disappeared. Eventually he set up a stall, then a shop, then two, now he owns three shops, employs a dozen people and has three or four flats.

"I thought they were poor. They live as if they hadn't a penny."

"Ciancimiglio is rich, but he spends it all on his family which is one of the largest in town. If you count all the cousins, nephews, grand-children and all the rest of them there must be at least two hundred of them, and he supports the lot. He's tough, but he's generous. He beats his wife and kids, he's a bastard with his employees, but when they ask him for something he always gives it them. He's a brute, but he has the residues of peasant sensitivity typical of the tribe. He's loved by everyone, his relatives adore him. His hands are hard, though: once he killed a three month old grand-daughter of his with a punch on the mouth because she was crying too much, now he supports his daughter-in-law in great style, he had to buy her a five-bedroomed flat so that she wouldn't report him."

"How do you know all this?"

"He's been coming to Addis every year for the last fifteen years. I've known him since he was as poor as a beggar, he's only become rich during the last eight years or so."

I lifted my head at the cheerful clacking of clogs which announced the arrival of the 'beauties'. They came forward indolently, all perfumed, dressed in gaudy colours, looking around with sleepy limpid eyes. There was one I hadn't seen before. Short, with a graceful body, fair, good-looking, suntanned and solid. He walked like a fragile stately queen.

"That one comes from Praia, he always comes in August when he's finished working in town."

"What does he do?"

"He's a hairdresser."

"He's good-looking."

"He's trying to set himself up in business, he's been saving for years, he puts everything aside. Last year he earned over a million lira, in one or at most two years he'll own a shop. He's married with a two-year-old daughter, but at the end of August he sends them to his parents in the countryside near Cesarta and comes here to prostitute himself. The rest of the year he's a serious and highly respected worker."

I looked at him more carefully. As a matter of fact he is less boyish than he looked at first sight. He has a way of turning his eyes half shyly and half seductively that attracts me. He has none of the others' look of casual brutality. His well-cared-for face, gentle and at the same time obstinate, expresses a diffident and yet fierce determination. I kept watching him as, light and nimble, he made his way amidst the crowded tables. His tight lilac shirt, bursting open at the buttons, reveals his fresh, smooth and hairless skin beneath. Vittorio was staring at him with a look of ironic contempt.

"His only aspiration is to become a died-in-the-wool petty bourgeois, a true home-bird and churchgoer, his belly full of piss and importance."

"They start all servile and obsequious, they slog their guts out, they scrape together a few dollars," said Faele sucking a big violet ice cream, "then they set up in business, take on a few underlings and exploit them to the bone."

"His name is Mario, he's nicknamed Pendulum, because he commutes to and fro between here and Naples, between one profession and the other, between his wife and his clients. He's very scrupulous, indeed meticulous. I believe he even goes to mass every Sunday."

"Do you know him?"

"He was a neighbour of mine, we grew up together. His mother was a washerwoman, his father owned a rowing boat and an oil lamp for catching cuttle fish. But what can you do these days with a rowing boat when the coastline has been plundered and if you want to catch a fish an inch long you need to go ten miles offshore?"

"If you know him, why don't you say hello to him?"

"He wouldn't like it, when I meet him in Naples we greet each other, but not here, here he's doing a dirty job and it's better if I pretend not to know him."

"He's the most handsome of the 'beauties'."

"His mother worked in a laundry and supported the family, his father caught a few fish from time to time, salted them and then sold them, but he didn't have any initiative. Besides he was always ill, he had liver trouble, backache, I don't know what else, but in spite of being ill he spawned a child every year. Fortunately they died, one of typhus, another of cholera, another of tuberculosis, the whole family lived in one room with no running water and no toilet. Every morning one of the children went out and emptied a large chamber pot into the street, and in the evening the same thing — after all everyone was doing the same. In the middle of the alley there was a narrow ditch into which ran a small black stream: that's where we played when we were little, and that smell was for me the smell of the world, a stench which I still smell sometimes even today."

"Wasn't your father a fisherman too?"

"No he wasn't, he used to infest the magistrates court like a sewer rat always squabbling over five liras with his customers who were even poorer than he was. We were better off, though, we lived on the fourth floor and had a toilet: it wasn't just ours, of course, it was a cubby-hole that stuck out from the landing and had to serve four families. Mario, anyway, is a year older than me, he was the second child. His eldest sister got married to a policeman and moved to Genoa. We did the first few years of school together, he, his sister and I. Then she stopped coming because the money ran out, he went out to work, and I carried on — so you see what privileges can do for you. He started with shampooing and washing the clients' hair, then he passed on to tinting — up to a couple of years ago his fingers were perpetually stained black. Now he wears gloves and is careful about his appearance — it's a working tool for him. Even so, in all these years of hairdressing he hasn't managed to save a penny because of his family. His father died, his mother has grown old, one of his sisters is a prostitute in Rome, well that's what they say. She was the best looking of the lot. She looked very much like Mario, a bit on the short side like him, but well-built, with thick curly blond hair." Faele looked cross. He told Vittorio off for not having tried to involve Pendulum in the Movement.

"Do you think I haven't tried? Do you know how often I used to go and pick him up from the shop? I knew his boss kept him cleaning the floor until eleven, he paid him when he felt like it, he forced him to eat standing behind a partition so that he wouldn't miss out on a single perm, and do you know what he got a month? 30,000 liras, until he was twenty one. What's more, since legally he was an apprentice all that time, his boss didn't pay his contributions and never gave him one day's holiday. I used to tell him: come with me to the Union, sue him, but he wouldn't — but then, how could you blame him? He knew that for an unemployed illiterate in Naples any job is like manna from heaven. Now he earns 120,000 a month, and he feels like a king: he's married, his wife is a manicurist, they've rented a flat with an indoor toilet and they mind their own business."

Faele, who was licking his ice cream with his thick violet-stained tongue, sneered sarcastically: "He doesn't do too badly, does he? He screws around, he eats for free, he drives around in a Mercedes, for God's sake what more does he want?"

"You cretin, you always say the first thing that comes into your head! These old bags are terrible, what do you think? They pay you, sure, but they also treat you like dirt, they pick you up with their fingertips holding their noses so's not to smell the stench, then as soon as they've used you up they chuck you out."

"They treat them the same way as men usually treat prostitutes", I said, surprised at my own courage.

"Worse in fact, since women are used to being passive, it's part of their nature, but a man, a man must watch out for his honour. How can he stomach it?"

"I've met lots of prostitutes" interrupted Faele, "and I can assure you they enjoy being treated badly. I'm positive, I've come across so many of them and the worse they're treated by their pimps the more they cling to them. You must admit that women are servile by nature, there's no doubt about that."

"It isn't servility, you ignorant cretin, it's masochism," Vittorio rebuked him curtly. "Women have a masochistic nature, men a sadistic one."

"Who's been feeding you that bullshit?"

I jumped at hearing Suna's shrill voice behind me. She put her head on my shoulder as if to transmit her friendship to me. "I'm a sadist by nature, and I'm telling you to your face, you're a prick."

Faele made a bitter face. He wasn't quite sure whether to give her tit for tat or keep his mouth shut. He looked at Vittorio with questioning eyes but his friend laughed sarcastically and said to Suna in a tender voice:

"Do you know how gorgeous you are?"

"If you want to change the subject, please don't resort to such stupid outdated tricks."

"No, I mean it, you know. There's no need for you to defend

women's sense of dignity because all men revere you spontaneously. Isn't that enough?"

"Don't give me that shit, Vittorio. You know what sympathy is?"

"Sympathy for the fur-coated ladies, for the industrialists' fat wives, for the German whores?"

"For all women."

"You're wrong there because you're quite different from those crones, you're young, beautiful, intelligent, you should make common cause with us, not with those other women."

"Class solidarity," said Faele peremptorily. "Wealth breeds wealth, I keep telling you."

"You get on my nerves, Faele. Why don't you piss off?"

Offended, Faele stood up and went off towards the harbour. He looks really funny when he walks: his legs are too short and his head too big, and he moves like a cowboy in a Western, cocksure and arrogant. Softening his voice, Vittorio stretched forward to Suna. "Do you know what I like most about you, Suna? Your mouth. I could die of love for a mouth like yours."

"Why do you butter me up, Vittorio? I've already told you I'll get you the money. Isn't that enough?"

"Give me your hand."

"Why?

"Please, Suna, just for a moment."

Suna stretched out her hand wearily. With a quick movement, Vittorio put it on his crotch, just where his trousers were bulging and taut. Suna withdrew her hand with a frown. But then she thought it over and replaced it on the same spot.

"You've a nice prick, Vittorio."

"So now will you believe that I'm dead serious when I say I love you?"

"Giovanna is here with us, and you treat her as if she didn't exist."

"I'm sorry, Giovanna darling, but I'm in love with Suna and I'm not so bourgeois that I have to hide it. I want everyone to know, I swear I'll be the perfect lover, full of respect and tenderness. Do you believe me?"

"The trouble is, though, that I don't like you at all."

"But you've just said that I've got a nice prick."

"So what? I don't have to make love to every man who's got a nice prick, do I? Goodbye!" She called Marta, who was sitting a little way off with Oliver, to help her to stand up. I knew she was quite capable of standing up by herself, but when there are people around she sometimes takes pleasure in being ceremonious. She levered herself up slowly, showing off her beautiful slender body, then, determined and self-assured, she walked away from us. She turned around for a moment to look at Vittorio with an ironic expression in her eyes, as if to say: you see, I'm handicapped, but you still need me, look how beautiful my body is in spite of my illness: look at me and feel that precious treasure you keep between your legs swelling up even more. I don't need you anyway, now or ever.

*25th August*

Immediately after Giacinto went out this morning I heard a knock on the door. It was only seven o'clock. I went to open it. It was Orio, all dressed up in a blue double-breasted suit, a white shirt and even a brilliant red dotted tie. He had combed his hair back with water and his face looked clean and scrubbed.

"Hullo, why are you all dressed up?"

"I'm going to Naples."

"Are you going with Santino?"

"No, I'm going by myself."

"What are you going to do in Naples?"

"I'm going into hospital."

"Are you ill?"

"No, I'm not, but last night they had to give me morphia. Did you know that when you take morphia it feels as if you're flying like a bird?"

"But what does the doctor say?"

"He says I must go into hospital."

"Can't your mother go with you?"

"No, she daren't leave the house, otherwise my brothers might snatch it away from her."

"What about Santino?"

"He's busy."

"Aren't you scared of going by yourself?"

"The man who works the motorboat is my cousin."

"So, you've come to say goodbye. Do you want a coffee?"

He didn't answer. He pressed himself tight against me. He was shaking. I lifted his chin. His eyes were dry, clear, transparent. His dreamy, absorbed face was disconcertingly beautiful.

"I want to make love to you."

"So do I."

I kissed him. His lips were soft and sweet. His breath was bitter, dry.

"When are you leaving?"

"In half an hour."

"How are you getting down to the harbour?"

"Uncle Tano is going to take me on his Lambretta."

"You must go immediately or you'll miss the boat."

We hugged each other once more. Then I saw him to the door. He went down the road with long nimble steps. Before rounding the corner he turned. From that distance his light blue eyes looked white and blind.

As I went back in I was hit on my arm by a smelly bundle. I flung it out of the door with a kick and shouted "Pigs!" I was answered by a muffled snigger. I went on shouting "pigs, pigs, pigs . . . " but I didn't hear anything else.

An hour later, while I was washing the sheets, there was another knock on the door. I wiped my hands and went to open it. It was Tota, sweaty, panting, her eyes shining. She looked drunk. She hugged me impetuously.

"Come, Vannina, let's go."

"What's going on?"

"Giottina is cross with you, she says you're going round with people who don't understand you and are harming you. She's terribly upset, I don't know whether she'll ever forgive you. Let's go."

I rinsed the sheets and hung them out on the line, and then followed her to the shop. On the way she made me buy a tray full of cakes of the most expensive sort, stuffed with cream and candied fruit. The launderette oozed moisture. I made my way through the dresses dangling from the ceiling as I swallowed lungfuls of bleach and sickly detergent. Giottina didn't greet me. She carried on ironing with concentrated energy, pretending not to see me.

"Vanna has brought you some cakes, Giottina."

"She might as well take them home, we aren't in a whorehouse where people come and go without you knowing who they are."

"You must forgive her, Giottina, she's a real friend."

"A bad friend."

"Look at her, you're upsetting her, Giottina. Look at Vannina's face, how ugly it's become, how weak, do look."

For a moment Giottina lifted her wild eyes at me. She stood dramatically upright and pointed at me with one finger, like a prophet.

"I don't want her, take her away."

"She's brought you some cakes so that you'll forgive her. Have one of the cakes for forgiveness, go on, just one, to sweeten the taste in your mouth."

"No."

"It's a pledge of love."

"No."

Tota picked up a cake and put it under her nose. Giottina kept on twisting her mouth up. With two rough dry fingers Tota opened a gap between her friend's tightly shut lips. She separated her teeth with her nails and pressed the cake on her tongue. Giottina gave in: with half-opened eyes she started sucking up the cream. Then still frowning she sank her teeth into the soft crust, slowly and greedily.

"That's it, now you are forgiven, Vannina, give a kiss to your loving friend." We were in full performance, it was like a theatre. My throat was blocked with nausea, I would have liked to run away, but at the same time I experienced a strange perverse sympathy for my two crazy friends. I went up to Giottina and kissed her on the cheek, like a sister.

"You've made new friends and now you're ashamed of us."

"Didn't I go up the mountain with you? Didn't I do what you asked me to?"

"But then you just forgot all about us."

"In a few days I'm going back to Rome, our friendship will finish anyway."

"Who told you that? When the almond falls off its tree it sets out on a dangerous journey, yet it is an almond still and has another tree in its heart."

"I won't forget you, I promise."

"Now though, you're still attached to the tree and are nourished by us. The people you go around with are horrible, I mean that disabled girl, the Neapolitan student and that repulsive Faele."

"Do you know Faele?"

"He's a piece of shit."

"Why?"

"Because . . . I can't tell you."

My curiosity was immediately kindled. I knew their stories were just scandalous figments of their imagination, yet I wanted to hear them. Giottina put on a triumphant face: I had swallowed the bait, the game of telling stories and lies could start once more. It was our game, the game of the three of us. I picked up another cake and gave it to her, but she shook her head.

"Don't you like chocolate?"

"I'm too busy, I can't work and eat at the same time. You can put the cake in my mouth for me, can't you?"

I raised the cake to her mouth, but she gave no sign of opening it. I had to separate her lips with my fingers. Only then did she bite reluctantly into the cake, leaving half of it on the palm of my hand. I waited for her to finish swallowing and then offered her the other half. But once again she closed her mouth into a pout and once again I had to open up her soft sweaty lips and push the cream puff between her teeth. It was an affectionate sort of violence and it sealed the ceremony of our reconciliation.

"You tell her, Tota, what Faele did last year."

"No, Giottina, you tell us."

I sat on a small bench waiting patiently for the story. The thud of the iron on the padded table had grown softer and more muffled.

"Do you know Don Ciccio's daughter, the idiot who makes noises?"

"The mongoloid girl — do you know her?"

I remembered seeing a young girl with a large head around the village, dressed like a child. Her eyes are ridiculously far apart from each other, her arms long, her mouth twisted to one side, and she talks to herself, gesticulating furiously.

"I think I do."

"People don't even know her name, so when they want to call her they whistle as if she were a dog."

"I've seen her a few times in the square."

"She can't speak, she just makes meaningless noises in her throat. The street boys bully her, there's always someone putting a lizard on her head or beating her up or spitting in her face, and she goes gh gh gh gh and runs off like a frightened piglet."

"What has Faele got to do with her?"

"He has everything to do with her. Just you listen."

"Faele was in love with this beautiful thirty six-year-old German woman called Gerda, but she was having an affair with somebody else, the pork-butcher's son Peppe, nicknamed Blackcock, and Blackcock was the mongoloid's elder brother. Have you got it?"

"Yes, I see."

"Well, to revenge himself, Faele took his rival's mentally deficient sister up into the mountains and there occurred what was bound to occur."

"Tell Vannina about it, so that she learns what sort of a stinking rat this Faele is."

Tota stretched a hand out towards the cakes. She seized a big round one with a cherry on top and put it in her mouth. Giottina carried on ironing silently with a grumpy frown on her face. Tota gave me the hint to offer her another cake. She smiled cunningly and winked at me, pointing to a large zabaglione cream puff. I picked up the cake and went up to Giottina. She shook her head sullenly but her eyes were cheerful and greedy. I had to go through the same rigmarole as before, prising open her closed lips with my fingers and pressing the cake through her teeth. For a moment her hard thick tongue lightly touched the fleshy part of my fingertips.

As soon as she had finished gobbling down the zabaglione she went back to her story, at the same time ironing with slow regular movements. As the story progressed her voice got graver and deeper and more portentous.

"He took the mongoloid girl into the woods and she was happy, poor kid, because no one ever takes her anywhere, they all avoid her and she spends whole days playing by herself with stones, so she kept running back and forth by his side like a happy dog, all she lacked was a tail to wag. Now and then she grabbed her benefactor's hand and kissed it all over, she was so happy. Meanwhile he was busy thinking about what Blackcock and the German woman were up to, to work himself up, the bugger."

"That German woman really was attractive!" interrupted Tota, jealous of the attention I was paying to her friend.

"Fuck your German woman!" With an offended gesture Giottina carefully folded the shirt and put it on top of a pile of other shirts. Intimidated, Tota sank her head into her shoulders and opened her eyes wide. Giottina continued with her story.

"At home in Munich, she was a waitress, just like one of us. She earned much more than us though, so during the summer she packs her suitcase and off she goes to the Pensione Miramare to idle her time away; every night an ice cream and then off to the cinema, another ice cream, off to the cinema again, then in the morning on the beach, a sandwich for lunch, she lived like a lady, this Gerda; then she got to know your friend Faele and for a while they went out together, they used to go and pet inside a cave near Punta Zafferana, where there are mosquitoes as big as wasps. They say that this Faele is well endowed, well, that his cock's so heavy that it won't stand up properly, and Gerda would say to him: 'You're OK inside your trousers but outside your legs are so short and bent they aren't worth a brass farthing, besides you're far too dumpy, you look like a young goose. I know a guy who's much better looking than you, he's called Peppe Blackcock and one of these days I'll leave you because I fancy him and I don't fancy you!' "

"So naturally Faele was a bit upset," interjected Tota.

"Especially because as soon as she told him she didn't want him any longer he fell head over heels in love with her, he just went crazy. That's what love is like, treacherous."

"Really crazy with love, he was."

"She'd started going out with both of them, Blackcock and Faele, hoping she'd be able to keep them hidden from each other, but in a village like ours not even a dream goes unnoticed let alone something like that. Even when you go for a shit you can feel people's eyes on your arse. So immediately someone went up to Faele and said: 'Watch out for that German girl, that Gerda of yours, she's messing about with Blackcock.' "

"You don't know that Blackcock fellow because he's gone off to Australia, but he was a really handsome lad, as straight as a rod, with a face like an angel."

"His cock was so dark that when women saw it they'd get scared, they thought he must be a negro or have some disease."

"His balls were white, though, so incredibly white that when you looked at them you'd go blind."

"Gerda spotted him immediately because she was as greedy for men as Giottina is for cakes. So in spite of the fact that he was engaged to some local girl called Concettina and was just about to get married to her and the documents were all ready, she grabbed him, undressed him and made him hers, black cock and all. They say his cock was so beautiful she'd keep on turning it over in her hands like a precious stone."

"All this time Faele was spying on the German woman from behind trees, and one day he saw them doing filthy things amidst the rocks up towards San Andrea."

"So next day he called the mongoloid girl with a whistle and took her up into the mountains."

A customer came in and they both stopped, their eyes sparkling with rage. Giottina asked her rudely what she wanted but before she had a chance to utter more than a word Giottina interrupted sharply with the assurance that her stuff wasn't ready yet. Then they pushed her out in a great hurry. As the door slammed, the clothes hanging from the ceiling fluttered.

Meanwhile Tota had stuffed another cake into her mouth, and Giottina started ironing again with an offended air. She showed no inclination to carry on with the story. The road with all its noises and clatter was a long way away, behind the glass door streaked with moisture. I had almost got used to that poisonous air and my head felt light, as if I had been drinking. I waited patiently for them to start again with the story, taking it in turn like a choir with two voices.

"I expect you know that up in the mountains there are wild tangled places where no one ever goes. Faele took the mongoloid up there, amidst the thorns and the rocks, and said to her: 'Come on, you bastard, come here, follow me and I'll show you.' "

"And the little bastard ran happily by his side, thrilled by this newly acquired freedom."

"Then he sat on the ground under a tree, on the fallen leaves, and said: 'Come here, you half-wit!' And the half-witted girl went to squat at his feet so happy that she picked little tufts of grass and ate them."

"He talked and talked to her, she didn't understand a thing, of course, and he said: 'You are a poor idiot, I know, a poor dumb half-wit, but I must revenge myself for the wrong your brother Blackcock is doing to me and now I'll take my revenge on you.' "

"The little cretin didn't understand, she laughed and ate the grass and rolled about on the ground, the crazy girl."

"Then he unbuttoned his trousers and took out that shameful thing."

"Immediately, as if it were the most natural thing in the world, she lowered her head on it and started drinking it up."

"And he says: 'What, you halfwitted whore, you do things like that? Who taught you?' "

"She didn't answer of course, she was too intent on her dedicated task, as if she was taking pride in performing it well. From time to time she would take a black hair out of her mouth and then she'd start again as serious as if she were a labourer, poor little mongoloid."

"So he pushed her away and said: 'So that's it, everyone takes advantage of you because you're dumb and stupid. They taught you to do this for their own pleasure without anyone knowing, the bastards. But who gets you to do it? Your dad? Your brother? Your cousin?' "

"And she kept on nodding, yes, yes, yes."

"So he threw her on the ground and lifted her skirt."

"He saw she didn't wear panties."

"He saw she was like a three-year-old, hairless, all white and chubby, her fat thighs creased and wrinkled."

"He closed his eyes and said to himself: 'now or never', and he tried to push that shameful thing into her."

"She kept still, but she was shaking, because she'd never done this before, the little mongol."

"He grabbed her and threw her down, and triumphantly thrashed away on top of her."

"But as he was about to come, he saw her face right next to his, and when he saw how ugly, how horrible it was, with its greasy skin, its nose like a cow, eyes like a Chinaman, pug chin, one inch of forehead, teeth bent and rotten, his cock went all limp."

"He said: 'Ugh, go away, you're too ugly, too stupid, you aren't even worthy of my revenge, get dressed, you idiot!' "

"But while he was talking like that the little cretin drew up to him and gave him a kiss on the mouth, and as she kissed him she looked at him with those cold, distant eyes of hers, like the eyes of a fly, and he got scared and pushed her away again."

"But she came back over to him, the mongoloid girl, and he looked at her at close quarters, straight into her fly-like eyes and deep down he saw something strange, a lustre, a sparkle of love, the sweetness of womanhood."

"Ever since that day he would bump into the mongoloid kid wherever he went, he'd throw stones at her, he'd kick her, but she would always go back to him. The whole village laughed at him, and at the great love he'd caused to blossom in her." Giottina wiped her forehead with her arm. She was panting. Her cheeks had turned red. Her chest went up and down, drenched with sweat, her little chain shone between her breasts.

Tota sat leaning against the wall, empty of all thought, exhausted, inert, her eyes lost and vacant.

I lifted my hand up to my neck. I crushed something soft. A huge grey mosquito stained my fingers red.

*26th August*

The police have discovered the American woman's corpse half eaten by rats. They don't suspect she has been undressed. They haven't noticed that the pendant has disappeared, or that other things are missing.

The body has been sent to the United States by air, according to her son's wish. The hut has been pulled down. The blackberry bushes round it have been burnt, together with the dead woman's rags and papers.

Tota told me all this. She also told me that in a few days they'll go and dig up the stolen goods and they'll take them to Naples to sell.

By now I've only got four days' holiday left. Suna hasn't mentioned her invitation to Naples again, so I think I'll go back to Rome with Giacinto as planned.

Every night I dream of Orio. When I go past his house on my way to the market, I seem to see him moving between the stalls, with his faded green canvas trousers, the blue beret on his head, his down-at-heel wooden clogs.

I asked Santino about him. He said he's "so so". I couldn't get more out of him. The brothers don't speak to each other. The mother is shut up at home. Orio is alone in hospital, without anyone to go and see him. In my dreams his belly is bandaged and a dog's head protrudes out of his navel. I'm searching for change so that I can phone him. I can't find the money. Or I have the money but the phone is out of order. At times I even manage to get through to him, but although I can hear his voice he can't hear mine. I'm wandering round a town which must be Naples, my feet are worn out, my head is empty. I clutch the change in my fingers, all I have left, and I'm looking for a telephone that works. This distressing dream repeats itself every night without fail. The idea of going back to school drives me to desperation. I think of Fidelio. I can't make out his face any longer. Instead of his eyes I see only those of Orio, faded and spectral.

Vittorio and Faele are always here. They eat with us, arguing fiercely about politics. They too are leaving for Naples on the first of September.

*27th August*

Giacinto came back at three o'clock with a large bream hanging from his belt, its throat ripped open. Santino followed him, carrying a nylon net full of sea urchins.

Giacinto started gutting the fish. Santino grabbed the bucket in which I soak the floor cloths and filled it with water. He sat on the camp bed in the kitchen and planted the bucket between his knees. Then he started splitting the urchins open with a knife, shooting black spines all over the room.

It's like a conjuring trick. I watched him spellbound. Giacinto too stopped struggling with the bream to follow his movements: the urchin in one hand, the knife that flashed down on it, the shell that split into two perfect halves, one falling into the water the other thrown into the air, then cleaned up with his fingers, filled with lemon juice and sucked up, the whole operation over and done with in just a few seconds.

In spite of being a king of the underwater, Giacinto was quite unfamiliar with sea urchins. Whenever he touches them he gets pricked. He can't open them without the spines penetrating his skin.

Santino laughed at our surprise, but he was flattered too. He got excited and became more reckless: he'd throw two urchins into the air at a time, catch them in the air and split them open with a single blow of his blade at the risk of the iron tip gouging his hand.

We all ate lots and lots. Some were swollen and juicy, but others were stunted and bitter and by the end I had a taste of iron in my mouth.

Giacinto put the fish guts aside for the cat. It's the same animal as was slung over the wall by our neighbours. Now it has quite recovered, even if it is slightly lame in one of its paws. It always comes in at lunch time for its portion of fish. It doesn't like being stroked and doesn't come if you call it. But from time to time, just when you least expect it, it jumps on to your lap, or even on your shoulders, and stays there purring for as long as it pleases.

Vittorio and Faele arrived at the last minute. We'd already eaten up all the spaghetti and sea urchins so we divided the bream into five. Vittorio grumbled that we were selfish.

They were tired and cheerful. They told us about some peasants from the village up in the mountains whom they'd been talking to all morning about crops, prices, political organisations and parties.

"We've got people on our side up there too, amongst the disaffected peasants and unemployed fishermen."

"I thought you were here on holiday."

"We don't believe in holidays, we work all the time."

"Well, I'm off for a sleep," said Giacinto, yawning.

"Your laziness'll be the death of us." Laughing and excited, Faele splashed some wine in Giacinto's face, but he wasn't at all amused. He gave his friends a black look and wiped his forehead with a handkerchief.

"You're just a couple of turds and you fancy you're jaguars," he said in a drowsy voice, and went off to have a sleep.

*28th August*

Santino has left for Naples. I asked Vittorio where he got the money for the journey. He answered: "From the Movement." Now they often have another holiday-maker from Trento with them, whose name is Renzo Bastiani. According to Faele he has "the wisdom of Lenin and the courage of Trotsky."

I don't like him much, I don't quite know why. He's kind and he speaks in a soft gentle voice with a strong Triestine accent. His eyes are light and shifty, his skin is always red, his hair brown and very short, his teeth protruding, his nose long and freckled, his body graceless. He stretches himself out towards other people, expressing a warped hatred against the world which is repressed and concealed beneath the rather formal correctness of his behaviour. He joined the Movement straight away and he's already working, writing and bustling about. He loves Vittorio like a dog loves its master and never leaves him alone.

"Tell me, where do you sleep?"

He was just on the point of sticking his fork into a piece of tuna fish. He raised his shifty eyes and replied: "I sleep at a friend's, in Casamatta."

"Are you a student too?"

"Excuse me, please, I'm studying law. And you?"

"How is it we never see you around in the square?"

"I've been at home, studying. I rarely go to the beach, I've got a sensitive skin."

Giacinto passed him some bread and poured him out some wine with exaggerated generosity.

"What does your father do for a living?"

"He used to be a commercial rep, but now he's retired."

"A rep for what?"

"Paint and varnish."

"Do you live in Trento?"

"No, excuse me, I live in Rome with an aunt who's a dressmaker."

Faele was fidgetting about restlessly in his chair. He interrupted Giacinto's questioning in a furious voice.

"People who ask too many questions are either spies or friends of spies."

"He comes to my house and eats my food, so why shouldn't I know who he is?"

"My, my, my, mine, mine, mine, you're as attached to property as any other dirty bourgeois, what sort of worker are you?"

"Oh, piss off."

Vittorio punched him on the arm. His fork with a piece of fish on it flew to one side and shot oil on to Renzo's shirt.

"Excuse me, comrades, I have only got one clean shirt, you know."

I ran into the kitchen to get a damp cloth. Faele was laughing. Giacinto was in a temper. While I was rubbing Renzo's shirt I was assailed by the sickly smell of his body. I wrinkled my nose. He must have realized for he snatched the cloth out of my hand and carried on himself, embarrassed.

"Vanna, bring us some fruit."

I went to get some. I made the coffee, did the dishes and rinsed the cutlery and glasses. When I went back outside they were asleep: Faele, lying on the ground under the banana trees, Vittorio on the deck chair, Renzo leaning his head on the table. Giacinto had gone back inside the house.

*11.00 o'clock*

The three friends stayed on till late, trying to convince Giacinto that he should join the Movement. But he said, no, he wouldn't dream of it — though he listened to them in silence, to the last word.

They were talking about four volunteers who are carrying out a 'softening-up mission', as they call it, in the most isolated villages in the Calabrian countryside.

"What do these comrades of yours do?"

"They talk to the peasants and try to make them aware of their rights."

"How?"

"By showing them the facts."

"Such as?"

"I'll give you an example: In San Bartolo's the seasonal labourers are people no party cares a damn about because officially they don't exist. If you go there and ask for them, they tell you there are no casual labourers in their village, they keep their mouths shut because they're scared. But then you take a closer look and you discover that every morning a rich landowner's mini-bus passes by and picks up a group of young lads between ten and thirteen, old age pensioners, and all sorts of unemployed people. They get on the bus and it takes them to Rio Nero and there, in shirt-sleeves and plimsolls, they start hand-weeding the cornfields, picking olives, pruning the vines, etc, and after eight or ten hours work, never planned in advance, but just according to how much there is to do, they earn between 400 and 600 liras a day." He stopped to light a cigar. He was staring at Giacinto with intent, hard eyes.

"The whole business is orchestrated by a certain Fandanzio, who organises the cash and the transport, and in exchange he gets an average of 1000 liras per labourer. The payment rates are never stipulated beforehand, so in the evening, according to results, this petty tyrant deals out the money as he feels like it, keeping at least 400 out of every 1000 liras for himself. Do you understand the system now?"

"So what do you do?"

"We go up, we try to organise them, to create some solidarity amongst them, some contractual power, and we set them up against this little Duce. We run quite a risk though: last month a comrade of ours was run over by a tractor as he was walking in the middle of the street, and guess what, the tractor belonged to Fandanzio, and even if he himself wasn't at the wheel someone else was. And that's how it is, that's our job over there."

"I'm going to Calabria with them. Student life in Rome makes me sick," said Renzo.

Vittorio turned towards him with an appreciative look. His friend sat as stiff as a rod, eating his fish with slow, deliberate gestures.

"Here's another example, Giacinto: the squatters in the San Quinto district in the suburbs of Naples. There's a group of buildings put up by the Institute of Workers Homes which have been occupied by the homeless for the last three years. Now the police arrive and want to chuck them all out because the houses have been allocated to other families who were down on the waiting list before them. There are eight hundred of them, including many women and children, and they're being evicted by force. Their move isn't taking place peacefully though: there are clashes, desperate resistance, assaults on the police, and the police for their part make use of every weapon they've got, tear-gas, armoured vehicles, truncheons — it's like a war. One child is killed by a teargas bomb, pandemonium breaks out, the squatters throw themselves against the police without stopping to think, against the advice of the political leaders."

"We are there to give the struggle an ideological content."

"Don't be so conceited, Faele. The communists want to run the occupation, but stealthily, with a smile on their lips and their arms open, planning among themselves when they start the battle and when they finish it, as if those poor sods had nothing to do with it. So in their local rag they write that this time the squatters are in the wrong, they must leave their homes to people who were registered before them, and then they must quietly and obediently put their names down on the waiting list so that, maybe, in ten years or so, they too will have a flat in the Institute of Workers Homes. Can you believe it? In a nutshell, this self-styled proletarian party demands that the homeless put their names down on the list, the same way as it demands that the sick put themselves down on the list, the students put themselves down on the list, the proletariat put themselves down on the list. In thirty years time, maybe, you too might have a bite of bread, this is the idea. You see? You want the revolution, comrades! Put yourselves down on the list! Join the queue!"

His eyes shone, his mouth, framed by his curly beard, glistened with saliva. "We don't want to put ourselves down on the list, Giacinto, we are for the head-on confrontation, for the immediate protest, for the power of the people."

"Who gives you the money for all this?"

"Anyone who's got it."

"But who?"

"Our friends, our enemies as well: we don't care, provided they don't ask for anything in return."

"They don't ask for anything in return, all right, but you're still in their clutches."

"Who says that?"

"I say it."

The two friends looked at each other downcast. Vittorio went back to his half-smoked cigar. Faele bit into another peach.

*29th August*

Today in the market there were two sharks that had been caught not very far off the coast. One of them was cut in half at its middle. The other was lying on its back on the floor of the fishmonger's, still in one piece.

I had to go and buy some fruit, but I stood there fascinated by that huge beast lying dead on the floor. Its silvery green skin, its open mouth, as if waiting to bite, the neat crescent-shaped row of sharp teeth. Its clear, wide open eyes stared at me enigmatically, as if wanting to communicate some evil secret.

I felt a nudge on my arm and turned round. It was Tota with her shopping bag hanging from her bare arm. She kissed and hugged me rapturously.

"Come, Giottina is waiting for us."

"I must go and buy some peppers and apricots first."

"Later, Vanna, let's go."

We walked along the road towards the harbour and turned off into Via del Pettine. We went into the dark, sweltering launderette.

Giottina put her iron down to come and hug me. She was chewing some mint leaves. The greasy smell of starch and steam mingled with the sharp pungency of the mint.

"Do you want some?"

"No thanks."

"Mint freshens you up."

She took a small plant with dull furry leaves out of a glass jar. She snicked off a couple of leaves with her nails and thrust them into her mouth.

Tota slumped with her full weight on the small bench. Giottina sprayed some water on her face, laughing. Tota backed away and they both laughed together. I sat down too.

"Do you know what happened in the Villa Trionfo?"

"Bedlam."

I already knew I mustn't ask questions. The tale will unfold in its own time, bit by bit, predictable and yet unexpected. Their voices will take turns, following each other swiftly, without ever getting entangled. And I will be drawn in against my will, my tongue will run dry, I will come under the spell of their infamous words.

"The maid is pregnant."

"But not by the chauffeur."

"Not by that little brown-haired chap who's always dressed in white — he's impotent, he hasn't got any balls."

"When he sees a woman he shits himself."

"He wears plastic underpants, like a baby, if you get too close to him you can smell that stench of shit, talcum powder and plastic that only babies have."

"So then, whose child is it, you'll want to know, won't you, Vannina?"

" . . . of the mistress herself."

"Yes, indeed, that's how it is."

"You'll say but a woman has no semen."

"A real woman has no semen in her womb."

"But she rules over her husband's semen."

"This too is the sacred truth."

"One day when the wind was blowing and the doors were open to let the air in, the wife and her husband sat at table opposite each other like a respectable married couple."

"The maid was going in and out of the kitchen with that homogenised mush they sometimes spread on bread and sometimes rub on their bodies to make them look young again. Anyway all of a sudden he says to her, that is to his wife . . . "

"'Wife, I want a son all of my own.'"

"And she says: 'No, I don't fancy it. I hate the idea of having a huge belly, swollen legs and swollen breasts, it would make me look ugly.

Besides I don't fancy all the pain a child causes when it comes out'."

"Then quietly quietly the husband starts crying, his tears drop into his soup, and he says: 'Why is this soup so insipid? It has no taste at all' and the wife replies 'It's all your fault, it's your sinful tears.' "

"And he says 'I'm crying because I want a child from our marriage which has indeed been long and cheerless,' and she replies 'It's absolutely impossible.' "

"So he starts crying again, and this time there are soles on his plate which drift in the salty water and begin coming to life again, but straight away the maid nails them down to the plate with one blow of her murderous fork."

"The husband was crying, giving off a sweet smell of jasmine, the wife was getting sick of it, and she says: 'For God's sake, stop crying, I'm choking over this sole I'm trying to eat' and the more she spoke like this the more the husband would cry."

"Seeing all this sorrow and anguish the maid says 'If you want a child why don't you adopt one from the orphanage? I was brought up in one for fifteen years and I can tell you this: living there's so bad that it would be better to die of poison.'"

" 'For heaven's sake,' the wife says, 'you never know what sort of thieves and whores those children have for parents — no, I don't want them.' "

"The husband though insists that he really wants a child because he feels an absolute need for one, that a marriage without children is a disgrace, and that when they are old who's going to look after them, and what about their property which is so large and valuable, who are they going to leave it to?"

" 'If you really insist,' says the wife 'I have an idea'."

" 'Would you really make this holy sacrifice for me?' he asks, fingering his shirt which was drenched with tears all down his chest and legs."

" 'Since I've no wish to be blessed with a swollen belly, let's get the maid to have the child for us.' "

"Taken by surprise, the maid drops the plate of homogenised pap, the husband stops crying and smiles happily with his eyelashes still wet, and says: 'That's the best idea in the world, I knew you were a loving wife, and this makes me really happy'."

" 'The trouble is, though,' he adds, 'I don't much fancy making love to this maid. I'm not a pig, you know,' and the wife replies: 'I'll see to that. Indeed I'll put something of myself in it, so that the child will come from all three of us equally'."

"After that they didn't talk about it any more at that time. The servant was a little nervous because even when you are the queen of a household, you're still the maid who is under the mistress and to whom you can't say no."

"But that night, while the husband is asleep, the wife takes his prick in both her hands and works on it so much that this mortified member becomes a porpoise, a great porpoise that sails and sails, rushes, jumps, dances, then all of a sudden starts spurting out its fireworks: the wife collects that precious treasure of his in her beautiful mouth, shuts it tight like a trap and then with her cheeks full of the divine milk she goes to the maid's room."

" . . . She tears the sheets off her, opens her legs and with her mouth she thrusts the family semen into her womb."

"So the maid got pregnant of the master without his touching her and the mistress goes around saying that the child will come from all three of them, because he ejaculated it, she sowed it and the maid nourished it."

*30th August*

I slept until late. Last night our neighbours had a party. They were up until three, singing, shouting and dancing. There was no chance of sleep. When I got up, Giacinto had already gone fishing. Before going out he had piled our neighbours' garbage to one side and set fire to it. But some of the stuff wouldn't burn and a thick grey smoke rose from the heap polluting the yard. I put it out by throwing some earth over it. As I was making myself some coffee, Suna and her brother arrived. He went straight away into the bedroom where he started messing about with Giacinto's fishing tackle.

"Well then, have you talked to Giacinto about our trip?"

"I thought you'd changed your mind."

"We're leaving tomorrow."

"But we've taken the house until the first of September."

"You can leave one day early, surely?"

"Giacinto won't want to miss a whole day's fishing."

"Well then, you come with me and you leave him here by himself for one day. Isn't that all right?"

"Can't we leave the day after tomorrow?"

"I can't sleep any longer, I'm in such a state I get furious with everyone. I quarrelled three times with Marta and I hit Oliver with one of my crutches."

"Why are you so angry?"

"Because of Santino, he doesn't telephone, he doesn't call, he doesn't write. I feel like splitting someone's head open."

"Well, maybe I can join you in Naples. I can't leave Giacinto to pack up our luggage all by himself. Besides we have to clean up and tidy the house before we give it back."

"Here you are again, the usual obsessed housewife who creeps out of her hole like a busy mouse. Let him do the cleaning, why not?"

"Giacinto can't do a thing around the house, I always do everything."

"He'll learn."

"I tell you, I'll join you the following day, what difference does it make?"

"I can't leave by myself. Someone must help me to get on and off the boat. Besides my father would give me hell."

"I'll ask Giacinto."

"Can't you decide yourself?"

"He's my husband."

"You say it as if he were your master."

At that moment Vittorio arrived wearing white tight-fitting trousers and a freshly laundered red T-shirt.

"I knew you'd be here."

"How did you know?"

"I just knew it. You two look like a couple of conspirators. It gets on my nerves, you should be my accomplice, not hers."

"Are you a woman by any chance?"

"Why, are you only able to team up with women?"

"Yes."

"Why?"

"Because we have some problems in common."

"Don't you have any problems in common with men?"

"Listen, I'll never make love to you, do you understand? I don't happen to like you and that's that."

"People change their minds occasionally. Today you don't like me, tomorrow maybe you will. I feel it."

"Tomorrow I'm going to Naples and I won't see you again."

"We'll see each other. I know where you live so I'll come and see you."

"Don't you have a girlfriend in Naples?"

"Yes I do. So what? I'm not a pathetic bourgeois, you know."

"Does she deceive you?"

"She doesn't want to."

"Or is it because you forbid her to?"

"No, she simply doesn't feel like it. She's faithful by nature."

"What does she say about this anti-bourgeois habit you have of pouncing on other women?"

"She approves of it."

"And you approve of her approval, naturally, your patriarchal voice becomes all sweet and sickly and says: 'Thank you, my treasure, this is just what I expected of you'."

"It's no good taking the piss. Anyway let's stop talking about her, I'm here because of you, and not because of her. Vannina, darling, can you make us a coffee, I'm falling asleep on my feet."

I went into the kitchen. I poured some water into the percolator, opened the jar where I keep the coffee, and turned on the gas. In the next room Suna and Vittorio were bickering. She was telling him off for behaving like a chauvinist pig and he was telling her how beautiful she was. I went to see what Oliver was up to in the bedroom. He was lying on the floor asleep. On his feet were the green rubber flippers, on his face the mask with the cracked glass, the mouthpiece tight between his lips. He was sleeping quietly, giving out a slight regular hiss. I burst out laughing and woke him up.

"Do you want some coffee?"

He took the mouthpiece off. He wiped his mouth with the back of his hand. He shook his head.

"Don't you have a mask and a pair of flippers at home?"

"Marta doesn't let me go underwater, she says it's bad for my ears because they've been inflamed. Besides there are sharks about. Will you give them to me?"

"They aren't mine. You must ask Giacinto when he comes back."

He got up and started prancing round the room lifting the large flippers, all dusted with talcum powder. The mask squashed his nose, and pulled at the skin on his forehead.

"Am I too thin?"

He had taken his shirt off and looked at me slyly, pushing forward his frail skinny chest.

"I could count your ribs, you look like a skeleton."

"Which is more beautiful, Suna or me?"

"Suna."

"You don't understand, you're stupid."

"You asked me for my opinion, and I've given it to you."

"My mother is a thousand time better."

"Is she beautiful then?"

"Compared to her, Suna is a louse, a crippled louse. My mother has blue eyes and long legs, Suna has grey eyes like my father, and legs like two sacks of sawdust."

"Which do you look like most? Your mother or your father?"

"My mother. In fact, I'll tell you a secret: I'm not the Turk's child like Suna, but don't tell anyone."

"Whose son are you?"

"I don't know, but certainly not his. That's enough, isn't it? My mother deceived him all the time, she never loved him. He spends his time wanking himself off, the damned Turk."

"Why do you dislike him so much?"

"Just because."

"Do you dislike Suna too?"

He didn't answer. His face became gloomy and frozen behind the thick cracked glass. His clear eyes became misty.

I was about to say something, but he turned round and went back to lie on the bed. He slipped the mouthpiece into his mouth. He didn't say another word for the rest of his stay.

*11.00 p.m.*

Giacinto was really put out when I told him I'll be leaving tomorrow with Suna.

"What the fuck are you doing that for?"

"She can't travel by herself."

"Who cares?"

"If I don't go with her, how's she going to manage?"

"You must stay here with me. We must hand back the house in good order. Look at it now, it's a real shithouse."

"I'll tidy it up today. You can go and eat at the restaurant tomorrow so's to avoid messing it up."

"You know I hate eating out."

"If you prefer it, I'll leave you something cooked."

"But why do you listen to that cripple instead of me?"

"I don't start school until October whereas you go back to work as soon as you get back to Rome, so I'll end up waiting day in day out for you in the heat. I don't fancy it."

"You've always done that before."

"Yes, but . . ."

He interrupted me with a hug. His anxious yellow eyes stared at me from close to.

"You do love me, Vannina?"

I nodded. He thanked me with a sweet loving kiss.

*31st August*

I cleaned the house thoroughly from top to bottom. I washed and scrubbed everything: the floor, the toilet, the walls, the sink, the windows. I took down the thick black curtain that separates the bedroom from the kitchen. I soaped it and washed it and rinsed it.

I packed up all the stuff we'd brought with us from home inside two large plastic suitcases. All I left out were Giacinto's fishing tackle, his light blue shorts, and his swimming trunks. I'm taking the yellow canvas bag with me to Naples.

Giacinto came back from fishing at four. He was in a dreadful mood. I watched him coming towards me from the far end of the yard: he's so blanched by the sun that he looks like an albino. His knitted eyebrows are almost white, and so are his eyelashes which blink lightly over his narrow hazel eyes. The freckles which cover his whole body give an impression of splashed coffee. His legs are muscular, his arms strong, his belly lean and taut. He looks like a peevish quick-tempered young boy.

"So you've decided to go to Naples with Suna, have you?"

"Yes, the ferry leaves at seven."

"Since we got married this is the first time you've acted off your own bat."

"Well . . ."

"What the fuck does it mean?"

"I don't know."

"It's that crippled girl that's set you against me."

"Why do you hate her so much?"

"Because I judge her for what she really is, a slut."

"But why?"

"Because she isn't natural. She gets on my tits."

"What do you mean by 'natural'?"

"That follows nature's rules."

"That is?"

"A woman's nature is something sweet, feminine, but that one keeps talking off the top of her head and getting on everyone's nerves."

"Am I natural?"

"You are, yes, up to now you have been anyway, but now you're putting yourself against nature."

"Because I've decided to leave?"

"By nature you're good-hearted, calm, affectionate, patient, submissive. Recently though you've been acting oddly, you're going against your nature."

"But I feel like acting this way, so this too must be part of my nature, isn't that so?"

"No, I know you so well, it's no use pretending: your real nature is quite different, at heart you're very feminine. But now you're acting like this just to imitate that runt of a woman."

"You're only saying this because you're annoyed that I'm leaving."

"No, I say it because I love you, and you love me too, even though you may sleep with someone else, you love me, you need me, you are dependent on me."

It's true. When he talks like this he is like an old man who has consciously renounced all desire for possessions. But there is a terrible strength in those blond arms of his and with that strength he keeps our marriage together. I'm in love with those arms.

*11.00 p.m.*

I went to say goodbye to Giottina and Tota. There were several people in the launderette and everyone was talking simultaneously. The moisture stuck to one's arms like slime. I was about to go when Giottina took my hands and burst theatrically into tears. I felt something between my fingers. It was a small parcel wrapped up in a piece of newspaper.

"Put it in your pocket without letting anyone see", she whispered in a hurried voice.

I obeyed mechanically. The other customers stood there watching us with astonishment. Giottina was sobbing quite desperately, gulping down her tears. I didn't know what to do. I saw that Tota was getting ready to repeat the same performance, with her eyes swollen, her face wincing with pain, her body stretched spasmodically towards me. Instinctively, I moved out of the way but, resolute and determined, she grabbed my arms.

Meanwhile Giottina was pushing her customers out, laughing, crying, swallowing her tears, making comical excuses. The heat was oppressive. The dresses hung from the ceiling like dark menacing phantoms. I turned my head round just in time to see Giottina bolt the door.

We were now alone in the fading light of the cave. Through the dripping glass the world outside looked like a sunny, fresh, unattainable seabed far beyond our reach. Tota gave a little angry scream and clasped me in her fat arms damping my neck with her tears.

"I'm not setting off for the States, you know."

"You're leaving, you're dying, and our tears will follow you."

"I'll be back next year."

"In one year the snake changes its skin three times."

Tota moved away from me when she felt Giottina's hands roughly taking hold of my shoulders. A minute later I was being tightly pressed against her panting chest and my face battered with dense, hot kisses.

I felt I was being engulfed by those suffocating hugs. I didn't want to be overwhelmed and I tried to free myself, but I was pinioned by four muscular arms.

The two women were now kissing my cheeks, my temples, my forehead, my mouth, my eyes, my nose, clinging to me spasmodically. I was wet with their tears and their saliva. The acrid smell of their sweat was making me dizzy. I don't know how long that frantic embrace lasted. Eventually someone knocked on the door, so we finally disentangled ourselves.

Red and panting, her face drenched and her hair dishevelled, Giottina went to open the door, displaying great naturalness and innocence. Tota dried her tears with a skirt that was hanging from the ceiling and Giottina flung herself at her.

The customer left and Giottina closed the door again. I remembered the parcel they had thrust into my pocket. I took it out and opened it. Between my fingers I found a roll of banknotes.

"What's this?"

"Your share."

They laughed at my surprise and looked at me with cheerful shining eyes.

"My share of what?"

"Of the American woman's stuff which we sold in Naples. It didn't come to much because they only paid us by weight for the pendant, the bastards. This is your share."

I put the roll down on the ironing board. I didn't at all like the idea of keeping it. Giottina frowned.

"If you don't take it, you'll offend us deeply."

"I don't want anything from that dead woman."

"Is it wrong to steal from the dead? To steal from the living, yes it is, but from the dead, no it's not, because they see you and if they're not happy about it they cause you to get caught. So if you don't get caught, it means they must be pleased." They burst out laughing, and I laughed with them.

"Anyway on this island everyone with their hearts in the right place steals."

"The mayor steals."

"The councillors steal."

"The police sergeant steals."

"The parish priest steals."

"The shopkeepers steal."

"The landlords steal."

"The restaurant owners steal."

"The hotel keepers steal."

"The bar managers steal."

"The fishermen steal."

"The maids steal from their masters."

"The masters steal from their maids."

"The only people who don't steal are the thieves because they're always in the nick so they don't have much time to get around."

"I've a cousin who was in jail for nine months for stealing a roll of wire."

"My niece was in jail for a year and seven months for stealing a bottle of oil."

"My uncle didn't steal anything at all and he's been in jail for six years."

They dropped on their chairs exhausted, laughing wildly, slapping their thighs with their palms, cheerful and crazy.

*NAPLES*

# *Naples*

*1st September*

I'm in Naples, in Suna's house on a dark narrow street, I don't even know its name. The house is old, the walls crumbling, the staircase dirty and stinking of cat piss.

The Maldrik's flat consists of four rooms on the third floor. Its windows look out on to the street, but the view is blocked right off by a new freshly painted building.

As soon as Suna switched on the lights there was a scramble of reddish cockroaches.

"This house is from the last century, it's as full of holes as a cheese. You can use as much insecticide as you like, it's no use, the cockroaches are here in their millions."

She took out some clean sheets, some white and pink striped towels, and a lemon-shaped bar of soap. She showed me the room where I'll be sleeping.

"This is Oliver's room, do you like it?"

It is lined with dark wood. In the middle there's a brass bed and by the window a table covered with books and exercise books. The smell of rubber shoes, chocolate and dust stagnates in the airless room. The walls are covered with photographs and posters of tennis tournaments. On a shelf there are four trophies of shiny metal. As I opened the wardrobe I thought I saw something dark move.

"What's that?"

"It's a mouse. Are you scared?"

"Mice disgust me."

"The place is alive with them, there was a time when Oliver and I spent whole days driving them out, we used to enjoy ourselves a hell of a lot, but now I don't think about them. Once my father gave me some terrible Dutch poison which strikes them dead in one second. Now and then I'd open a drawer and find a big fat mouse lying there as hard as cement."

"Why did you get such an old run-down flat?"

"Because it's near my father's. His flat is beautiful, larger and much brighter than this."

She showed me an inlaid wooden chest of drawers, the most precious object in the house. Inside it there was a whole collection of white tennis shorts, rackets, dirty tennis balls, white and blue shoes.

Along the corridor leading to the kitchen hung some small pale-coloured paintings, crowded with human figures.

"My father painted those. Horrendous stuff, but he's very fond of them, if he comes and doesn't find them he's quite capable of making a scene."

I looked at them closely. They've been painted with great care. They illustrate domestic scenes — a peasant family gathered round the table in a smoky kitchen, their faces lit by the fire; a husband and wife busy decorating a room with bunches of gladioli, the room picked out in a sugary light blue; a mother breast-feeding her baby, her arms enclosing him lovingly, her head bent, the whole scene frozen in a syrupy pink.

"He's sentimental in his paintings because everything in his life is going wrong. Even his present wife isn't too good, she insults him, drinks too much and fills up his house with relatives who steal from him non-stop."

"Whose photograph is this?"

"Elizabeth."

"Who's she?"

"My mother."

The photograph is large and clear. There is a background of trees, and on a bench sits a minute fragile woman in a pair of trousers too large for her. Her calm beautiful eyes stare at the camera with a look of determination. There is something uneasy and proud in the way she sits there staring straight in front of her which immediately endeared her to me. Perhaps she's less beautiful than Suna, yet she's more glowing and more delicate.

"She looks like you. Is she English?"

"Irish, actually. She comes from a family of shepherds in Galway, her surname is O'Connor, her mother died in childbirth when she was born, she has an elder brother whom I've only seen once, he's a big tall man who always stoops, whereas my grandfather is short and robust. That's it, now I've given you the lowdown on my family."

"Have you ever been to Ireland?"

"Yes I have once, when I was ten. I went to stay with my Uncle Robert who works for the Post Office in Dublin."

"Did you go by yourself?"

"No, I went with my father, but as soon as we arrived in Dublin he left me in the lurch and went back to London on business, or so he said, though he'd promised to stay with me and I'd even thought it'd be a sort of honeymoon for the two of us, all alone, without that little terror Oliver. Instead he abandoned me in a very squalid guesthouse covered with Virginia creeper and told me to wait for Uncle Robert who'd come and pick me up before the end of the day. I can still remember that cold damp room. I filled up the bath tub with steaming hot water, slipped into it, and there I stayed for a couple of hours swallowing my own tears, masturbating desperately. It was one of those old cast-iron tubs with lion's paws for legs. I remember it all perfectly, the window with white curtains, and beyond it the creeper with its red leaves. I'd been dreaming about that journey for months and there I was, as soon as we arrive he ditches me with my bad legs into that foreign bath tub, immersed in steaming hot water, all by myself like a waif, with my hands between my legs tormenting my cunt. What an idiot I was."

"But didn't he love you?"

"He arrived back on the last day, breathless, loaded with suitcases, he hugged Uncle Robert and my grandfather and then we were off."

"Where was your mother then?"

"Elizabeth hadn't been on speaking terms with her father for the past eighteen years, since she got married to the Turk against his will. The funny thing is that the Turk has made it up with him and the rest of the family and she hasn't."

"Have you ever been to visit your Turkish relatives?"

"We did decide to go once, I'd packed and got everything ready, then there was a terrible row between my father and mother so we didn't go after all. A year later she ran off with Salvatore and my father never left Naples again. He says that Turkey gives him the creeps, that his relatives are all shits, grown rich from dishonest rackets — as if he'd become rich himself from honest ones. Anyway he doesn't want to go by himself."

"What about his new wife?"

"Emma? She has deep roots in this neighbourhood, an earthquake wouldn't budge her, if she takes one step out of town she feels sick. She needs to live in the street where she was born, chatting with the neighbours, eating fried aubergines and drinking iced coffee topped with cream, to go to the same shops, to sleep every night in the same bed with the same satin linings, and if you take a single one of these things away from her she gets depressed and falls ill. When they went to Switzerland on their honeymoon, she wouldn't eat, she turned green and she spent every night tossing and turning as if she'd been bitten by a tarantula. The Turk keeps telling us about it, in the end they had to come back straight away and since then they've never gone away anywhere."

"What does your father do?"

"I don't know exactly, he trades, he deals with money, with foreign currencies, he's never told me a thing about his job. I know that after the war he made a lot of money with the Americans, now he doesn't make as much, he even went to prison once but he'd cut off his tongue rather than talk about his business. I know he has two other flats in this neighbourhood, he's a mean, greedy landlord, a menace, his tenants are poor mediocrities with no money, the whole neighbourhood is poverty-stricken, but he doesn't care a damn about anyone, when they don't pay he throws them out and if they refuse to go he 'persuades' them in his own way, by sending round the 'sappers'."

"What are the sappers?"

"He sends over these big bouncers and for a few thousand liras, they break everything up, smash everything, turn everything upside down and steal whatever they find. If it doesn't work the first time he just goes on repeating it, once, twice, three times, until the tenants get fed up and move out."

"This father of yours is a bit of a criminal."

"Not just a bit, a lot, but he's quite a special criminal of great beauty and charm, everyone who sees him falls in love with him."

*Midnight*

The shops were already closed. We ate biscuits and tinned sardines. The house is hot, one doesn't feel like eating at all. Fortunately the fridge works well, and we filled it with bottles of milk and coke.

Suna went to sleep early. I heard the phone ringing: it was Giacinto. He says he's back at work, that it's very hot in Rome, that our house has been taken over by lice. "When are you coming back?" he asked me anxiously. I said I'd be back in a couple of days.

Oliver's bed is too soft, it sinks right down in the middle as if it were a hole. The oppressive heat prevents me sleeping. I open the window. Outside there's an old woman singing. She's sitting on the ground right in the middle of the street.

*2nd September*

We slept until about ten. As soon as we got up, we gorged ourselves on biscuits and milk. At eleven we went out in search of Santino. Our first destination was the Movement headquarters. We took two trams and eventually arrived in Via Serbatoio: a stone front door, a small courtyard, a staircase with broken stone arches, and along the wall some revolutionary slogans half covered over with whitewash.

We rang the bell. Vittorio came to open the door for us. Behind him came a youth with large frog-like eyes. Everywhere there were gaudy coloured posters and rolled up red flags propped against the walls.

Vittorio hugged Suna impetuously and happily. He said he knew she would come. He tried to kiss her on the mouth, but she dodged him. He grabbed her hand and covered it with tender kisses.

"Why don't you come to the pizzeria with us? We were just about to go and have a bite."

"Where's Santino?"

"He's at work."

"Where?"

"Why are you so interested in that half-wit? He's a spineless guy, only good for making a fool of himself. He hasn't a scrap of initiative. Okay, he's quite a meticulous worker, but since he's been with us he hasn't changed his peasant mentality a jot."

"I like him the way he is."

"Do you know what he does every evening? Goes dancing in some totally tasteless nightclub, with the orchestra all dolled up in silver jackets. He's obsessed with this fantasy of posh restaurants and fashionable bars, he's a washout."

"Who does he go to these places with?"

"Some short-arsed chunky girl he's picked up God knows where. The truth is that lad has no balls, he's a wet blanket. If we were fascists instead of marxists he'd do exactly the same things with exactly the same meticulousness."

"You talk like this just because he's better looking than you are."

"Don't talk bullshit, good looks don't count for a thing."

"It counts for me. When's he coming back?"

"He's gone out to distribute leaflets with Mafalda."

"Who's Mafalda?"

"She's a new member. The daughter of a monarchist lawyer, just imagine!"

*1.00 a.m.*

We went to the pizzeria. Suna was absent-minded and hardly spoke. The other lad whose name is Antonio never opened his mouth either. Vittorio talked all the time about the Movement, about his passion for Suna, about terrorism, about the war in the Middle East, about the Americans, about sex, his father, and many other things.

I ate a pizza that tasted of cardboard and a salad that was yellow instead of green. However, the bill wasn't too much, we paid less than 1,000 liras each. Suna paid because Vittorio's pockets were empty. He turned them inside out for us, all stained with ink and grease, as if they were two flags.

"What on earth do you do? Do you keep pens in your trouser pockets?" Suna burst out laughing. Vittorio took out a biro broken into two and gave us a demonstration of how he could write with both pieces. I burst out laughing too. Antonio watched us all contentedly, his large bulging eyes wide open.

Suna ordered a beer. Vittorio looked at her with comical supplication.

"What's wrong?"

"Not Italian beer, please. It tastes like piss."

"What beer do you want?"

To earn himself a Dutch beer he made a fork appear out of his sleeve, then he made it disappear with quick comic gestures. He embellished the whole performance with monkey-like grimaces and childish whimpering.

We drank eight cans of beer. Then two more. And then two more again. Vittorio was becoming daring, hands and feet up in the air, balancing himself on a chair. Suna laughed, though without much conviction. As a reward he asked her for a kiss. Suna gave him one.

We went back to the Movement's headquarters, but Santino still wasn't there. He didn't turn up at all during the afternoon. Vittorio became as forceful and impetuous an executive manager as ever. He went out, came back, discussed, wrote, gave orders, determined and obsessed, with at times a gentle and at times a harsh tone of voice. The others listened, and did what he told them.

At about six we went back home, tired from having hung about in the heat all day without doing a thing. Suna was in a bad mood. She flung herself on the bed and said she didn't want anything to eat or drink.

"If you want to go to the cinema, Vanna, the money's in my bag."

"I have my own money."

"Go then."

"By myself?"

"What are you afraid of? I'd like to stay here alone for a while, without anyone around. Byebye."

I went to the cinema even though I didn't feel like it. I chose a thriller which was on at a local cinema and as soon as I went in I realized I'd made a mistake: the cinema was full of men. They sat in groups or alone, made loud comments about the film, ate sunflower seeds and spat the shells on the seats in front of them.

I sat in a corner, at the end of a row of empty seats. Five minutes later someone came and sat next to me. I turned my head for a second. It was an old man with a cold. He watched the film with his mouth open, breathing heavily through his nose. As soon as I turned back to the screen I felt his cold hand getting under my skirt. I stood up and changed seats.

On the screen brightly-coloured cars flashed past, pursued by other coloured cars. A hand brandishing a pistol appeared in the foreground. It fired. The car windscreen shattered. A blood-spattered face stared at us with dead yellow eyes. The car took a bend at great speed and launched itself down a steep slope, hitting the rocks, losing its wheels and bumpers. It somersaulted three times and ended up in a pool of stagnant grey water with a splash.

I let out a sigh and leaned against the back of my seat. I felt a naked hairy arm. I turned and bumped against the face of a middle-aged pater familias with a twisted greedy mouth. I stood up and went out.

I had only been away from home for three quarters of an hour. Suna had told me she wanted to be alone, so I strolled along the narrow streets of the neighbourhood. I crossed a square. I bought myself an ice cream in a café just as it was putting its shutters up. I emerged into a larger road flanked by acacia trees encased inside iron cages. I was walking slowly thinking of Orio and of his worried anxious face.

Suddenly I was assailed by a screech of brakes. I turned and saw a large flashy car coming to a standstill by the kerb. Out of the window appeared two ugly young heads. They asked me if I wanted to go with them and how much I charged.

I walked on without looking at them, hoping they'd realise they'd made a blunder. A minute later I heard them start up the car, and gave a sigh of relief.

But after walking twenty paces or so, I heard them pull up again. The car stopped alongside me and proceeded at exactly the same pace as I was walking, its rackety engine revving noisily.

I carried on resolutely, as if I hadn't seen or heard them, hoping that they'd weary of it. But a moment later I heard the car mount the pavement with two of its wheels just behind me. An arm stretched out of the window and tried to grab my blouse.

I began to run, but this only spurred them on and they started zigzagging noisily, driving on and off the pavement. I was scared. The road was empty: there wasn't a single person in sight. I stopped by an entrance, protected by a kerbstone.

The car slid near me and out jumped a young man with thick long sideboards, a sly face and pot belly. He wore a pair of tight-fitting strawberry-coloured trousers and a black shirt open to his chest.

"Are you scared, pussy cat?"

I knew it was better not to answer. I started walking towards home.

"Why in such a hurry, babe? Come on, hang on a minute! If you get inside the car with us we'll give you a nice present."

I walked with my head down, sweating, panting, biting my lips. I hoped that my refusal to answer would eventually make them give up.

"Just listen, you dope, I don't have a knife or a pistol! I've only got a beautiful throbbing cock and you, what do you have? No money, I can see that, you're a poor sod like me. You've got a beautiful arse though."

His friends burst into raucous laughter. I saw a bus coming and waved my arms frantically to make it stop. The driver looked at me for a moment perplexed and then continued his merry rush along the empty road.

I started walking again with long strides but the youth with sideboards continued to follow me. Behind him came the low, dirty car with the noise of its powerful clapped-out engine. Every so often they would rev up the engine and the empty road would resound like a train going through a tunnel.

"Well then, when are you going to show us this arse of yours?"

I had thirty yards to go before the turning into the street that took me home. I wondered whether I should take out my keys, but I decided not to. They would have noticed. I had to do it at the last minute, surreptitiously.

I started walking faster, keeping close to the wall, though without running. I felt they weren't too sure what to do. Maybe in a minute or so they'd jump on me, or they might drive off laughing. The youths in the car were watching to see how their friend with the sideboards was getting on.

"You're wearing a wedding ring, I see. So you're married, eh? God, what a swine of a husband you must have! To let a pretty young wife like you roam the streets at night, all alone."

"Get a move on, we're dying of boredom in here," shouted one of his friends from the car.

"A beautiful arse means a beautiful cunt, isn't that so? Can I lift up your skirt, may I?"

His hands took hold of my skirt. I turned round and kicked him on the shin. He bent down swearing. We were only a few yards from the door and I ran the last few steps, slipped the key in the keyhole and went in. But I didn't have time to close the door and the youth with the sideboards reached me and thrust his foot in the opening. He pushed it open with his shoulders and followed me in. The others were laughing at him, waiting with curiosity to see how he was going to behave. Fortunately they didn't get out of the car as I had feared.

I had already run up the flight of stairs taking the steps two at a time, when the youth caught up with me. For a moment we stared into each other's eyes. A flash of hatred passed over his childish face, I saw him lift his clenched fist and felt it crunch heavily on my nose. He bent towards me, gave me another punch on my temple, grabbed my handbag and ran off.

For a moment I couldn't see a thing. There was a black wall in front of my eyes, a hammer beating inside my head. I touched myself. I was bleeding. I sat on a step and rested my burning face against the wall.

When I got my breath back I went downstairs to close the door. I had a nasty feeling they were about to come back. Then, holding my nose with my fingers as best I could, I went up to the third floor.

Fortunately I still had the keys in my hand. The house was dark and silent. I went to the bathroom and washed myself. Then I went to my bedroom but found the door was locked on the inside. I knocked.

"Giannina, do you mind sleeping on the sofa? I'm with Santino, see you tomorrow."

I wanted to tell her what had happened, but her cold voice discouraged me. I heard Santino's soft, gentle laugh. I couldn't understand why they were in my room. Provoked by a sort of childish curiosity I bent down to look through the keyhole. I could see a bit of Santino's naked body, his limp penis the colour of corn, and Suna's head resting tenderly on his thigh.

My head ached and my nose started to bleed again. I went into the kitchen and drank some cold milk. Then I made myself up a bed on the sofa in the living room.

*3rd September*

I must have screamed in my sleep, because all of a sudden I woke up to see Santino's face above me. Suna stood there in her long nightdress, leaning on her crutches.

"What have you been up to? You're all black and blue, and you're bleeding."

I told them of my adventure. Santino laughed softly and sleepily. Suna told him off and he became more serious. She listened full of indignation and kept interrupting to ask for more details.

"You did fine to kick him, but you should have aimed at his balls, that would have paralysed him."

Santino sat on the sofa and stared at me in a daze. I asked him how Orio was.

"So so," he answered, opening his beautiful hands in front of him.

"But when is he coming out?"

"Who knows? They keep saying tomorrow, tomorrow, but he's still there. He asked about you."

"I'll go and visit him tomorrow."

Suna drenched my face with hydrogen peroxide and made me

gulp down some cognac. She was pleased that I was there to witness her reunion with Santino.

"He came at eleven, I thought it must be you, but it was him. That cretin Vittorio hadn't told him I was looking for him, a real shit, isn't he?" Santino was looking now at me, now at her. His pale blue eyes were dilated with sleep and he laughed apologetically as his eyelids fluttered together.

"This neighbourhood is changing," said Suna. "It wasn't like this before, I used to go out at night by myself without any worry. But tell me, what was this guy like, describe him to me, I know all the lads in this neighbourhood."

Santino fell asleep, his head dangling on his chest. Suna drank some cognac too, as I retold the story for the third time.

"What was in your bag?"

"15,000 liras and all my documents."

"Tomorrow we'll go and report it."

"I don't want to make a report, I've still got Ciancimiglio's one on my mind."

"Don't worry about that, I'll tell Hasan and get him to have it quashed. You'll see, he knows lots of people at police headquarters."

I was falling asleep on my feet too. I saw my face reflected in the glass of a painting: my left cheek and eye swollen and greyish-blue, a black bruise just above my cheekbone. Luckily I had at any rate stopped bleeding.

"Isn't he handsome? Look at him!" said Suna, gently putting her hand on Santino's sleeping face. She bent down to kiss him, tenderly sucking his upper lip. Santino woke up and put his arm round her shoulders. They went back to bed.

*4.00 p.m.*

I found the documents together with my empty wallet. They had been thrown on the pavement just outside the entrance. A neighbour found them as he was taking the chain off his motor-scooter. He handed them over to me with a self-assured look, sleeking his greasy hair down with his other hand.

I asked him if he had heard anything last night. He denied it over-confidently, his eyes looking down and a false jarring note in his voice. I realised that he had heard, but he had purposefully taken care not to interfere.

At two, while Suna was asleep, the bell rang. I went to open the door and found myself confronted by a massive solid man with a handsome gypsy-like head and cheerful grey eyes.

"I bet you're Giovanna."

"Yes, that's me."

"Let's take a look at you. Well, you're pretty, black eyes, curly hair, long eyelashes. You're married, yet you look like a girl. Who beat you up?"

He couldn't have been anyone but Suna's father. His large, strong body, his long arms, his whimsical mouth, even the scent of carnation and the jersey of soft, expensive wool, emitted a feeling of calm self-confidence.

"I'm Suna's father, the Turk, I guess you've heard about me already."

"Well yes . . . " I was about to add something, but he cut me short with his warm nervous voice.

"Don't listen to what my daughter says about me, she's quite a liar. But you are not from Naples, I gather?"

"I live in Rome."

"Nasty, dirty town that. I've always been had there, once they even sold me a house that had been demolished a month earlier. Thank you for escorting Suna. A disabled daughter is a real burden. How's Oliver?"

"He's well."

"Don't tell me where you're from, I want to guess. You've got a vaguely Roman accent, but underneath that there's something else, let's see: Apulia?"

"My mother is from Caltanisetta, my father from Marsala."

"Why did you tell me, I wanted to guess myself, anyway it's obvious you're a Southerner, your legs are six inches too short, and your eyes are so suspicious. But why didn't Oliver come with you?"

I was about to answer, but this time too he interrupted me with a mischievous look.

"Of course, yes, it's too hot, that's right. Anyway, here's 30,000 liras for your expenses. Now I must be going because I'm very busy."

As he started to take the money from his wallet Suna came in, leaning wearily on her crutches, her eyes puffed, her face haggard, her hair unkempt. They embraced each other tenderly.

"Now Suna, go to the doctor straight away, today, ask him to take new X-rays, bring me the bill, then go back to Addis. It's too hot here. What about you, Giovanna, are you going back to the island with her?"

"No, I can't, I must get back to Rome."

"Who's going to accompany Suna then? You won't leave her on her own, will you? If it's a question of money, I'll pay for the journey of course."

"It isn't because of the money, my husband is waiting for me at home."

"Well, let him wait. You accompany Suna, then you can go back to Rome, I'll pay for that ticket as well, of course."

I was about to reply, but I noticed that he wasn't listening to me any more. He had stopped in front of one of his pictures and was contemplating it with fascination. His face had softened, his lively grey eyes had become sentimental and dreamy.

"Daddy, will you have lunch with us?"

The gypsy didn't answer. He stood there in front of the painting, enchanted by the elegance of that domesticated family scene.

*Midnight*

As soon as the Turk went I rushed to get the bus to the hospital. I wanted to see Orio and I was afraid I would be late for the visiting hours.

The bus was crowded. Gusts of air came in through the windows, but they couldn't disperse the strong smell of sweaty shirts, badly digested onions, coffee, fried food and cigarettes. Pressed against limp overheated bodies I felt nauseated as I jolted along, counting the minutes.

Three stops before the hospital I got off. I walked the rest of the way. The soft asphalt sank in under my shoes. The sun shone on my aching face.

When I got to the ward Santino had mentioned, Orio wasn't there, and I had to go through four wards before I discovered him. Finally I found him at the end of a passage amidst hundreds of beds, by a large open window. He was playing cards with an old man.

When he saw me he became very serious. He put his cards down and buttoned up his toothpaste-stained pyjama jacket. Meanwhile, the old man gave me a hostile look and went off limping.

"How are you?"

"I'm well."

But he didn't look well. Two dark blue rings stood out against the dull skin under his eyes. His lips were dry and feverish. He had lost weight and his belly was swollen and taut.

"And you? Have you had a punch-up with someone?"

"Yes."

His grey face relaxed into quiet, childish laughter. There was something withered about him that made him look ugly. Only his eyes were the same as ever, clear and joyful, the colour of milk flecked with green.

"Sit down."

I sat on the edge of the bed. He moved his legs aside and I saw his little round belly sticking out from underneath the sheet, hard and protruding.

"How do you feel?"

"Well."

"Have they operated yet?"

"No they haven't."

"When are they going to?"

"I don't know, they never tell you a thing here."

"Do you need anything?"

"No, I don't. Santino brought me a pile of comics that big, but I read them all in one day, then I sold them. If you want to bring more comics, they sell well here." I took his hand. It was ice-cold. I warmed it up by rubbing it between mine.

"If you do that, it makes me want to make love with you."

"Do you want me to stop?"

"No, I don't."

He closed his misty eyes. I unclasped his fingers and caressed his open palm, pressing the small hard yellow callouses with my fingertips. It is the hand of an adult, solid and yet yielding. I clasped it tightly, and sensed a spasm in my belly, and a warm sensation welled up in my throat. I wanted to make love too.

I looked around. There were beds everywhere, even in the middle of the ward, and the passages were cut down to a bare minimum. The patients, though, didn't seem to mind at all, they were going back and forth bumping into each other and climbing over the beds, the chairs and the bedside tables. Some were playing cards in groups of three or four, others were eating, others were asleep. Some were listening to the radio half buried under their sheets. There was even someone pissing in a chamber pot, with his face towards the wall.

Two beds away from us there was a white screen hiding the bed of one of the patients. Orio followed my look.

"That's someone who's dying, last night he screamed and screamed. Now thank God he's quiet. He got on everyone's tits, let's hope he dies quickly."

No one seemed to be attending to the dying man. Behind the screen, I caught a glimpse of an oxygen bottle. From time to time you'd hear a deeper breath, like a death rattle.

I tried not to think of all these people. I stared at Orio's dry hand. All my excitement had evaporated.

"Are you asleep?"

"No, I'm not."

"Are you in pain?"

"Why didn't you come earlier?"

"I didn't know you were waiting for me."

"Will you come tomorrow?"

"Yes, if you like."

"Now you must go, because I have to play cards with those two, they're waiting for me to play a game."

I looked at the old man who was leaning on the window sill. He wore a pair of baggy trousers fastened round his waist and his thin wrinkled neck emerged from a filthy shirt. Next to him there was a young man with a bandaged arm, who stared at me with eyes as icy as a snake's.

I moved to stand up but Orio pulled me back by my hand. I bent over to give him a kiss. I felt his delicate, slightly damp skin against my lips. A whiff of bile came from his beautiful soft mouth, and I shuddered.

*4th September*

"You could be doing something in that school of yours."

"Like what?"

"You should work out a 'softening-up' process; you could talk to the boys, do some propaganda for our ideas."

"Yes, of course, so that they kick me out straight away."

"You're scared, aren't you? Now I know what sort of person you are, I've got you sorted out, Giovanna: you're honest, I can't deny that, sensitive to other people's problems but shit scared, and it's this fear of yours that fucks you up."

"You're right, I'm scared."

"It isn't an ordinary kind of fear, I can see that. I look at people and I suss them out right down to their guts. Yours is the fear of someone who lacks confidence. You don't believe in yourself, do you?" Vittorio looked at me sternly with his clear, insolent little eyes. Suna was eating an ice cream and didn't seem to be listening to what we were saying. Santino was operating the duplicator with Mafalda.

"I don't think I could do anything good in that school, I'm helpless. Besides, I find my colleagues too disagreeable, and the pupils too, they're cocksure, idle, sadistic, I just hate them."

"It's your own fault, and of people like you. You dish out these half-baked ideas, dead-as-mutton teaching and repression and you make the kids just like their parents, if not worse, just morons. If you only had some enthusiasm, passion and also of course a clear capacity for historical analysis."

"I just don't have the enthusiasm."

"You say it as if you were saying: 'I have no saliva'. Your fear is cultural and social, a typically evil result of your fucking petit-bourgeois background."

"It's a fear which results from thousands of years of servitude, you arsehole."

"You always have to defend women, Suna. According to you no woman ever has any defect; she's just a pathetic victim with no responsibility and no blame."

"Fuck off, Vittorio."

He was about to make an angry reply, but something made him hold it back. He grabbed Suna's white nervous hand and pressed it against his cheek.

Suna rudely drew her hand back and carried on licking her ice cream. Her eyes were fixed on Santino who was fiddling about with the duplicator with slow, indolent movements.

Next to him Mafalda looked like a bear. She picked up the sheets, put them in order, cleaned the grease off the machine with a rag, turned the handle, doing everything with careful, heavy, clumsy gestures.

The two didn't look at each other, but there was some secret bond which drew them together, a complicity they couldn't completely hide.

Mafalda is 28. She's tall and dark, she has thick legs and large breasts, and her face is dark and heavily lined. At first it appears almost ordinary and anonymous, though slightly brutal and introspective. But when you look more closely you discover something sensual and tender which lights up her heavy features.

"One of our lot teaches at a grammar school in Pozzuoli, you should talk to him. Until a few years ago he was a slavering drifter like anyone else. Then he met us and joined the Movement and now he's a good militant comrade. I want you to meet him, but just now he's on holiday with his girlfriend."

"As far as holidays go he's still a drifter."

"Faele, you've always got something to be critical about."

"I'd like to know why we should be here working our arses off while he's having fun in Yugoslavia with that pest of a girlfriend."

"Just watch it, and mind your own business. Have you made that list of what we want?"

"What about the money?"

"I'll see to that. You just make that list and shut your mouth."

Meanwhile Santino and Mafalda had disappeared. Next to me, I felt Suna stiffen. I turned and saw that she was biting into her ice cream with bare teeth, sullen and gloomy.

"The trouble is that the fascists are carrying out 'softening-up' missions too, so how do we distinguish ourselves from them?"

"Don't talk bullshit, Renzo."

"What a bore."

"It's you who's the bore, you're never satisfied with anything. What the fuck is it you want?" interrupted Suna. She stood up and, dragging on her crutches, went towards the door to the balcony. Vittorio, Faele and Renzo carried on quarrelling, but I couldn't follow their argument. I wondered whether I should follow Suna or wait for her.

She came back a minute later, her face stony, and sank into her chair. One of her crutches fell to the floor, and Vittorio bent down solicitously to pick it up.

"What's wrong, are you sick?"

"Let's go, Giovanna, I'm fed up with this shitty place."

I helped her get up. We walked to the door, but Vittorio ran after us.

"Where are you going? Wait, Suna, what's wrong with you? You promised to come to the pizzeria with me."

"I don't feel like it."

"Are you coming back later?"

"No, I'm not, in fact tomorrow I'm going back to Addis. Byebye."

"Wait, what are you saying? But listen . . . "

Suna took his head in between her hands and kissed him passionately on the mouth. Vittorio tried to clasp her in his arms and she bit his lip violently. He staggered back in astonishment, and she ran off limping, her long black skirt and large fringed sleeves ballooning out behind her like a great black bird dragging itself along on its wings. I remembered Giottina's words: "beware of the evil wings of the one who can't fly!"

I found her at the bus stop, leaning against the lamp post. She was staring in front of her, her muddy grey eyes clouded with rage. She told me she had found Santino and Mafalda in each others' arms on the balcony.

I helped her get on the bus. I didn't know what to say to comfort her and we travelled home in silence.

I was hungry and cut myself two slices of bread. Suna refused to eat, and went to lie down on her bed. I had lunch by myself on the table crawling with flies: cold potatoes from yesterday, milk, a banana.

While I was eating, I suddenly found her beside me, her face sweaty, her lips pale.

"I can't sleep, Vannina, I'm too hot. Have you ever been jealous?"

"Yes, once three years ago when Giacinto had a fling with a girl called Lillina who worked as a cashier in a guesthouse in Monte Mario."

"What did you do?"

"Nothing. I saw this girl once when I went to visit Giacinto at his garage, and she was there having her Fiat 500 repaired; she had hair down to her waist and her trousers were so tight they could have split on her bum; from the way they looked at each other I realised they'd been making love, I understood it straight away."

"How did you react?"

"I stood there like an idiot with such a terrible guts ache I thought I was going to shit myself. Later I asked him if he was in love."

"What did he say?"

"That he didn't know."

"And you? What did you do?"

"I threw up, then I didn't feel like eating any more."

"And then?"

"I started spying on him, I followed him like a half-wit, I'd go and visit him at the garage all the time, to put it in a nutshell I became an unbearable nuisance. I realised that from the way he started treating me, like a stupid boring little girl. He continued to see her anyway. Then just as I was getting used to it, they left each other."

"I get so mad at Santino standing there like a sack of potatoes, anyone who wants him can have him, he's got no character, he doesn't even know what he likes and what he doesn't like, he makes me sick, he disgusts me. If he comes, tell him I don't want to see him any more — no, don't tell him anything, just kick him out, throw him down the stairs, tell him he's a toad, that I hate him, that he can go and hang himself, and now I'm going to go and masturbate, when I feel depressed that's the only thing that cheers me up. Byebye."

She went banging her crutches on the striped floor-tiles. I poured some more milk into my glass. I peeled a peach.

While I was eating I heard a sob, and I went in to see if she needed anything. I found her lying on the bed, naked, one hand on her groin, her eyes full of tears.

I didn't know whether to go in or stay. I asked her if she wanted something to eat. She lifted her beautiful troubled eyes and smiled at me with seductive sweetness.

"Come here Vannina."

I drew closer. She beckoned me to sit next to her. I did so. She took my hand and placed it on her belly.

"Can you caress me, do you mind?"

It was the first time I'd touched a woman's belly. It felt disagreeably soft. I played a little with her hair in the way I sometimes do with my own.

She closed her eyes. She stretched her arm and pressed my hand on her damp flesh. My body was icy, my throat blocked up. I touched her more deeply and her soft tender sex opened timidly to my touch. It relaxed between my fingers like a small open sea-anemone down in the depths of the sea.

A few seconds sufficed. I felt her spring, stretch and all of a sudden relax with a small stifled cry.

Her warmth roused me and I would have liked to kiss her, but she pulled the sheet over herself and with an abrupt gesture turned her back on me and huddled against the wall.

I stood up and went back to the kitchen.

*Midnight*

I went to see Orio in hospital. He looks better. I took him some comics and this made him happy.

Giacinto rang me up at about nine to ask when I'm going back. I said: tomorrow, if Suna goes to Addis, otherwise in a few days. He says I'm letting myself be mesmerised by a witch. I laughed and he slammed the receiver down in a temper.

At dinner Hasan showed up wearing a summery lilac shirt through which one could see his lean muscular chest. He was cheerful and self-assured.

"Use 'tu' with me, Vannina, okay? Has Suna been to see the doctor yet?"

"I don't know."

"In my opinion this doctor business is just a cover-up, I think underneath it all there's something else, a love affair perhaps. Do you know anything about it?"

"No, I don't."

"You're afraid of spying on her, aren't you? Well, you're a discreet girl. You're quite right, remember that in this life the less you talk the better. Where is Suna?"

"She's asleep."

"Okay, let her sleep. How old are you, Vannina?"

"Twenty five."

He fixed his unsmiling grey eyes on my face. His large red mouth is of a coarse, striking beauty.

"Do you think Suna will ever be any good for anything in her life?"

"What do you mean by 'good for anything'?"

"Well, find a decent husband she won't split from after living together for a couple of months; have children, become a good mother. I'm afraid she'll always be a misfit."

"If she carries on studying medicine she could become a doctor."

"Bullshit. Can you imagine a crippled doctor? And on top of everything a woman doctor? I'd be happy if she doesn't end up in a home for the subnormal."

"Why should she end up in a home?"

"I shan't live for ever, and I haven't saved enough for her to live on the interest. I've got all the others too, wives, children, the fact is I just can't give her enough to live on without working. And left to her own resources I just know she'll never make it."

"She could work."

"There's no work for a cripple, besides haven't you understood yet what sort of a person Suna is? Intelligent, talented, I don't deny that, but fickle — after a while she gets bored with everything."

His voice is deep and caressing. When his grey eyes light up they flicker with sharp, steely reflections.

"If I were in her shoes, I'd kill myself," he continued. "True, she's only a woman, for a man it would be much worse. Let's hope she finds a husband who will take her as she is, with a good dowry perhaps, and then she could have children. She's beautiful, she should make the most of that."

"But Suna can do everything, she can walk, travel, work."

"She can do everything all right. She can make love, too, I know, but that's the problem because to convince herself she's attractive in spite of her legs she makes love left, right and centre."

I was about to ask him why she shouldn't make love when she chooses but he cut me short with a sharp affectionate gesture.

"It would have been better if the paralysis had affected her up to her navel, then there wouldn't be any problems and I wouldn't worry. What's she going to do if she gets pregnant, can you tell me that?"

"She won't get pregnant, she's careful to take precautions."

"I can see you're an emancipated girl. I'm all for women's emancipation. When I think of all those poor Turkish women shut up at home I feel like crying. All the same a woman shouldn't try to behave like a man or she'll lose all femininity, she'll become vulgar and promiscuous. For me a woman must more than anything be shy and mysterious, like you for example. I'm sure you don't go around making love to all and sundry."

I didn't feel like answering him. I knew just what he was after — to drag me in and get me to talk about myself and then about Suna, giving away all her intimate secrets.

"You think I'm being moralistic, I know that, but you don't say so because you're a kind girl. You know, amongst all Suna's friends you're the one I like most, you're not arrogant, you're not over-confident, you're not conceited. Besides, a woman doesn't need to make love as much as a man, so why not preserve that discretion that is so beautiful in a girl?"

To answer him would have been equivalent to giving in to him. I looked him up and down. He arched his slim graceful body in front of my eyes, showing off his narrow hips, his crutch and his long shapely legs.

"When I was in Turkey I knew women who'd only made love two or three times in their lives, just after their marriage, and that was all till they died. They didn't have a clue what sexual pleasure was, yet they were healthy, plump, happy — much more cheerful and content then girls like Suna who take the initiative as if they were men, make love day and night, and then have nervous breakdowns."

"Daddy, why are you tormenting Giovanna with your stupid ideas?"

"Ah, you're awake then!"

Suna came forward, limping, her muscular arms bare to her shoulders, a yellow towel wrapped round her neck, her wet hair hanging in shiny compact locks over her frowning face.

She went up to her father and kissed him on his cheek. I noticed that in front of his daughter he loses a lot of his confidence. He still talks arrogantly but can't avoid showing a certain embarrassment.

"Have you been to see the doctor?"

"No, I haven't."

"What are you waiting for?"

"I'll go, Daddy, just leave me in peace."

"It's not good for you to be in town in this heat, in this sweltering house. Besides, what's the point of my renting a house by the seaside?"

"You should give me some money, Daddy."

"What for?"

"I want to buy myself a rubber dinghy."

"A rubber dinghy, with your legs? Are you crazy?"

"So that I can go into the sea."

"Aren't you ashamed of showing yourself in a swimming costume in your condition?"

"No, I'm not."

"How much do you need?"

"300,000."

"I'll buy it for you for half as much."

"But I want a special one, a large one, with an engine and everything."

"I'll see to that, my darling. I must go now, Emma's waiting for me."

"I'll ring you at your office tomorrow."

"What for?"

"For the money."

"Well, we'll see, I'll think about it."

He hugged his daughter, and me too. The scent of his carnation and lavender water penetrated my nostrils, cloying and sensual. He left, gently closing the door behind him.

"He forces me to tell him a whole lot of lies to get round him. I hate him, did you see how suspicious he is? He prefers to waste his time buying all the stupid things I ask for rather than give me the money direct, the swine."

"Have you decided to give some money to the Movement?"

"I haven't decided yet . . . well, perhaps I will. I think they're doing some good. I like Vittorio, he's sincere, even if he does have a bee in his bonnet, especially about women. I think I will, yes, I'll give him some money, that is if my prick of a father forks out."

*5th September*

"Pardon me, please, I'm against it myself."

"Your personal opinion doesn't count. The last national assembly decided for it."

"In a country where opposition is legal it doesn't make sense to go underground."

"Yes, legal, but when you lay your hands on someone's property see how they all jump."

"Property is theft."

"You always talk in clichés, Faele."

"And you're just a bloody intellectual. I couldn't care less about words, it's the concept that counts."

"The concept is in the words, if you talk platitudes you also think platitudes."

"You're just a fucking intellectual show-off."

"What are you then?"

"Vittorio, Faele, do stop arguing! In my opinion, anything of this kind is a mistake at this moment."

"Mistake or not, it's the assembly's decision."

"The assembly made me the person responsible for the southern region, so it's my job to organise softening-up operations."

"Pardon me, Vittorio, I don't agree."

"In other words, you're scared to death."

"No, pardon me, I'm not. But I'm against any action that could be exploited by the right."

"You're shit scared, you prick! Take a look at Santino, he's semi-literate, yet he doesn't make half such a fuss."

"Santino is a babe in arms."

"Look at Suna then, she's middle-class and loaded with money but she doesn't make such a fuss either! She's joined the Movement and she does what she's told."

"Suna doesn't know you're intending to use illegal methods."

"You're just shitting yourself with fear, Renzo."

"Please, control your aggression, you're just an irrational extremist."

"You're shitting yourself, you bloody conformist."

Mafalda sat at a folding table writing. She didn't say a word during this discussion between Vittorio, Renzo and Faele, and neither did I, nor did any of them ask me what I thought. Santino was working next to Mafalda. He was paying careful attention, not to his comrades' words, but to Mafalda's movements as she handed him the sheets for him to staple together.

Suna didn't look at them at all. She was nervous and edgy, and her restlessness infected everyone. Shortly afterwards Antonio turned up as well with his bulging yellow-veined eyes and sad kindly air. Vittorio, Faele and Renzo went to discuss the plans for their mysterious project in the other room.

Mafalda and Santino went out, and Suna followed them. I was left alone with Antonio. He was staring out of the window, and I stared at him.

"Are you hot?"

"Yes, I am."

"So am I." He smiled, revealing his large white teeth.

"Are you a student?"

"Yes, a law student. And you?"

"I'm a teacher."

"Have you joined the Movement?"

"No, not yet."

"I've just joined it. Have you ever been active in any movement?"

"No I haven't."

"I belonged to another group before this, but I had to leave it."

"Why?"

"Because of this itching."

"Oh?"

"Well, it was like this: I was very happy in the group, I got on with my comrades, I liked the feeling of cooperation that existed amongst us, there was a strong sense of brotherhood, a lot of affection, we struggled against selfishness, we lived simply, ate little. It was really good, we never quarrelled, each of us had to live on the equivalent of a worker's wage and the rest went to the party. We had a leader who made really smashing speeches and everyone listened to him as silently as if they were in church. Then, I don't know why, I started this itching: whenever we had a meeting for self-criticism my back and my legs started to itch. When the leader made his beautiful speeches on how to serve the people my eyes and nose itched and I scratched and scratched and they'd all say: 'Keep still, Antonio, keep quiet.' And then in the morning I'd read the timetable with all the tasks for that day, and my bottom itched, my feet itched, I became scabby and covered with red sores all over. I looked disgusting, I couldn't sleep because of the itching, I didn't even feel like eating any more. One day, the leader, who's a good hearted young man, says to me 'What's wrong with you, Antonio, are you ill?' I said 'No, it's this itching of mine that drives me mad.' He says 'Go and see a doctor, here's the money.' I went to the doctor and he says 'There's nothing wrong with you, it's just that your nerves are in a bit of a mess, an allergy perhaps. Have some rest and get a lot of fresh air.' So I did what he said and my itching got better. I went to the seaside, I breathed clean air, I spent a lot of time reading all by myself, and I recovered. So then I said to myself, now's the time to go back to the party when there's such a lot to do. I felt a real worm to be there doing nothing while all the others were slogging away, so I went back but the moment I went into the meeting room I started itching again so violently that I writhed about like a dog, trying to scratch my neck, my back, my legs and my feet, all at the same time, as if I had St Vitus's Dance. So to cut it short I had to give up."

As he was speaking his hand mechanically went up to the nape of his neck and he started scratching furiously with his nails, his frog-like face contorted into a comical harassed grimace. I pointed this out to him and he burst out laughing. He looked at his nails, blinking his eyelids, and said he'd been totally unaware of it. We laughed together.

*6.00 p.m.*

The visiting hours at the hospital are from three to five, but by tipping the nurse I am allowed in earlier whenever I want.

As a matter of fact today I didn't meet a soul, neither the porter, nor the doorkeeper, nor the nurse. I dashed up the stairs taking two steps at a time.

When he saw me, Orio propped himself up on his bed. But I could see he was having to make a big effort. He's losing strength, he no longer plays cards with the people from the nearby beds. He lies still, staring at the window with his head twisted to one side.

"I've brought you some more comics."

"I sold the last lot for 2000 liras; I'll sell these for what I can get, I don't feel like haggling."

"Are you in need of money?"

"I'm putting it by for when I come out."

"How do you feel?"

"Guess who came to see me this morning. Toto."

"Was that nice?"

"Sit down, let me have your hand."

I sat down and gave him my hand. He lifted his faded aquamarine eyes. He looked frightened.

"How do you feel?"

"Well."

"What do the doctors say?"

"Not a thing. The sister says they're going to slit open my belly."

"What's the name of the doctor who's treating you?"

"He's an old man, he rushes in, says two words, then rushes off again. He doesn't even look at me. He's got a twitch all down one side of his face."

"What about the nurses?"

"There are five of them, but there's too many of us, everyone keeps calling for them so in the end they get fed up and shut themselves in the porter's lodge and refuse to come out. Yesterday three people died. Do you see those beds over there?"

He pointed to some beds at the other end of the passage. I couldn't see any difference between them and the other beds: there were sick people lying in them just like the others.

"They've taken the dead bodies away. Those are new people."

"Are you still in pain?"

"They give me something to make me sleep. It's quite nice, it tastes of raspberry. Toto says that Gigi is coming tomorrow, but I don't feel like seeing anyone."

"Why?"

"Because they're only coming to see if I'm going to die, so that there'll be one less to share the inheritance."

"So you tell them to mind their own business."

"When I'm well, I'm going to sail off to Australia, like Blackcock."

"Do you still read the comics?"

"My eyes are weak. I think it's that raspberry stuff that makes me sleepy, even now I feel like dropping off."

"Do you want me to go?"

"No, I don't."

He clasped my hand in between his hot dry hands. He closed his red-rimmed eyes. His breathing was short and laboured.

"Will you promise to come back tomorrow?"

"Yes, I promise."

"Can you give me a kiss?"

I kissed him on the mouth, looking round ashamed of myself. But no one was paying any attention to us, except for a sick man with a cropped head who was crying softly in a bed at the far end of the passage. The others were too busy chatting or playing cards or listening to the radio to take any interest in us.

I stayed there with his hands in mine for I don't know how long. Perhaps he was sleeping. From time to time he opened his eyes like those of a blind man. His yellow skin perspired around his nose and temples.

I looked up to the window. You couldn't see the sky, only buildings, identical to the one we were in, painted blood red. Some large windows opened on to the façade of the building opposite and inside you could see stacks of beds laid out in every direction, even right in the corners.

Along the side wall was a row of balconies, thronged with clusters of patients huddled together. They wore striped pyjamas and were enjoying the fresh air, just like prisoners. On a balcony by the corner two boys were playing at who could spit farthest. The only refreshing thing was the feathery top of a poplar springing up from the yard. Its lightly coloured leaves fluttered at the slightest puff of wind, with a soft silvery glitter.

I fell asleep too, sitting where I was with one foot in the air and the other resting on one of the iron bars of the bed. I dreamt that Orio was my father. He had two deep wrinkles each side of his mouth, his eyes were stained yellow, his teeth were worn and broken. He held my young girlish hand in his gnarled fingers and spoke to me in a language I couldn't understand.

I understood the meaning of his clasp though. It said that our love and affection was deep and wild, that his old burning peasant's hand was holding mine tight for ever. 'I'll never let go of your fingers' said the soft light pulse in his veins, 'your wildness will stay with me, imprisoned by my iron hands, I'll never let you go, for your sake, for the sake of my own child, my daughter.'

I woke up with a start of fear. Orio's hands still clasped mine, but his face was twisted by pain.

"I'm going to call the sister," I said, frightened.

But just then a man in a white coat arrived carrying a syringe in his hand. He beckoned me to move aside. Then, with a quick confident movement, he stuck the needle into Orio's emaciated flesh and went away without saying a word.

A few seconds later Orio's face regained colour and his body relaxed. He fell into a deep profound sleep.

I stood there watching him sleep so sweetly and quietly: I felt a passionate desire to kiss him.

I was about to go, and was getting ready to leave when I was stopped by his faint voice asking me to stay. I don't know how long I stayed for. I started getting a pain in my back from the effort of sitting still. But eventually it was supper time and I had to go. On my way out I asked to see the doctor, but I couldn't find him. They sent me from one ward to another and eventually a kind china-faced sister advised me to come back tomorrow.

*Midnight*

As I came into the house I was met by a strong smell of roast meat. I went into the kitchen and found Suna cooking a meal. She moved clumsily, propping herself on her crutches, but with great skill and dexterity she managed to avoid dropping anything. I saw she was happy.

"Where have you been, I was looking for you everywhere."

"I went to see Orio."

"How is he?"

But she didn't give me time to answer. She thrust three plates into my hands and told me to set the table.

"Who's the third person?"

"Santino."

"What about Mafalda then?"

"I've decided to share him with her. I've chucked away my pride, he'll sleep one night with her and one with me."

"Won't she object?"

"Santino will tell me that tonight. He's gone to talk to her about it, and afterwards he'll come here for dinner."

"What's cooking?"

"Rabbit braised with rosemary, it smells good, doesn't it? Santino loves roast rabbit."

She burst out laughing, opening her mouth wide and turning up her nose like a five-year-old girl. Then she went on cooking, humming 'Avanti Popolo' to herself.

I set the table. I was perspiring, and could still smell the odours of the hospital clinging to me. I put the glasses and the wine on the table, sliced the bread and then went to have a shower.

When I returned to the kitchen the rabbit was ready, and Suna was dressing the salad with oil and vinegar. We sat in front of our empty plates waiting for Santino. I was famished, but I didn't dare stretch out my hands to grab some of the succulent meat. To cheer me up Suna poured me out some wine.

"I told him to bring Mafalda if he wants to."

"What time are you expecting him?"

"At nine."

"It's ten o'clock already."

"I told him that as far as I'm concerned he can do what he likes, even get married to her, provided he carries on making love to me.

Do you think that's crazy?"

"What if she doesn't agree?"

"She will agree."

"You won't like it either after a while."

"The rabbit's getting cold. Put a serviette over it and pour me out some more wine, please, Vannina."

"Couldn't we eat while we're waiting?"

"No, you're crazy! What's Santino going to have, just leftovers?"

I did what she told me. Her mood was changing quickly. Her previous cheerfulness was giving way to a frantic anxiety.

"Why did you join the Movement?" I asked, to distract her from her thoughts.

"Because I want to stop just thinking of myself and my ridiculous preoccupation with my disabilities. I want to dedicate myself to something strong, something real."

"Will you give him some money?"

"I'll give him everything, money, time, labour, energy."

"When do you want to go back to Addis, then?"

"I'm not going back at all, I'll stay here and work with them."

At eleven Santino still hadn't turned up and we decided to eat the rabbit. Suna no longer spoke, she sat with her ears pricked up, ready to catch the sound of his footsteps on the stairs.

We sliced the melon and had some more wine. I went into my room to write and she stayed in the kitchen waiting. She put 'Norma' on the record-player and the house was flooded with shrill and despairing voices. The music swelled like a storm bursting into sudden explosions, then flowed, smoothly and tenderly, slipping under the doors and through the cracks in the windows.

*1.00 a.m.*

A short time ago Santino at last arrived. I had opened my window because of the heat. I could hear his voice as he started talking with Suna. They locked themselves in and I could hear them laughing.

I felt randy, I wanted to make love too. I picked up the phone and called Giacinto. He was in bed. He was glad to hear my voice.

"When are you coming home?"

"Orio is very ill, he's all alone, I can't leave him."

"So does that mean that if he's ill for a month you'll be staying in that shitty town for a month too?"

"As soon as he's a bit better, I'll come back."

"You're a cretin."

"How's it going at work?"

"There's stacks of work, what with overtime and everything, we're all pissed off. Yesterday Moretti threw a screwdriver at Vargas and Vargas fired him on the spot, but we grabbed Vargas by the neck and told him that either he takes Moretti back or we go on strike and occupy the garage, so eventually he gave in and agreed to take him back."

"I'd like to have you here."

"Are you taking the piss out of me?"

"I'd like to make love to you."

"You're still there, though."

"And you?"

"How's Santino?"

"He's in the other room making love to Suna."

"So that's why you want me all of a sudden because of those two pigs. You make me sick."

"What does it matter why? I want you, that's all."

"Go to hell."

"All right then, goodbye."

"Hang on, do you love me?"

"That's why I rang you up."

"Come back soon, and don't come back different from how you used to be, otherwise I'll strangle you. Goodbye."

*6th September*

Mafalda has agreed to share Santino with Suna. He's happy. Suna told me everything this morning as soon as she got up. She came and sat on my bed naked, sipping a glass of hot milk. She had thrown her emaciated legs to one side and held her suntanned bosom upright like a statue. When you see it at close quarters her skin is covered with an almost imperceptible white down. Her small fair breasts look incredibly fragile under her strong muscular shoulders. Her slender neck barely supports her beautiful feline head.

I looked at her with admiration for the simplicity and naturalness with which she exhibits her naked half-diseased body without embarrassment.

"What did Mafalda say?"

"That she doesn't love him, but likes him a lot and she doesn't give a damn whether she shares him with me or not."

"What about him?"

"Santino is head over heels in love with her."

"So why don't you leave him to her?"

"Because I'm head over heels in love with him."

"What about him?"

"Santino never falls in love with anyone."

"But you've just said he's head over heels in love with Mafalda."

"Yes, in a way, yes. He's obsessed with her, but it's outside himself, it's almost as if he's acting a part. But he needs me anyway, because of the money."

"Does Mafalda give him money too?"

"Mafalda doesn't give him a thing, she hasn't got a bean. Her father's a lawyer but he doesn't fork out a penny. Besides, since he got to hear that she's had an abortion and got involved in politics and doesn't give a damn what her relatives say about her, he's refused to see her."

"Aren't you jealous of her?"

"Yes, I am, a lot. I just have to control myself, don't I?"

"What would you do if she wants him one night when you want him too?"

"That's why I want to talk to her, I want to come to a clear agreement over our shifts. Santino is so muddle-headed about it all."

"Why was he so late last night?"

"Because he was making love to her."

"Did he make love to you too?"

"Yes, he did. But it won't be like that all the time, otherwise he'll get worn out. We'll share him, one day me, the next day her, like good friends."

At two I went to see Orio. But he wasn't in his bed.

The china-faced sister told me he was in the operating theatre and that he would be coming out in an hour. They advised me to come back tomorrow because he'll be sleeping all day today.

"What's wrong with Orio? Can you tell me honestly? I haven't managed to find out yet."

"Are you a relative?"

"No."

She bent her head slightly forward, covered by its heavy black veil.

She stared at me with her two shining eyes, full of perplexity.

"Can you contact his mother?"

"Yes, I will, but they aren't on the phone. I'll have to send a telegram. What am I to say?"

"They suspect he might have cancer. But perhaps you'd better wait till tomorrow for the result of the operation. You'll be able to talk to the surgeon then."

"I've tried to lots of times, but I've never managed to catch him."

"He's ever so busy. You must understand that on this floor alone we've over six hundred patients and he can't trust the young doctors to take his place, he prefers to do everything himself. He's very conscientious, he's seventy but he's as bright as a button. Have you seen him? His hands are a bit shaky when he operates, but by now he's so experienced he could take out a lung blindfold. Unfortunately there are just far too many patients. More and more arrive every day, we don't know where to put them, we don't have enough beds, we don't have enough staff, it's a real crisis. The porters are leaving because they haven't been paid for months, we're short of medicine because we have no money, the hospital has a deficit of four thousand millions, so now anyone who needs an operation has to wait ages for his turn and some of them die in the interval. What can he do, the surgeon is one, the patients are so many."

"Can't he get his assistants to help him?"

"Well, yes, he does that, but he's cautious, you know. What with meetings and strikes and demonstrations these youngsters don't study any more. According to the surgeon all they're interested in is politics, and he can't trust his patients to them."

"How much does he earn for each operation?"

"Well, he's not a novice, he charges his price, a high one in fact. But with him you're safe, you see, with the others you're not."

*11.00 p.m.*

At five Suna and I went to carry out the first assignment the Movement had entrusted her with. This was to go to one of the working class districts and investigate the sweated labour done by the local women at home, and then try to organise them into a political force — so spoke Vittorio in his most didactic paternalistic manner.

We took the bus. It was very hot and gushes of steaming hot air came in through the open windows. Suna got annoyed with two youngsters who helped her get on the bus by lifting her up by the waist.

"Who asked these louts to interfere?"

"They were only trying to help you."

"They don't give a damn about helping anyone, they do it so that they can prove to themselves how healthy and virile they are."

We went down to the Piazza de Miracoli and turned into a steep narrow street, out of which opened a succession of dark holes, each one a single windowless room. Higher up, strung from one balcony to the next, there were washing lines carrying wet laundry and flowerpots with parsley and basil suspended by strings; below the stench of cats, fried food, sewage and soap, the deafening noise of a radio mingling with the screams of children, the screech of an electric saw and the regular rhythm of sewing machines; and in the middle of the alley a trickle of black frothy water.

We went past several doors without plucking up the courage to go in. We stopped in front of a shop the size of a telephone box inside which we could see mountains of shoes waiting to be mended; by the window a bald man with a small hammer in his hands and some nails held tight between his lips, was working with his head bent.

We watched him in astonishment as the flies strolled undisturbed over his shiny bald patch. Suddenly we became aware that he was swearing at us, but we couldn't understand why. He made angry gestures in our direction and shouted something incomprehensible until eventually we realised we were blocking his light. Mortified, we moved off quickly.

After that we went into the first doorway we came to. The entrance was shielded by a curtain of coloured nylon strings. Inside it was dark, and we groped our way down three steps. It was silent, the room looked uninhabited and abandoned.

Then a child's voice mumbled something in an unintelligible dialect. Meanwhile my eyes were getting used to the darkness and I began to distinguish a few things: some beds crowded against a wall, a glass display cabinet, a gigantic television set framed with gilded metal, a bicycle hanging from the ceiling, a pram, a sink set into the wall, a gas stove half hidden behind a partition.

A naked child stood upright on one of the beds talking in his own mysterious sing-song language. His belly was swollen and protruding and his nose was snotty. As soon as we drew close he stopped talking and shot like lightning on all fours to hide under the bed.

Someone laughed in a soft hoarse voice. We turned and saw that in one of the beds at the far end of the room a woman with a fat, pale face was lying. She didn't ask us what we wanted, she didn't get up, she just looked at us with benevolent curiosity.

"Who works at home here? Does anyone take in work?" asked Suna.

"I haven't got through this week's yet, I know today's delivery day, but I haven't finished because I've been ill. Well, not really, only a touch of heartburn, I'll be up in a minute, make yourselves at home."

"We aren't here to collect things. We're investigating work done at home, so do you mind if we take down a few notes?"

Suna spoke with a level confident voice, but I could detect that she was anxious because of her determination to start her new job well.

"Please, do take a seat. Oh, but you're crippled, how did that happen? Was it an illness or did you have an accident?"

Suna knitted her brow, irritated. She was about to tell her to mind her own business but the woman's concerned voice disarmed her.

"I had polio when I was a child, but now I'm quite well and I can move and walk around, even though I do need crutches."

"My niece, Vincenzina, had polio like you, but she's not so mobile as you are, she's shut up at home and she can't go out without someone to help her. You were brave not to lose heart. How long ago did it happen?"

Suna had run out of patience and answered curtly that she had come to talk about work done at home and not about her illness. The woman lowered her head embarrassed.

"What do you do?"

"I make gloves."

"How many do you make in one day?"

"Eighty."

"How many hours do you work?"

"Well, it depends, sometimes seven, sometimes ten or fifteen. If I've fallen behind one day I have to do a few hours extra the following day. It varies, the important thing is that by the end of the month I must have made 2004 gloves."

"How long does it take to stitch up one glove?"

"Six or seven minutes. They're made of thick leather, you see, and the needle breaks every minute or so, even the cotton snaps — the cotton you get today is no good at all. Sometimes I make two in five minutes, that's when I feel strong early in the morning, then by the evening I feel too tired, I work slowly so's not to make mistakes, and I only do one glove every ten minutes, even twelve, it depends."

Meanwhile the child had come out of his hiding place and plunged into his mother's bed. You could see his small bony body roll under the blanket towards his mother's feet. When he got to the end he stopped, all curled up like a hedgehog.

"How much do you get for a pair of gloves?"

"Ten liras."

"Do you have only one child?"

"No, this is the youngest, there's also Salvatore, and then Stella who's going to be thirteen soon. Do you want to see how pretty she is? Angelino, show these young ladies Stella's picture."

The woman kicked the child, who was hiding even further down in the bed. She watched the small ball moving under the blanket and bashed him repeatedly on his head with her foot. The child came out straight away, puffing and panting, his hair dishevelled and his face flushed. He stared at us for a moment, frightened, and then scurried towards the door. He thrust one of his hands into the pocket of a dress which hung from a nail, pulled out a purse of red plastic and took it to his mother.

The woman sat up and adjusted her hair which cascaded on to her fat shoulders like a shower. She covered her front with the edge of an egg-stained sheet. She opened the purse and took out a small crumpled photograph.

Suna didn't stretch out her hand, so I reached over and took the photograph. From within the small shiny square stared out the face of a stunted underdeveloped little girl with bouncy curls and sad feverish eyes. I passed the picture to Suna who looked at it for a minute without any interest and then returned it to the woman.

"Where is Stella now?"

"She went to Capri with her eldest brother. She's found a job as a maid that brings her 50,000 liras a month. She was lucky. She deserved it though, my poor dear Stella, because she's so good, even when they trample all over her she never complains, she just says thank you and smiles. That's why people take advantage of her, she even became pregnant by her uncle and she didn't breathe a word, my poor baby, then we found out because he died from a stroke and she miscarried because of her fright."

"How many children do you have?"

"Eight, well, not eight now because four of them have died."

"Well then, four are alive."

"Salvatore, Rina, Stella, Angelino."

"What does your eldest son do?"

"What does he do? What do you think he does? Nothing, he's unemployed."

"How old is he?"

"Sixteen."

"What about your other daughter?"

"Rina? She's got a good husband, a man from Caserta who's a policeman in Rome and they have one son. She's all right, she's even got some chickens on her balcony."

"What does your husband do?"

"He's a dealer."

"What does he deal in?"

"Paper, he goes out and picks up bits of paper with his wheelbarrow, then he sells it."

"He's a ragman then, isn't he?"

"He prefers to call himself a dealer."

"And how much does he earn?"

"It depends, if he finds cardboard, which there's a big demand for, he might get up to 2000 a day, but there are days when he finds nothing, so he earns nothing."

"Do you get any medical aid?"

"Well, no, I don't, neither does my husband, we're loners, we mind our own business. We manage without it because fortunately we're never ill."

"You're ill now, though."

"It's nothing, it's just some liver trouble, every so often I have this liver complaint, so I have to lie down on the bed because that's what a liver needs — a bed. But it's nothing really, I'll be up again tomorrow."

"Have you been to see a doctor?"

"Doctors are too greedy, my liver's reduced to the size of a tennis ball because my blood's cold and doesn't flow too well. You see, when the blood is cold the liver is in trouble too and it tosses and turns."

"Why is your blood cold, though?"

"Because I have this passion for sitting down. When you don't move, your blood becomes like a slab of marble, didn't you know?"

"Do you never move then?"

"Never, ever, my job keeps me nailed down to the chair, so my blood stagnates and becomes as hard as a stone, even my feet become icy and hard. Would you like to feel them?"

With an agile movement she pulled out a fat white foot from underneath the blankets and stretched it towards us. Suna stretched out one finger but she was too far away to reach it. Smiling, the woman turned towards me. I took her foot in my hands. I shuddered when I came into contact with her cold, flaccid flesh.

"Do you want some coffee?"

"No thanks, we must go now."

"To tell the truth, it's not real coffee, my husband makes it from roasted chickpeas, have you ever tried it? It's real good, do you want to taste it? Angelino, heat up the coffee for the visitors, be a good boy."

But Angelino had gone out stark naked and was playing with other boys in the alley, yelling and screaming.

"Are there any more women who make gloves round here?"

"The whole district makes gloves."

"What's the name of the firm you work for?"

"Who knows? This man, Mr Merchandise, comes here, they call him that because he always calls out 'merchandise', collects the stuff and off he goes, always the same."

Outside, the light hurt our eyes. Stupefied, we stood there in the doorway looking at the alley swarming with children. The stench of drains was abominable. We started walking again, but Suna dragged herself along heavily.

"Are you tired?"

"No, I'm not."

But she only said this out of pride. She was pale from the effort and was sweating in an unnatural way. Her shirt was glued to her back, the veins on her neck were swollen.

"Shall we go home?"

"No."

"We could always come back tomorrow."

"No."

She was moving forward with her head down, ready to give battle, her hair twined round her ears and over her eyes in untidy locks.

We went into another house, less dark and less sweltering than the first one. We were met by cheerful bursts of laughter coming from three women who sat there sewing gloves in the light that filtered through the door.

They were laughing at Suna who almost fell after slipping on the steps in the entrance. They laughed at me too as I rushed clumsily to hold her up. Suna was annoyed but didn't react, though the women were openly laughing at her. Their fingers hadn't stopped sewing for an instant, they moved nimbly with amazing dexterity.

"We are doing an investigation into black labour."

"Black labour, and what's that?"

"What you're doing, working at home, outside the protection of the trade unions, without any medical aid and without a guaranteed wage."

"We are within the law, even the police sergeant told us that. Isn't that right, Mariella?"

"You are, but your boss isn't, because he's exploiting you and can't be held accountable for your exploitation. Do you know your boss?"

"No one has ever seen him."

"I have, in my dreams. He's white and fat and whenever he speaks roses sprout out of his mouth," said the youngest woman, a self-assured girl of about eighteen. They burst out laughing loudly, though without breaking the methodical rhythm of their sewing.

"So he has all the rights bosses always have, but not a single responsibility. Do you understand that?"

"Of course we do, little madam." Another malevolent clownish laugh.

"But what have you, little cripple, to do with all this?"

"I've already told you, some comrades and I are doing an investigation on sweated labour done at home."

"You can shove your investigations up your arse, little princess. Isn't that right, Marie?"

More mocking laughter.

Suna was sweating. She had trouble holding the notebook in her hands while propping herself up with her sweaty armpits on her crutches which were on the point of slipping on the floor. I had offered to write for her, but she had refused. I asked her again:

"Let me write, Suna."

She was tracing some black scribbles. This time she gave in and handed me the notepad covered with damp fingerprints.

"Our Movement is fighting black labour."

"We only know one movement, and that's our hands."

The oldest of the three thrust her swollen red hands under Suna's nose and improvised a conjuring trick: she made the glove disappear into her mouth, then she made it reappear from underneath her skirt.

"Our aim is to organise all those women who work at home so that they can defend themselves from their bosses."

"And what do you call yourselves, you movement people?"

"Proletarian Victory."

"Do you have any money?"

"Very little. The Movement isn't financed by anybody. It's autonomous."

"And you, little cripple, do you have any money?"

Suna, who is normally so quick-witted and self-confident, was totally lost here. The three women's crude sarcasm paralysed her completely. She looked at them dismayed, not knowing what to retort. I asked her whether she wanted to go. Coldly she said no.

"We want you to organise yourselves against exploitation."

"Listen, cripple, do you want a piece of advice straight from the heart?"

"Well?"

"Go home."

"This is not the right place for you, little cripple!"

"Get out of here, lame girl!"

By this time they were openly laughing at her, without any restraint, with pigheaded, cruel malice.

"You're like sheep, without any eyes, without a mouth, without a mind. They're sucking your blood and you sit there quietly laughing and if someone says to you: watch out, they're sucking your life away, you turn round and fart in their face."

"Did you hear that, Maria, she's calling us sheep now, the cripple."

"If my husband turns up, he'll bugger her straight away."

"Mine would throw you on the bed for your cheek and push something that big right up you."

They laughed frantically, tears glistening on their pale cheeks, happy, noisy, rowdy, vulgar.

They were all three fat, but an unhealthy, flabby, jaundiced fatness. One was about fifty, the other thirty, and the youngest was the girl in her teens. The older two were dressed in black with their arms bare, their hair permed, each wearing a golden cross on her chest. The youngest one wore a pair of faded jeans and a pink T-shirt with OKAY printed on it. In her ears were two horn-shaped coral amulets the colour of blood.

"If you want to beat me up, why don't you do it yourselves? You could throw me down in no time at all, you're big and strong and I'm crippled. But no, you hand it over to your husband, your defence, your survival, your honour, everything, and he's your boss too, second to the gloves. In fact he's your worst boss because he owns you completely, flesh and spirit, and you don't even know it."

"Do you by any chance hate men, little cripple? Would you by any chance at all be butch, little cripple?"

They were laughing so much they were doubled up, and bumping their heads against their knees.

"If you laugh like that you'll all have convulsions."

"Piss off then, little cripple."

We went out and searched for a taxi. Suna slumped on the seat and shut her eyes. She was deadly pale and breathing with difficulty.

At home she went to bed without drinking or eating. She didn't say a word. She only asked me to put on 'Norma' and then she went to her room.

At nine I brought her some broth. She was breathing heavily and her face was mottled with red marks. I put my hand on her forehead. It was burning.

"How are you?"

"Fetch me the thermometer from the bedroom."

The thermometer went up to 102. I asked her if she wanted me to send for a doctor, but she answered with a short no. I was about to go, but then I heard her speaking in a low, furious tone of voice. I drew close to her to listen.

"I'm a middle-class washout, Vittorio's right, I understand nothing, I can do nothing. I'm a real turd, that shit of a Faele is right, tell him, no, don't, I'll tell him myself. Get out of here, you cripple, did you hear them? They wanted to insult me with their pricks of husbands, they would have strangled me, but not with their own hands, oh no, with those of their men, they defer everything to them, everything but one thing, their work, did you see what a lousy job theirs is, for a thousand liras a day if they're lucky, and on top of it there's the pots and pans, the dishes to do, the washing, the cooking, the kitchen, but even then they aren't their own bosses. 'Get out of here, cripple.' I'll never go back there, never, tell Vittorio, thank you very much, he can go. How cold I am! Can you put a blanket on me Vannina? And get me some water too, please, my throat's so dry."

I put a blanket over her, and went into the kitchen to get the water. When I went back I found her asleep, with her mouth half open, a lock of hair glued to her cheek, her arms folded, her body curled up in a ball. I closed the window. But her teeth were still chattering with cold. I took a coat hanging inside the wardrobe out of its cellophane wrapper and spread it on top of the blanket.

*1.00 a.m.*

At about eleven I heard the bell ring. It was Santino, looking radiant, a lock of blond hair dangling softly on his forehead, an open and happy smile on his face.

"Where's Suna?"

"She's not feeling well."

"Can you give me something to eat?"

We went into the kitchen, and I fried him a couple of eggs and cut him some bread. I could feel his serious light blue eyes fixed on me.

"I went to see Orio. They've operated on him and I think you should tell your mother."

"My mother's in bed with pneumonia."

"It looks as though Orio might have cancer."

"Who told you?"

"The sister."

"The sister doesn't know a thing. I spoke to the surgeon, he told me it's just something that's got to come out and then he'll be all right."

"Did you talk to him after the operation?"

"No, I didn't, but he also said that Orio has a strong body and that he'll live to be a hundred. We're of strong stock, we are, you know."

He gave me a proud, disarming smile. Then he pounced on the frying-pan and devoured the eggs and bread in about half a second.

"How's Mafalda?"

"She's well."

"Suna tells me you've agreed to stay together, all three of you."

"Yes, that's right."

"Are you pleased?"

"Yes."

"Do you love Suna?"

"A hell of a lot."

"And Mafalda?"

"A hell of a lot too."

He put his fork down. He lifted his milky, gentle eyes. He seemed anxious that I should believe him.

"Tell me something, are you in the Movement just because of Mafalda?"

"I like the Movement, all my friends are in it."

"Do you know what the Movement is aiming at?"

"To dislocate the nerve centres of the capitalist structure."

He said this all in one breath, worried that he might miss a word. Then he asked timidly for something more to eat. There was nothing but eggs in the fridge, so I fried him a couple more. He started eating again, looking very cheerful, and giving me a sweet seductive smile.

I heard Suna moan. I went in to see if she needed anything and found her completely uncovered, tossing in a sort of frenzied delirium. I pulled up the blanket and went out. I persuaded Santino to sleep on the sofa, and then I washed the dishes, scraped the pans, cleaned the cutlery, rinsed the glasses, and put away the bread, the wine, the butter, the salt and the vinegar.

Santino watched me out of the corner of his eyes. He was waiting for me to prepare his bed. He helped me stretch out the sheets absent-mindedly. I said goodnight to him and went to bed.

Something turbulent started stirring in my womb. The idea of Santino's naked body stretched out alone in the next room, his availability, kept me awake. I knew I only had to call him to have him beside me, amenable and ready. His sweet, light body excited my imagination.

I was on the point of calling him, but then I changed my mind. I thrust my head beneath the pillow. I don't know whether it was out of loyalty to Suna, or whether I was afraid of getting entangled in a relationship that was already too complicated. I don't know. I plunged into the warmth of my own body and I came alone in the darkness beneath the blankets, silently and secretly.

*7th September*

Suna's temperature has gone down. She's weak, though, and isn't yet able to get up. Bare-chested, her back resting on a heap of pillows, she gives me order after order. She isn't bossy, but issues her demands in a playful capricious tone of voice. Yesterday's mood of despondency seems to have vanished along with her fever. She chats and giggles, hassles me to put on 'Norma', then a moment later asks me to turn it off again.

Today Santino and Mafalda are coming to lunch so I went out shopping for the four of us. I bought a rabbit, aubergines, lettuce and plums. When I got back home I found Suna putting make-up on her eyes with a black eyeliner. She was sitting half naked in front of a mirror humming a tune from 'Norma'.

Around one o'clock Giacinto rang. He's angry because I haven't made up my mind about going home yet. I told him I'll have the whole winter to spend in Rome. He retorted that Suna has caught me in a trap and bewitched me. He put the phone down without saying goodbye.

At two, Santino and Mafalda arrived. When I opened the door to them they were kissing each other. They were cheerful and excited.

We sat down in front of our heaped plates. Santino started eating greedily without looking at the two women sitting next to him, as if to say: 'all right, you two get on with it, sort it out between yourselves, it's got nothing to do with me.'

Suna and Mafalda were only slightly embarrassed and weren't looking at each other like rivals. Their expressions were those of complicity rather than hatred, and they looked ready to burst into laughter. Santino couldn't understand. He sank his head between his shoulders, vaguely alarmed, all ready for a sudden outburst.

"Well then, what about you having him on Tuesdays, Thursdays and Saturdays, I'll have him on Mondays, Wednesdays and Fridays, and on Sundays he can have a day off."

"What about if one day he doesn't fancy it? We can't do it that way, he must decide for himself."

"So?"

"Do you think Vittorio will be angry?"

"I don't give a damn about Vittorio."

"The Movement has its own code, you know that, don't you?"

"A new code for a new world," mocked Suna sententiously, taking off Vittorio. Mafalda looked at her with amusement. Santino raised his eyebrows, perplexed.

"Sensuality will no longer be an end in itself, like in today's filthy cattle market, but a means to sincere communication which has its own role in society, without being confused with our other needs . . . "

Suna raised her eyebrows and pressed her lips together, and her eyes turned hard and cold. She put on a disguised voice in a skilful, light-hearted imitation of Vittorio.

"Will sensuality be forbidden then?"

"No, it won't, my dear Mafalda, it will come to an end just as all other injustices will; once the structure is changed, the superstructure crumbles like mud in the sun, personal relations will change, no more sickness, depression, neurosis . . ."

"What will the new concept of love be like?"

"Without ambiguity."

"Without jealousy?"

"Without selfishness."

"Will a man be allowed to love another man and a woman another woman?"

"Homosexuality is a symptom of bourgeois shit, there won't be space for mawkishness of that sort."

Santino burst out laughing. The effort of imitating Vittorio's voice had caused the veins in Suna's neck to become swollen, her face to become mottled with red patches and her eyes to become fierce and shining.

Mafalda stretched one of her arms across the table and clasped Santino's hand. Suna immediately followed her example — and grasped the other one, raised it to her mouth, and gave it a kiss.

Santino smiled happily with both his hands imprisoned, his mouth still full of food, his eyes greedy and vacant.

*Midnight*

In the afternoon I went to the hospital. At first they wouldn't let me in because visiting time was over, but the porcelain-faced sister came to my rescue and let me steal in through the side door.

"How's Orio?"

"Not very well."

"How did the operation go?"

"They opened him up and then closed him again straight away."

"Will he get better?"

"Did you get in touch with his mother?"

"She's in bed with pneumonia."

"Poor boy, he has no luck at all."

"Did any of his brothers come?"

"I didn't see anyone. I think he's waiting for you."

We stopped at the entrance to the ward. I noticed the drops of sweat on her lips, and the coif which framed her broad face was soaked.

"Aren't you hot?"

She smiled meekly. Her clear skin curled slightly around her lips and revealed her small yellow teeth.

Suddenly she turned her back on me and rushed off at the call of one of the nurses. She walks in a funny way, swaying on her too short legs.

I went into the crowded ward. It was almost impossible to make one's way through it. They had added a few more beds since the last time I'd come. The large room looked like a lazar-house, a bit like one of those pictures they show you in schoolbooks to illustrate some epidemic during the Middle Ages.

In spite of the fact that the windows were wide open, a suffocating smell of sweaty bodies, medicine, urine, soup, and disinfectant hung heavily round the unmade beds like a fog.

The patients didn't seem to notice the smell however. They were busy wheeling and dealing as if they were in a noisy, seething Sunday market. Only a few were in bed, mostly they walked about, some in their pyjamas, some in their singlets, and others barechested, up and down the big room, climbing over the beds, bumping into the bedside tables, with a great clatter of dragged slippers, banging of metal plates, laughter, snorting and swearing.

Some of the patients get their relatives to bring them everything from home, their bedside tables are cluttered up with objects like the shelves of a grocer's shop: jars of fish in oil, bowls of oven-baked pasta, small sticks of bread wrapped up in checked cloths, stacks of biscuits, paper bags full of fruit, and bottles of wine with paper tops. On the other hand there are others who never get a visit from anyone, so to avoid passing for down-and-outs they display the few things they've got on the bedside tables in full view: scattered cigarettes, rolled up pyjamas, folded-up newspapers, a nibbled pear, a pair of shoes, an empty chamber pot.

There were two sets of screens today. That's the sign that two patients are about to die. The only privilege they get is this improvised isolation, though it seems to have been arranged mainly in order not to upset the other patients rather than to give comfort to the dying.

Fortunately Orio's bed is at the end of a row, in between the wall and the window, so he can have a little bit of freedom and is to some extent isolated from the others. I immediately saw there were no screens where he was, and gave a sigh of relief.

As soon as he saw me, he lifted himself up to hug me. He looked better; he was pale and worn out, but his eyes were bright and he moved without too much effort.

"Are you better?"

"Yes, I don't even feel my usual pain any more."

"I'm glad."

"Last night I dreamt I made love to you."

"That means you're better and are getting stronger."

"But just as I was about to come I saw that it wasn't me who was making love to you but my brother, Santino. Have you ever made it with him?"

"No, I haven't."

"You like him though, I can tell from the way you look at him."

"Yes, I like him."

"More than you like me?"

"I made love to you, not to him, didn't I?"

"When I'm dead, will you make love to him?"

"I want to make love to you, alive."

"If Suna wasn't there, would you make love to him?"

"Why do you torment yourself, I won't make love to Santino, I promise."

"What a bummer!"

"What is?"

"Having a good-looking brother."

"You're better looking than him."

"You just say that because I'm ill."

"No, I don't, I really mean it."

He relaxed into a happy burst of laughter. He became alive again. He lost that air of being an old man that he's had recently. The two wrinkles on the sides of his mouth suddenly disappeared.

I bent down and kissed him. He fastened his arms firmly round my neck. I drank up his dry acid breath.

*8th September*

"I'd really like to know what the morality of the proletariat is."

"It consists of rejecting all moral values, you imbecile!"

"Pardon me, that's sophistry."

"Silly Renzo, you come from the North, that's obvious."

"So what?"

"So the proletariat is the star of the South."

"But what a star! Pardon me, the North too has its own proletariat."

"It comes from the South though. Wherever you turn you see our star shining out, our poor wretches who leave, suitcases under their arms, for the factories of Turin and Milan, for the Charleroi pits, for the Ruhr steelworks, for the Munich car factories; and if it isn't our Calabrians, our Sicilians, and our Neapolitans, it's the Algerians, the Moroccans and the Portuguese, it's still the star of the South, you cretin, our star of fire whose light shines forth vigorously, its strength tied by magic to the wheel of exploitation."

"How poetical! Excuse me, let's stick to facts."

"Stick to facts! You don't understand a thing about facts, don't you know that stars are worlds larger than ours?"

"Excuse me, Vittorio, don't change the subject. I tell you, we went to occupy their houses for them but what did we get out of it? Hostility, dislike and the police against us."

"It was just lack of organisation."

"Excuse me, you can't organise people's characters: we annoyed them with our arrogance, our hastiness, our internal squabbles."

"That's it, organisation, our members' personalities shouldn't take precedence over the unity of the Movement."

"The unity of the Movement, what the hell is that? Underneath it all, you mean yourself, don't you?"

"You talk like Faele."

"Take that demo against the rise in the cost of living, you sent the youngest, most inexperienced members, the others took one look at them and laughed in their faces. Do you understand what I'm talking about, you half-wit?"

"Lack of discipline."

"You sent a disabled girl to investigate the work done at home, that too was a total failure."

"What the fuck do you mean, a disabled girl? What has the fact she's disabled got to do with it? Are you a racist now as well?"

"You sent the most inexperienced, the least politically sussed out, the most childish of us lot to talk to ex-prisoners, thieves, the unemployed, then you wonder why we go from one failure to another."

"It's the only human material that's available to us, and anyway it isn't true, we're on very good terms with the prisoners."

"Yes, but only because a couple of bankrobbers and a few pimps make use of us to get free legal assistance."

"You're a shithead!"

"Excuse me, I would also like to know what is revolutionary about stealing a handbag from an old lady to go and buy drugs."

"You have a very abstract idea of what theft is, just like the fucking bourgeois sod that you are; theft is a negative value in the history of private property. Shut up and fuck off!"

" 'Shut up and fuck off' — what a contribution to the discussion. You still haven't explained anything."

"Fucking Jesus, you start from universal values, but the universal values thieves, prostitutes and pimps infringe are the values of a capitalist society, values that our class society has made into the norm."

"So, in a socialist society thieving would be allowed?"

"No, you half-wit, the difference between a capitalist regime and a socialist one is that the first is imposed on people and serves only the interests of a fistful of employers, for fuck's sake, whereas in the future society it'll be established by the great majority of the people for the common good. Do you understand that, you cretin?"

At that point Mafalda, Suna and Santino came in. They'd finished distributing the posters and the leaflets. Renzo, who doesn't like Suna, moved away and hunched his shoulders in irritation, and Vittorio followed him to continue the discussion.

Immediately afterwards Antonio arrived as well, with a skinny young lad I hadn't seen before whose name was Giampiero. They were arguing.

"If I tell you it isn't mine, that's good enough."

"It's your father's, so what's the difference?"

"I attack private property from within."

"That's just crap."

"I'd like to know why you always poke your nose into other people's business."

"You can't go round in a Jaguar, you'll just make us a laughing-stock."

"I do what the fuck I want, we aren't in a boarding school here."

"I'll tell you what you should say to your wealthy father — dear dad, you get on my tits, I'm off, cheers, here's your car, shove it up your arse."

"Of course, your father's poor, so it's easy for you to talk."

"As long as you accept his money, you're his property."

"I'm no one's property, for fuck's sake, I treat him like shit."

"The bourgeoisie doesn't tolerate any attack on property, even by its most beloved son."

"In fact he's denounced me three times and if it wasn't for my mother I'd be in clink by now."

"It's always the mother who saves daddy's sons."

"Do you know her? Then what do you talk like that for? She isn't a pain in the neck with a black skirt like yours who lives just to serve you and stinks of washing-up water."

"It's you who's the pain in the neck."

"I'm telling you, she's so beautiful that you'd wet yourself right there on the spot. She's the best cunt in Naples and she screws around because she enjoys it. She gets laid by all the sailors in the dock area, she even pays them, you know. She protects me because she steals too, in fact I help her, we're business partners."

"Ah, she's also trying to break the system from within."

"My mother? You must be joking. Even if she was on her deathbed she wouldn't give up a single diamond, a single jewel."

"Just the same as you then. You wouldn't give up that Jaguar on your deathbed, would you?"

"I shall drive that fucking hearse into the sea one of these days."

"Anyway, don't you dare say 'get laid' like that in front of me, do you understand?" interrupted Suna imperiously.

"What did I say to offend you so, madam?"

"What is your mother, is she by any chance an egg that she gets laid? The trouble is you don't even realize how sexist your remarks are."

"Oh fuck off, Suna."

"Fuck off yourself."

"If you don't pipe down I'll chuck you out of the Movement."

"You can't chuck anyone out, you aren't the whole Movement, you know."

"Stop arguing, please, comrades." Renzo had come in, looking as remote and haughty as ever. Vittorio followed him, light-footed and fiery.

"Suna, you'll go back to your investigations on work done at home. Renzo, you take the loudspeaker to the Osmon factory gate. Faele and Giampiero, you come with me."

"Can't you get someone else to go in my place?"

"No, Suna, I can't, that's your task. Only a woman can succeed in gaining the trust of other women. Go and just don't worry, be kind and considerate and you'll see, you'll be all right."

"Can I take Mafalda and Santino with me?"

"No, Mafalda and Santino are needed for duplicating."

*10.00 p.m.*

Almassunta is a woman of thirty but she looks fifty. She is a widow, has six children and lives in a room with light blue walls, with her old mother and three of her children.

"Alfonsino lives at the monastery, he'll become a priest. Carlos has at last got a job as a ship's cook, Nino is working as a labourer in Germany, and Carmeluccia has gone to Lisbon to become a nun."

The four women, Almussunta, her mother, and her two eldest daughters sit working outside the front door to save electricity, with their feet in the drain. They sew rapidly with an even rhythm, listening drowsily to a radio which hangs from a nail on the door.

"Do you draw any social security?"

"No, Miss."

"Would you like to?"

"Of course we would."

They looked at one another and smiled timidly.

"In this district there are hundreds of women doing your job all without any public relief. They don't even know who their boss is, they just slave away for a pittance."

"That's very true."

"Your factory is here at home, but no one calls you workers."

"That's God's truth."

"If you got together you could become a political force."

"We don't meddle with politics." They spoke softly, their eyes glued to the thread, their agile fingers moving nimbly.

"Your wages are miserable."

"God's truth."

"Well then, why don't you get together and protest?"

"People who protest lose their jobs."

"If you protest all by yourself, yes you will, but if you are all together, that would be different."

"We don't know the other women."

"But they do exactly the same as you, they sew gloves like you."

"Who knows them?"

"Here we all know each other, but we all keep to ourselves, there's no trust," added the eldest daughter shyly.

"Do you know who your boss is?"

"No, Miss."

"If an animal is sucking your blood, the first thing you'd want to know is what sort of animal it is, wouldn't you?"

"Once Mariuccia drank some milk and then she found a leech attached to her throat, didn't you, Mariu?"

Mariuccia lowered her head again. She looked at us with her pitch black, anxious eyes. Out of shyness she faltered and made four wrong stitches. Her mother pointed it out to her in a complaining but affectionate voice. The girl stopped, completely confused.

"We had to take her to hospital to get that leech out of her. It was so strongly attached to her throat that not even my strong hands could pull it off."

"And that thing was hiding in the milk bottle."

"The doctor said it wasn't possible, that leeches don't live in milk, but everyone knows that you can find all sorts of things in milk."

"Once they even found a dead mouse in the milk."

"God's truth, that is, you find pins, cockroaches, nails, playing cards, anything, you name it, there it is, in the milk."

"Where's your husband?"

"He's dead, thank God."

"Why thank God?"

"He didn't work, he was as treacherous as a snake, and he beat us all up."

"Was he unemployed?"

"When I married him he was a fruit vendor, then they took his licence away from him so he carried on selling under cover, but every month they'd catch him and throw him inside. While he was inside he behaved well enough, but when he came out he was worse than a jackal, he'd break our necks with one blow."

"How did he die?"

"He got stabbed in the stomach. Poor angel, they say it was revenge. You see he had a girlfriend, a prostitute, and towards the end he had lots of money but he wouldn't even let us smell a whiff of it, and then they killed him, bless you, Saint Gennaro. But you, miss, what party do you work for?"

"No party at all, we're a movement, we work for the poor."

"Like friars, then."

"Yes, a little bit like that."

"Is it a new religion?"

"It's not a religion, it's political."

"I like that priest so much, what's his name, Father Smiley, he speaks on the radio every Wednesday night, do you know him?"

"No I don't."

"He speaks so well, with his heart full of love."

"Yes, sure, but what good does that do you?"

"He speaks to us."

"And what does he do for you by speaking?"

"He makes us feel . . . content, happy."

"As far as we're concerned this contentment is bad because if you feel content you let people trample over you without saying a thing, and that won't get you anywhere: contentment, obedience, resignation, that's all wrong."

"Do you believe in Heaven?"

"No, we don't."

"And in hell?"

"You're already in hell."

"Here, in our own homes?"

"When someone works twelve hours a day to earn 30,000 liras a month, then she's in hell, no doubt about that."

"Where are the devils?"

"Your bosses are the devils and they're eating you up alive."

Almassunta had stopped sewing in order to talk to Suna in her shrill voice, half joking and laughing, half serious. Her two daughters and her old mother looked at her in alarm and amusement.

"I think it's all hot air you're talking."

"To get out of hell you need to smash open the iron door which you can never do by yourself, only by the concerted effort of lots of people."

Suna was becoming heated, her cheeks were red, her eyes sparkling. She had propped her crutches against the wall and was sitting unsteadily on a very high stool, her dead legs thrown one on each side, her shirt opened up on her sweating chest, her skirt rolled up over her knees because of the heat. The four women watched her with curiosity but also with fear, spellbound by her dogmatic fury.

"Do you know how much your boss earns on each glove you make?"

"I don't even know how many teeth there are in my mouth, miss."

"10 liras per glove, that's what you get, which makes 20 liras a pair, and he sells them at 2000; take out the cost of the leather which is 400 a pair, that's 1,600 liras profit on each pair of gloves. Take off the cost of the thread which is 20 liras a pair, and it's 1,580, take out the cost of the transport which is 10 liras a pair, that makes it 1,570, which multiplied by the number of gloves per day, that is 80, makes 25,600 liras, which multiplied by 26 working days, gives you 3,265,600 liras a month. Multiply this by the number of all the women who work in the district and you'll understand how much he's robbing you of."

"The rich are rich, the poor are poor, and everyone looks after themselves."

At these words the four of them all nodded solemnly and there was no way of carrying on the discussion. Almassunta sent her daughter inside to get some dried figs and Marsala. The figs were wrinkled, soft and very sweet. While they melted in our mouths she explained how they dry them by keeping them for months hanging underneath their beds in the dark. That's why they are so white and soft: they never see the sun and they slowly dry up underneath the bed springs. In fact, when you sniff them, they give off a faint smell of old mattresses and dried urine.

When we took the bus back it was already late. I had to give up my visit to Orio.

*Midnight*

At home we found Santino and Mafalda making love on Suna's bed. No one said a word. Suna went into the kitchen and started cutting up an onion with slow calm movements. I broke six eggs into a bowl to make a large omelette.

While I was beating the eggs with a fork, Mafalda came in barefooted, her hair all dishevelled, doing up her shirt over her chest.

"Are you angry, Suna?"

"No."

"We don't know where to go to make love, you know how things are with me, I sleep in a sleeping bag in the hall of my friend's flat, Santino stays with Vittorio who's now got his mother and three brothers living with him, so we just don't have anywhere to go."

"You don't need to apologise."

"I'm sorry."

"It's nothing."

This last sentence came out of her suffocated and bitter. The plate she was holding in her hands slipped and broke into small pieces on the floor. Mafalda bent down to pick up the pieces.

Santino rushed in at the crash and immediately went to help Mafalda. Suna watched them crawling on all fours with a smile of satisfaction. Then all of a sudden she grabbed Santino by the wrist, pulled him up and kissed him furiously on the mouth for a long time.

Mafalda raised her large hazel eyes and watched them without moving, pale and inert.

*9th September*

"Why didn't you come yesterday?"

"I was late."

"I waited for you all day."

"How are you?"

"Well."

"Your pains?"

"They give me that raspberry stuff and I just sleep."

I took one of his dry feverish hands into mine. In one day he had become drained and stripped of flesh, but I didn't tell him that. I kissed his fingers and bit his pale, wrinkled fingertips.

"Have you made love to Santino yet?"

"No, I haven't."

"Yesterday he came to see me, the shit, and I asked him, 'Do you screw?' and he says 'Yes, all the time'."

"Yes, sure he does. Not with me, though, with Suna and Mafalda."

"With both of them?"

"They take it in turns."

"And you?"

"I want you."

"Promise me that even when I'm dead you won't do it with him."

"I promise."

He lifted up his suffering face, dried out by fever, and stared at me with his colourless empty eyes. I bent over to kiss him and he quietly lowered his eyelids. I rested my lips on his half open mouth and sucked his bitter, muddy breath.

I was about to move away, but he made an effort to keep his lips pressed against mine. I kissed him again, more forcefully. The contact with his soft burning skin gave me a sudden overwhelming faintness.

I looked round, no one was watching us, with the exception of the usual bald man at the end of the passage, and anyway it's not clear whether he's really watching or whether he sleeps with his eyes wide open. A nearby screen hid us from the sight of three quarters of the patients in the passage.

I lifted up the sheet a little on the wall side of the bed. I stretched out my hand towards my little lover's body. I touched his belly. He opened his eyes, smiled with contentment, and closed his eyes again with a sigh of joy.

His outsize pyjamas opened up like torn paper under my shameless fingers. Beneath my fingertips I could feel the smooth, warm, completely hairless skin of his broad, swimmer's chest. I placed my open palm on his taut belly which was throbbing as if inhabited by a tiny famished child. With the back of my hand I touched the bristly curls of his pubic hair and a little further down a small fragile snail. I clasped it tenderly in my closed hand and it started growing, swelling up, putting out its head from between my fingers. Orio made a little grimace of joy.

At that moment someone moved the screen away and I quickly withdrew my hand. Orio opened his eyes, filled with disappointment.

The next door patient had died. There was a moment of silence in the passage. All eyes turned towards the thin pointed face of the boy who lay on his stomach with his head on one side, his mouth open, his strong shoulders outlined by the straps of his singlet, his black hair stuck to his temples, a blood clot on the corner of his mouth.

Three orderlies arrived. They put the dead boy on a stretcher and hurriedly took him away. Two nurses came to change the dirty sheets and re-make the bed. The sister emptied the bedside table drawer, passed a rag dipped in disinfectant over the plastic surface of the table and the iron tubes of the bed.

A new patient stood there waiting, with a parcel wrapped up in newspaper under his arm. At a sign from the sister he sat down calmly and decorously, his large peasant-like hands open on his knees. He waited there quietly, while the other patients weighed him up with their critical gaze.

As soon as the sister finished and the man was huddled down under the clean sheets, the passage all of a sudden regained its festive market air, with its trading, shouts, swearing, games, strolling about, haggling, arguing and laughing. No one seemed to notice that the new patient had leapt out of bed shouting that his mattress was soaking with piss and that he wasn't going to sleep on a dead man's piss. He was shouting it though more with fear than conviction, in fact more to himself than to anyone else.

A boy with a pear-shaped head came up to Orio's bed and tried to sell him some cigarettes. Orio shook his head. The other went off unruffled, imperturbable, flicking his long black eyelashes.

*Midnight*

I was about to go out with Suna when Hasan arrived. He came in with his usual self-assurance. He took off his linen jacket, the colour of wrapping paper. He sprawled on the divan and demanded a glass of lemon and water.

"I hear you've become involved in politics. Good for you, I'm glad you're doing something useful."

Suna looked at him in amazement. He smiled maliciously, satisfied. "When I was a youngster, I was involved in politics myself. I used to go fly-posting on the walls of the university with some hand-made glue. I was energetic and merciless, I'd advocate beheading all the rich and glorifying the poor."

"You've already told me all this, Daddy."

"But what I didn't tell you is that one day they caught me while I was making an inflammatory speech and took me to the police station where ten of them raped me. I've never told you that before, have I?"

"No, you haven't, not that."

"Horrible customs over there in my own country. Although I hear that they do much the same everywhere. Last year in Chicago a young lad died of it."

"What are you driving at, Daddy?"

"I know of a girl who was raped by fifteen policemen and then left to bleed to death."

"Don't worry Daddy, no one rapes a cripple."

"A woman is always a woman, especially if she's young and beautiful."

"How did you change your ideas so much from when you were a student?"

"I discovered that things are more complex than they seem."

"When did you discover that?"

"About twenty years ago."

"Was it just when you started earning stacks of money by your fiddles, by any chance?"

"Anyone'd think you hate me, Suna. But it doesn't matter, it's good for children to hate their fathers, it helps them grow up. And now give me a cup of tea, my treasure, I'm sleepy."

He slipped off his yellow leather shoes by pushing one heel against the other. He waved his feet in their red and green silk socks in the air, shook his large head of curly grey hair, and stretched himself on the divan, smiling gently with his tender, malicious eyes.

"If you want tea, go and make it yourself."

Hasan looked at his daughter as if she were a mouse, with quiet commiseration. Then he turned towards me with a winning smile.

"You Vannina, I bet you are more kind-hearted than Suna. I'm all for cooperation within the family, Suna's right. But just at this moment I'm tired, and so fed up with walking and talking. You see, I work too hard, after all if I didn't who would bring the money home to enable my beautiful disabled daughter to live by the sea, without doing a thing? I need a good mint tea."

I went into the kitchen. Suna lunged after me.

"What are you doing, you idiot, are you getting it for him?"

"It's no hassle for me, and he's tired."

"Oh yes, he's tired and tired! He always talks like this when he wants to be waited on. I know him, he acted like this for years with Elizabeth and now he's doing the same with Emma, who's always there at his disposal like a lap-dog."

"Anyway, I'm a guest here, so I do have some obligations."

"What obligations, don't be silly!"

"It's easier to do certain things than not to do them."

"I know, that's why I'm telling you to refuse. But whenever there's a man around you immediately become weak and servile."

Hasan had followed us barefooted and silent without us noticing. As soon as we saw him he burst into a cheerful teasing laugh.

"You see what a beautiful daughter I have, Vannina? Her shoulders are a little bit too muscular, they look a bit like a coalminer's shoulders, but what a neck, don't you think it makes her look like a swan? In Turkish Suna means swan, did you know that? And her face, lift up your face, darling, look at it, what a sweet, delicate face. She takes after her mother, the bitch, but her eyes are just like mine, they're grey, look at them, have you ever seen a grey more grey than that?"

"Stop all this mawkishness, please, Daddy. As a matter of fact I'd rather be the daughter of a cockroach."

But he didn't take offence. He laughed at her goodnaturedly. He opened his long arms, like two protective wings, and closed them softly round his daughter's nervous body.

*10th September*

On my way back from the hospital I met Suna getting into a light blue

Volkswagen. I asked her where she was going, and she beckoned me to get into the car. Inside were Vittorio and Antonio.

"Where are we going?" I asked, thinking we might be off to some cheap café for dinner.

But from the grave intent expressions on their faces I understood they had something more important in mind. Suna was twisting the handle of her handbag as if she wanted to break it and Vittorio was driving sullenly, staring intently in front of him. Antonio sat all hunched up in a corner, lost in thought.

I didn't ask any further. I looked out of the window at the town as it flashed by over our heads, grey, massive, dirty, rowdy. We stopped for a long time behind a bus, enveloped in a cloud of smelly exhaust fumes. Vittorio drummed the steering wheel with his finger. Suna knitted her brows and repeatedly checked her watch for the time.

"See if they're following."

Antonio turned and nodded, and I looked round too. I saw Giampiero's Jaguar with two well-known heads inside: Mafalda's and Santino's. In addition there were two other people I had only seen once or twice at headquarters.

At last the bus moved on and Vittorio turned into a side street. We reached the dock area and passing the Port Railway Station sped along Via della Marinella. Within ten minutes we were turning on to the motorway to Pompeii. Gusts of warm air came in through the window, ruffling my hair. The smell of the sun-scorched asphalt blended with the acid smell of fertilizers: we were passing through farmland.

We left the motorway at the fourth exit, crossed the railway line and turned down a country road. The car wheels sank into the white dust. The car jolted over the holes in the road which were steadily becoming worse. But we continued to press on, bouncing on our seats for about ten kilometres until at last we turned down a grass track over which our wheels slid with a smooth hiss. All around there were only tomato fields and vineyards, and in front of us the sky had turned red.

Suddenly we stopped in the middle of a field — or at least that was what I thought at first. Suna got out and I followed her. Behind the vines, in the semi-darkness, I made out a low house with its green plaster peeling off.

Vittorio walked towards the house with determination, dodging the puddles, followed by Suna and Antonio. Meanwhile the Jaguar had arrived with the others. The door of the house opened and Faele and Renzo appeared on the threshold.

"Where are we?" I asked.

Suna beckoned me to keep quiet. The windows of the house were nailed up, the walls were chipped, there was grass sprouting out of the roof, and the whole place appeared abandoned.

"Get inside quick."

Inside it looked completely different: the wallpaper was brightly coloured, the furniture was new and glossy, and an oil lamp shed a wavering light over two large dark mirrors. Against the walls there were shelves loaded with tinned food. There was a coal fire, a portable radio, an imitation Persian carpet and a few small plastic covered armchairs.

"This is Giampiero's secret house where he brings his women," whispered Suna, squeezing my arm. Vittorio beckoned us to sit down and we all took a seat, some on the armchairs, some on the other chairs, and the rest of us on the floor.

"Where is he?"

"In the other room."

Renzo was smiling with satisfaction and Vittorio looked at him with approval.

"Giovanna will have to go, though, she isn't a member," said Faele: his voice was hard-edged, and he looked at me searchingly, with angry dark eyes. "What if she reports us?"

"Come on now, if she'd wanted to do that she'd have done it ages ago, you idiot."

"Now it's different."

"I'll stand guarantee for her."

"You can stuff your guarantee up your arse."

"Please, Faele, stop it."

"I don't trust her, as far as I'm concerned she should go."

"Where can she go to? There's nothing here but fields. Don't be stupid."

"I don't trust her."

Suna grabbed her crutch as if she was going to hit him on the head, but Vittorio snatched it away from her.

"That's enough, you imbeciles. Giampiero, go and fetch the prisoner."

Vittorio took a large black revolver out of his pocket and handed it to Giampiero who took hold of it as if it were the most natural thing in the world. He slipped into the bedroom and came back a moment later pushing in front of him a man with a black hood over his head.

He sat him in the middle of the circle face to face with Vittorio, and pressed the nozzle of the revolver into his back. He removed the hood from his head, handed the revolver back to Vittorio and then went back to his seat with a negligent self-assured air.

The man looked about fifty. A red blindfold cut his face in two: the top part thin and lean, furrowed with deep horizontal wrinkles, the bottom puffed and perspiring, disfigured by two large pale lips. His bald head was covered with freckles and encircled with a fringe of greasy hair at the level of his ears. He was panting with apprehension.

"What do you want from me?"

Nobody answered. The man tried to free his hands from the ties, but to no avail. He writhed in his chair, and his bright blue shirt clung tightly to his chest.

"Who are you?"

Faele opened his mouth to say something but a threatening glance from Vittorio stopped him. The man shuddered, frightened by our silence. He sniffed the air, twitching his nostrils, which were squashed underneath the handkerchief, as if he were trying to make out where he was and who was standing in front of him from the smell.

"What do you want?"

Vittorio looked at him with a satisfied smile. He settled himself comfortably, lit a cigarette and then, after two or three slow puffs he began the interrogation:

"How did you become a Governor?"

"All thanks to honest hard work, I assure you. I started with the Civil Service competitive entrance exam, like everyone else."

The man had brightened up. He was glad to have a chance to speak. He answered all in one breath, shaking his sweaty head.

"How did you become a Governor?"

"I've already told you."

"How did you become a Governor?"

"By taking this Civil Service entrance competition, I won it, it's all in order."

"How did you become a Governor?

"Are you deaf? I've already told you."

"How did you become a Governor?"

The man lost the relieved air he had begun to assume. Vittorio, cool and composed, repeated the same question over and over again, in a clear, monotonous tone of voice, remorseless and inexorable, without a trace of emotion. The others listened, their mouths shut, their eyes and ears alert.

"How did you become a Governor?"

"With this competitive examination, you see, how can I explain it to you? Thanks to my experience, I'm a scrupulous Governor, I am, honestly, the prisoners think of me as a father, I've never given them an unfair punishment. Ask around, just ask the prisoners."

"How did you become a Governor?"

"I've told you, I've told you, you're driving me mad." His voice was becoming gradually more shrill and uncertain.

"How did you become a Governor?"

"I don't know, I swear I don't know, maybe because I've never got across anyone, and I've always respected those in power. If that's what you want, that's it, I'll tell you anything you want."

"How did you become a Governor?"

"I'm a member of the party in power. Is that what you're getting at? Okay, it's perfectly natural, I'm not ashamed to admit it."

"How did you become a Governor?"

"It's a matter of favours, of course, I agree, I agree. Before that I was Mayor of a village in the Marche region, I procured votes, of course, well, that's how it is . . . then this post became vacant and considering the salary was good and . . . well, I'd wanted some peace and quiet . . . I tried to . . . " his voice petered out.

Vittorio seemed satisfied with this last admission. Drops of sweat streaked down the prisoner's cheeks and round his lips. You could see he was bothered by it but his arms were tied together and fastened to his belt and he couldn't move them.

"Can I have some water?" he asked, licking his lips.

No one replied. Vittorio stubbed his cigarette out on the sole of his shoe and threw it in the middle of the room. He stared for a long time in silence at the man sitting in front of him. Then he began again, ice-cold and serious.

"Now tell us what your working day as a Governor is like."

The man gave a deep sigh as if he'd rid himself of a burden. The question had changed, the nightmare was over. Now he'd be able to stand up to that enigmatic interrogator. He smiled feebly and began to speak in a calmer tone of voice:

"It's a working day just like other people's: I write, check up on things, do some of the accounts, make a few telephone calls, and that's about it."

"Tell us your day."

"I get up at seven, I spend the day in my office, I go to bed early; it's a solitary life, I live like a hermit."

"Tell us your day as a Governor."

"What do you want, more details?"

Silence. Then there was the sudden click of the safety catch of Vittorio's revolver. The man looked scared.

"What do you want of me? You won't do anything foolish, will you? I haven't done anything wrong, I swear."

In between Giampiero's feet I could see a tape recorder with the tape turning and its microphone on the floor facing the prisoner.

"Tell us your day as a Governor."

"I've told you, for God's sake, in the morning I get up at seven, well sometimes it might be eight, my wife brings me a cup of coffee in bed, then immediately I'm up I go to my office, I start work, I sign papers, I write letters, I read reports, petitions, at midday I have lunch with my sons, then at three, well not really, at half-past four or five maybe I go back to work, I see one or two of the prisoners, I talk to the warders, the administrator, then at eight I knock off and at nine I'm home again having dinner. I watch TV with my family and by eleven I'm in bed. That's all."

"Tell us your day as a Governor."

"I've told you all I can."

"Tell us your day as Governor."

"Perhaps you want to know some details about my job. All right then, I hadn't thought of that. Well, my job is a bureaucratic one: approving expenditure, signing passes, writing letters to the Ministry, filling in registers, it's a job which gives very little satisfaction, I could do without it, but it's my duty, I'm paid to do all this and I do it conscientiously and loyally."

"Tell us your day as Governor."

"I've told you, I've told you everything, what else is there to tell you? You ask me and I'll talk about it, but this question repeated over and over again, always the same, is becoming obsessive."

"Tell us your day as Governor."

"Do you want to know how much I earn? 300,000 a month. I can't exactly squander money, can I? I can't understand why you're taking it out on a poor bureaucrat like me. Why don't you kidnap some industrialist, that would be a bit more worthwhile, or perhaps a Minister, or an Undersecretary — but me, what power have I got?"

"Tell us your day as Governor."

"But what, what about it? Tell me, please."

"Tell us your day as Governor."

"Well, all right then, there's the chicken business. I'd forgotten about it, so some prisoners have told you perhaps. I've got this hen-house which is looked after by some of the prisoners, I get about thirty eggs a day and I sell them to the prison authorities and they in turn sell them to the prisoners, after all I must earn a living, mustn't I, with two growing sons who demand motorbikes, clothes, travel, how can I cope?"

"Tell us your day as Governor."

"I own a pigsty too, if you really want to know. They've probably told you about that too, they're inquisitive, these bastards, inquisitive and interfering, there's no worse nosey-parker than a prisoner, he doesn't miss a thing, every time you sneeze everyone gets to know about it in half a minute. All right then, I have a pigsty which is looked after by some of the best-behaved prisoners who get rewarded at the end of the year with a few pieces of bacon. I sell the pigs to the police sergeant who in his turn sells them to the barracks and who of course gets his cut on it. Are you happy now, I've told you the lot, even things I've always kept a secret, so now will you let me go?"

"Tell us your day as Governor."

"But what more can I tell you? I've told you the truth, everything, I've disgraced myself, what more do you want?"

"Tell us your day as Governor."

"There's nothing else to tell, nothing, I swear to God."

Vittorio pressed his revolver on the man's bare arm, and he started backwards.

"Okay, then, I get money from the building and cleaning contractors, but I don't defraud the inmates, only the State, after all everyone swindles the State. The big shots invest their money abroad illegally to avoid paying taxes, what are they doing, aren't they swindling the State? Aren't they more guilty and more important than me? My fiddles are petty, it's just a matter of a few thousand liras, and after all, all Governors do the same: there are these contractors, hundreds of them, all at each others' throats, and there are some who are prepared to pay more so I make the most of it. I'm not hurting them, in fact I'm doing them a favour, and I'm not harming the State either, except well perhaps some jobs are a little bit more expensive than they might be . . . And now I swear I've told you everything, the lot . . . "

"Tell us your day as a Governor."

"But what? Well, all right, I have three informers amongst the prisoners, Okay? But again this is something all Governors do, it's part of routine procedure, it isn't something I've invented, you can't be a Governor without having informers amongst the prisoners."

"Tell us your day as Governor."

The man was sweating. He was frightened and confused, and he couldn't understand what was wanted of him. From time to time Vittorio gave him a jab with the revolver and he would give a jump. Then he would start talking again, wildly and anxiously.

"Perhaps you'd like to know who these informers are. Well then, one is a homosexual, he's very short and fragile, and I can blackmail him into spying for me because he knows that if he refuses to cooperate I can always hand him over to one of his rivals who'd butcher him with a penknife. He's had that happen to him before, you see. The second one is a surveyor who made a lot of money as a police informer before he ever came to my prison; the only problem with him is that he demands to be paid, and quite well too, because he's under the protection of the Chief of the Flying Squad. The third chap is a very influential character in the prison, a Mafia boss called 'The Ripper', he's up to his neck in the drug trade. I know that, but I turn a blind eye to it in exchange for the information he gives me: he too is certainly more powerful than I am, he gets just what he wants, he's really good at the job: three times he's helped me foil an escape, and twice he's informed me about three guys who were spreading political propaganda. But don't get the idea that I punished those people myself. I handed them over to the fascists. I think they really knocked them about, but it wasn't me who told them to, the whole thing was just between them, in fact in the end I got those fascists punished for their violence. They're protected, though, those guys never stay in for very long. One of the politicians committed suicide after being beaten up which I was sorry about, it's one thing to give people a lesson, that's fair, but death, no, that's going too far. He was a nutcase though, a poor sod with no rhyme or reason to him."

"Tell us your day as Governor."

"I've nothing else, I swear, on the head of my mother. Honestly, there's no more, I don't have anything else to say."

Silence. Vittorio didn't reply. The man sat there still, contracted, shrivelled, waiting. The silence went on for a long time. Vittorio didn't show any sign of breaking it. The others hardly breathed either. The man was gradually becoming more nervous. He heard a chair move and gave a jump.

"What are you going to do?"

Silence.

"Tell me what you want from me . . . money? I'll give it to you, but speak . . . tell me something, for God's sake."

Silence.

At the slightest creak or movement from the youngsters, the man jumped as if he'd just had an electric shock.

"Do you want more details? I'll give them to you, you know it all by now, but perhaps I've forgotten something. Tell me if I have, just ask. I suppose you've been given inside information on me from those bastards who hate me. How many slanders did they tell you? God Almighty! Prison Governors are the favourite target for the entire scum of the country."

Silence.

"Well, yes, I've sacked a teacher because she was spreading political propaganda during her lessons, I expect you think that's a crime. But I didn't want to do it. It was an order from above. Are you satisfied now?"

Silence.

"All right then, I made a half-witted prisoner work for me as a dishwasher and waiter, in exchange I'd give him a bottle of wine, he was an alcoholic anyway. But actually I'm doing him a favour, because when he's with the others they take advantage of him, they take the piss out of him. I got him a beautiful tailor-made uniform and a green apron, and I keep him busy sweeping, cleaning and washing dishes. Of course you'll say this is exploitation, but it's not really, because he's very happy; if I took away his job he'd die of misery. He's even become fond of my cat Marco Polo and gives it his wine to drink. He's such a weird guy, you can't imagine . . . "

He began to laugh to himself, but it was an unnatural, almost hysterical laughter. The silence continued. The man moved his blindfolded head trying to see through the cloth but he couldn't. Suspicion filled him with anxiety: he didn't trust us, and thought we might be going to kill him at any moment. He shivered at each click of Giampiero's lighter, and his shirt was soaking with sweat.

"Yes, I abused my authority to get . . . well . . . one of the prisoner's wives to give me a mouth job in exchange for a prison pass."

Silence.

"Now I've told you the most shameful thing of all, which I regretted immediately afterwards but to tell the truth she was a loose woman, more or less a prostitute, she had several lovers. But I regretted it all the same: if I could go back in time, I wouldn't do it because everything gets around in that den of gossip, and one cuts a sorry figure . . . I'm so tired . . . I'm exhausted . . . please take this blindfold off me . . . "

Silence.

"I've told you everything, the lot. I've disgraced myself for good. It's the end, there's nothing more, I swear."

Vittorio lifted his hand and held the revolver against his forehead. The man gave a scream of terror.

"I suppose you want to know about last month's uprising. We've gone round and round in circles for an hour. I know that's what you're after, isn't it?"

Silence.

Vittorio withdrew his revolver with a slow, cautious gesture. The man started talking in a hurried voice.

"For all I know the three rebels may have belonged to your crowd. I hadn't thought of that, is that why you've kidnapped me? Well, yes, it's fair, it's because of your mates that now . . . Those comrades of yours were making things hard for me, that's it, you know it already, they were continually organising small disturbances, rows, they'd managed to set up a school of 'ideology' as they called it, which was nothing more than a school of organised crime: they taught karate, hand-to-hand fighting, how to defend themselves from tear gas, how to burn the cells down, how to disarm the warders, etc, etc . . . Ideology, my foot! Well, to cut a long story short I couldn't let them become the prison's bosses, not for my sake, of course, but for the others, I have to set a good example, you see, the prisoners kept coming to complain, first of all The Ripper, the drug dealer, says: 'Governor, those people are vicious dogs, they're destroying our peace, every minute there's some act of violence.' In fact, it was him who had the idea of infiltrating a friend of his into their group, not himself, of course, because he's too well known, but a person called 'Agony', who is always calm and quiet and would do anything for a gram of heroin. I said: 'Do what you like, but let's be quite clear, I don't know a thing'. So he went to talk it over with Agony and after a few days Agony joined your rebellious friends as part of the group. God, it's hot, I'm suffocating, couldn't I have some water?"

Silence.

I could hear a large moth striking its felt wings against the glass of the oil lamp. From outside came the continous screeching of crickets. For a moment it would stop, then it started again with its insistent rhythm. Beyond the fields I could hear a dog barking.

Behind the man the bedroom door had been left open. By stretching my neck a little I could see a bed covered with a red and white checked tablecloth and a large mirror which reflected the prisoner from behind and some of us sitting on the floor.

"Well then, one day Agony comes up to me and says: 'Governor, sir, we're ready, we've organised the whole thing for Friday morning.' I say: 'Well done, Agony! You're a genius.' I can't imagine how he'd succeeded because he's the type who's half asleep all the time, a good for nothing, thin, dumb, bald, teeth rotting . . . anyway, however it came about, your lot accepted him. So I said, 'We'll let them go ahead with it, and then we'll catch them redhanded and I'll see to it that they're sent to solitary confinement. It's time they were taught a lesson. I don't want any injuries or deaths, though, I don't want bloodshed, is that clear?' "

He stopped, panting. He was out of breath. Some drops of sweat had run down on to his upper lip and he licked them up with his rough pallid tongue.

"But you see I hadn't reckoned with The Ripper and the soldiers and the police. To put it in a nutshell they were determined to have those four guys out of the way. Dead, that is. So Agony says: 'I've done my duty, now leave me in peace. I'm not going with that lot, I'm not risking my life for you arseholes.' That's fine with me, I say, but The Ripper didn't agree, and neither did the police. The Ripper says that if Agony backs out now it'll arouse their suspicions. Well, in a nutshell, they forced poor Agony to take part in it too . . . So the appointed day came and your friends locked themselves in the infirmary, they held a doctor, a nurse and a warder as hostages. They were armed of course, it was us who had provided them with weapons, that's to say it was The Ripper through various exchanges and fiddles — and even then he'd sold them at an inflated price, the scoundrel. Well, to cut it short, they say: 'These three are our hostages, the people's prisoners, now send an armoured car and we'll make our escape to Cuba.' Straight away we say: 'Of course, yes, anything you say.' To tell the truth I had very little to do with it, by that time the police had taken over, they were the ones who tossed and turned this hot potato in their hands, I didn't want to have anything to do with it, in fact I was against it from the very beginning: a good beating, yes, okay, but death, corpses, oh no, I don't agree with that. Instead they sent for God knows how many tanks, special corps, snipers, machine guns, even a TV crew was there, it had become a big thing. Those guys had barricaded themselves in and wouldn't budge, they demanded orange drinks, ham sandwiches, bars of chocolate, but I say 'people in such a situation asking for ham sandwiches, that's ridiculous, won't garlic sausage do?' Oh no, they demanded ham and ham it must be. But ham is expensive, it costs money and who's going to pay for it? But they said ham it must be, nothing but ham or they'd throw the nurse out of the window. That damned hell went on for three days, three bloody awful days during which even my chickens started losing weight because there was no one there to feed them, the whole prison was plunged into turmoil, there was no way of keeping them all quiet. I get really annoyed and I say 'How long are you going to keep up this masquerade, let's put an end to it all now. You've trapped them and you've caught them, what those guys need now is a jolly good lesson. Pretend you're going to take them to the airport, and then seize them all inside a net and throw them into a dungeon and shut them up there for a while.' But of course what the Governor of a prison says doesn't count, the whole thing was now in the hands of the police and I couldn't even open my mouth. All they'd say is 'Please, Signor Almirata, stay out of this!' Just like that, without a bit of respect. Well then our guys were still there in that hell, threatening to kill the doctor and the nurse, a poor woman who'd learnt to do only one thing in all her life, to give injections, an illiterate who Doctor Calogero had made a nurse so that she could get a rise in salary, a poor half-witted old woman who didn't understand a thing. And he too, poor Doctor Calogero, a good man, generous, kind to everyone, well, to tell the truth slightly obsessed with his own ideas because according to him the prisoners are all suffering from neuroses, and they should be cured and not punished. Then the warder, Puntasecca, a twenty three year old lad from Avellino, illiterate, who'd got his job through his parish priest's influence; sturdy, a great glutton, tough with the inmates, but at the same time cheerful, oh yes, a good lad. Well then, these three were in the hands of the criminals, including of course poor Agony who had nothing to do with it and was now pretending to be in the plot with the others, and was holding a machine gun in his arms and shouting through the megaphone to the policemen: 'You're slaves to the system which is oppressing you! They send you to fight against your brothers for a mouthful of stale bread! They call you in to murder the people and they rip off all the benefits! Comrades, put down your weapons and join us!' He said it though with such intensity that at one point I wondered whether he really had been converted. Poor Agony, I saw him dead afterwards, his head was shattered, one of his eyes had slid down over his ear, he was the sort of person who wouldn't hurt a fly, and he got dragged into it because of that stupid craving for dope . . . Well anyway, on the third day I say: 'Watch out because if you don't get cracking the whole prison will blow up. I'm not taking responsiblity.' And they answer 'Calm down, Signor Almirata, we're negotiating with them, but anyway we have complete control over the situation.' It wasn't true at all, though, they were scaring the shit out of everyone, the prison had stopped functioning, the kitchens didn't cook, the launderette didn't do the laundry, the workshop was shut, in a word a real shambles, besides all those big cops wearing heavy boots who charged about in the garden, trampling on my roses and hyacinths, and two of my fattest chickens, Mimi and Fifi, disappeared, two real jewels who laid eggs as big as pears, and my wife wasn't well and my dearest Pepe, the cleaner, had lost his last spark of reason, he didn't understand anything any more, he sat all day huddled up in a corner of the kitchen with his hands over his ears. 'What's wrong with you?' I say. 'Why are you stopping your ears up, Pepe dear?' but he wouldn't look at me, he just kept on stopping his ears as if it were wartime and he was waiting for a bomb to explode. On the fourth day it looks as if finally they've come to an agreement, which of course as we know now was just a sham. To put it in a nutshell the rebels were to come out pushing the hostages with their hands up in front of them, they'd then slip into a Black Maria which would take them to the airport, but it was all just a sick comedy because in the meantime the police were preparing themselves and getting armed, and as soon as they opened the door there would be *wham*! And that's how it was, the rebels opened the door and straight away a sniper shoots and kills — as luck would have it — poor Agony himself. The others answer back and pandemonium breaks loose. This was the signal they'd been waiting for. Hundreds of them rush into the room with their machine guns blazing and they kill Doctor Caligero, the Nurse Assunta Stella, and the Warder Antonio Puntasecca, as well as the three lefties. Of course they kept the journalists and television people well out of the way, and later they put out the story that they killed each other off by mistake, in a desperate attempt to do away with the hostages; and the police and the rest of them are great heroes, and off they all go leaving me up to my neck in problems, everyone's nerves were shattered, nothing functioned any more and of course I had become the scapegoat. It was me who saw those prisoners, their poor bodies like hares after thirty hunters had shot them up, full of holes, broken, torn to pieces, some with their bowels hanging out, some with their skulls smashed and their brains spilt, some with their throats ripped open, a massacre, and on top of everything I had to send Pepe, poor fellow, to a mental hospital because when he heard the shots he started screaming and wouldn't stop, he was shaking all over and pissing himself, what rotten luck! I'd always told him he was too much of a coward, what lousy bad luck, why should all this happen to me, of course, with those eyes hanging out of his skull so that I couldn't even recognise him any more, Agony I'm talking about, and the ham sandwiches — such a thing that — and meanwhile the police stole my chickens and of course later no one would know who it was and all the responsibility was mine and I . . . "

By now he was babbling on as if he were drunk, stumbling and gobbling his own words, drinking the sweat from his lips, with his whole body stretched forwards towards his invisible audience.

Vittorio looked at him satisifed. He swivelled his eyes round as if to say 'now do you see what I'm capable of?' The others admired him silently. Santino was the most scared of the lot: he was crouched in an armchair beside Mafalda, his head sunk between his shoulders, his eyes wide open in dismay.

Undaunted, the Governor tried to continue his story, but Vittorio was no longer interested. He went up to him unobserved and hit him over the head with the butt of his revolver. There was a single muffled thud and the man slid to the floor hitting his face against the tape recorder.

Giampiero covered him up with a large yellow striped towel. Faele lifted him up by his armpits and Renzo by his feet, and they carried him over to the Jaguar like that. Then they drove off at speed, without switching on the headlights. Vittorio gave them half an hour to drop the prisoner off somewhere around the port area.

We were the last to leave. Antonio locked the door and Santino and Mafalda got into the Volkswagen with us. Vittorio was cheerful, he whispered something into Suna's ear and kissed her lightly on her lips.

The air was calm and peaceful. The crescent moon, yellow and oily, was rising up out of the dark mass of the vines. The song of the crickets and the frogs had become deafening.

*Midnight*

I was already asleep when I heard the door of my room open. It was Suna in her long, white nightdress. She came in and sat on my bed.

"They were talking about it on the radio, they say he's been kidnapped to get ransom money, they're talking about bandits."

She didn't seem frightened. She spoke in a soft, calm, almost amused tone of voice. All of a sudden she undid the buttons of her nightie and let it slip to her feet.

"Vannina, at this very moment Mafalda and Santino are making love."

"What are you doing?"

She didn't answer. She stood there for a moment, fair and naked, propping her beautiful muscular body firmly on her crutches. Then she lay down next to me and slipped between the sheets.

I turned towards the wall, I wanted to get back to my interrupted sleep. I felt the warmth of her against my back.

"Do you mind if I masturbate here, next to you?"

"Do as you like."

I couldn't keep my eyes open, but I half turned round for a moment and caught a fleeting glimpse of her belly covered by its veil of golden down and of her hand moving delicately between her legs. It was a distorted image, as if I were looking at her through a misty steamed-up glass.

Then in a twinkling I fell asleep. I dreamed I was stabbing the prison Governor. I struck him ten times with rapid precise blows. Then I cleaned my knife on Suna's nightdress. I cleaned it very meticulously and all the time tears were pouring from my eyes because I knew that the Governor was none other than my father the peasant, his face cut across by the red bandage, his piggy lips damp with sweat, his head hairless, his hands like mine, short, smooth and knotted. I took the blindfold off him and I kissed his wide open eyes lovingly, in desperation.

*11th September*

I strolled up and down the streets waiting for the visiting hour to start. I stopped in front of a shop that sold knives, fascinated by the glitter of the blades.

Suddenly I thought I recognised something: the knife I had used in my dream to kill the Governor — my father — was there, resting on an ivory-coloured cloth. It had the same slightly curved handle of light-coloured wood, and the same long sharp blade.

As I examined it at close quarters I saw that the blade was covered with brown stains. My breathing came to a halt, and I could feel my heart beating; with a painful clarity I once again felt my arm thrusting the blade into his back, and heard the horrible noise as it ripped his flesh.

I don't know how long I stood there motionless in front of that window, my inside numb, my eyes frozen. Then, with a sudden shock I became aware that there was another face reflected in the dirty glass next to mine. It was the head of an old man with narrow, watery eyes, wearing a black woolly balaclava.

I turned and met his pupils staring at me, sad and lecherous. He clutched my bare arm with withered fingers. I freed myself roughly and ran along to the road to the hospital.

The passage was more crowded than usual. It was almost impossible to fight one's way through the beds, which had again increased in number and were taking up every inch of space. There was great confusion and noise, and a horrible stagnant heat.

I climbed over chairs and edged round bedside tables, stumbling over slippers, crashing into beds and sick bodies. At last I made it to Orio's bed, and was about to hug him, when just in time I saw it wasn't him.

In the old man's sly smiling face I recognised the man at the shop window. The black balaclava hat had slipped over his eyes and he had a disconsolate look as he tried to free himself. I stretched my arm over to pull up the bandage and my father's eyes smiled at me beseeching, insane.

I stood still staring at him, dazed and confused. Then someone came up to me from behind and patted me lightly on my back. It was the porcelain sister.

"The boy died last night. If you want to see him he's downstairs in the mortuary. We've contacted his mother, but apparently she's very ill too."

"Did he suffer?"

"Well, he did have a lot of pain, but we filled him up with morphine."

Laboriously we made our way into the corridor. There were beds even there, lengthwise against the walls, one patient's head against the next one's feet.

On my way out I passed the bald old man, who was crying continuously and stared at us from far, far away. He huddled up under his bedclothes as if he were freezing. He followed me with his two glassy eyes, without moving his eyelids, as large tears gathered on his emaciated cheeks.

"Yesterday five people died, we've hardly got time to move the corpses out of the beds before new patients arrive. We've even had to set these beds in the corridor. I'm against this mess but the ward is chock-a-block. We can't throw the patients out in the street, can we?"

"Where's the mortuary?"

"Downstairs, this way, I'll take you there."

We went through corridors crammed with people walking about, sitting, settling down for a long wait. The smell of medicine, mingled with the acid stench of all those sweaty bodies, was unbearable. A male nurse stopped the sister by pulling her black veil.

"Sister, I need some blood for that boy whose leg has been amputated."

"Tell his parents they have to go and get it on the black market, they'll find it there, here we haven't a single drop left."

"What about the bandages, where are they?"

"There aren't any, make do with some gauze or else tear up an old sheet. Ermina can tell you where they are."

The young man went off grumbling, his violet-stained white trousers hanging down over his whitened canvas shoes, his long hair falling over his lean shoulders.

"Until the money comes there'll be no bandages, they've shut off the supply because we haven't paid for the last seven months. But where's the money? The speculators sell blood on the black market so what can I do? I can't stop them!"

The sister lifted the veil off her perspiring cheeks.

"Once or twice I've given mine, but then I can't work the usual twelve hours."

We walked in silence. We descended a steep grey stone staircase and walked along another corridor, making our way between more patients queuing for X-rays. We entered a dark narrow corridor that smelt of fried food. All of a sudden we emerged into a yard with some shabby flower beds. Amidst the clusters of red, pink and white oleanders lay scattered broken plates, dirty bandages, plastic containers, torn pieces of dirty cotton wool, all looking as if they'd been there since the beginning of time.

"We'll have to go through the kitchen, do you mind?"

I said that I didn't and she led the way with her short, tottering steps, her rustling skirt, her upright head and her rosary with its metal beads jingling against her hip.

Propped against the kitchen door there were several large black sacks bulging with garbage. As soon as we opened the door a fat glossy mouse sped through a hole in the plastic bin-liner and scuttled under the stove. An old woman with a filthy apron grabbed hold of a large insecticide can and rushed off after the mouse. The sister did not even bother to look at her.

A little further on I stumbled over a pan lying on the floor and knocked off the lid, revealing some black liquid sprinkled with islands of rancid fat, out of which stuck an assortment of chicken bones.

"What are you doing? We must get on."

The sister stamped her foot impatiently and I replaced the lid on the pan and followed her. Other huge pans full of cold food stood on the ground. The floor was scattered with debris: empty bottles, bits of stale bread, fish bones, apple peel, old lettuce leaves, heaps of dirty gauze. On a marble-topped table lay some bits of meat with clotted blood, seething with large blue flies. A nauseating stench of washing powder, onion, burnt pans, disinfectant, bad fish and rotting vegetables assaulted me from every corner.

The sister noticed my bewildered expression, and pursed her delicate lips.

"The dustmen packed up two months ago. The staff hadn't been paid, so the contractors cut off their services. Now they've promised us another loan — we carry on by dint of loans, but the trouble is loans cost money, and the interest is destroying us. A stay in hospital used to be 300 liras a day, now it's gone up to 4,000, no wonder the patients complain."

She spoke in a bored off-hand voice, without ever pausing in her walk. The jingling of her beads produced a funereal music.

"On top of it all a new employee turns up every day, someone who's quite useless and who only got the job by graft, and that means another extra salary, another extra mouth to feed. That seems to be the hospital's main purpose, and meanwhile everything goes down the drain."

Even after we had come out of the kitchen and had crossed more corridors, I kept on sensing round me the nauseating smell of the kitchen.

At last we descended a staircase with high yellow-painted walls, and stopped in front of an iron door.

"Are you afraid of the dead?"

"Well, yes, a little."

"Would you prefer not to see him?"

"I'd like to see him."

The sister pushed the door with her shoulders and it opened with difficulty, scraping against the floor with a noise like crushed sand. A whiff of cold air greeted us as we went in. The room was large, cool, and built entirely of concrete. Lined up along the walls were stretchers covered with sheets of blue plastic beneath which could be identified the outlines of the corpses.

The sister went up to a small table against the far end of the wall. She lifted the plastic sheet and beckoned me to come closer.

Orio lay there, as beautiful as the first time I had seen him: his face was pink and relaxed, and an incredibly pure light-blue sparkle shone through his half-closed eyes. His hair had been combed backwards with water and he looked like a small boy who's just finished playing football and has rushed under a steaming hot shower and is now sleeping happily wrapped in a large adult bathrobe.

I bent down to kiss him, but the sister held me back. I wonder why — is it for some reason forbidden to kiss the dead? I didn't fancy asking her though. I was about to lift up the rest of the sheet because I wanted to see his beautiful naked body for the last time. But once again the sister stopped me.

A minute later we were in the open, in a sunny garden. The sister sat down on an iron bench and beckoned me to sit next to her.

I had never seen that garden, which is invisible from the upper floors and is virtually unreachable except through the mortuary or directly from the street. It was a square of ground closed in by high walls and comparatively tidy in spite of being uncultivated. The grass was long and of an intense green, with a few wild anemones growing in it.

I bent down to feel what was scratching my ankles and found myself grasping a small rosebush. I pulled a rose off and lifted it to my nose. It had no scent, only the slightly acid smell of grass.

"Hic jacet Orio totus," said the sister.

"What does that mean?"

"It means here lies the whole of Orio, flesh, body, spirit, soul."

"Don't you believe in eternal life?"

"No, I don't."

"Why don't you give up the veil then?"

"I'm all right as I am, thank you."

"Do you go to church?"

"Yes, I do, of course."

"Do you pray?"

"Yes, yes, I do."

I looked at her with astonishment. Her large face with its prominent cheekbones and smooth compact skin was animated; there was an ironic, ambiguous smile in her narrow heavy-lidded eyes, which made you think of something secret and powerful struggling vainly to take shape.

"I must go back upstairs now, you can get out into the road directly from here, through that small door over there."

"Thank you."

"His funeral will be tomorrow. If his mother doesn't come, do please come yourself, or he'll be alone."

"I'll come."

"If you're upset say some prayers, even if it's only with your lips. Words are rules and rules are our salvation."

She gave me a tender smile and kissed me on my forehead and eyes. Her breath smelt of dried figs, sweet and clean. Her tongue stretched out timidly and licked the tears that had welled from my eyes. I hugged her, then all of a sudden she moved away and went off without saying a word.

*Midnight*

At home I found Suna packing. She had pulled a suitcase out from under her bed, taken all her clothes from her wardrobe and piled them up by her pillow, and was now in the process of folding them carefully. She was red in the face from the effort of balancing herself on her crutches.

"Hang on, I'll help you."

"Vittorio says we must disperse, it's dangerous to stay on here. It seems that someone has been grassing on us."

"Who?"

"Giacinto rang earlier, I told him you were at the hospital. How's Orio?"

"He's dead."

"Fuck! A fourteen-year-old boy, what a shame! Did he suffer?"

"Apparently he didn't, much. Where's Santino?"

"He's coming later. It's Mafalda's turn tonight."

"Tomorrow I'm going to his funeral, then I'll leave."

"No, you must leave today, now, you can't go to the funeral nor can Santino. We must clear off immediately."

"Have you talked to Hasan?"

"I've told him I'm going back to Addis. He's pleased, so he's given me some money."

"There won't be anyone at the funeral."

"Who cares? The dead are dead, and that's that."

"I promised the sister I'd go."

"What sister?"

We were interrupted by the doorbell. It was Santino and Mafalda. They had some rice croquettes in a paper bag and a bunch of grapes. We ate them standing while getting ready to clear off.

Suna was nervous. Santino smiled calmly: he was the happiest of all of us to be leaving. I didn't know whether to tell him about Orio, and decided to put it off so as not to spoil his good mood. But then he asked me how his brother was and I couldn't avoid telling him.

He gaped at me incredulously. Then all of a sudden, he threw himself on the floor screaming. He started rolling about hitting his head against the kitchen tiles, writhing and crying desperately. Suna and Mafalda looked at him bewildered. Neither of them had any idea what to do. Eventually Mafalda knelt down at his side, took his head on her lap and rocked him gently as if he were a child. He let her comfort him for a few minutes, but then he shoved her away with an angry gesture and carried on sobbing furiously.

We stood there without saying a word, helpless witnesses to his blind, passionate distress. Mafalda muttered a few words of affection, but he didn't hear her; his body was shaken in violent spasms that convulsed him like a puppet. Then, just as suddenly as it had started, it finished. His voice died in his throat, his head fell to one side exhausted, his whole body calmed down. A minute later he was asleep, stretched out on the dirty tiles, his face smeared with a mixture of rice, tomato sauce and tears.

I called Giacinto to tell him I'd be home today and he said he'd come and meet me at the station. I looked up the timetable and decided to take the first available train to Rome.

The fact is, though, I have no money left and I don't fancy asking Suna for it since she's put me up and fed me all this time. Unfortunately it has slipped her mind that I've been robbed of my last 15,000 liras.

In the end I decided to hitch tomorrow and rang Giacinto to tell him of my plans. He said that if I liked he'd come and fetch me by car, but I refused to put him to so much trouble.

*12th September*

As far as Caserta it was easy. A farmer in a car full of boxes of peppers gave me a lift almost as soon as I took up my position at the entrance to the motorway.

In Caserta I went into a bar to have a coffee, so I spent my last 100 liras. I reckoned I'd be back in Rome within a few hours. The sun was baking outside, and I made myself a little hat out of a piece of newspaper, like the ones bricklayers wear. I went back to the entrance to the Rome motorway, with Giacinto's yellow bag hanging from my shoulders. After waiting for half an hour my lips were dry and my head was throbbing. I moved under a sycamore tree which was in a rather unfortunate spot right on a corner where I could only be seen at the very last minute; but the heat was too much to stay in the sun.

An hour later I started feeling terribly hungry. The cars were zooming past me, green, red, yellow, blue flashes, and I didn't have time to raise my hand before they had vanished. I thought after all I'd better change places and I went back to my old spot at the beginning of the bend, in the full heat of the sun. I sat on the metal barrier. I sat there with my eyes closed trying not to think of anything. Then I heard a screeching of brakes and a large silvery car pulled up beside me. A man's arm stretched out to open the door.

"Get in."

"Are you going to Rome?"

The man bent down to look at me. He gave me a stupid smile and closed the door abruptly, almost catching my fingers, and drove off leaving me there dazed and bewildered.

I went and sat on the metal barrier again. Hunger was gnawing at my stomach and I had a splitting headache. Sweat was trickling down my back in rivulets.

Around one o'clock a car eventually slowed down at my raised arm. It was a large American car with a middle-aged woman and man inside it. They made a sign for me to sit in the back next to a child's bike and then they drove off again without a word. I leaned my head back, happy to be in the shade and sitting on a soft comfortable seat. I wanted to tell them how happy and grateful I was, but the two seemed to be not in the least interested in me.

The man drove in an upright position, holding the steering wheel with his arms outstretched, and the woman sat quietly on his right.

She was so still and motionless that she could have been asleep. All I could see of her was her suntanned neck and her black hair gathered behind her ears and fixed with a crown of golden hairpins. From time to time the man turned to look at her. His bloated profile stood out indistinctly against the glass for a fraction of a second: his heavy double chin, his blurred lips, his snub nose, his large receding forehead, his cloudy eye.

To begin with their silence disconcerted me. But after a bit I felt relieved that they weren't talking, for it meant I could sit back and relax with my eyes closed. After resting like this for a while I could feel my headache melting away.

They stopped at a motorway service station and went to have something to drink without asking me if I wanted to go with them. They came back a few minutes later arguing furiously, and carried on quarrelling just as if I weren't there. They were squabbling over trivialities. He told her off for not asking him if he wanted more sugar in his coffee. She retorted that he was in such a hurry to carry on with the journey that he hadn't even given her time to go to the toilet.

However, they didn't seem to be in much of a hurry: the car sailed along calm and serene. The woman sat there motionless, staring straight in front of her. The man drove deep in thought, from time to time turning to look at her.

At the next service station we stopped again to get some petrol. The woman got out, slamming the door, and the man started singing in a shrill voice: "What do I care . . . I don't give a fig . . . .what you do to me . . . "

She came back with a packet of biscuits, sat down heavily and started munching them. She didn't for a minute think of offering me one, and neither did I have the courage to ask her.

On the floor I found a box of tissues and used them to wipe the sweat off my neck. I looked round for something to eat, but I could see nothing but old newspapers and empty packets of cigarettes. The smell of the cheese biscuits floated back to me, fresh and inviting.

I tried to stop thinking of food. I leaned against the back of the seat and closed my eyes. I stretched out my legs, putting them round the wheels of the bicycle, and tried to sleep. I sank into a state of sultry drowsiness, dulled by the sharp smell of petrol and biscuits. Straight away Orio's face appeared in front of me, contracted with pain, his pale blue eyes beseeching me for help. A stab of pain in my stomach made me suddenly open my eyes.

The car had stopped in a parched layby. The two had gone off, I didn't know where, and I was sitting alone in the broiling hothouse. I opened the door but there wasn't a breath of air, so I got out into the stagnant afternoon heat. I could see the owner of the car about a hundred yards away, standing next to a multicoloured kiosk, waving and making incomprehensible signs to me. Then his commanding voice reached me:

"Stay in the car, please, and keep an eye on the luggage!"

With my usual cowardly meekness I got back into the car and waited for them patiently. After a quarter of an hour I got out again to try and see what they were up to. I caught a glimpse of them at the end of the steep road, next to a row of lorries, sitting and eating some sandwiches under a large blue and yellow sunshade.

I felt so angry I would have liked to hurl the car down the precipice. If I'd been able to drive I would at least have moved it into the shade of a small coppice of oaks that stood out in the nearby field. But I was stuck there in the sun and couldn't do a thing except what they wanted.

I opened all the doors and sat in the only seat that got any shade, where the woman had been sitting. I felt something hard under my foot: it was the packet of biscuits. I stretched my hand down, looking round as if I were a thief, but the packet was empty except for a few broken bits at the bottom of the box. I thrust these greedily into my mouth.

It was almost an hour before they came back. They had a satisfied, well-fed air and were both smoking cigarettes. They got into the car and drove off, without saying a word. He turned on the radio and she leaned over to say something in his ear. He burst out laughing and she grabbed his head, pulled him towards her and kissed him; he smiled at her, wrinkling his sun-tanned skin.

I curled up on the seat and closed my eyes again. I tried to remember my last visit to Orio, the contact with his feverish skin, his parched mouth, his calm voice, the sour wind from his sick belly. His tongue melted in my mouth with a taste of open sea-urchins, and I caressed his blond head, passing my fingers through his hair, stiffened by sea salt. We were swimming together in the deep waters off Punta Zafferana and the clean fresh water swathed my hot body. Orio was swimming slowly by my side, agile and relaxed, when all of a sudden he moved away from me, descended between the rocks and sank amidst the reddish seaweed. I tried to reach him and dived beneath the water, holding my breath and clinging to the rocks; but I couldn't see him any longer, he had disappeared, sucked down by the dark still water.

I woke up distressed and breathless, gasping for air. The two in the front seat were silent. I could only hear the monotonous drone of the engine and the swoosh of the wind through the half-closed windows. They had turned off the radio and I thought 'at last a little bit of peace and quiet.'

The silence was broken by a low moan, and I opened my eyes. I couldn't see the woman, she had disappeared down behind the back of the seat. The man sat stiffly, his head nailed down on his shoulders, his body held rigid with tension.

I closed my eyes again, and there was a gasp followed by a muffled moan. Then something warm touched my ankle. I looked down: it was the woman's fingers searching impatiently between the seats. Her hand, loaded with rings, clutched one of my shoes, felt it all over and then let it go to start its search again. The arm was stretching out further, like a long shiny snake jingling with bracelets, and instinctively I pulled up my legs. At length her hand lighted on what it had been looking for: the box of tissues. A minute later I saw one of the tissues fly out of the window rolled up in a ball. The man was doing up his trousers, his shoulders relaxed, his neck pushed forwards, his arms resting on the steering wheel.

Half an hour later we arrived at the exit for Rome. The man paid, staid and dignified, straightening his tie. Then he turned into the road to the town centre. When we got near the Via Salaria I opened my mouth to ask him to drop me off. But I couldn't utter a word. I was seized with a sudden sense of shame. Perhaps they had forgotten all about me, I thought, and by speaking I would give away the fact that I had witnessed their intimacy.

I let them take me as far as their home, in Via Archimede. I got out without their noticing me, whispered a feeble and awkward thank you and disappeared as quickly as I could. As it turned out they were so involved in the problem of finding their door key that they didn't notice my departure at all. She was swearing she had given it to him and he that he had given it back to her.

I walked all the rest of the way home.

*ROME*

# *Rome*

*12th September*

*Midnight*

When I got home it was already dark. Giacinto was waiting for me sitting on the floor in the entrance, with the radio switched on by his feet. He opened the door as soon as he heard the lift. When he saw me all dirty and sweaty, my face drawn with exhaustion and my hair glued to my head, he looked worried.

"What's happened to you?"

"Nothing. It took me a long time to get a lift and I haven't eaten since yesterday."

We hugged each other and the smell of car oil wafted over me with reassuring familiarity.

"Do you want to have a shower?"

"I want something to eat first."

I dumped my bag on the floor, took off my shoes and sat down in front of a huge plate of cold spaghetti. Giacinto took a piece of cold roast beef out of the fridge and cut me off a couple of slices. As I stuffed my face with mouthful after mouthful, I could feel his eyes scrutinising me anxiously.

"I'm not sure, but I don't think you've changed."

I shook my head, my mouth full, my hands busy breaking off some bread.

"I was afraid you'd come back different."

"How's it going at Vargas's?"

"They're talking of redundancies. He says that what with debts and increased costs he can't manage. We're threatening to go on strike though, and he says if we do he'll close down. He'd even close the business, the shit!"

"Has the letter from the provincial education office arrived yet?"

"You've been allocated to a school in Centocelle, off the Prenestina. That's good news, isn't it? It means you can get up an hour later and only have to take two buses instead of three."

"You know Orio's dead?"

"Don't tell me about your secrets."

"He died the day before yesterday."

"I don't want to know, okay?"

"Don't you want to know about Santino and the Movement?"

"No, I don't. All I want to do is to make love, and that's all."

"I'm tired out."

"I've been waiting all day."

"Didn't you go to the garage today?"

"Today's Sunday, you idiot. I slept till eleven this morning; then I went to Mario's for lunch and since then I've been waiting for you. As a matter of fact I was getting worried because you were so long."

"How's Mario?"

"Under the weather. He's got to do his military service soon."

"Does that upset you?"

"He's the only friend I've got, of course I mind."

"I'm so sleepy."

"How's Santino?"

"He left for Addis with Suna."

"Don't tell me anything about anyone. To hell with them all, come with me."

He took my hand and dragged me towards the bedroom. He kicked the door wide open. The smell of carbolic soap was the first thing to hit me. I looked around; the low iron bed, the imitation wooden wardrobe, the battered slippers, the frayed mat with a picture of Diana the Huntress, white on blue, a photograph of Giacinto with a ten-pound grouper, the nightlights with its dusty glass with two dead midges stuck to it, my books crammed on the shelf by the window, the curtain with its faded flowery pattern all shredded by the cat's claws: nothing had changed since I had left a month ago.

I threw myself on the bed as I was, fully dressed, with my shoes on. Giacinto undressed me gently as if I were a little girl. I said I wanted to sleep but he pressed himself passionately against me.

"I want you."

"I'm too tired."

"It doesn't matter, leave it to me."

"Do you want to make love with me or against me?"

"Shut up darling, keep still, don't say a word, don't move, don't deny yourself to me."

He wanted me to stay there like a corpse, until he had satisfied himself. Whether I wanted him or not, felt desire or not, didn't seem to matter to him in the least. I gave in to him, but something inside me rebelled and made me feel like throwing up.

*14th September*

Dear Vannina,

Something terrible has happened — Santino has been arrested. Someone must have talked. Vittorio says there must be a spy amongst us. They arrested him as soon as he got off the ferry at Addis, and once inside apparently he told them everything.

Vittorio has left for France with a false passport, and Mafalda went with him. Renzo went back home somewhere up in the Trentino, but no one knows his address. Faele is in hiding with some friends in Naples, and Antonio has disappeared. The only one who isn't scared is Giampiero, he just keeps driving about in his prune-coloured Jaguar as if nothing had happend.

I was summoned to Police Headquarters in Naples, and went through a long interrogation. I said fuck all, but they knew everything already. All they wanted was to know how much money I had given to the Movement. Naturally I didn't give any satisfaction to the bastards.

The first night they shut me up in a room that was more like a shit-house. They left the light on all night and all they gave me to rest on was a chair. No food, no water. The following day they dragged me from office to office for more interrogations.

During one of these treks I caught sight of Santino passing by at the far end of a corridor between two policemen. I called to him, but he didn't hear me — or perhaps he just pretended not to, I don't know. He was smoking calmly and chatting with his two escorts as if they were old friends.

They asked me a whole lot of idiotic, offensive questions such as 'who was your lover?', 'who did you sleep with?', etc, etc. According to them the only reason a woman gets involved in politics is to follow the man who screws her so as to keep a check on him. It's perfectly logical for a woman to join a movement for the sake of a man's prick; it's perfectly illogical for her to have any loyalty to the movement and refuse to grass.

After three days of the same old story they released me. I was dirty, hungry and furious. I had caught lice as well as some stupid eye infection that caused my eyes to become all swollen and red and water continuously.

As soon as he got to know I was inside the Turk sent me a lawyer. Then he started to pull strings to get me out. But it wouldn't have worked if I hadn't been a woman without a prick and on top of it legless, so by their standards I was harmless.

As far as you're concerned, you've no need to worry: Santino didn't mention your name and anyway you're not on the list of members.

Write to me c/o Poste Restante, home is not safe.

Ciao,
Suna.

*Midnight*

"Just what your friends deserve, bunch of amateurish politicos and bunglers," commented Giacinto when I told him about Santino's arrest.

He pulled out his dirty greasy overalls and handed them to me to wash. Then in addition to the overalls he disgorged a mountain of dirty shirts he'd been keeping aside for me. I filled up the bathtub with hot water and poured washing powder into it. Meanwhile I put the dinner on to cook, scrubbed the floor, changed the sheets and cleaned the cooker: the house was in a terrible mess.

Giacinto was watching the box. Our neighbour's child started screaming and Giacinto turned up the volume to cover his screams. Someone hit the wall with a shoe, and I told him to turn the volume down, but he ignored me. A little later they rang the doorbell. I went to open it and the neighbour stood there and shouted that her child was sick, her father-in-law was dying, and that she couldn't put up with this racket. Giacinto switched the television off and went out slamming the door behind him.

The toilet is blocked. I tried to unblock it by sticking a thin bent bit of wire down the pan. I extricated pellets of cotton wool, clots of hair and two used condoms. I threw everything into the bin and started cleaning the floor.

Giacinto and I never use condoms. So there must have been another woman around. But I know full well that he'll never tell me about it, not even if it was a matter of life and death.

*18th September*

I went to Centocelle to visit the school I'll be teaching in during the winter. It's a recently modernised district, but it's already on the downgrade. There are no gardens, no tree-lined squares, no swimming pools, no gyms, no libraries, nothing. Every street seems to stink of bad food: fried fish, cabbage, beans, tripe, chips, stale fat.

The school consists of two prefabricated huts stuck right in the middle of a football pitch. It's built of plastic panels, sheet metal roofs and plywood doors, and looks like some huge gimcrack toy.

The headmaster is a tall, fashionably dressed man. He was the only person around the empty sweltering school. He greeted me with a well-bred bow, and displayed a self-assured, pleasant smile.

"The school is new, I do hope you'll like it. Unfortunately, the pupils leave much to be desired, in fact they are the children of petty bourgeois families just moved in from the countryside and are therefore coarse, cunning and superstitious. Do you know the district?"

"No, I don't."

"Well, it's one of those hybrids so typical of Rome, the result of immigration and urban disorder. Thrifty labourers and thieves and hooligans live wretchedly together, ignorant policemen and ultra-leftist students, small terrified office workers, cynical mean-minded shopkeepers; one could say that we have a real melting-pot of classes here. I can tell you straight away, your task won't be easy, but don't panic and I will help you."

He gave me a winning smile, half closing his dark genial eyes. "This is your classroom. It's nice, don't you think?"

I looked round. The room is bright in spite of the very low ceiling. The end wall, which abuts on to the road, is entirely taken up by a horizontal window which consists of multicoloured glass representing a stylised design of sunflowers and light blue moons. The designs are painted in pink and blue. The teacher's desk has a futuristic shape: a transparent yellow plastic rhombus with a protruding iron tube that functions as a chair.

"Do you like this stained glass effect? The children have smashed the bits of glass several times but I always have them replaced, don't you think they give the room a cheerful tone?"

I thought they looked horrible, but I said nothing, not wanting to offend him.

"It's been proved that if one works in a pleasant environment one produces twice as much work. In the staff room too, which I'm going to show you in just a minute, I had some murals done by the same painter, a dear friend of mine, a genius, I got him to paint African skies, Egyptian pyramids, mosques, Pharaoh's tombs, pretty girls carrying water-jars, and lumberjacks: everything just about recognisable, though in an impressionistic style, modern, you know, atmospheric type of work. As a result the room looks enormous, twice as long and twice as large, I'm sure you'll like it too."

"How do you heat this room?"

"Unfortunately we have no money for a proper heating system; when it's very cold we use a small electric heater. It will be enough for you, and as for the pupils they're used to the cold, they don't have any heating at home either, you know. Your only problem, my dear, will be to keep them quiet and in their places. The fact is they tend to overwhelm the teacher, to eat him up, and especially you — you're so young, so obviously new to teaching, they'll eat you up in one mouthful."

He laughed softly and maliciously, looking askance at me. He took out a packet of cigarettes from one of his extremely tight pockets and offered it to me.

"You don't smoke? Well done, but do you know how many cigarettes I smoke a day? Ninety. My doctor says that by now my lungs have the consistency of torn paper, and one of these days they'll crumble for good and all. But you see I don't really want to go on living, I've already tried to kill myself twice."

To show me he wasn't joking he rolled up his striped shirt sleeve and shoved a long reddish scar under my nose.

"Once like this with a razor blade, and another time with gas. But I'm lucky, there's always some dolt there to save me. The first time my wife, the second my son: mine is a very affectionate family, as you can gather, they're afraid I'll leave them destitute and without anyone to support them. Not that I get much as a headmaster anyway, but the articles I write for the 'Daily Sport' give me a little bit of breathing space. I don't know how I'd manage otherwise."

"Are you a journalist?"

"A sports columnist, to be precise. Do you think that's odd for a teacher who delights in studying Leopardi? The thing is that I've always been very fond of football, I simply exploited my passion.

We've even got a school football team, as a matter of fact it's the most together thing around here. The children have a lot of respect for me as a sports reporter, far more than they've got for me as a headmaster."

I looked at him more closely. He's without doubt the most eccentric headmaster I've ever seen. His face is lean, cut by deep wrinkles which cross his cheeks, lips and forehead lengthwise; his eyes are large and sorrowful; his nose thick and flattened; his teeth are protruding and black. When he smiles the wrinkles become twisted and grow deeper, they make him look like an old gloomy gorilla.

"Perhaps you're wondering why I'm in such a hurry to die . . . "

"Well . . . "

His whole suntanned and athletic body was taut with his desire to unburden himself.

"The thing is I don't even like myself. I don't like my face, I don't like my body, I don't even like my character, which is simultaneously shy and outspoken, moody and serene, an unbearable hotchpotch. In addition I detest the life I'm leading, which is one idiotic continuous compromise: I've always had many talents, but none which could really take me out of myself and make me stand out, I can do lots of things but none of them really well. And here you are, even this tendency of mine to confide in people I've only just met, who obviously couldn't care a damn about me, is disconcerting, don't you think?"

I didn't know what to answer. I could feel his mournful eyes on my face. I would have liked to leave; but there was something sincere in all that histrionic vanity which prevented me from disliking him: he puzzled me and roused my curiosity.

Meanwhile he'd lit another cigarette from the stub of his old one. His fingers trembled as he drew the two cigarettes together.

"Smoking reconciles me with myself — do you understand that?"

I nodded awkwardly. He inhaled deeply, his head thrown backwards, his eyes half-closed in blissful contentment. Out of his blackened nostrils unrolled two small white snakes of smoke; at the same time a grey curl wriggled from his lips, floated up into his nostrils and emerged again in shreds.

"I live to smoke."

He pronounced that sentence with a dramatic air in a hoarse

affected voice. Without meaning to I must have smiled because he hastened to giggle with a sly air of complicity.

"You think I'm a bit of a sham, don't you?

"Well . . . "

"You're a very kind person, I understood that straight away, a sensitive, graceful, introverted, stubborn and sensual type of woman, completely unfitted for the role of a teacher. Why do you teach?"

"I need money."

"Terrible. One should never enter a school unless one is dragged into it by a demonic urge to teach. Why don't you do something else?"

"I can't do anything else."

"Nonsense. You should have become a scholar. You have a propensity for observation and study; you're not afraid of being by yourself, you have powers of reflection, you're slow and deliberate. Perhaps it's my smoking which gives me these prophetic skills, I only need to take one look at you to understand what you're like: I know for sure you're not a gossip, I know you don't like me, I mean physically, but you're curious about my personality, like everyone else for that matter. You see, I'm not just any ordinary man, I'm aware of that. Am I right?"

"I don't think I'm an academic sort of person. I'm too lazy and too unsure of myself."

"You don't know yourself well enough, and anyway you have a tendency to play yourself down, just like me after all, we have something in common, you and I, Signora Magro."

He took a last puff of his by now miniscule fag end, which was burning out in his yellow-stained fingers.

"It's strange, we are both here, in this classroom flooded with unreal light at this time of the morning. Don't you feel the bitter lingering weight of destiny?"

"How many pupils am I going to have?"

"How like a woman! I roam through a world of metaphors and abstractions, and you pull me down by my feet. You're too preoccupied with mundane reality, you never dare to take a risk, to dream, you're narrow-minded, you women, too prosaic, too humdrum. Probably even now you're thinking in your prosaic fashion that I'm trying to make a pass at you?"

"I'm not in the least."

"If you say so it must be so, because you are not a liar, your little girl's soul is transparent and honest. I feel we are going to understand each other. The other teachers are terribly banal and predictable! Two lefties who think like tanks, without even a spark of imagination, and talk in clichés: capitalism, proletariat, exploitation, direct action, class struggle, and most of all they use the word 'mass' indiscriminately. Up to now you haven't used it once and I'm duly grateful to you for this."

I didn't point out to him that up to then he had been the only one to speak. "The others are uncommitted drifters: except that we have two reactionaries who also happen to be women, two angry cynical heathens even if they do claim to be regular church goers, attached to superstition like two leeches. They're also very ugly people, and they hate me. They sent a letter of complaint against me to the provincial education office and as a result a ninety-year-old inspector came and visited the school. He was in his dotage, totally cuckoo, but not so much that he couldn't make out what was going on: that's to say, that those two women are too ugly to be able to tell the truth, and perhaps also they're a little bit in love with me. Women's ideological drives always have their roots in the uterus, their sex cries out for me and in order to keep it under control, they give me a lot of shit. That's logical, isn't it?"

He lit another cigarette in his carefree manner. The ashtray on his desk was full already. He gave me a quick sly look and then carried on smoking nonchalantly, completely absorbed in his own thoughts.

"We also have the school lunatic, Rosa Colla. You'll get to know her soon enough, she'll take you to her home and introduce you to her 'family'. She's as ignorant as a goat, but she can keep the children under control all right, some magic trick she must have learnt from her animals. She's stupid enough but she doesn't do anyone any harm. She even has some measure of gentleness unexpected in a woman whose body is the shape of a treetrunk. Well, now I'll let you go because I'm busy, it was a pleasure meeting you. And don't forget, be punctual on the first day of school, come and see me half an hour before the start of the first lesson and I'll give you the registers. Take care and try not to hate me too much. Goodbye."

His wrinkled face twisted into a sad, fatuous grimace. He shook my hand with his hot knotted fingers, stained by nicotine. A minute later I saw his bowed back moving off down the corridor.

*Midnight*

I told Giacinto about my encounter with the headmaster but he didn't show much interest. He had toothache and was tearing at the potatoes on his plate with nervous energy. He asked me to cook him some apples.

After dinner we lay on the bed. I wanted to read and he wanted to make love. I told him I was thinking of Orio and that annoyed him.

"Let's do it all the same."

"I don't feel like it."

"All you have to do is to lie there quietly, what hassle is that for you?"

"That's exactly what I want to avoid."

"You've always done it."

"I don't want to do it now."

"You see, you have changed, I was wrong then. That cow has put you against me. You've lost your sweet nature, you've become hard, moody, just like that shit Suna. You've become spoiled, and what's happened to that sweetness of yours which I love so much, where has that gone?"

I gave in to him against my will. Out of meekness, out of habit, out of love, I don't know. I waited for the end to savour his explosion of joy, to feel a weary satisfaction at having him cling to me, frenzied and relentless in chasing blindly towards a pleasure I did not share.

My satisfaction however soon turned to anger, indeed into hatred against the inertia of my body, against the perverse sense of duty which held me from rebelling against the submissiveness which I always allowed to dominate me. Something was burning my throat and I couldn't spit it out.

*22nd September*

Dear Vannina,

Now Giampiero has been arrested too. I'm sorry I had bad thoughts about him. His girlfriend, Mirella, came and brought me the keys to the new headquarters which we are paying for with his money.

The trial will take place in November. Or so they say, but you never know. They'll drag it out, as usual, leaving those poor devils they've put inside in the shit. It's not enough for them to have treacherously killed those three in prison. Only the women have been kept out of it because thank God in this case they don't count. I'm collecting money for the lawyers. I managed to wheedle 3000,000 liras from my mean bastard of a father. I even had to sell the pearl necklace I was given for my eighteenth birthday. If you can send something too, please do — it's urgent.

Addis is deserted. Yesterday it rained all day long and the sea is very rough. Oliver and Marta are always screwing. I caught them the other morning sleeping together, hugging each other. She has the body of a young girl. It doesn't look like that when she's dressed because she always stuffs herself up with all those long aprons that make her look so awkward. But underneath she's very beautiful, and just think, she's fifty! Her grey hair that she always twists up into a plait was lying loose on her shoulders. I was shocked, I felt almost as if their love-making was incestuous.

The Turk is bombarding us with telephone calls because he wants us all to go to Switzerland. But Marta and Oliver are putting up a passive resistance campaign against him: one day Oliver is sick, another day something breaks down in the house, another time the sea is too rough and the ferries aren't running, and so on. As for me, I don't know what the fuck I'd do in that Swiss dosshouse of his.

If it was up to me I'd go back to Naples; here I'm getting as lethargic as a dormouse: I eat and sleep and die of boredom. No one knows what's happened to Mafalda and Vittorio. Who would have thought they'd get it together — suddenly they discovered they were just right for each other.

That idiot Santino doesn't write. I've sent him a dozen letters but he's never answered one — not a single word. They tell me his mother often goes to see him. After Orio's death she's aged a lot and can hardly see. She's persuaded Santino to study, she wants him to become a surveyor; every week she embarks for Naples carrying a load of books and note pads. She's got him to take a correspondence course. I can't imagine Santino poring over a book, he hates books, and there he is studying to become a fucking surveyor just to please his mother. When I think of his body I get a belly-ache. I'll never again find such a sweet loving body. I wake up during the night with a craving to see him, even if only for one minute. It's such a violent craving that I'm breathless: just to see him, without even touching him, just to see him going around naked with that jolly little prick of his. I keep on masturbating and masturbating from morning till night, my cunt is as sore as hell, my body aches and so do my legs and my back and my arms. I tell myself I should look for another prick, but I don't feel like it. I think of Santino all the time and I come like a moron in my own hands. Ciao, write soon.

Suna.

*25th September*

Giacinto is worried about my sexual listlessness. He thinks it's due to passing dissatisfaction brought about by the bad influence of that 'devil of a Suna'.

"You're going against your own nature, love."

"What nature?"

"Your nature is good, soft, sensitive and you're making it become hard and aggressive."

"Am I being aggressive if I don't feel like making love to you?"

"Yes, you're aggressive against yourself, you're repressing your own character."

"Perhaps my character was moulded on yours, it wasn't really my own."

"Oh fuck off! When I met you you were already like that, I didn't do anything to change you."

"I just wanted you to like me."

"That's right, because you loved me."

"I wanted to be a good wife."

"And you've been a good wife, but now you're changing, now you're rejecting the best side of yourself."

"Best because most convenient for you."

"You don't understand a fucking thing, Vannina, about either yourself, or me, or marriage. Come here, kiss me, I love you."

I gave in to his embrace. But perhaps I didn't. Perhaps I kissed because I wanted to. I hugged him, savouring the warm bitter smell of grease and peppermint. I made love with my eyes closed in a state of artificial intoxication. Giacinto was happy, he kissed my eyes, my mouth, my throat, my hair, with fierce tenderness. He was rewarding me for my submission.

But even this time he could not remember there were two of us. He let himself plunge into a solitary breathless race which ended up with a broken, triumphant scream.

*4.00 p.m.*

Dear Vannina,

We left Addis and here we are back in Naples. Guess who was the first person to ring the bell at home? Mafalda. Alone, with an exhausted, angry expression on her face. Vittorio got married to a Swiss girl who's 'beautiful, rich and a virgin.' So he says in a letter he sent her, making a lot of stupid comments on the woman's chastity and more nonsense of that sort. He left Mafalda at the frontier without a penny, with a bag full of papers. She had to hitch all the way down. It took her three days. Now she's staying with me. Her father doesn't want to see her, her mother is dead, she doesn't know where the hell to go. Compared to her father the Turk's a liberal. Now he keeps asking all the time if I need more money, he no longer bothers me with questions about political activities, he's stopped using his threatening tone of voice, I don't know what's wrong with him, he encourages me to study medicine and he's given up that project of sending me to the International College in that shithole Lausanne.

Marta got pregnant. She went to a back street abortionist without telling me a thing, the stupid cow. She came back very upset, she looked as if she'd fallen into a well. Now she's in bed, she's still bleeding, but she won't let me send for a doctor. I'll end up sending for one anyway. She's there sprawled on her bed in her dark little room, and she doesn't speak and doesn't eat. Her eyes are fierce and wicked. Since she's been in bed Oliver seems to have lost his affection for her. In fact he couldn't care less, he goes around the house bored to tears and every afternoon he goes and plays tennis with an American girl he met in the street. Her name is Sandy and she's like a boiled potato.

Mafalda is furious with Vittorio, she says that with women he's brutal and fickle, and that deep down he only loves himself and he's shit scared to commit himself. To cheer her up he told her he's only marrying the Swiss girl because of her money, so as to finance the Movement. He says the girl knows this and agrees: they're going to buy an offset litho press, print a newspaper and open new centres all over Italy.

Meanwhile, Mafalda is trying to pull the Movement together. But it's a mess, because none of those who were most active are around any more: Vittorio is abroad, Renzo is in Trento, Antonio is God knows where, and Giampiero and Faele are inside. But she doesn't lose heart. She works, rushes about, does everything at the risk of being put inside herself. She tries to bring in new people and at the same time round up all those old members who dispersed after the arrests. Now and then someone turns up and we have meetings of a sort, but everyone speaks at once, there's terrible confusion — 'not a fucking bit of discipline', as Vittorio would say.

Meanwhile, it turns out that Mafalda can do everything: she knows how to spell, she's articulate, she writes like a real leftist, she's a good organiser; it's she who's keeping the Movement together for the time being. Someone proposed she should be made coordinator of the South while Vittorio is away, but the idea was rejected. Some real twit with a beard, who only joined two weeks ago, said that people would laugh at us. The others didn't dare to breathe, the fuckers!

This new thoroughbred is called Rino, he's the most fanatical of the lot now that Faele's not here. He's for ever eating sunflower seeds, he talks like a lawyer, he has small, babyish hands, cold jealous eyes and he spits these bloody sunflower husks everywhere. The floor is always covered with his shit, and of course he never dreams of cleaning it up, that's a task for us women, Mirella or Mafalda or me. I was absolutely furious — 'Why should they laugh at us?' I asked him when we were talking about Mafalda. Do you know what he answered? 'Because it's not on.' And that's that, finito. Decided. Impossible to go back and rethink it, Rino has spoken.

This guy has also proposed my expulsion from the group for reasons of lack of discipline and 'ideological divergencies'. I asked what divergencies he was talking about. 'You're bourgeois,' he shouted in a strangled voice, 'we're aiming at the revolution and you're wasting time on frivolities whose only purpose is to divide men from women.' I don't know why I get on his tits so much, every time he sees me he twists his mouth as if someone was thrusting a lemon between his teeth.

If I could, I'd kill him. It's not a very nice feeling towards a comrade, I'm afraid, but if he had a foot as big as a millstone I know he would't have a second's hesitation about squashing me on the floor.

Vittorio is a nuisance but he does know how to keep people together. Okay, intrigue, authoritarianism, bullying, arrogance, coaxing, fear, whatever, but at least when he's there the Movement is united and when he's not it goes to pieces.

It's not only me and Rino who are pissed off with each other. Everyone is at war with someone in the nastiest way possible. Lots of them are thinking that Vittorio won't come back so they're conspiring to put their bums in his chair. Any excuse is good enough for a row. For instance yesterday an argument broke out between two students from Pozzuoli and an unemployed guy from Caserta: the students were accusing him of political laxity and opportunism; he accused them of being abstract and dogmatic. In the end they had a punch-up and fell on to a window breaking the glass. The crash calmed them down a bit and they went off like angry wolves, without looking at each other, threatening and resentful.

But also, the fact is, I must admit it, we're going through bad times: we've no money, we're scared that more arrests are in the offing, and we've fallen down on three quarters of our political programme. Vittorio is the only person who can find money when there isn't any. Luca, Fidenzio and Peppe, who were in prison, are killed. Tino and Ciccio have been inside for two years without a trial or anything. That's the real reason everyone is so nervous, it's understandable. Besides, there's another reason, no one works full time at headquarters except Mafalda. All the others are doing something else as well: they're either studying, or teaching or have some other job. And when we meet in the evening we're worn out, ready to flare up at the least provocation.

Yesterday Antonio reappeared, with his frog-like eyes bulging more than ever. He stays quietly on the sidelines with a suffering expression on his face, I asked him where he'd been and he answered: 'in hell'. He speaks in a strange, half-hearted, feeble way. He says he has no faith in the future, that our group is too small and bloodless, that we speak in a language no one understands, that we suffer from authoritarianism and paternalism, and that soon war will break out and we'll all be thrown up in the sky like dirty old rags. Luckily, though, it's only me he tells all this to, otherwise he'd risk being expelled. To tell you the truth, I can't understand what he stays in the Movement for. When there's anything to do he slogs away and wears himself out but during discussions he doesn't open his mouth once, and when there's nothing to do he falls asleep.

He's the only friend I have in the Movement. He's always broke, he wears a pair of stinking plimsolls, his nails are filthy, His father isn't poor, he owns a pasta factory in Torre Annunziata, but he's broken off from his family and lives near the station in a rented room crawling with lice.

He's fallen head over heels in love with Mafalda, but he never says a fucking thing to her. I can tell from the way he looks at her. I'm a bit jealous, actually, but I don't know whether of him or of her. I'm scared that they might become friends and leave me out in the cold.

I've started my investigation into work done at home again. I get Antonio to come with me. Mafalda can't, she's too busy down at headquarters. I'm better now, I don't scare off the women with my prying: I sit down, I chat and laugh; I'm learning to get information out of them without asking too many questions, I make myself familiar with their problems and gain their trust.

Ciao, Vannina, write to me soon,

Suna.

*28th September*

Today I spent 5,000 liras for the usual two thin slices of meat plus a lettuce, a couple of pounds of grapes and two ounces of coffee. Until recently I always managed to spend less than 4,000 liras a day.

Giacinto got angry when I asked him for more money. He says I let people rob me and that I don't know how to bargain.

"Prices have gone up."

"It's you, you let yourself get had."

"They go up every day."

"So what? You must find ways of spending less."

"Why don't you do the shopping then?"

"Because I'm working."

"So am I."

"You fling that in my teeth all the time, for fuck's sake! If I earned more I wouldn't let you go to work you know that."

"But I like working."

"Don't talk nonsense."

He gave me a kiss and went out slamming the door. When I put up a fight against him he treats me like a spoilt, pigheaded, slightly comical little girl whom one treats indulgently out of affection.

About eleven the door bell rang. It was Vittorio with a beautiful girl with wavy blonde hair, a good few inches taller than him.

"Hello, Vannina, how are you? This is my wife, Dominique. She's quite a beauty, isn't she? I'm on my way to Naples, without me the Movement is falling apart."

"Suna wrote to me that you'd got married. You're back a bit soon, aren't you? Isn't it dangerous?"

"I've always got my false passport. And by the way remember that officially my name is Valerio Scavolini. In any case we avoid staying in hotels, so do you mind if we sleep here tonight? I must talk to some comrades and I can't leave before tomorrow."

"If Giacinto agrees, that's fine."

"I'll see to Giacinto. Get a bed ready for us so that he'll find the whole thing already settled. Is there any grub to fill our bellies with?"

He went into the kitchen, leaving his wife in the hall holding a large leather suitcase. I looked at her for a moment before relieving her of the weight. She's tall but she looks like a little girl: frail, bony and shapeless, with two anxious eyes. I carried the case into my bedroom, then took her into the kitchen. Vittorio was sitting listening to the radio and eating a cheese sandwich. He'd even poured himself out a glass of wine.

"Would you like a bite, love?"

The girl took a bite of his sandwich, giving him a grateful look. She was obviously hungry but she didn't dare to ask for a sandwich all for herself. I made her a roll with meat in it.

"Rino is a bully, Mafalda thinks she ought to be the boss, and they argue and waste time. Suna has become aggressive, this way it'll all end up in the shit. What the Movement needs is a bit of discipline and morality, it needs balls."

"How do you know this? Who told you?"

"A trustworthy comrade. I know everything that's going on, even if I went to Australia you can be sure I'd know everything about everyone. There's a a lot of confusion, too many new, untried and untrustworthy people, no one knows who they are, spies probably, who can tell? The membership system must be changed, we must start all over again. Dominique will help me, we'll produce a newspaper, we'll change everything."

After he'd finished eating, Vittorio went out and Dominique stayed. I asked her if she wanted to rest. She said she needed a shower so I showed her into the bathroom. She came back into the kitchen a little later wrapped in Giacinto's yellow bathrobe, and asked me for a drink of cognac.

"I've got no cognac, I'm afraid."

"Never mind. Can I stretch out my legs? Vittorio made me walk for hours; I wanted to take a taxi, but he wouldn't let me. When he's got something in his head nothing holds him back. Do you know him well?"

"So so."

"He's obstinate, but he never stands firm just on a whim. He's got a precise idea in his head, and he's ready to do anything for that idea."

"How is it that you speak Italian so well?"

"My mother is from Venice."

"Have you ever been to Naples?"

"No, but I know I'll like it; I like everything to do with Vittorio, even his weak spots."

"What weak spots?"

"The importance he gives to my virginity, for example. Didn't he write to you too about that? He tells everyone, it makes me blush. But his weak points are very powerful."

"How old are you?"

"I'm twenty four."

"How come you were still a virgin at twenty four?"

"At home they're puritanical; petting, yes, but only as far as the waist. From the waist down it's forbidden, and I always obeyed them, not out of sacrifice, it's just that I'm not a very enterprising girl, I have a great sense of duty. And also perhaps I'm a bit frigid."

"Is it true you're very rich?"

"Yes, my father is. He's a merchant banker and he gives me a million a month. Are you wondering whether that's why Vittorio married me? Yes, it is, he told me straight away, he's not the type that tells lies, he hates empty words and sentimentalism. He would never say to a woman he loves her, he'd rather have his tongue cut off. But I know he does love me anyway."

"Did you ever meet Mafalda?"

"Yes, in Geneva. She's very clever, and kind as well, but she isn't Vittorio's type; she has no gentleness or charm, she's always got that long sullen face. Vittorio doesn't want a woman like that."

"What does he want a woman like?"

"Quiet, available, deeply in love, affectionate, interested in politics but without ambition; a woman who can cook, have children, look after the house, and who can make love and laugh and joke without too many problems."

"Can you do all these things?"

"I've had so many kind, thoughtful boyfriends, but they bored me to death, they never talked about my money, it was as if it didn't exist. Vittorio's different, the first thing he said to me was: 'Dominique, you're rich, and you're living in a shitty situation, you must throw away your bourgeois habits and go hungry with me in Naples'. He said it just like that, to my face, and I understood immediately that I'd do whatever he asked me to do. He was the first man who demanded something of me, in fact he demanded everything, the others never asked me for a thing."

"Crushed and contented."

"What do you mean?"

I heard the key in the front door. It was Giacinto, his hands still black with grease. He looked at the girl wrapped up in his bathrobe in amazement and turning towards me said in a tense tone of voice: "Who's this?"

"She's Vittorio's wife, Dominique. They're spending the night here and tomorrow they're off to Naples. Is that okay?"

"Come next door for a minute."

I followed him into the bedroom. His face was smudged with grease and he was frowning. He locked the door and turned on me with a savage voice:

"I don't want those two in my house. He's even wanted by the police, that fellow, and I don't want him here."

"Only for one night, what's the hassle?"

"I've never wanted to be part of that fucking Movement, so why should I risk jail now just to please that cretin?"

"They haven't got anywhere else to go."

"Throw them out. I'm not having them in my house."

"This is my house too."

"Don't talk rubbish. If they stay here, I'm going."

*Midnight*

Vittorio and Dominique stayed. Not because I could convince Giacinto but because Vittorio asserted himself. Giacinto kept his word: he went to sleep with his friend Mario at Mandrione.

The two visitors bagged the double bed for themselves, and I made do with a rubber mattress on the dining room floor. They talked a lot before going to sleep and then they made love — I could hear the bed squeaking. Then I heard the water running in the bidet, and I realised I'd forgotten to give them a clean towel. I got up to fetch them one, but I didn't have the courage to knock. I could hear them laughing and then Vittorio came out, stark naked, and almost bumped into me. He pretended not to notice me, and went into the kitchen to get something to drink. They knocked off a bottle of wine, which I found empty in between the stained sheets in the morning.

They left at six. Vittorio had borrowed a Fiat and some new false documents. Dominique was beaming. She got into the driving seat because Vittorio had to study some papers on the journey. They said goodbye to me with a honk on the horn as they disappeared round the bend of Via Torrevecchio.

*29th September*

Dear Vannina,

Vittorio is back. Together with his beautiful amiable Swiss wife. I tried to have a row with her but to no avail, because she's terribly scared of doing anything Vittorio might not approve of.

Marta is sick. She isn't bleeding any more, but she doesn't seem to be getting better so I called the doctor. He says she's run down, she has kidney trouble and pains in her back. He prescribed a course of injections, but she doesn't want to know; on top of it all she won't eat or sleep or talk. Oliver spends a lot of time with her, he does his homework squatting on the end of her bed and takes along his records and the radio. But as soon as it's six o'clock he grabs his racket and rushes off to play tennis with his American potato.

Marta doesn't say anything, but she's as peevish as a cat, she never leaves her bed and she doesn't speak a word. She perks up only when she hears him coming up the stairs, then she tidies up her grey plait and rinses her mouth with eau-de-Cologne.

Oliver acts the swell, brings her flowers and talks to her like a fucking father. But as soon as the phone rings he loses his airs and tumbles bare-footed along the corridor to answer that potato-face from Boston.

Marta thrusts her head underneath her pillow so's not to hear his sweet voice and all the nonsense those two burble at each other on the phone.

Amidst all this misery there's one cheerful note: I've fallen in love with Mafalda. And she with me. We've made love only once, but it was fantastic. I'm in love with her heavy body, with her sombre character, with her hoarse voice, with everything. I like how she moves, how she speaks, how she laughs, how she hugs me, how she sleeps, how she wakes up to kiss me with her eyes still closed, grumbling in her sleep.

Antonio is with us all the time these days and the three of us have been back to the slums to carry on with our investigations on work done at home. This time though I keep my mouth shut and things turn out better because Mafalda is much more skillful than me. She can find just the right words to make herself understood by the women, even the most difficult and indifferent ones. Antonio doesn't say a word and neither do I. He doesn't speak much anyway, as I told you before. Besides his ideas are too negative and depressing to be of any use. But he likes being with us, and we like being with him. He's the only one in the Movement who doesn't put his prick into every discussion and doesn't feel diminished talking politics with us. He's in love with Mafalda, but he doesn't do a thing to win her over. He knows we're screwing together, and isn't scandalised by it.

Hasan is always talking about you: he says I should follow your example. But it isn't a compliment, as you can guess. What he likes about you are the most pathetic sides of your character: your submissiveness, your meekness, your docility, your cowardliness.

How is it going with Giacinto? If you don't feel like screwing, don't. His prick can wait, you can't. You've been waiting for too long, in fact, with your fad of being the kind and obedient wife. Look at Dominique, you wouldn't want to become like her, would you? All the more so as you have no money.

Ciao,
Suna.

*Midnight*

"I read Suna's letter."

"That's bad of you."

"She talks about me."

"So what?"

"You must break off with that witch."

"Why should I?"

"It's so obvious that she wants to seduce you: she says things about me so that she can carry you off with her, she's head over heels in love with you."

"She's in love with Mafalda, not with me, you've read it yourself."

"Bullshit. That cow wants to snatch you away from me, she wants to gobble you up like a chicken, haven't you noticed her eyes like vultures?"

"I don't understand why you hate her so much."

"And you'd leave a man who loves you to get it together with a paralysed fucking cripple!"

"I haven't the least intention of getting it together with her."

"You don't want to make love to me any longer, do you think I'm stupid?"

"Suna has got nothing to do with that; even before I met Suna I didn't like making love with you much, did I?"

"For fuck's sake, listen to me, Vanna, look at me, stop acting like a little girl. Here I am, me, a man, your husband, and I want you to take me seriously, I want you to look me in the face and tell me what the hell is going on in your mind."

"I don't know. I wish I could think for myself without you hassling me so much."

"I didn't want to tell you this before because I was waiting for a better opportunity, but now I must tell you something. Can I?"

"Tell me what?"

"Let's have a child, shall we? I swear to you blind, I swear it's not some flighty brainwave I've just thought of: I've been thinking about it for months, but I didn't know how to tell you. Well then, Giova, shall we have this son of ours, shall we, love?"

"Do you think a son will make everything okay?"

"I've been thinking about it for a long time, it's not a bit of nonsense I've come up with by chance, a sort of surprise from Father Christmas. I've been thinking about it, I tell you, and I've come to this conclusion: you're fed up because you don't know what to do with your life: quite right, all my respects, a woman needs to have children — fair enough. And you're fed up with me too, you've become as dry as a twig because of this wild idea that I don't want children. It's all my fault, I admit, I've been thinking too much about money and too little about natural things, but now, Jesus fucking Christ, the music is going to change, now we start all over again from scratch. Well then, Vannina, love, let's have a child between the two of us, shall we?"

"I don't fancy it."

"Fuck me, you're as stubborn as a mule: a married woman without children is just like a cat without kittens, she moans and flings herself about and bites her own tail in despair. It's sad to see the way she bites her own tail."

"I don't fancy it and it wouldn't change a damn thing."

"But it's natural to have a child, then you can give up that shitty job you've never liked, we'll even please my boorish mother who keeps on asking: 'When is it due then? When?' I don't want to force you into it, Vannina, of course not, I only want you to find yourself again, my lovie, I want you to go back to what you were before, when I married you, so natural, so spontaneous, so much in love, sweet, shy, so hardworking." He hugged me in a paroxysm of joy and kissed my eyes, my mouth, my cheeks, my hair.

*2nd October*

School has started. Getting to Centocelle takes me almost as long as getting to Zagarolo. The Via Prenestina is always jammed with traffic and the bus crawls along at a snail's pace.

I've been allocated a class of forty children, twenty three boys and seventeen girls. When I went in I found them all sitting in their new uniforms, with clean hands and serious expressions on their faces. A little girl came up to me and offered me a bunch of anemones and recited a few conventional words of welcome. I opened the register and called the roll, Aiello, Bartoli, Candidi, Di Domenico . . .

But silence and order lasted only a short time. At the end of the roll-call, a few small groups had already formed in which the children were talking amongst themselves, laughing and playing cards.

Halfway through the morning the headmaster came in, dressed in light blue, with a lilac tie with green dots, patient and amiable. He talked about the school, about discipline, about lessons; but most of all he talked about football. The boys listened to him enthusiastically, pulling at his sleeves with questioning eyes. Everyone wants to be in the school team, so they all boast of their successes in the summer competitions, and insist on showing off their muscular calves, all ready for the great test.

The girls sit demurely on one side, smiling, a little bit disdainful, already well accustomed to being excluded from these football fêtes.

Later on, I met the other teachers in the staff room with the big Egyptian frescoes. They looked at me with curiosity and suspicion, without any sense of friendliness. They smiled politely but there was nothing spontaneous in their greeting. I had the impression that my arrival had upset a complex balance of forces.

Rosa Colla, the woman the headmaster had talked about as an idiot, was the only one who looked at me with any real interest, perhaps seeing me as an ally. Her colleagues treat her as a half-wit; the headmaster even says it to her face, enjoying a wink of complicity from the others.

Back in the class I had to separate some of the boys who were fighting. I got them to be quiet only with great difficulty. They listened to me with obvious condescension, they were paying attention not out of respect or interest but out of curiosity: they were studying me. I raised my head from the book several times instinctively looking for Fidelio. My return to school brought a nostalgic yearning for the wild boy of Zagarolo.

The most annoying thing is the noise: the walls are made of paper and the school stands right next to a steep road. You are constantly interrupted by the shrill hiss of the buses as they brake. To make myself heard I had to keep on raising my voice and shouting.

The blue, red and violet light comes in through the large glass window, falling on to the desks and colouring the children's heads. Even the blackboard changes its colour: the chalk writes sometimes in red, then in yellow, according to the position of the sun shining through the gigantic stylized flowers.

The children have chosen their desks according to a precise social hierarchy. I twigged this by the end of the first morning after four hours observation of them as they moved about and chatted.

In the first row are the duffers, the poorest ones, the ones who can't speak much Italian and those who wear shabby clothes and re-soled shoes. In the middle rows are the girls, divided into two sub-groups: the first group are boisterous, insolent and cunning: the second awkward and shy. The better-off girls, the daughters of the butcher, the shopkeepers and the doctor belong to the first group, and the poor ones, the daughters of the streetsweepers, the barrowmen, the labourers and the unemployed to the second.

Amongst the latter there's a very small, stuttering girl who looks five instead of eight. She wears a tattered dress and a small pair of red wellingtons and she hardly knows a word of Italian. Her name is Maria Stella Capra.

At the back of the class sit the ring-leaders: tall well-fed boys who are always playing practical jokes, laughing noisily, interrupting with dirty remarks, and attacking the little ones — in a word they are the rulers of the class.

I tried to get them to talk. I asked about their families, but I couldn't get much further than their fathers' jobs. They are already playing out established roles. They asked me about myself and I replied with something innocuous. I disappointed them, I was too much like so many of their mothers: my southern origins, my husband working as a garage mechanic, my house in a working-class district, nothing new or exciting about me.

Once their curiosity was satisfied, their fear ceased too. When I called Maria Stella to the front the boys at the far end threw themselves into taking the piss out of her, jeering, and throwing paper darts at her. The girls in the middle rows shared in the general laughter, though without malice. The small ones in the front looked at me with surprise, gaping at me with their blank eyes. I had to get angry to force them to behave.

*3rd October*

At home Giacinto has left some flowers on the kitchen table — as an apology. The reason being that last night, while I was asleep, he made love and came inside me. He was so quick I didn't have time to react. He knows very well that during the night I never wear a diaphragm, so he took me by surprise.

I rushed to wash myself. I was so sleepy that I went to sleep on the bidet. Then, consumed by rage at that deceitful love-making, I grabbed a pillow and went to lie down on the couch in the living room. I slept badly, with my feet uncovered, my head wedged in between the arm of the couch and the pillow. I could have got out the rubber mattress we use at the seaside, but the idea of sitting there and pumping it up put me off.

I didn't see him in the morning. I went out while he was asleep. At two, when I got back from school, I found his flowers: some small pink, mauve and green daisies.

*4th October*

Dear Vannina,

Marta has run off. She filled two suitcases with our stuff, Oliver's and mine, and cleared off leaving her room in a real state.

Oliver went berserk, he smashed up all his rackets, hurled all the dishes out of the window, and then tried to throw himself out too. It took two of us, Daddy and I, to hold him down because he was wriggling like an eel. To keep him still we had to tie him down and in the process he bit his tongue so severely that he drew blood. Then he got scared and started crying and screaming. What a mess. What a disaster!

Naturally the Turk is pretty upset. I told him that Marta had fallen in love with Oliver and he replied that wasn't a good reason for stealing all our stuff. The funniest thing is that she's even taken five of his small paintings of the family. He'd like to report her: he says that he's really pissed off with all our stupid love affairs. But I think I may have succeeded in persuading him not to report her.

Also she's run off with my portrait of Elizabeth, Oliver's radio and record-player, my waterproof watch, the bread knife, the mirror in the hall, the Turkish scimitar with its hilt of imitation turquoises, and God knows what else. I can't imagine what the hell she intends to do with all this stuff.

Ciao, see you soon,
Suna.

*4.00 p.m.*

On my way out from school I found Rosa Colla waiting for me at the entrance. She insisted that I should go to her house for a coffee. We had come out an hour earlier than usual because of the caretakers' strike, so I did.

Her flat is only a short distance from the school, in an old working-class block of council flats dating back to 1958 which is now in such a bad state that it looks like a pre-war building.

She shot in front of me up a staircase with chipped steps and walls covered with scratches, graffiti and stains.

"Hold your nose as we go in."

"Why?"

"You'll see."

"Why?"

"And don't get scared, okay?"

"What of?"

"You'll see."

She was taking the steps two at a time, as if her heavy body was made of feathers. She stopped in front of an ill-fitting door, gnawed all along the bottom. She took out a heavy iron key and opened the door. The house was full of light, but the strong stench of animals which filled the atmosphere took one's breath away. Rosa pulled me in by one arm and immediately closed the door behind her as if she was scared that someone might be following us.

From the two rooms that opened out of the hall there appeared a succession of inquisitive snouts. A massive dog with large tufts of yellow fur and one leg missing, rushed out to greet us, barking joyfully and wagging its tail. Two other little chestnut dogs hurled themselves towards us also wagging their tails.

Something darted across the room at great speed and I felt a blow on my head. I jumped back startled and Rosa Colla burst out laughing.

"That's Trallala, the naughtiest of all my children." She stretched out her hand towards my head and withdrew it with a grey crow poised on her index finger, its wings battered, its beak sharp and pointed, its eyes round, yellow and wicked.

Meanwhile, I felt something scratching my shoes. I looked down and saw two tortoises with faded shells trying to climb up on to them clawing shakily with their rough feet.

"Well, this is my family. Do you like it?"

I was trying to get away from the two tortoises but she was already off to the bedroom, smiling to herself with amusement, and beckoning me to follow her. She opened the door and pointed to the bed. In the middle of the rolled-up blankets lay a striped tiger cat with four newly born kittens. As we drew closer the animal lifted her head sniffing the air, and opened her eyes wide in a strange vacant way.

"Her name's Castagna and she's blind. I found her half-dead in a dustbin, where some boys had set fire to her. But she's better now. Isn't she beautiful?"

The cat stood up casually, shaking off the little ones that clung to her tits. She walked towards the edge of the bed with her huge golden-green, sightless eyes wide open. Rosa picked her up in her arms and delicately caressed her swollen belly. Then she held her against my chest. She was heavy and yet so soft as I took her in my arms.

"Isn't she sweet?" she said laughing.

A moment later we were in the kitchen. There she showed me a kid that had climbed on top of the sideboard. "This is Panama. They were just about to slaughter her when I rescued her. Come down, Panama, or you'll fall off."

The sideboard, the chairs, the floor, the table, were covered with a veil of tiny black balls the size of lentils — Panama's excrement. Rosa wiped a seat with one of her sleeves and sat wearily on it. Then with a shrill resentful tone of voice she told me about her neighbours who are trying to get her evicted, and her landlord who wants to put up the rent, and the postman who has stopped delivering her mail out of spite. Her pale snub-nosed face bears a strange resemblance to that of her kid. Her lipless mouth, crammed with protruding teeth, looks especially suitable for chewing the cud. Her sparkling yellow eyes express something very sweet, but at the same time demented and foolish.

"Well then, I'll make a cup of coffee."

The two small fat dogs went to lie down at her feet. "I found them in the rain, at Mandrione, both of them with distemper. I called them Rain and Wind; Rain is the male, and Wind the female, and they both eat like wolves."

She took a jar of coffee down from a shelf and opened the lid. The smell of animals and of all the excrement had completely cured me of wanting a coffee. I told her, and she looked at me suddenly downcast as if I were putting myself on the side of her enemies, of those who rejected her odd ways in the name of normality.

"All right, I'll have some", I said to cheer her up, and immediately I saw her spirits rise again.

Meanwhile, the yellow dog had come close to me and was sniffing my ankles. Rosa stretched a hand out towards its black wet muzzle, and pulled it towards her. She spoke to it in an affectionate tone of voice, as if it were a child. I noticed she was wearing a gold wedding ring.

"Are you married?"

"Yes, to someone called Gianni, but he ran away with my friend Anna. Now they send me lots of postcards from Germany."

"Do you have any children?"

"Once I brought back a young lad I found in the park; he hadn't eaten for three days, his clothes were all in rags, he was dirty and unshaven. He was very good-looking, though. He told me he was twenty-two. He stayed with me, ate, drank, slept, and three days later he left without even telling me his name."

The coffee came up hissing. Rosa poured me out a little cup. Then she moved her hand over to the sugar bowl, picked up a lump and dropped it into the boiling liquid. I followed the movement of her short fat fingers with their bitten nails and dark creases in the skin.

"A month later I realised that poor creature had made me pregnant. Where on earth could I get hold of him by that time?"

"Did you ever see him again?"

"He came back when I was in bed just after having an abortion. I was depressed and bleeding, all alone, the animals were nervous because I wasn't feeding them. Trallala shrieked like an eagle — oh, that one is the most over-bearing and cheeky of the lot. Rain and Wind barked without ceasing, the tortoises gnawed at the door, Panama had invaded the house with her piss and shit, only Castagna lay quietly on the bed with me."

"What did he do?"

"When I told him I had got pregnant and had an abortion, he punched me all over. Then he left, having first rummaged through my handbag and stolen my last 10,000 liras, and I haven't seen him since."

She swallowed the boiling coffee in two sips. Trying to imitate her, I burned my tongue and palate. Meanwhile, the tortoises had started climbing over my shoes, slowly and mulishly. I didn't know how to get rid of them without hurting them. I must have pulled a funny face because Rosa burst out laughing.

Then all of a sudden she half closed her lips, pushing them forward, and out of her throat came a muffled, gutteral sound. Immediately the yellow dog got up from the floor, picked up one of the tortoises delicately between his teeth and put it down on the small balcony. Then he came back and picked up its mate and carried it outside too with the same delicate movements. Finally, proud and beaming, he came back to be caressed and hugged by the woman.

"Do your pupils know about all these animals you keep?"

"One day I brought them all back here; but while I was preparing some jam sandwiches two of them locked themselves in the bathroom and thrust a stick up Catagna's bottom."

"The headmaster says you're the only one who can keep the children quiet."

"It's easy, I let them do whatever they like, I amuse them, they put together a class journal, they write, they play. I don't even know what a lesson is. I teach them how to count with beans, we cultivate a vegetable patch in a garden that belongs to the grandfather of one of the boys — well, in short they don't have time to get bored."

"Are they all well-behaved and nice?"

"Oh no, some take advantage of it, some don't give a damn, some are bossy, some just clear off. But I've organised them in teams and they must cope amongst themselves, the class is in their hands, they elect their own bosses, I have hardly anything to do with it. They just ask me anything they want to know and I try to help them."

*6th October*

Today Giacinto didn't come back at the usual time. He rang me to say that he'd be doing overtime. He had the same uneasy tone of voice that he had when he used to lie about his affair with Lillina. Perhaps he's seeing her again, perhaps he's screwing her, I said to myself. But this thought didn't hurt me, it just gave me a vague sense of discomfort.

I had lunch by myself: rice with tomato sauce, two fried eggs and a plate of fresh young lettuce. I don't know what to do about money this month. The landlord sent a letter demanding a rise in the rent. Our lease expired two months ago, so I don't know whether we can refuse. I must look into it.

I spent the afternoon correcting homework. At about six o'clock Mario came, with his dirty white mackintosh thrown over his shoulders, a long red scarf round his neck and walking boots on his feet.

"Is it raining?"

"Where's Giacinto?"

"He's still at the garage."

"I wanted to go fishing with him."

"In this weather?"

"Round Orte."

He was on tenterhooks. During all the years we've known each other we've never talked together alone. When Giacinto is here he talks to him quietly as if I didn't exist. If I intervene he looks at me with irritation. Theirs is a man's friendship based on male solidarity, complicity, warmth, jokes and games: all things which I'm obstinately excluded from.

"Do you want to stay and have dinner with us?"

He raised his pock-marked face in alarm and thought about it for a while. Obviously he was scared of staying alone with me. "Perhaps. Maybe I'll come back later. What time will he be back?"

"I don't know. Nine o'clock perhaps, perhaps later. He'll ring me, I daresay."

"Okay. I'll come back. Goodbye."

Later on I went to the window, and I could see him walking up and down the pavement, his red scarf dangling on his chest, his mackintosh fluttering round his legs.

*12th October*

"To keep her children happy
The mother sits and sings

A song she learned from Granny
An old old song that brings
Memories of the cradle —"

A little girl lifted her hand. "How many 'ls' are there in cradle, one or two, Miss?"

I went over to her desk. She was writing in large flowery letters. I struck off an l with my pencil. Then I continued the dictation, with a feeling of impatience towards the stupid school book I was forced to use.

"The children listen quietly,
They open wide their eyes.
They're never tired of listening
To her sweet lullabies.
They love to see their mother,
Calm and madonna-like."

"Is there a comma after mother, Miss?"

"Yes there is."

"Is madonna written with a capital letter?"

"No, with a small letter."

The lesson is interrupted by the caretaker who comes in to ask me to go to the headmaster's office. We have to decide whether to join the strike announced for tomorrow. The headmaster is silent and gloomy, chain-smoking one cigarette after another. The teachers discuss the matter ferociously. Rosa Colla cleans her nails with a bit of paper folded into four.

When I went back to my class I found everything upside down: the desks had been moved to one side so as to form a sort of circular stage. The children were all huddled together perched on the benches. In the middle of the arena, lying on the floor, was Maria Stella, and on top of her were four scrambling boys.

They were so involved in the performance that they didn't hear me return, and I stood there by the door trying to understand what they were up to. Then all of a sudden it dawned on me: they were mimicking a rape.

Two boys were holding her by the feet and arms while two others had climbed on top of her. One was sprawled on top of her, wriggling with ridiculous, exaggerated movements, pushing his bottom back and forth. I recognised Vicari, one of the tallest boys, the son of the owner of the local supermarket.

The other boy was astride the little girl's neck so that his shorts were pressed against her face. He too was wriggling, red in the face and sweating, and as he wriggled he was shouting: 'Suck it, go on, suck it, you whore.' It was Maurizio Gelosi, another one of the boys who sit in the back row, a lad who comes to school on a moped and whose father owns a pork butcher's shop.

Neither of them looked at the girl, their mischievious sparkling eyes were turned on their schoolmates, seeking their approval.

All the girls had gathered to one side and were giggling with amusement. Only two of the smallest ones stood there in silence, dumbfounded, gaping with their mouths open and blank looks on their faces.

Maria Stella tossed feebly about, her face hidden by her taller schoomates' trousers, breathless, half choking, but also somewhat gleeful and satisfied. Her faded skirt was rolled up on her legs uncovering her white, skinny thighs and a pair of tattered grey woollen panties.

I rushed over to free her. I slapped the first boy I managed to grab hold of with such fury that it surprised me even more than it did him.

Vicari and Gelosi reluctantly obeyed me, puffing and grunting. They expected me to chuck them out of the classroom. Instead, I sent them back to their seats. Then I asked Maria Stella to come to my desk. I wanted us to talk about what had just happened, all together.

"What were your schoolmates doing a little while ago, Stella?"

"Dunno". She raised her mottled face and smiled stupidly at me.

"Was it a game or was it for real?"

"Dunno."

"When you're playing a game everyone should enjoy themselves. Were you enjoying yourself in this game of theirs?"

"Dunno."

"You lay there underneath them choking. I saw you tremble in spite of the fact that you were showing off a bit too. The two of them were on top of you, you couldn't move, you're small, you're weak, and you couldn't fight back. What sort of a game is that?"

"I'm not weak, I can bump them all off if I want to."

"Well then, why didn't you free yourself from those bullies?"

"They were keeping me down."

"And why were they keeping you down?"

"Because they're all yobs."

"Do you know what Maurizio and Giancarlo were doing?"

"Dunno."

"They were imitating the grown-ups."

"I once saw a monkey with its willie out."

"Do you know what scene your mates were trying to act out?"

"It was biting its own bum, and my dad laughed so much that he wet himself."

"Answer my question."

"Dunno."

"A rape, do you know what that is?"

"Dunno."

"A rape is an act of violence that one man or more than one man performs on a woman or on a little girl like you. Do you understand?"

"They screw her, then, Miss."

"Why do you think the other girls didn't come to help you?"

"Because they're all big yobs."

"Or was it perhaps because they think the boys have a right to do these things?"

"Dunno."

"Why do you think they chose you and only you as a victim?"

"They're always putting their hands up my knickers to see whether I've pissed myself."

The boys burst out laughing. Maria Stella looked at them cockily, twisting her fingers and hitting her red rubber boots against the chair.

"Well, just explain to me why your schoolmates chose you and not another boy for this stupid game of theirs."

"Because I'm little."

"Do you think that if you were a boy, even if you were little, they would have played the same games with you?"

"No, of course not, the girl does the woman and stays underneath, and the boy does the man and stays on top and fucks her."

"So do you think this is how one makes love?"

"Dunno."

"With violence, pushing and laughing, without caring for the other person?"

"They're all big yobbos, Miss."

"Love is something that two people share with gentleness, with tenderness, and without bullying, and both people should be happy, don't you think?"

"They're filthy arseholes."

The boys guffawed and Stella rejoiced at the wisecrack. The other girls laughed softly and demurely.

I started to explain what the man and the woman's genitals are like, how they copulate, how the eggcell becomes fertilised, how a child is born. I cleaned off the blackboard and I started drawing plants, seeds, animals and eggs on it. My hand moved fast and confidently. The children had calmed down but I don't know whether they were following me. I felt that they had been somehow infected by my indignation. I was talking to them about rape, about sexual roles, with passion and anger, in a way that had never occurred before in so many years of teaching.

For once when the bell rang I regretted not having more time. I was excited, my hands were covered in chalk, my head was full of more things to say. The classroom emptied in a second, with a great confusion of school bags being quickly closed, uniforms being pulled off, chairs toppled over, laughing, swearing and shouting.

I was left behind alone, immersed in the sugary light of the glass wall. I finished drawing the eggcell as it meets the sperm. I wiped my hands and left the room.

Only when I got to the gate did I realise that someone was calling me. It was Rosa Colla. She asked me if I would like to go and have lunch with her. I said no: I was tired and wanted to go back home. She looked sad and incredulous as she said goodbye to me. I clutched her hand vigorously and promised I would go with her another day. Her goat-like eyes stared at me a second, wondering whether I was telling the truth. Then she smiled, convinced, and walked off clumsily on her high heels.

For the first time, on my way back home shut inside the crowded bus, all perspiring and tired after five hours of teaching, I didn't feel demoralised and empty, but seized with a fever of happiness and fulfilment.

*Midnight*

I ate two plates of pasta, the usual grilled slice of meat, some lettuce and a few biscuits. I felt desperately hungry. I told Giacinto about what had happened in school and he looked at me with a grim expression on his face, not at all reassured.

"You're becoming a real fucking nuisance like Suna."

"What do you mean?"

"You want to do good instead of which you get on people's tits, you're just a fucking do-gooder, ready to force people into being good at gun point."

"I don't want to be good, it's just that before teaching was so boring and now I enjoy it."

"That's it, that's the trouble, you all enjoy yourselves: you enjoy yourself teaching those girls not to be girls any more, just as those cretins from Naples enjoy themselves teaching the proletariat not to be the proletariat."

"When I was bored I did everything badly."

"Work is work, there's nothing amusing about it, it's a serious thing which you've got to do whether you like it or not, and that's where your life is, in other people's hands, what is there amusing about that?"

I didn't feel like arguing. I was tired, sleep was pressing up my throat and causing a pain in my nostrils. I cleared the table quickly, washed the dishes, scrubbed the pans, rinsed the cutlery and glasses. Then I undressed and got into the ice-cold bed. Suddenly I sat up on the bed confronted by the image of one of Giacinto's shirts which had been lying rolled up in the kitchen for a week waiting to be ironed. And tomorrow he won't have any clean shirts.

I got up and went to plug in the iron. I had a sip of coffee and then I started ironing.

From the kitchen I could see Giacinto's fair body huddled up on the bed, his head wedged in between his shoulders, his legs bent, his arms folded, his fists clenched as if he were occupied in furious self-defence. I watched him sleep, his short heavy breathing, his brows knitted and his temples sweating.

When I'd finished ironing, I wasn't sleepy any more. I sat on the bed. I put my hands on Giacinto's knees and tried to stretch his legs out straight. He tried to send me away with a kick. I persisted, gently caressing his freckled chest and his lean belly with its sleepy muscles. His pink wrinkled penis lay dangling on one of his thighs.

I held it in my fingers and pressed it tenderly. Giacinto pulled a resentful face, a sort of silent hostile growl; then all of a sudden he went back to his usual contracted unyielding position.

*15th October*

Dear Vannina,

I've been expelled from the Movement for 'convicted and confirmed homosexuality'. They had to keep Mafalda because without her they wouldn't know what to do — as I told you before she's the one who takes charge of organising everything.

Vittorio gave me a very complicated and even affectionate talking to, explaining how I'm not a real revolutionary because I think too much about sex and too little about the class struggle, because I seduced Mafalda who is a 'normal' girl and took her down the path of 'bourgeois corruption'.

In the face of all this Mafalda reacts in an ambiguous way which gives me belly-aches. Secretly she tells me I'm right, publicly she makes strict speeches about group discipline and the Movement's morality which should never be betrayed.

She explained to me that for her this is the only way of staying inside the Movement, that she's doing it deliberately, in cold blood, and that it helps her continue her political struggle, the only thing she really cares about.

I asked her whether she's going to carry on making love with me. She answered yes, she thinks so, but secretly. 'So how will you square this with your political conscience?' I asked. She answered very seriously: 'Homosexuality is not contrary to revolutionary morality, but at this moment we aren't strong enough to start discussing these secondary topics, besides we must set an example to the working class, we can't present ourselves as a group of happy-go-lucky hedonists more preoccupied with our sexuality than with our work'.

The result is that now she very rarely comes to my house. And I'm always there like a twit waiting for her. I spend hours on end by the phone just hoping to hear her voice for a moment. I never know when she's coming, she appears all of a sudden, at about three in the morning, in her lined cloth jacket, her face drawn, her eyes red, her breath sour.

She knocks on the door with her fingers, softly, and I run to open it. For fear I'll miss that discreet tapping I'm always glued to the door, with my belly throbbing and my throat dry, night after night.

Sometimes I fall asleep with my head against the wall almost convinced by then that she won't come. Then, there she is, she slips into my bedroom without making a sound, like a conspirator. She undresses quickly, gets into bed and calls me. It takes me an hour of caresses and tenderness to loosen her up. Then she turns into a loving ferocious tiger. She bites, laughs, jumps, kisses me, hugs me and I'm so happy I wish I could die.

I don't know yet whether I'm more hurt or pissed off at being chucked out of the Movement. I'd like to send them all to hell, fucking moralistic cretins. But then I think that they're right: it's true, I'm incapable of living communally with a group of people, I don't even know what discipline is, I say what I think, I don't have any political sense, I don't understand a damn thing about strategy, I only care about women's misfortunes.

Women, that's what I think of all the time. I'm gradually falling in love with women more and more, I wish I could kiss them all with love, on their folds of fat, on their sweaty wrinkles, on their fleshy bums, on their old ruined cunts, on their haunted eyes, on their ramshackle dilapidated mouths, all over where they are insulted and torn to pieces for the triumph of the great God prick.

Mafalda says I'm going mad, that I'm a maniac, a write-off, that politics is something quite different, but I'm not sure whether she's right.

Ciao Vannina, a big strong hug from me,
Suna

*10th November*

Oh God, ten days late. I have this feeling of hardness in my belly, as if something was pulling and coiling inside me. Giacinto is spying on me. He's waiting for a sign of change. With a child he believes I'll become the sweet, submissive, ever-available woman I was before.

I haven't told him about my period, but he seems to know. He looks at me with a cunning expression and the other day I caught him rummaging amongst my knickers in the dirty washing basket. I must go and have a pregnancy test.

*15th November*

I had my pregnancy test. Result: positive. Giacinto found the piece of paper, I don't know how, in spite of the fact that I'd hidden it. He woke me up in the middle of the night to tell me about it. He was happy, he hugged and kissed me almost in tears. I told him I have no intention of having a child I don't want and that was forced on me so deceitfully. He hit me on my chest with his fist. He says that the child is his and no one can take it away from him.

*18th November*

I feel sick. I bring up everything I eat. At school I have to go to the toilet continuously. I've lost three kilos. My teeth hurt. I always have a bitter taste in my mouth.

Giacinto rings me up every five minutes from his garage to ask me how I feel. I read and my head starts spinning. I do the dishes and my back hurts. In the evening I go to bed at nine o'clock without eating. Giacinto never gets impatient over the dirty floor or the shirts of his I've forgotten to iron. He walks around the house barefooted, moving pieces of furniture to make room for the child. He kisses my neck, my shoulders. He talks about the future in a paternalistic voice.

"You'll leave that shitty school, no more buses, no more fits of anger, even if you're enjoying yourself now, enjoyment at work never lasts anyway, you know. The study groups, the seminars on sex, the class run by the students, you can leave all those trendy novelties to that lunatic Rosa Colla, you must dedicate yourself to him, to our son. I enquired about the hospital: with the medical benefits it's 18,000 liras a day. Do you prefer the Policlinico or the Gemelli? The latter's more expensive, but I could manage, I've already started doing overtime, I've run up quite a few hours: besides now we're opening a new garage and I'll be dealing with the customers and with the other mechanics. They're going to promote me to head-foreman of the garage, I have that arsehole Vargas's confidence. If I work at it I can be even tougher than the boss, it's a matter of order, organisation. They're lazy sods and they think they can work a fiddle. Who do they think they can cheat? Me? Those shitheads of customers? Sure, they can cheat them left right and centre, and they won't know. But they can't take me in, so they've already found out that I'm pretty good, I've already told them that they should give me a rise considering my responsibilities, I should set the conditions, shouldn't I? Besides, who knows, one day I might buy them out, I've got the necessary skills, it's just a matter of money.

Meanwhile Vargas is looking after the other garage and here I'm the manager, then in a few years from now I might have put a few million aside, let's say ten, with that I'll take over the shop, you see, but perhaps no, I open a new different garage myself. The secret is this: money makes money, sure as God's in Heaven my son isn't going to sleep in a shithole like I did, he won't eat bread and onions like me, and I'll be able to give a little bit more to my bitch of a mother who's never in her life managed to eat a plate of ravioli in peace, with a cushion under her arse, but always on her knees as she scrubbed and cleaned. I'll buy her a flat so that she won't throw her money out of the window. Eh love, can you hear me? Are you asleep? If you want you can leave your job tomorrow. I won't say anything, indeed I'll be glad, by now I can manage by myself, I swear, love, I've always said that I don't want you to work, what I earn is enough, isn't it?"

I told him I'd no intention of stopping teaching. He clung to me passionately and affectionately. He bit one of my ears, he kissed my neck, he spoke to me as if I were a little girl who had to be cajoled for her own good. I told him to leave me alone. But he continued to press against me from behind. I could feel his naked chest against my back, the warmth of his legs against mine. I went to sleep with that weight against me, like a child astride my back.

*22nd November*

Dear Giovanna,

I don't know why I'm writing to you: I guess by now you'll have heard all about it. But I'm here, in her house, and I think she loved you and I feel the need to talk to you. I think I'd better tell you how it all happened. You know that recently she'd started doing medicine again. She seemed satisfied. She would go to the University by herself, she didn't want any help from anyone; her legs were getting better, she studied really hard. She wasn't seeing her political friends any more, I don't know why. Even Mafalda had disappeared. But she would never speak about her. I believe she was suffering from loneliness, but when I asked her about it she answered me rudely — you know how short-tempered and impatient she was with me. She would be for ever buying books, she spent days on end reading and studying. I bought her a real skeleton, it cost me all of 120,000 liras. Every so often I'd visit her, but she didn't seem happy to see me. She's always been so argumentative with me, which I've never told her off for — you know how it is, it's essential to break free from one's father some time in one's life and she'd so much idolised me that she was finding it more difficult to free herself than most people do.

In these last few days she was always alone. Oliver had gone to London with some friends. She had shut herself in the house night and day to study. She had to take four exams in February. I had told her not to overdo it, but you know what she was like, either all or nothing. She was slogging her guts out and I didn't like to interfere.

She came to our house for lunch on Sunday. She seemed quite serene. She had a plate of pasta al forno that Emma had cooked for her. She was cheerful: she played with Nina, my youngest daughter. She insisted on going home by herself. She did seem to me a little bit thinner and much too pale: because of this I urged her to stay out in the sun a little bit, to breathe some fresh air. She answered me: 'Daddy, mind your own business!' with that sarcastic air you know so well. Then nothing more — that was all.

I never saw her alive again. On Wednesday morning they rang me up. The porter was screaming, I couldn't understand a thing. I rushed over and there she was on the pavement dead. She hadn't broken anything: no blood, nothing, it looked almost as if she'd simply fainted. She had hit her head though.

Inside the house I found books open on the table, her crutches propped up against the window sill. In the kitchen there was a terrible mess: tins half empty, stale bread, biscuits, food that had gone mouldy, dirty dishes, just like a slum. I'd suggested to her that we could send over our Rina who is so good, but she didn't want it. She insisted she could do everything herself.

Oliver doesn't know yet. I'm afraid how he'll react. I'm waiting for him to come back from London: he has to go back to school in a few days. Emma cries continuously. I have to go out to avoid listening to her. It's not because she loved her a lot, but she feels that the family is like a tribe, and she wails in despair at any dwindling of the strength of the group: whether it's Suna or someone else makes no difference.

This is the second day I've come here. I wander about going through her things. The skeleton which hangs in her room makes me jump every time I bump into it. I look at her medicine books underlined in pencil, I pick up her used shoes, her clothes. I lie on the sofa and stay there in a daze for hours. I wonder why she killed herself, I don't know, probably never will know. She hasn't left anything in writing, anything at all.

I found a tape recorder with her voice recorded on tape. A Latin lesson or something like that, something a couple of years old, when she was still at college. I put it on, I turn up the volume and I sit there like a moron listening to her.

Well, that's all. Forgive my outburst, but I don't feel very good at all: I don't feel like working, like talking to anyone, or doing anything. And yet they're waiting for me, sooner or later I'll have to go back to my normal life.

Yesterday I did something strange. I was searching through her books. I found a photograph of her at the seaside, naked on top of a rock. Her legs were thrown awkwardly to one side; her chest was all tensed up in the effort of balancing on top of some sharp-pointed rocks, her face half hidden by one of her arms folded over her head. Her sweet grey eyes were smiling, I don't know who she was with, but she looked happy. I stared at it for a long time. Then, without knowing what I was doing, I began to tear it up. I reduced it to tiny little bits and then, still hardly aware of what I was doing, I put them in my mouth. I chewed and chewed them and then swallowed them with great care, almost in a trance as if I were hypnotised.

I understood what I was doing only when I had finished swallowing the last bit of paper. Then I started laughing; but my laughter loosened up the muscles I'd been keeping tight and constrained for days, and I started crying uncontrollably, unable to stop.

Tell me please whether she's written to you recently and what about, whether she talks about me, her studies, her love affairs. Did she tell you she was upset? And why? Even if you know nothing, write to me all the same: I would be so grateful to receive a letter in which you tell me about her.

I hug you, dear Vannina, with affection,

Hasan Malrick

*3rd December*

After reading Hasan's letter I slept for four days, my bones ached, my tongue was swollen and furred. I was cold and all the blankets we have in the house weren't sufficient to cover up my trembling shoulders.

Giacinto would draw close to me; he'd rub my feet with his hands; he'd tuck the eiderdown under my chin. Yet I kept on shivering with cold.

I was sunk into a dark and painful sleep for days. On the fifth day I had a strange and obscurely revealing dream which changed the course of my life.

I dreamt my arms had been transformed into long feathery wings and I was flying, my body light and contracted, my nerves as taut as ropes under my armpits. The effort I was making to lift myself up was painful, but once up in the air I was gliding in the wind with a soft intoxicating sweetness. If I looked down below me I took fright, but was also excited. I could see spreading trees, I could see ripe cornfields, I could see shiny streams in the distance, I could see wild copses and cultivated fields. In an outburst of happiness I let myself swoop down as if I were riding on top of a smooth wave, and almost brush my belly against the soft tops of the pine trees. Then I swooped back up, once again the muscles of my body contracting in the effort. I started flying high up, above the clouds, I went beyond the countryside and drew close to the town, I went beyond the roofs spiked with aerials, the balconies decked with flowers, I flew over a shining road swarming with people, then I started feeling giddy, the saliva dried up in my mouth; yet the joy of flying was so strong that I'd keep on forcing my aching arms to go even higher up, amidst icy currents, letting myself be enveloped by the bitterly cold wind.

Then all of a sudden I lost my strength, the air offered no more support beneath my body. I gradually became heavier and heavier, more and more clumsy. My fall started, I could feel myself being sucked down towards the earth by a piercing force. I tried desperately to keep afloat, to carry on my flight, I made tremendous efforts with my arms and legs, but my body plunged to the ground, my throat tightened and my stomach churned.

I hit the hard, muddy ground. I lay there motionless, unconscious. I was dead. My limbs were in pieces, my blood spread around me. I had no eyes, no mouth, I was crushed, destroyed, wiped out of existence.

But something was still alive. I tried to draw breath. I could. I was safe. I tried to prop myself up. A stabbing pain in my legs stopped me. I looked down: they were broken, mangled. I touched my torn stumps, crying not only because of the pain, but also because I would no longer be able to walk.

I was there like that, desperate, screaming without a sound, shedding bitter tears which encrusted my face with salt, when I heard a rustling sound. I raised my eyes: Suna was coming towards me, sinking her crutches in the mud, her face rapt and serene.

"Stop crying, you idiot!" she said in a hoarse voice like that of an old man. "Take the crutches and clear off."

But I couldn't make up my mind whether to take them or not. So she took off her night dress and stood there naked in front of me, staring at me sternly. I took the crutches she was offering me, but when I took them off her she fell to the ground. I bent down to help her and she said: "Go, you blockhead." I wanted to kiss her and to thank her. I bent down but instead of her I found her sex: a white marble shell with a red pulsing interior. From the shell poured out a stream of very sweet milk. I brought my lips close to it: I drank some of that milk which tasted of seaweed, and as I drank it I felt it was filling me up with strength, with courage.

Then I thrust the crutches under my armpits: I stood up. My frail shoulders had become sturdy and I found myself walking, without my legs, walking along lightly without any strain.

I turned round and saw Suna laughing happily, her body immersed in milk, her very long lashes waving softly over her pale face.

After that dream I woke up feeling better. I threw my blankets up in the air. I went back to school. I asked Rosa Colla to give me the name of the doctor who operated on her.

*7th December*

Doctor Petal, that's his name. He didn't have any petals, though, only pink, fluttering eyelids. He thrust his hard, icy hands into my body. He opened me up, he ripped me apart and scraped me thoroughly. I bit my hands with clenched teeth to endure the brutal pain; I could feel the blood gushing out in streams from my tortured uterus. I fainted. I woke up again. The hours, the days, the years were passing by and the excavation never finished. All the pain in the world had accumulated at the bottom of my belly, amongst the torturer's metallic hands.

Later, I only wanted to rest. Instead, they pushed me out. The money? Have you got the money? It's 200,000 liras. Yes, yes, I've got it. I had borrowed 200,000 liras partly from Rosa and partly from the headmaster as an advance on my next salary.

After I came out from the doctor, I didn't go home. I went to Rosa's who made room for me on her bed, together with the cat.

Every morning, the crow Trallala wakes me up with a sharp raucous cry, the tortoises sleep inside my shoes, the goat Panama sows her shit balls inside the coffee cups. As soon as I'm better, I'll start looking for a cheap flat.

*15th December*

Today I found Giacinto waiting for me outside the school. Dressed in blue, clean-shaven, clean, he looked all ready for a formal occasion.

"Aren't you working today?"

"I've taken an hour's leave. Can I talk to you for a moment? I've got the car, I can take you home."

"I don't live far away, I'll walk."

He took my arm, conciliatory, anxious, kind.

"I'm not bothered about what you've done, Vannina, I know you've been ill over Suna's death, the lunatic, I told you there was something wrong with her, didn't I? I'm sorry, don't think I wanted her dead. She thought of it herself, it means she wasn't happy, something was going all wrong, she was out of place there with the others, and after all poor girl, she paid with her own life, I don't deny it. But you can understand why I was angry seeing you being dragged down by her, even after her death, dragged into madness, into irresponsibility, you and your child that was also mine, you shouldn't have decided for both of us, you snatched it off me and didn't even ask me for the money, which I would have given you anyway, out of love. Or perhaps no I wouldn't, I don't know if I'd have given you the money to bump off our child, that treasure you've thrown away, out of irresponsibility. I know because you let her trap you, against your own feelings, against our love, against your own intelligence, you've ruined it all, out of pride, out of pigheadedness, I don't know: but I swear to you I'm not here to reproach you, I'm here to ask you to come back with me anyway, just as you are, with all your faults, which I won't throw in your face ever, I swear it on my mother's head, but I want you; without you the house is empty, it's filthy, I never know where the fuck things are, I don't even fancy eating there any more, and the bed is like a cold empty square, and how can I sleep on that bed we bought together? I'll take you as you are, Vannina, with your fancies, your fits of anger, if you want to carry on teaching I'll let you, I won't say a thing, only later on, perhaps, shall we try and have another child again, would you like that? When you go back to being the sweet Vannina I used to know, that I married, for God's sake, but do you realise Vanna, that when you marry someone that person must stay the same; you must eat, you must get better, you can't live in that house with a raving lunatic, they told me everything at your school, you know one of your colleagues says that Rosa Colla is a slut, that she's had a child with an unknown vagrant, that she keeps animals in her house, that yes to put it bluntly she screws those filthy dogs, they say she lives in the midst of shit and she's into sorcery and corrupts the children. It's not very nice for you to get mixed up with someone like that, people start throwing mud and you find yourself in the middle of a nasty situation without even knowing it, look at the state you're in, I didn't even recognise you when you came out of your class. You're pale, you're thin, your hair is dirty. Vannina, promise me you'll come back to me, tell me something, please."

I didn't feel like talking. I said goodbye to him at the front door. He answered goodbye, disappointed, anxious, imploring. I felt like kissing him, hugging him, feeling his strong arms around my waist. But then he would have dragged me home. I told him I wanted to be left alone and I closed the door in his face. I walked up the stairs, two steps at a time. I opened the door, I sat on the bed. Castagna lifted up her head towards me and stared at me with her blind eyes, so beautiful and so empty.

Now I'm alone and I must start everything again from the beginning.

*This Book Was Typeset by Margaret Spooner Typesetting*
*Dorchester, Dorset. It Was Printed on*
*55 lb Glatfelter Natural Paper with*
*a Smyth-Sewn Binding by*
*McNaughton & Gunn,*
*Ann Arbor, MI*
*USA*
* *
*